BOLD EMBRACE

"You don't think much of me, do you?" River asked.

Taken off guard by the hurt in his voice, Aidan shook her head. "That's not true. I—"

His eyes were bright with accusation. "Yes it is. You think an Indian should do your bidding. You don't care about anyone but yourself. Have you given any thought to what you're doing to me?"

"What I'm doing to *you!*" Tears flooded her eyes but she made no effort to wipe them away. "I'm not the one who can't decide what I want!"

"What I want *is* the problem," he said, his voice husky with pain.

"You want to improve conditions on the reservations. And we agreed that I'm going to help you do it, in exchange for your taking me to Cuba. How is that suddenly the problem?"

Frustrated, he grasped her upper arms. "That's not the issue here!"

"Then, what—?"

"This, dammit." He kissed her as if he could stamp out the torturous desire growing inside him.

At first she tried to push him away. But as quickly as the will to resist possessed her, it was gone, leaving behind a longing so intense she didn't question it. All she knew was she wanted this, too. Wanted it more than anything she'd ever wanted in her life . . .

SAVAGE ROGUE

MICHALANN PERRY

ZEBRA BOOKS
KENSINGTON PUBLISHING CORP.

ZEBRA BOOKS

are published by

Kensington Publishing Corp.
475 Park Avenue South
New York, NY 10016

First printing: April, 1989

Printed in the United States of America

DEDICATION

To Pat and Marge Flanagan. No dreamer could have asked for better parents. No matter how high above my own limitations my dreams may soar, you are always there, encouraging me to believe in myself and to follow my heart—no matter how impossible to achieve my goals may seem to the rest of the world.

Forward

By the time the nineteenth century neared its end, the Indians who had survived the great American expansion of the past fifty years had been totally and brutally humbled, and they were neatly tucked away on remote reservations, where they could not disturb the national conscience.

Consequently, in 1898, instead of being disturbed by the oppressive conditions people in their own land were forced to endure, Americans became caught up in concern about the supposed atrocities committed by the Spanish government in Cuba.

It is true that the Spanish authorities had misgoverned Cuba, but few Americans realized that Spain had made many concessions and was, in fact, willing to give up Cuba to avoid war with the United States. In truth, there was no reason to go to war at all.

Unfortunately, the excitement and misguided patriotism incited by newspapermen, those who practiced sensationalism and "yellow journalism" to sell more papers, were too strong to be overcome by reason. The cry for war simply became too loud to be denied.

So Americans from all over the United States went to fight in a senseless, made-up conflict in Cuba, while the Indians on the reservations continued to live in abject poverty and virtual imprisonment.

7

Chapter One

San Antonio, Texas—May 1898

Her blue eyes wide with terror, Dawn Donovan gaped at the kneeling man who was tugging a chest from under the bed.

"What are you doing in my sister's room?"

The intruder's head jerked up. "Close that door" he ordered with an angry hiss, "before you have the whole household in here!"

Dawn hesitated, a suspicious frown forming on her face as familiar brown eyes glared up at her. "Aidan?"

"Of course," the trespasser growled, raising the lid on the trunk. "Who'd you think it was?"

"But you're . . . " Excitement exploded in Dawn's mind, quickly transforming her surprise into curiosity. Here was a chance to be in on one of her older sister's schemes at the beginning, instead of learning the details after it was over—as she usually had to. "Why are you dressed like that?" she asked, closing the door behind her and locking it. "Why is your hair all slicked back, and where did you get those clothes? And that mustache!"

"Out of the trunk of costumes that acting troupe left behind when they stayed here last year," Aidan answered, wincing as she tore a spirit-gummed mustache from her

9

sensitive upper lip. "Ouch!"

"What are you doing in them?" Dawn moved closer, her tone animated and secretive. "Is this another one of the disguises you use to get a big story?"

Aidan studied her eighteen-year-old sister for a moment, her own enthusiasm difficult to contain. Shaking her head, she turned her attention to unbuttoning the brown double-breasted reefer jacket she wore. "I can't tell you. I don't want to risk spoiling everything."

"I won't give you away. I give you my word. In fact, I can help. When you need someone to cover for you with Mama and Da—and you know you will—I'll be able to do it! Now, tell me! What's going on?"

Shrugging out of the coat, Aidan dropped it into the trunk and regretfully shook her head. "I'm sorry, Dawn. I would if I could. But I've come close to getting my big break too many times to take a chance on losing this one."

"But I'm your sister! I won't ruin it for you."

Aidan untied the spotted silk necktie and removed it from around her neck. She pitched it, along with the high-buttoned waistcoat, into the open trunk. "All I can tell you now is that this story has the potential to make me even more famous than our renowned father and Nelly Bly put together."

"Oh, Aidan, you've got to tell me!" Dawn pleaded, her golden blond curls bouncing up and down as she clasped her hands together and fell to her knees in a begging pose. "I won't give you away. I promise!" She placed a hand on her heart and assumed her most solemn expression. "May I end up a miserable old maid if I so much as breathe a hint to a living soul. Please!" she wailed.

Aidan smiled at her younger sister's theatrics. "I wish I could, Dawn. But I can't. And there's no use nagging me about it." She stood up and walked toward the bathroom that had been built between her bedroom and Dawn's two years before when Rancho Camila had been equipped with

10

electric lights and indoor plumbing—which included the added luxuries of hot water and flush toilets.

Slipping the suspenders from her shoulders, Aidan slid the flannel trousers down her boyishly slim hips, then stepped out of them. Unconcerned with where they fell, she directed her attention to the buttons of her shirt front.

Having taken off the shirt, she draped it over the back of a chair, and closed the bathroom door. "Now, I've got to get this hair oil washed out before anyone else sees me. I hope there's enough hot water. Will you go and ask someone to put extra wood in the boiler, just in case I need—What are you staring at?"

"Your hair!" Dawn exclaimed, her eyes bulging with dismay as she finally realized that Aidan's red hair, which was usually gathered into a long tail that curled down her back, had been cropped off just below the nape of the neck. "You cut your hair!"

"Well, of course I did." Aidan glanced in the mirror at her reflection, and her nose wrinkled distastefully. Parted in the middle, her natural curls were held flat by the oil of Macassar she had pilfered from her cousin, Richard, who lived with his family in the other house on the ranch. "I had no choice."

Seeing the heartsick look on her sister's face, she felt compelled to explain further. "I tried to tuck it into my collar, but it didn't work. My hair's so thick, I looked like the Hunchback of Notre Dame." Aidan grinned, but when Dawn still looked appalled, she shrugged and turned to the bathtub. "Besides, where I'm going, it would just be in the way. Don't worry. It'll grow back."

"But your beautiful hair!" Dawn said, still unable to believe Aidan had cut it off. "How could you have done that to yourself? No story can be worth that much!"

"Believe me, this one is," Aidan declared, kicking off her masculine shoes and stockings. Bending over the tub, she inserted the plug in the drain hole, then turned on the

11

hot water and waited. The pipes thumped and groaned for a full minute before they finally produced a slow but steady stream of hot water. "Thank goodness." She peeled the elasticized union suit she wore from her body and, unabashed by her nakedness, kicked the discarded underwear aside before dipping one foot into the tub to test the water.

"How are you going to explain your hair to Mama and Da?" Dawn asked as she watched her sister lower herself into the water and lie back in the tub to wet her hair. "They're going to know you're up to something."

Aidan poured a large dollop of thick shampoo into her hand. "They'll never know. I saved my hair and I'm going to pin it back on," she said with a self-righteous smirk as she worked the soap into her hair. "So I don't have anything to worry about—unless you tell them." Turning her head, she peered out from under a bent arm at Dawn. "And you won't tell them because you gave me your word you wouldn't, didn't you?"

Recognizing the leverage she had suddenly acquired, Dawn gave her sister a wide, taunting smile.

"Daaa-wn," Aidan dragged the name out, her tone uneasy. "Why are you grinning like that?"

"I only promised I wouldn't tell them what you were up to . . . if you confided in me. But you didn't tell me anything so my vow isn't binding."

Aidan's massaging fingers stilled in her lather-whitened hair. "You wouldn't dare," she said, her voice threatening.

"Are you so sure? Of course, if I knew your secret, I'd be bound to silence by my own promise, but as it is . . . " Leaving the implied threat unspoken, Dawn turned to leave the bathroom.

Aidan straightened in the water. "Come back here," she hollered. "If you tell them, I'll never forgive you."

"I'm not sure I could sleep nights if I kept this from our parents," Dawn goaded over her shoulder as she entered her own bedroom.

Aidan bolted out of the tub and followed her sister, unconcerned with the watery trail she left in her wake. "All right, I'll tell you," she snarled. "But so help me God, if you betray me, the life of a miserable old maid will look wonderful compared to what I'm going to do to you!"

Clapping her hands together, Dawn cheered.

Aidan gave her a final warning glare, then wheeled around and retraced the wet trail to the tub. "I mean it, Dawn. If you so much as breathe a word of this to anyone, I'll—"

Running to her sister, Dawn swore, "I'll die before I betray you. Cross my heart! You won't be sorry you trusted me."

Aidan angrily splashed back into her bath. "I'd better not be."

Picking up a washcloth, Dawn started to scrub her sister's back. "Just wait and see. I'll be a big help! You're going to wonder why you didn't ask for my assistance before. Now, what is it? Is it like when you sneaked into the mental institution at Terrell to see if the patients were being treated cruelly, and then couldn't get back out?"

Aidan shrugged off Dawn's reminder of the frightening three days she'd spent two years ago. After all, that was in the past. Besides, she'd gotten her story, and that was the important thing.

"This is much bigger than that," she said with a taunting grin, her secret dying to burst from her lips.

Dawn's eyes widened. "Bigger than getting locked in a hospital full of crazy people!"

Aidan nodded and lay back in the water to rinse herself off. "What would you say if I told you I'm going to Cuba with the Rough Riders?"

"You're what?"

Filling a pitcher with fresh water, Aidan handed it to Dawn. "Can you help me rinse my hair?"

Acting automatically, Dawn took the pitcher. "You can't

13

be a Rough Rider," she protested as she worked the clean water through Aidan's shorn tresses. "They're all men . . ."

"Exactly," Aidan said with a self-satisfied chuckle. "And so are all the reporters they're taking with them—except one, of course. But I didn't mention that little fact to Lieutenant Colonel Roosevelt when he agreed to take me."

"You mean you—?"

"Señoritas," a voice called from the hallway. "Your mama, she says you are to hurry."

"Oh, no!" Dawn gasped, dousing Aidan's head with all the water at once.

"Hey! What are you doing?" Aidan sputtered, spitting out soapy water and rubbing her eyes.

"We have to hurry. I got so caught up in your plan, I forgot to tell you we're having company for dinner! Come on! We don't want to be late."

"Company! I don't have time to spend the evening with some dull old politician or a publisher friend of Da's" Aidan snatched the water pitcher from Dawn and refilled it. "I'm going to stay in my room tonight and start writing my story. I want to get my first impressions of Mr. Roosevelt and the Rough Riders on paper while they're fresh in my mind." She bent her head over her legs and rinsed her hair again. "Just tell Mama and Da I have a headache, and asked for dinner in my room."

"But you have to come!" Dawn grabbed a towel and held it out to her sister. "Our guest isn't some stodgy old friend of Da's. This is a friend of yours. One I think you won't want to miss seeing."

"A friend of mine?" Aidan asked, accepting the towel and stepping out of the tub. "Who?" She dried her body briskly, then wrapped the bathsheet around her hair and strolled into her bedroom. "Well? Who is it?"

"I ought to let it be a surprise," Dawn teased. She examined her reflection in the mirror, then pinched her cheeks to enhance their natural rosiness. Tilting her head from side

14

to side, she scraped her teeth over her lips to make them red.

"I'm in no mood for games, Dawn." She whipped up a dressing gown and put it on. "Tell me, or I'll tell Mama and Da about the time we got into his liquor cabinet."

"You'd be in just as much trouble as I would."

"But they expect things like that from me. While on the other hand, you—"

"All right, I'll give you a hint. We played when we used to visit Grandmother Quiet Rain on the reservation before she died. We called him Danny then, but now he's changed his name to—"

"Danny? Danny Edwards?" Aidan shrieked remembering the one-quarter Indian boy she'd had such an agonizing crush on for the major part of her childhood. "Why didn't you tell me?" Excitedly, she tore the towel from her head and ripped off the dressing gown. Dropping both on the floor, she made a dash toward the tall chest of drawers beside her bed.

"What's he doing in Texas? Have you seen him yet? How does he look?" Aidan hurled questions at her sister, not waiting for answers, as she yanked open a drawer and whisked out fresh underwear. "Do you think he's still as handsome as we thought he was when we were kids?" she mused, stepping into lace cambric drawers that fell to just below her knees. A sudden smile curved her lips as she took out a chemise. "I wonder if he remembers the time he . . . "

Her dark eyes glowing nostalgically, Aidan hugged the lace-trimmed undergarment to her, recalling the good-bye kiss she'd received from Danny Edwards when she had just turned twelve and he was thirteen. That was the last time she'd seen him because her grandmother had died the following winter and they hadn't gone back to the reservation again. But she'd never forgotten that sweet kiss—or the tall boy with the dazzling blue eyes who had given it to her.

Without realizing what she was doing, or the way Dawn

was watching her, Aidan pressed the palm of a hand to her cheek. "Imagine. Danny Edwards. After eight whole years."

"There's one thing you should know," Dawn said. "He isn't Danny Edwards anymore. Now he calls himself River Blue Eagle."

"River Blue Eagle?" Aidan wrinkled her nose. "What kind of a name is that?"

"It sounds like an Indian name to me."

Aidan shot her younger sister an annoyed look, then jerked her chemise over her head and poked her arms through the armholes. "Of course, it's an Indian name. He's an Indian."

Rummaging in her drawer for a slip, she pulled out a corset and eyed it with suspicion, as if wondering what she was supposed to do with it. Deciding the stiff garment was definitely not necessary, she tossed it aside and returned to her search. "But he's only one-quarter Indian. Aha!" she swept up a shamelessly crumpled petticoat. Continuing to talk, she stepped into it, shimmying it up to her waist as she walked across the room. "Indians are taking white names these days. So why would someone who had a perfectly acceptable name change it?"

Dawn shook her head, her horrified gaze fixed on the wrinkled slip. "You'll have to ask him. You aren't going to wear that, are you?"

Surprised, Aidan looked down at herself and shrugged. "Why not? No one's going to see it." She wrenched open the door to the oak-lined clothes closet she and Dawn shared. "Have you seen my pink blouse with the green dots?" she asked, riffling through her clothes. Stopping when she came to a black skirt, she ripped it from the hanger and put it on, stuffing the unironed petticoat out of sight as she did. "I know it was in the closet when I got dressed this morning."

Glancing disapprovingly at the items strewn over the

floor of Aidan's half of the closet, Dawn stooped down and dug under a pile of discarded clothing. "You don't mean this blouse, do you?" She grimaced as she revealed a wad of dotted fabric.

A smile lit Aidan's face, and she grabbed for the unkempt garment. "There you are!" she said to it. "I knew I saw you this morning."

Refusing to give up possession of the blouse, Dawn snatched it back from Aidan, certain her sister still intended to wear it. "Aidan! When are you going to start taking pride in your appearance? Can't you see this blouse is in no condition to be worn to scrub floors, much less entertain a guest? What was it doing in that heap, anyway?"

Aidan grinned sheepishly. "I suppose you're right," she admitted. "I was in a hurry when I left this morning and couldn't decide what to wear. Then I thought of the clothes in the trunk, and I — "

"Spare me the rest of the story," Dawn said, shaking her head and laughing. How could she stay mad at Aidan? "I've heard it before, and right now, we have more immediate things to worry about. Like what you're going to wear and what we're going to do with your hair!"

Giving Dawn a quick hug and an affectionate peck on the cheek, Aidan turned back to the closet. "I'll do better. I promise." She held out a yellow- and black-striped blouse with large ballooned sleeves and a high, gathered collar. "How's this?" she asked.

"A little gaudy for my taste, but at least it's ironed." Dawn took the blouse from the hanger and held it out for her sister to slip into. "And it's in style."

Aidan turned around so Dawn could button the blouse up her back. "Lucky me." She laughed. "For once, current fashion is in accord with my 'unique' tastes. But even if bright colors weren't the rage right now, I would still wear them."

17

"How well I know." Dawn shook her head in a gesture of wry disapproval. "You always had to 'dress up' the tasteful pastels and browns you wore when we were little. Remember the time you 'borrowed' a red petticoat from a Mexican servant? The trouble you got into!" Dawn giggled at the memory. "Your bottom matched that petticoat for a week if I recall correctly. And I'll never forget the day you showed up dressed for church in that purple matador's jacket. No matter what you wore, you could always be counted on to be unique, couldn't you? And we all loved you—even if at times we can't understand why you do certain things."

Aidan tweaked her sister's plump cheek playfully. "And love you—even if you stop fussing over me and trying to turn me into what the etiquette books proclaim a lady should be." She combed her fingers through her short hair, noticing it was almost dry and already curling. "Now, are we going to stand here all day, or are you going to help me with my hair?"

Sighing, Dawn tugged on Aidan's arm. "Come on. It's probably hopeless, but let's see what we can do."

Glancing around the main living room at the center of the large hacienda, River couldn't suppress his resentment. He was certain this *sala*, which was what the servant who had shown him in had called the room, was larger than the combined living areas of a dozen reservation families. And he had no doubt that the furnishings alone cost much more than those twelve families could earn in a year.

Everything about the room was a blatant example of the opulence and waste whites were known for. And he hated it all, from the stuccoed walls decorated with Mexican blankets and serapes woven in hues of burnt orange, cherry red, and rust, to the massive dark oak and leather furniture and the wide-planked hardwood floors gleaming beneath his boots.

Hooding his gaze to disguise what he was thinking, River eased his lanky frame down onto the cowhide sofa, determined to make it through the next few hours without offending his parents' friends by telling them what he thought about their luxurious lifestyle. But it was going to be very difficult.

"What do you think of Texas, so far?" Clay Donovan asked, handing River a glass of whiskey.

Halfway expecting to hear some snide joke about Indians and "firewater," as he usually did when he socialized with whites, River hesitated an instant before reaching for the drink. Oh, the remarks were always accompanied by a jovial show of treating him as an equal, when in fact their actions were only vague attempts to disguise their own prejudices.

When the comment expected remark, River gave his host a strained smile and accepted the drink. "I haven't seen enough of your state to form an opinion, Mr. Donovan. But what I've seen has been interesting." There. No one could find fault with that answer.

"Hold on there, son." Clay lowered his still youthfully lean body into an upholstered chair covered with a patchwork of different colored cowhides. "None of that 'Mr. Donovan' stuff. Call me Clay. I already have far too many reminders that fifty's less than two years away" — He ran his fingers through thick blond hair just beginning to gray at the temples and sideburns " — without the likes of you coming in here and adding to the list."

Oblivious to the teasing gleam in Donovan's blue eyes, River stiffened, his own sapphire gaze hardening to granite.

Sensing how River had taken Clay's words, Gentle Fawn shot her husband a disapproving frown, then turned to River. "We were so happy when your mother wrote and told us that you would be calling when you got here. It's a shame she and your father couldn't come too. We would

19

have loved to see them."

The petite, dark-haired woman, who didn't look more than thirty, though River knew her to be at least forty, had a friendly, soft-spoken manner that immediately eased the tension gnawing at his insides. Embarrassed by the way he had reacted to Clay's casual remark, he forced himself to sit back in his seat. He could see from Clay Donovan's guileless blue eyes that the man hadn't meant anything untoward by his comment. But after years of attending white schools, and of working with politicians, it was impossible to forget old slights. Yes, it was going to be a very long evening.

He cleared his throat and took a sip of whiskey. "Mother considered coming with me, but my father couldn't get away—and her work on the reservation doesn't allow her much free time. She's hoping she'll be able to include San Antonio when she goes on her next lecture tour."

"Yes, the tour," Gentle Fawn said. "She asked me to join her, and I am seriously considering it."

"Ah!" Clay rose, a broad grin splitting his handsome face as he turned toward the entry from the bedroom wing on the south side of the house. "Here are my girls. Late as usual."

Twisting his head around, River saw two of the loveliest women he'd ever seen in his life. One blond and the other red-headed, they were both small—not more than two or three inches over five feet, he judged. And though the blond with her shiny gold curls and delectably generous curves might be considered the prettier of the two by many, River's gaze immediately went to the less curvaceous girl with the red hair.

Seeing the gleam of joyful recognition in her dark eyes as he gaze met his, he felt his heartbeat quicken. The skinny little girl he remembered from his childhood had become a beautiful woman. Never had a female affected him like this. It was as if he'd been kicked in the belly.

20

Remembering his manners, he bolted to his feet, grinning sheepishly. "Hello, Aidan," he said huskily, forgetting how much he had dreaded this evening. "It's good to see you again."

"Good to see me, indeed!" Aidan said, stepping down into the *sala* and, in long, unladylike strides, covering the space that separated them. "Is that any way to greet a friend you haven't seen in nine years? The least you can do is give me a hug." Without waiting for his response, she wrapped her arms around his lean waist and squeezed.

His expression stunned and helpless, he returned her exuberant greeting with a stiff embrace.

Suddenly becoming aware of how inappropriate her actions had been, Aidan looked up at River, and was surprised to realize he was at least a foot taller than she was. In fact, he was several inches taller than her father, who was just under six feet. "I'm sorry, Danny," she apologized, dropping her hands from his waist and stepping back , her gaze fleeting over him from head to foot.

How could this handsome man possibly be the boy she remembered? For one thing, long, gangly limbs had been replaced with muscular shoulders and arms that never strained against the confinement of the jacket he wore, as if his strength were imprisoned by the white man's clothing. And though Danny had worn his glistening black hair in long braids, this man's hair was cut short in the style of the times.

A wave of sadness rocked Aidan. She'd felt the same sick feeling when she'd seen a caged tiger one time at the zoo. True, River looked more "civilized" than he had in those long-ago summers when he'd worn nothing but a breechcloth and moccasins, and had run free over the Dakota plains; but despite his perfectly turned-out appearance, River Blue Eagle was completely out of place here. Like the tiger, he looked trapped, as though he longed to bolt and run back to the wild at the first opportunity.

River gave Aidan a half-hearted smile and released his grip on her. "Don't worry about it."

"I'm afraid a lack enthusiasm isn't one of Little Fire's shortcomings," Clay chided, prodding Aidan toward the opposite end of the couch on which River had been sitting, then taking his own seat.

"Little Fire?" River asked, sitting back down, his interest piqued by the Indian-sounding name.

"Mama and Da wanted my name to be symbolic of both their backgrounds. Indian for the years Mama spent with the Lakotas and Irish for Da's ancestors," Aidan explained with a grin, making the mistake of looking directly into River's eyes.

Her stomach did a funny little flip-flop, and her hands grew clammy. He still had the bluest eyes she'd ever seen, even bluer than her father's or her sister's. Looking into them actually took her breath away, just the way it had when they were children. But these were not the happy, laughing eyes she remembered from her youth. Now they were the eyes of an old man, an old man who had known such pain in his life that he would never be able to laugh again. It was as if River had aged five years for every one that had passed since they had last met.

Wrenching her gaze from those sad blue eyes, she cleared her throat nervously, certain that she was imagining things. Now, what had she been saying? Oh, yes, her name. She'd been explaining the meaning of her name.

"So they settled on Aidan because it's Gaelic for Little Fire," she said in a hoarse rush of words.

River nodded seriously, as if weighing what she had said. "I see." He couldn't stop staring at the fiery wreath of hair that circled her head. He wished she'd worn it loose instead of pinned up. It seemed wrong to contain something so obviously meant to be free.

"And never was a person more aptly name," Clay teased, with a wink at Aidan.

"Unless it's Dawn," Aidan said, desperate to escape the heat of River's intense blue gaze and to divert his attention elsewhere.

Aware that he was staring, River shook off the spell that had entrapped him the moment he'd seen Aidan in the archway, and he forced himself to turn to the Donovans' other daughter.

Feeling better now that River wasn't watching her in that way that made her feel he could read her mind, Aidan found her voice again. "Speaking of names, my sister tells me you've changed yours from Danny Edwards to River Blue Eagle. Why would you do that when most Indians are choosing to adopt white names?"

The muscles in River's jaw bunched. His fists, which rested on his thighs, clenched into tight balls, and his spine straightened. "Choosing?" He turned a menacing scowl on her, the expression on his face suddenly hard and filled with hatred. "Tell me, Aidan, would you call it 'choosing' if a stranger who didn't even speak your language came in here tonight and announced, "I'm making a list of all the people in your household, but I can't be bothered with learning to write or pronounce your name so I'm changing it to Ska-Peta-Winyan'?"

Momentarily stunned by River's assault and the loathing in his voice, Aidan was at a loss for words. What could have happened to make him change so drastically? Well, whatever it was, there was no excuse for his attack on her. She had merely asked a polite question, yet he had jumped on her as if she alone were responsible for whatever had caused him to be so angry.

Nostrils flaring, Aidan leaned toward River and returned his black look. "No, I wouldn't call that a situation of choice," she said through a tight smile. "However, according to what I've read in the newspaper, this is quite a different matter."

"Ah! The newspaper," River said with a sardonic nod of

his head. He slapped his knee. "How could I forget the trusty newspaper? If something is printed in the newspaper, it has to be the truth, doesn't it? Well, for your information, Miss Donovan—"

"River," Gentle Fawn interjected, her expression uneasy. Her gaze zigzagged between the two equally adamant opponents before she leveled a warning glance at Aidan. "How long do you expect to be in San Antonio?"

"Excuse me?" River asked, his hostess's tactful interruption reminding him of his own poor manners. "Oh," he said, registering her question and answering it before she could repeat herself. "We hope to have all the men outfitted and trained by the first of June."

Aidan's brown eyes grew round with surprise, all thoughts of arguing with River now gone. "What did you say?" she choked.

"Oh, we forgot to tell you girls that River is Theodore Roosevelt's personal aide," Clay announced.

Dawn and Aidan exchanged trapped glances. Dawn stuttered, "That means you're with the—"

"Rough Riders!" Aidan finished for her, all her own plans exploding in her mind at once.

Chapter Two

Dawn inhaled loudly. "You can't be a Rough Rider!" she protested, sneaking a frightened glance toward Aidan, who was staring wide-eyed at River, her mouth hanging slightly open.

Narrowing her eyes in a silent statement to her sister, Aidan forced her lips into a tight grin. "Of course he can, Dawn. Anyone who wants to join can be in the Rough Riders."

"Why would you think otherwise?" Gentle Fawn interjected, the frown on her usually smooth brow shadowing her eyes as her gaze whipped back and forth from one of her daughters to the other.

Dawn's blue eyes filled with tears, and she shot Aidan a pleading glimpse. "I . . . it's j-just th—"

"I would think," Aidan interrupted with a forced smile, determination not to let River Blue Eagle cost her the story keeping her voice steady, "a man who is so adamant about the way the Indians are being forced to change their names would want to stay here and help them correct their problems. You're a lawyer, aren't you? From Harvard, no less. Shouldn't you be filing some sort of legal action or something? It seems to me you would want to be fighting for the Indians in the courts here, rather than going into battle in someone else's war?"

River felt as though he'd been slammed in the chest with a

battering ram. Aidan Donovan had unknowingly pinpointed the exact argument he'd been waging with himself for weeks now. His fists tightened again, and he sucked in a steadying breath of air, then blew it out in a long, hissing release. "You don't know what you're talking about."

Realizing intuitively that she had hit on River's most vulnerable point, Aidan was gripped by a spasm of guilt. His hurting blue eyes looked even more tortured than before, and her immediate impulse was to change the subject. But unless she wanted all her plans for greatness to go awry, she had no choice but to pursue this. Besides, why should she feel guilty? She hadn't said anything that wasn't true, had she? It wasn't her fault he was so defensive. "Then suppose you enlighten me. Exactly why *are* you going to Cuba with the Rough Riders?" The challenge in the question was undisguised.

Clay cleared his throat pointedly. "I think we've about exhausted this subject, don't you?" He stood up and reached for the glass in River's hand. "May I freshen your whiskey?"

River glanced at the barely touched drink and lifted it to his lips. "No thanks. I'm fine." Without thinking, he slugged back the contents of the glass in two hefty swallows. Grimacing as the liquor burned its way down his throat, he rose and followed Clay to the bar. "Maybe I will have another."

The instant River's back was to her, Gentle Fawn bounded out of her chair and caught Aidan by the arm, her mouth fixed in an angry smile. "And while your father and our guest fix their drinks, you and I will go check on dinner, won't we, dear?"

"But —"

"Don't say another word," Gentle Fawn warned in a demanding whisper.

Recognizing the tone her mother used only on the rarest occasions, Aidan obeyed and followed her from the room.

Once they were out of earshot of the *sala,* Gentle Fawn spun around to face her daughter, her face red with anger.

"What's wrong with you? That young man is a guest in our home, and you have done nothing but goad and bait him from the minute you came into the room."

"I haven't been baiting him," Aidan said defensively. "Can I help it if he's so serious that everything I say to him hits a nerve? What would you have me talk about, Mama? The weather?"

"That would be a nice start," Gentle Fawn said, her irritation with her oldest daughter mellowing slightly. She gave her a conceding smile. "I must admit, when it comes to certain subjects, River Blue Eagle seems to have a bit of a chip on his shoulder."

Relieved to see her mother's anger ease, Aidan smiled conspiratorially. "It does make you wonder, doesn't it? Why does he become so hostile whenever there is any mention of the Indians? It's as if he hates the whites."

Gentle Fawn shook her head and grinned at Aidan's tendency to overdramatize every situation. "Hate is a very strong word. Perhaps 'guarded' would better express his attitude."

"Can't you see it in his eyes? He disapproves of us — everything about us. And it's not as if he hates just us. I think he resents his own white blood as well!"

"Now, you *are* reading things into his behavior that are not there." Gentle Fawn prodded Aidan toward the *sala*. "But whatever it is that causes him to act the way he does, it is not our business. He is a guest in our home, and he will be treated accordingly. By all of us. Is that understood?"

Aidan opened her mouth to argue, then closed it. She knew that look on her mother's face. When Gentle Fawn's mind was made up, there would be no further discussion. She would just have to find another time to approach River Blue Eagle about his plans — when they could be alone. She wasn't going to give up on finding a way to make him change his mind about going to Cuba. "I'll try to be good."

"You will do better than *try.* I expect you to go back in

27

there and find something to talk about that won't antagonize that young man."

Throughout dinner, Aidan managed to stay on her best behavior — which was a major feat under the best of circumstances. Her father had always said she was born with two things that could only lead her to more harm than good: the curiosity of a cat and an extra-large foot in her mouth. And there had never been any evidence to the contrary.

During the long meal, she had squirmed under the unsettling stare of River Blue Eagle, but she had mercifully kept her silence because her mind was churning with possible ways to convince him not to go to Cuba with Teddy Roosevelt's Rough Riders.

As the group returned to the *sala,* Gentle Fawn gave Aidan an approving smile that said, *Now, that wasn't too bad, was it?*

Seeing this moment when she was in her mother's good graces as an opportunity to set the stage for her planned absence, Aidan seized it. "By the way," she announced jubilantly, "I have some exciting news!"

"Oh?" Clay paused, holding the brandy bottle above an empty snifter. "What kind of news?"

"I have an assignment to do a wonderful story!"

"What kind of assignment?" Gentle Fawn asked uneasily. She still hadn't fully recovered from the experience with the mental sanitarium. "It had better not be anything like your last 'wonderful story.' "

Aidan swallowed the lump in her throat and forced a laugh. "Goodness, no! Believe me, I learned my lesson. No, this is perfectly safe."

Clay eyed his oldest daughter warily. "We'll be the judges of that. Somehow, your idea of 'perfectly safe' and ours is not always the same."

"Well, this time it will be. I've learned that plans are al-

28

ready getting underway for a huge exposition to be held in 1904 in Saint Louis to celebrate the one-hundredth birthday of the transfer of that city to United States under the terms of the Louisiana Purchase."

Clay gave her a puzzled stare. "Go on. . . ."

"So I mentioned it to Mr. Knight at the newspaper, and he agreed that readers might be interested in a series of bi-monthly articles reporting the exposition's progress from the beginning."

"And of course you volunteered to do these articles," Clay said with a knowing nod of his head.

Aidan squared her shoulders. "Well, of course. After all, it was my idea. I should at least do the first one. Surely, you can't object to my going to Saint Louis."

"Alone?" Gentle Fawn asked.

This might be more difficult than she had anticipated, maybe she should have said she was going to do a story in Dallas. No, that was too close to San Antonio. She had to be far enough away to discourage any surprise visits from her parents. "Nellie Bly went all the way around the world when she was only a year older than I am," she argued. "If she could do that, surely I'm capable of going to St. Louis by myself."

Clay threw back his head and laughed. "We might as well face it, Mama. Our little girl will be twenty-one this fall. We can't keep her in the nest indefinitely."

Gentle Fawn shrugged her shoulders and offered an apologetic smile to the group. "I suppose you're right. When I was eighteen I left everything and everyone I'd ever known behind in the Dakotas and came to Texas with you, didn't I?"

Clay winked a mischievous blue eye. "That you did! Any regrets?"

Her dark brown eyes gleaming with love, Gentle Fawn smiled more broadly. "Only occasionally," she teased.

"Occasionally?" Clay blustered, pretending to be enraged. "Is this the thanks I get for taking care of you all these years?"

29

Shooting Aidan and Dawn a playful grin, Gentle Fawn asked, "Who has taken care of whom, Clay Donovan? If it weren't for me, you would have left your scalp in Montana a long time ago — and not just once!"

Clay ran an open hand down his clean-shaven face and grinned, pretending to be embarrassed. "The way I remember it, she was the first one to try to make me prematurely bald."

Dawn giggled happily and clapped her hands together. "Tell us again how you met Mama, Da!"

Relaxing, Clay shifted his gaze from his daughter to River, then shook his head. "Some other time, Sunshine. We don't want to bore our guest with family stories."

"You're not bored, are you, River?" Dawn coaxed. "You want to hear how Mama tried to scalp Da, don't you?"

River forced his mouth into a smile. No, he didn't want to hear the story. In fact, he'd had about all of lighthearted white-man's company he could take. He just wanted to leave.

Besides, his parents had told him more than he wanted to know about the Donovans before he'd left South Dakota. Though Gentle Fawn's natural parents had been Spanish Texans, she had been taken by an Indian when only three years old and had ended up in the Dakotas as the adopted daughter of a Lakota warrior and his childless wife. Evidently no one, including Gentle Fawn, had ever suspected that she was not one of the People — until the white man, Clay Donovan, had unraveled the mystery of her true identity and had brought her to Texas to claim her white heritage.

"I'd really like to hear it," he lied. "But I have to leave quite early in the morning. We're expecting a trainload of volunteers from Missouri tomorrow, and I need to be back in San Antonio in time to help get them signed in and situated." He pulled a watch from his pocket and flipped it open, giving it a cursory glance. "I know it's early, but if you don't mind, I'd like to go to my room and get some rest."

Before his hosts could comment, he shoved the timepiece

30

back into place and stood up. "I'll probably leave before you awaken, sir, so I'll take this opportunity to thank you for your hospitality." He held out his hand to Clay. "Dinner was delicious, Mrs. Donovan," he said as he turned to Gentle Fawn. "My mother and father will be pleased to learn that you are both doing so well." He gave Aidan and Dawn a stiff smile and nodded his head. "It was good seeing the two of you again."

Without waiting for a response from the stunned family, he walked briskly toward the doorway leading to the bedroom side of the house, where he'd washed up when he had arrived at Rancho Camila that afternoon.

Clay turned to Aidan and shrugged his shoulders. "Has he always been so intense?"

Dawn shook her head. "I remember him as a happy, carefree boy who was full of energy and mischief. What do you think made him become so serious?"

"Well, whatever it was," Aidan said sarcastically as she rose, her gaze on the archway through which River had disappeared, "he couldn't get away from us fast enough, could he?" She stretched her arms over her head and yawned. "But at least he had one good idea. I think I'll call it a night, too."

"Damn!" River muttered as he closed the bedroom door behind him. He reached up and loosened the knot in the necktie that had been choking him throughout the difficult evening, then shrugged out of his jacket and tossed it onto the four-poster bed on his way to the glass double doors on the opposite side of the room. Tearing both doors open at once, he sucked in a long, greedy drag of cool night air. He felt better almost immediately, once the clean spring air wended its way to his lungs.

Turning back to the room, he realized the bed had been turned down by some invisible servant, and an electric lamp had been lit for his convenience. Anger and bitterness

31

churned anew in his gut. How could he sleep here even one night knowing entire families on the reservations would consider themselves rich to have a house half the size of this very room, to say nothing of having running water and electricity?

He strode angrily over to the bed and gave the string that dangled from the lamp an angry tug. The room was instantly pitched into darkness. He waited, allowing the blackness to seep into his pores and relieve some of the ache the artificial glare had burned on his soul.

Sitting down on the bed, he wrenched the celluloid-lined collar and cuffs from his neck and wrists and dropped them on the bedside table. Right away, he could feel his tension easing with the removal of each of the *wasicun* trappings. *Interesting word: trappings.* He smiled bitterly as he unbuttoned his stiffly starched shirt. *White man's clothing and luxuries are traps.*

Anxious to be as free as possible from the uncomfortable evidence of 'civilized living,' he kicked off his square-toed shoes, pulled off his socks, and stood up. Ah, much better. He quickly lowered his black suspenders and gratefully shed the rest of his white-man's clothing.

At last he wore nothing but a breechcloth and the beaded necklace his great-aunt, Prairie Moon, had made for him in the fall of 1890 — just three months before she and hundreds like her had been murdered by soldiers' at Wounded Knee.

Releasing an anguished moan, he dug his fingertips into his eye sockets, as though if he pressed hard enough he could rub out the grisly visions that filled his thoughts every time Wounded Knee came to mind. But the visions never faded. In fact, they'd remained vivid and constant for nearly eight years.

It had been late in the Christmas season, the time when his white mother, Star Blue Eagle, observed the one *wasicun* custom she had refused to abandon. Of course, River and his younger brother and sister had never objected to annual visits from Santa Claus, or to any of the other exciting Christmas traditions their mother had insisted they uphold, such as decorating a tree and exchanging gifts with each other. And that year had been no exception.

In fact, their house in Yankton, from which River's father, Daniel Blue Eagle, carried on his struggle for Indian rights, had still been draped in holiday greenery and red ribbons when the wire had come that had changed River forever.

Recalling his father's stunned face and the tears streaming down that strong man's cheeks as he'd read the wire aloud to the family, River walked out onto the private patio attached to his room.

His own eyes moist, he threw back his head and stared with unseeing eyes up into the sky. He could still hear his father reading the fateful message from the Indian agent at Pine Ridge, so clearly it might have been only yesterday. *On the morning of December 29th, 1890, U.S. soldiers fired on and killed a band of ghost dancers under the leadership of Chief Big Foot at Wounded Knee Creek on the Pine Ridge Reservation in South Dakota. Your presence is urgently requested to help prevent further complications to this unfortunate incident.*

Visions of dead bodies frozen in grotesque positions and buried in deep snow exploded in River's mind. Writhing inwardly at the grisly sight he couldn't forget, he pounded his fists against the stone wall that edged the patio. " 'Unfortunate incident!' " He groaned, reliving what he had felt when he and his father had first seen the corpse-littered field at Wounded Knee three days after the slaughter.

The winter's first blizzard had started only hours after the massacre, and the civilians hired to bury the dead at two dollars a body had not been able to start dragging the remains out from under the snow until New Year's Day, 1891.

In an instant, River had felt his youth evaporate. Dry-eyed, he had stood beside his father and watched woodenly as, one by one, the stiffened bodies had been heaved into a

33

single pit — after they had been stripped for "souvenirs" by members of the burial party. Even little children, some still clutched in their mothers' rigid arms, had been thrown into the pit.

Afterward, Daniel Blue Eagle had told River how proud he was of the way his son had handled himself at the site, but River had felt no pride that day. Instead, he'd been filled with shame and hatred of his own white blood. He had come to Wounded Knee a child, with a heart full of excitement at being allowed to accompany his father on such an important trip. But he had left it an old man. An old and bitter man.

"River?" a voice whispered over the screech of gate hinges twisting open.

Startled, he pivoted and stared at the vine-covered, seven-foot wall between the patios, in time to see a hidden door swing open to reveal a petite feminine form.

"What are you doing here?" he snarled.

"I came to see if you need—" The words dried up in Aidan's mouth and she stopped in the doorway, her astonished eyes taking in his broad, hairless chest. "Y-you're wearing a breechcloth!" she stammered, her gaze dropping from his bulging pectoral and arm muscles to his narrow waist and hips. "I mean, why aren't you wearing your clothes?"

"Is spying on guests a *wasicun* custom?" he asked, his tone caustic, as he approached

Her feet seemed to have taken root in the stone floor of the patio, but his verbal attack revived her spirit slightly, She curled her lip, returning his stormy stare. "No, spying on guests isn't a white custom. I only wanted to be certain you had everything you needed before I went to bed." She turned back toward her own patio. "Please forgive the intrusion. I won't bother you again."

"Wait!" His hand whipped out to stop her.

Chills tripped up Aidan's spine, and goosebumps popped out on her skin—except where River gripped her arm. There, she was painfully aware of the imprint of a palm and fingers

34

searing through the material of her blouse and into her flesh.

"I'm sorry I barked at you," he said, his voice hoarse.

His apology sent the scalding heat on her arm raging through her body. It turned her limbs to liquid, settling in the pit of her belly. She swallowed back the lump in her throat that threatened to strangle her. "You don't have to apologize. I shouldn't have intruded on your privacy," she managed to croak out, again unable to make her feet move.

"Now that you're here, would you like to talk?" he asked.

Aidan turned and stared up into his pensive eyes. "You don't have to invite me to stay just to be polite."

"I'm not being polite. I'd really like you to stay."

Uncertain, Aidan frowned. "Earlier, I had the definite impression that you didn't want to have anything to do with me."

"Yes, well, I'm sorry about that. I have a lot on my mind," he explained, walking back to the lower outside wall of the patio.

Aidan studied River's back, the angry retort on her lips suddenly silenced by the way the moonlight played over his tanned skin, giving it a golden sheen.

Muscles rippled beneath his flesh, filling her with a confusing need to know the feel of that flesh beneath her fingertips, and she took a step toward him.

Astounded by her reaction to him, she stopped. She had to get away before she did something foolish. Her breathing became ragged pants. "I will leave you to your thoughts," she said, wheeling about and making a desperate dash for her own patio.

Safe on her side of the wall, she started to close the gate. Then the reason she had sought River out came back to her, and she paused. If she ran away now, she might as well forfeit her plan to go to Cuba. This could easily be the only chance she would have to convince him that he should go back to South Dakota. So, unless she intended to give up without a fight, she had to return to the other patio. She would just have to ignore what he was wearing—or not wearing!

Aidan drew in a fortifying breath and again stepped onto the adjoining patio. "You know," she began, taking care to keep her gaze on the wrought-iron grillwork that extended several feet above the patio wall in order to keep out unwanted visitors while affording occupants a view of the landscape, "dressed like that, you remind me of a boy I knew when I was a little girl. His name was Danny Edwards. He was always happy and fun to be with. I don't suppose you could tell me what happened to him."

Gazing out into the darkness, River shook his head, his mouth twisting into a sad grin. "There's no such person anymore."

"Why not?" she asked, his melancholy affecting her as she drew alongside him.

"He grew up and realized happiness is only an escape from reality."

Forgetting her vow not to look at him, Aidan turned to gaze up at his strong profile and, without thinking, placed a small hand on his forearm. "I don't believe that!"

He glowered down at her hand, milky white against his darker skin. "No, of course not. How could you?" He shook off her touch and walked to the other side of the patio, making a wide sweep in the air with his arm. "Look at the way you live!"

"What's wrong with the way I live?" she asked indignantly.

River threw back his head and laughed. "Nothing, Aidan. That's just it. There's nothing wrong with the way you live. Except that it's an illusion. Because of this 'happy' life you have, it's never occurred to you that thousands of Indian families could live well on what your family probably wastes each year."

"Are you saying we have no right to live well?" she asked belligerently. "I'll have you know my grandparents worked hard to build this ranch, and my father fought his way up from the New York slums to become one of the world's most

36

famous journalists! Yet you suggest they have no business enjoying the fruits of their labors!"

"I wasn't suggesting anything like that. I was just pointing out that there can be no such thing as happiness when thousands are suffering."

"What would you have the more fortunate people do, River? Renounce everything they've achieved — earned? Give it all away? Besides, I don't see you giving up anything. Or do all the young men on the reservations have the opportunity to earn Harvard law degrees?"

River spun around and scowled down at the fiery redhead. "I got that degree so I can help my people and all the Indians of this country," he ground out through clenched teeth.

Seeing the perfect opening to steer the conversation where she wanted, Aidan seized it. "Oh? If that's the case, then why are you going to Cuba? How is that going to help the Indians? I would think you could do them more good if you stay in the United States."

River's broad shoulders slumped ever so slightly, and he shook his head in defeat. "If I believed that, I'd be on the first train north in the morning."

Her expression confused, Aidan tilted her head to the side, temporarily more interested in the mysterious man Danny Edwards had become than in her own problem. "I don't understand. Why would going to Cuba do more good than going home? That doesn't make sense. What can it possibly do for your cause?"

"Mr. Roosevelt," he said.

"Mr. Roosevelt? What kind of answer is that?"

"You may know he's taken an interest in more than one cause in the past, but he is also a personal friend of my father, and he owns a ranch in North Dakota where he lived for several years. Consequently, my father and I feel that he is the likely man to help us expose the plight of the Indians on reservations to the American public, and to assist us in bringing about improvements. So, when he invited me to work in

37

Washington as his aide, I really had no choice but to go. Then this Cuban war came up, and . . . Well, I'm sure you can figure out the rest."

Of course, I can figure it out, Aidan thought dismally. *If you don't go with the Rough Riders to Cuba, you an no doubt say good-bye to the promise of help from Theodore Roosevelt.* So where did that leave her? *Between a rock and a hard place,* a voice groused in her head. If she continued with her plan to stop him from going, she might be hurting thousands of people. Was a story worth that?

On the other hand, what guarantee is there that Roosevelt will actually help when the war is over? I don't remember reading that he's particularly sensitive to the Indians. Who knows? He could take up some other cause—or he could even be killed. Then, where would we be? River will have wasted months he could have used to look for other ways to help the Indians, and I will have lost the chance to get my story.

"If you tell Mr. Roosevelt that you are needed in South Dakota and can't go to Cuba with him, don't you think he'll still be willing to help you when the war is over?"

River studied her upturned face. "I don't know. Maybe he would. But I can't risk it."

"When he comes back from Cuba, he'll still be your father's friend," Aidan argued. "And he'll still be a man who believes in fighting for oppressed and mistreated people. So, why wouldn't he still be willing to help?"

River tilted his head as though he was giving her words serious consideration.

A seed of guilt twanged through Aidan. What if she was wrong? She shook her head to rid her mind of the unwanted thought. Right or wrong, she couldn't stop now. Not if she wanted to go to Cuba.

She forced herself to go on, her voice oddly strained. "And while he's in Cuba, you can continue to work to help your people—rather than wasting what could easily be a year or more in Cuba."

River took in a deep breath and released it slowly. His well-shaped mouth slowly spread into a grin. "You may be right, Aidan. In fact, the more I think about it, the more I think you are. Thanks," he said, pulling her to him in an impulsive embrace. "I guess I just needed to hear someone else say it."

The twinge of guilt Aidan had been feeling had now swollen into a full, gut-wrenching spasm. She opened her mouth to tell him to forget what she'd said. Then closed it.

What was wrong with her? She should be ecstatic! He was going to do exactly what he really wanted to do, wasn't he? So, what did she have to feel guilty about? It wasn't as if she had forced him to change his mind about going. He had made his own decision. Besides, whatever reasons she had for wanting River Blue Eagle to stay out of Cuba, she hadn't made any points that weren't true. In fact, she had probably done him a favor by convincing him to resign from the Rough Riders.

So why, if she hadn't done anything wrong, was she suddenly overwhelmed by a terrible sense of loss at having tricked River into going back to South Dakota?

39

Chapter Three

Her expression serious, Aidan stared out the second-story window of the room she had taken at the Menger Hotel in San Antonio, only a few hours after her family had watched her board the late afternoon Missouri Pacific bound for St. Louis. She was still ashamed of how easily she had hoodwinked her parents by getting off the train at the first stop, then hiring a coach to bring her back to the city. But it couldn't be helped. They would never have understood how important this was to her, and they would have found a way to stop her. They had been worried enough about her going to St. Louis, even though she'd reminded them over and over that she was an adult and capable of taking care of herself.

Now, if Dawn would just live up to her end of the bargain, everything would be perfect. All her "accomplice" had to do was make certain that once a week the family mail on the hall table produced one of the postcards Aidan had prewritten, affixed with a stamp, then canceled with a bogus—and deliberately smeared—St. Louis postmark.

Turning away from the view of the street, Aidan raked her fingernails down her neck and into the open collar of the blue wool flannel shirt she'd been issued as part of the official Rough Riders uniform. She knew the more she scratched, the more her skin would itch, but she couldn't stop herself.

With a vow that this would be the last time she gave in to the temptation, she tilted her head back to better get at her neck and upper chest with both hands. "These shirts must be a secret weapon of the enemy," she grumbled. "How do they expect men to go into the jungle wearing these? Cuba's supposed to be even hotter in the summer than San Antonio."

Her itching relieved for the moment, she quickly unbuttoned the shirt and tore if off. "That's it. I'm not going to be defeated by a shirt!" She snatched up a tailored white cotton blouse and stabbed her arms into the sleeves. *Two shirts will be hotter, but at least this one will keep the wool away from the part of my skin that isn't protected by my chemise.*

The cool, smooth texture of the cotton immediately eased some of her discomfort, giving her the strength to put the hated wool shirt on again. She hurriedly buttoned it over the blouse, then tucked both into the dusty brown cavalry fatigues the government had issued the Rough Riders. "You'd think they could have given spiffier uniforms to men who are going to war to defend their country. These look as if we're being outfitted to plow fields."

With an annoyed yank, she pulled her belt around her padded middle, taking care not to draw it in so tightly that she would betray her sex by revealing her tiny waist. Turning sideways to scrutinize her reflection in the mirror on the wardrobe door, she looked for any telltale curves that would give her away. Satisfied that she looked like all the other enlisted men, she draped a blue bandana around her neck and tied it in front, then sat down and covered her trouser legs and boot tops with the knee-high leather gaiters she had been issued.

With a final check to be certain her mustache was on straight, she plopped a regulation, floppy-brimmed slouch hat on her head, hefted her blanket-roll — which was all she

41

was allowed to pack — onto her shoulder, and moved toward the door.

Aidan concentrated on advancing through the overcrowded Southern Pacific rail car as the last trainload of Rough Riders finally rolled out of San Antonio at six A.M. on May thirtieth. Jostled and pressed from all sides by soldiers wearing uniforms like hers, she fought to keep her balance.

The rocking, Florida-bound train gave a sudden lurch, sending her back sprawling the meager few feet she had managed to move forward. The only thing that kept her from falling was the crush of the crowd from behind.

This is ridiculous! she said to herself, beginning to believe it was probably going to be impossible for her to find Lieutenant Colonel Roosevelt in the midst of the boisterous volunteers. Supposedly, there were ten coaches just like this one, all packed with singing and cheering men, in addition to twelve livestock cars and one Pullman for the officers. Roosevelt could be in any one of them.

Never one to turn down a challenge — even when she had issued it to herself — Aidan clenched her teeth, hugged her bedroll to her chest, and assumed the posture of a bull ready to attack. "Make way for the press!" she ordered, yelling to be heard above the noise of the train and the excited shouts for vengeance against the Spaniards. Head down, she charged.

Parting and then coming together like a puddle of mud when a stick is trailed through its thick, watery mass, the soldiers allowed Aidan to move through one railroad car after another.

Forcing her way into what she determined to be the last day coach on the train before the officers' sleeping car, she slumped back against the end wall. *This is it. If he's not here, then I give up!* Taking a moment to catch her breath, she glanced around.

Instantly she noted that there were very few blue-shirted enlisted men present. The soldiers in this car almost all wore brown khaki jackets with blue stand-up collars and epaulettes. *Officers!*

Her vigor and enthusiasm immediately revived, she raised up on her toes and strained to see. At that moment, a loud laugh rose over the noise that vibrated through the crowd.

That's got to be old Laughing Horse, she told herself with relief, remembering the name her parents had told her the Indians in North Dakota had bestowed on Theodore Roosevelt because of his prominent teeth and strange laugh. Certain there could be only one man on the train who had such a distinctive laugh, she pushed away from the coach wall and started toward the middle of the car, where the peculiar laughter seemed to have originated.

"Excuse me . . . . Coming through . . . . Excuse me . . . . Coming through . . . , she said over and over, filled with new determination, she shouldered and wedged her way through the crowd.

At last, she spotted him and stopped her advance. Though his back was to her, the sight of this solidly built man sent an unexpected pounding of self-doubt cannonading through her blood. This was the biggest moment of her life so far. From this time on, if everything went as she had planned, she would be solidly positioned on the trail to success.

But what if she wasn't up to all this? What if she just couldn't take the grueling hardships of going to war? What if . . . ?

She looked back over her shoulder toward the exit. It wasn't too late to change her mind. She could just turn around and disappear into the crowd, then get off the train at the first stop it made. No one would even have to know she had been here.

43

No! she told herself vehemently, resolutely turning her head forward again. *I've never been a coward, and I'm not going to be one now. Right or wrong, I'm going to finish what I started.*

Checking one last time to be sure the spirit gum still held the thick mustache in place, she ran her fingers over the correspondent's insignia on her hat. Her pride and confidence revived, she straightened her shoulders and pushed on.

"Ah! There you are, young man!" Theodore Roosevelt greeted her, turning his near-sighted gaze on her and giving her an exuberant slap on the back. "I didn't see you when we loaded at Union Stockyards, and I was afraid you didn't make it back from your trip to Saint Louis in time."

To keep the risk of exposure in San Antonio at a minimum, when she had signed on with the Riders, Aidan had told Mr. Roosevelt that she had an unfinished assignment in St. Louis that must be completed before the end of the month. "Oh, I made it, all right, sir!" she said, keeping her voice low. "Just barely. I wouldn't be surprised to find out I was the last man on the train though."

"Well, I'm glad you got back. I'd hate to admit I was such a poor judge of character," he said, with his famous laugh, his pale, watery eyes glittering behind the thick lenses of his wire-rimmed spectacles. "Come here. I want you to meet somebody." He gripped her upper arm and drew her to the side, addressing the officers he'd been talking to. "Will you gentlemen excuse us?"

Her apprehension completely relieved by the enthusiastic reception she'd received, Aidan followed him to another group of officers.

"Lieutenant," Roosevelt boomed, tapping a tall, broad-shouldered officer on the back. "I want you to meet A. D. Donovan, the son of the famous writer, Clay Donovan. He's going to . . ."

An alarm went off in Aidan's head, and she didn't hear

44

the rest of what he said. She was watching the way the muscles in the lieutenant's back suddenly stiffened against the seams of his brown jacket. If she didn't know better, she would swear . . .

It's just a coincidence, she told herself, annoyed by the ripple of excitement that had tripped up her spine at the thought of seeing River Blue Eagle again. *He's gone back to South Dakota. You've got to stop thinking every tall, broad-shouldered man you see from a distance is him! This man's probably old and has brown eyes,* she tried to convince herself, but finding it impossible to imagine this perfect male physique belonging to an old man. If only his hair weren't hidden under his hat . . .

"Son?" the officer asked, his muscular body starting a slow turn in her direction. "I didn't rea—"

Despite her situation, Aidan felt her heartbeat accelerate with happiness. He even sounded like River!

"—lize that Clay Donovan . . ." The lieutenant faced her squarely now, his memorable blue eyes gray with disbelieving recognition.

Aidan's split second of happiness plummeted into panic as the heat of River's barely disguised rage blazed into her.

"I've hired A. D. to act as my official biographer for this little war of ours," Roosevelt announced proudly, his thick-lensed spectacles not correcting his vision nearly enough for him to notice the tension that suddenly existed between his aide and his biographer.

Knowing it was only a few seconds before her entire ruse was exposed, Aidan refused to show alarm at River's presence. Her great opportunity for fame and success might have been nipped in the bud, but no one was going to say Aidan Donovan hadn't taken her defeat like a "man."

Drawing her tiny frame to it's full height, she glared defiantly into River's eyes and offered him her right hand. "Lieutenant," she said through clenched teeth, determined to keep her voice steady.

45

Ignoring her handshake, River turned to Lieutenant Colonel Roosevelt. "Sir, I must speak with you in private—immediately."

Roosevelt laughed. "Did anyone ever tell you that you're too serious, Lieutenant? Why don't you relax and enjoy the celebration like the rest of the men? We can talk later. Right now, I'd like you to get young Mr. Donovan settled in. I've put him in the compartment next to mine—with you." Roosevelt started to walk away.

River reached out to stop the older man. "But, sir, this really can't wait!"

Roosevelt shook his head in defeat, giving River a toothy grin. "All right, boy. Go on, if it's that important. But I'm warning you, I've waited a long time for today, and I'm not going to look too favorably on anyone who puts a damper on it for me. Now, what is it?"

Hesitating, River hurled a scathing glance in Aidan's direction. "I guess it's not really that big a problem," he said. "I'll handle it myself."

Roosevelt gave him a pleased nod. "Good boy. That's the way I like to hear my officers talk. Now, take care of Donovan, and I'll see you both later."

"Yes, sir," River mumbled, then turned back to Aidan, his eyes filled with a threatening gleam. "I'll be more than glad to take care of *Mr.* Donovan." Clamping his fingers around Aidan's upper arm, he dragged her in the direction of the exit that led to the Pullman car. "Let's go!"

"Hey! You don't have to be so rough!" she complained, running to keep up with River as he forced his way through the coach in stone-faced silence. "What are you trying to do? Tear my arm out of its socket."

River stopped abruptly and spun around to face Aidan. Bringing his face down close to hers, he spoke in a harsh whisper. "Another word out of you, and I'm going to revert to my ancestor's way of dealing with unwanted visitors!"

Of course, she knew he wouldn't literally scalp her, but

46

Aidan couldn't quite bring herself to challenge River Blue Eagle further. Not here, anyway. Clamping her lips together in an exaggerated expression of silence, she frowned at him, her angry brown eyes matching his blue ones challenge for challenge.

Satisfied that she would behave, at least until they were alone, River relaxed his grip on her arm slightly. Hauling her in front of him, he prodded her forward, resuming his original course toward the sleeping car, unconsciously adjusting the length of his strides to accommodate her shorter steps.

When they reached the compartment assigned to the two of them, River opened the door and propelled her into the tiny cubicle with a rough shove. "Now, suppose you tell me what the hell you're doing here!"

Tripping, she stumbled forward, sprawling onto the divan that lined the opposite wall. "What am *I* doing here?" Aidan grunted as she struggled to sit up. "That's what I should be asking you! Why aren't you in South Dakota?"

Her question sliced painfully into River's mind, and settled in a dull throb in his chest. He had believed Aidan Donovan understood how he felt about his duty to the People. She had actually convinced him that she, too, cared. Yet all the while, the plight of the Lakotas had meant nothing to her. She had merely wanted to get him out of the way so she could accomplish her purpose.

He grimaced with self-disgust. He should have known better. All white people were alike. No trick or deceit was too low for them. The only thing that mattered to whites was that they got what they wanted. It had been that way from the first time they'd set foot in America. And despite Aidan's lifelong connection to the Lakotas, it was clear to him that she was no different.

His expression showing none of the hurt and anger he felt, River closed the door behind him and locked it. "I repeat," he said, forming the words precisely, giving each

47

syllable equal emphasis, "what are you doing here?"

Aidan glanced from side to side, as if looking for an escape, then back to River. Her expression wavering between defiance and embarrassment, she shrugged and smiled in defeat. "What difference does it make now? You've ruined everything anyway!"

River's anger evolved into amazement. "*I've* ruined everything? You didn't really think you were going to fool anyone with that ridiculous disguise, did you? And where did you get this thing?" he asked. Moving with lightning speed, he stepped forward. His hand shot out at her surprised face.

Unable to stop herself Aidan flinched and snapped her head to the side. But she wasn't fast enough to escape his reach.

With a faint tearing sound, the mustache separated from her upper lip in one agonizing rip. "Aagh!" she screamed, slapping her hand to her mouth, her eyes watering from the stinging pain. "Why did you do that?"

Unable to ignore the tears that sprang into her large, hurt eyes, River felt a twinge of remorse. But damned if he was going to show it. "You may as well get comfortable, since you're not going anywhere until this train stops. Then you're going back to San Antonio." He snatched her hat off her head and tossed it onto the divan.

Crushed by the flash of surprise and distaste that crossed River's features when he saw her hair, Aidan grabbed her hat and plopped it back on, pulling it low on her head with both hands. Although she should hate him because he had ruined her plans, she felt hurt because he thought she was ugly. "You can't force me to go back," she stated hostilely.

"Oh, can't I?" He tucked the key to the compartment into his pocket and crossed his arms over his chest as he lazed back against the wall. "We'll just see about that."

"Yes, we'll just see about that," Aidan repeated, forcing herself to return his hard scrutiny.

They stared at each other in silence for several minutes, the longest minutes Aidan had ever experienced in her entire life.

Finally, unable to stop herself, she broke the gaze first. She looked down at her lap, then glanced back over her shoulder at the landscape appearing and disappearing outside the train window. Admitting to herself that she couldn't stand the silence any longer, she tried a new method of attack. "Why do you care whether I go to Cuba or not?" she asked, using her most conversational tone.

River continued to watch her silently, obviously not planning on answering her.

With forced nonchalance, Aidan stood up and walked over to the small sink in the corner. "On the other hand"—she gave the water spigot a quick twist on and off, then turned back to face River—"it means everything to me."

Still, he didn't respond. So much for the casual approach.

Aidan crossed to him and looked up into his solemn face, her expression beseeching. "Can't you just forget you recognized me? Please, Danny, for the sake of our childhood friendship, don't take this opportunity away from me. Let me write this story!"

River shifted his weight. "There'll be other stories," he said.

"Not like this one!" she insisted. "Can't you see? This is my chance! If I don't take it, I may not get a second one!"

"What about your Louisiana Purchase Exposition articles in Saint Louis? Isn't that big enough to satisfy you?"

Biting the inside corner of her mouth in a frustrated attempt to control the sudden trembling of her bottom lip, Aidan nodded in resignation. "Yes, I can see how a *man* would think that. Give the helpless little lady the simple, safe jobs to keep her happy—and out of the way. But leave the important things, like wars, to the big strong men."

49

"Important?" He spit the word out. "You call going off to write about men killing each other important? Maybe even getting killed yourself? If you want to write about something important, why don't you write about people in your own country who are suffering? The conditions most Indians are living under could—"

"The Indians!" she huffed. "You want me to write about the Indians? You're a fine one to talk. In fact, that's all you are—talk. I don't see you rushing back to the reservation to do anything for them. If the situation is as dire as you say it is, what are you doing here?"

River nervously shifted his blue eyes to the side, then back to Aidan's face, his unrelenting facade back in place. "I couldn't go back on my word to Lieutenant Colonel Roosevelt."

The indication that she had hit a nerve had lasted only a fraction of a second, but it had been long enough for Aidan to see it. And long enough for an idea to take form in her mind. "Danny . . ." she said with a smile.

His eyes narrowed suspiciously. "River," he corrected her.

She started to explain that he was still Danny to her, but caught herself. There were already enough differences standing between them. She didn't need to add an argument over his name to the list. If he wanted her to call him River, she would call him River. "I'm sorry. I forgot. I'll try to do better in the future."

He shifted his weight uneasily. All of a sudden, Aidan Donovan was awfully agreeable. It was obvious she was up to something. But what it was, he didn't know—not that it mattered. *Whatever it is, it won't do her any good. I may have been fooled once by that sweet personality she turns on and off like an electric light, but it won't happen again.* He stifled a disinterested yawn with his hand, then resumed staring at her.

Momentarily losing confidence in her new plan, Aidan pivoted away from him and studied the scenery whizzing

50

past the train window. After several minutes, she spun around to face him again. What did she have to lose?

"I know you think I tried to trick you into going back to South Dakota just so I could protect myself." She glanced up to see if her words were making a dent in River's armor. Nothing.

"And you're partially right. I did want you out of the way because I knew you would expose me if you went to Cuba. But that's not the only reason I tried to talk you into going home."

"Oh?" One dark eyebrow arched and his face twisted in a disbelieving smirk. "Whites have lied to Indians for centuries for no other reason than to get what they want. Why should you be different?"

Wounded by the hatred in his tone, Aidan dragged in a deep, fortifying breath before she went on. "I know it looks like the only person I was thinking of was myself, and I suppose it's true. But I really did mean the things I said to you that night on the patio. And I still do. I think we should all follow our own hearts and do what we believe in—even if it isn't the accepted thing to do."

Irritated by the seed of trust springing back to life in his heart, River snorted. "Well, whatever your reasons were, it makes no difference now. You're not going to Cuba, but I am. And that's the end of the subject."

Not yet, it's not, Mr. River Blue Eagle! Aidan went on speaking as though she hadn't heard him. "Have you ever wanted something so much you couldn't think of anything else?" She didn't wait for his answer, certain one was not coming. "It fills your every waking and sleeping thought, doesn't it? And has that thing you wanted ever seemed to be so close you could almost reach out and grab it? But no matter how hard you worked, and no matter how many times you tried for it, was there always some obstacle standing between it and you?"

"What's the point, Aidan?" he asked, doing his best to

51

sound bored, but struggling to hide the raw feelings her words evoked.

Aidan nodded her head understandingly. "The point is, I don't think you and I are so different after all. We both want something so much it colors everything we do and say. But no matter how many times we think we've found the way to overcome our obstacles, something always stops us, doesn't it? It's as if there's a giant glass wall that lets you get just close enough to see what's on the other side for the taking. But no matter how hard you try to get past that wall, it always stops you cold, always keeps what you want just out of your reach. Do you know what I mean?"

River was amazed by her sensitive description of his own feelings of frustration, though he'd never expressed them to her or anyone else. Without thinking, he extended his hand and placed it on her shoulder. "Surely, you aren't that committed to this war."

Fighting the desire to press her cheek to the gentle hand on her shoulder, Aidan shook her head and smiled. "No, I'm not 'that committed' to the war in Cuba. It's just a stepping stone, but a very large stepping stone. If I'm the first woman correspondent to write articles from the front lines of a war, I'll instantly become famous. I'll be right up there with people like Nellie Bly and my father. People will read my stories from coast to coast, maybe even all over the world."

Disappointed to learn that her goal was so shallow, and annoyed that he'd let himself be taken in by her words — again — River dropped his hand to his side and turned away from her. "Well, you'll just have to find yourself another stepping stone to fame and fortune, because you're not going to Cuba."

Trembling with frustration, she grabbed his arm. "Wait, you didn't let me finish!"

"What's to finish? You want to be famous, and you see me as the obstacle standing in your way."

"Nooo!" she groaned impatiently. "My obstacle isn't you! The obstacle I have to overcome is the fact that I'm a woman, and no one is willing to look at me as anything other than a helpless female who must be protected from all the ugliness in the world. I don't want to be famous just for vanity's sake. By making a name for myself in the jealously guarded male domain of war correspondents, I'll show women everywhere that there are no limits on what they can do. Most women have been convinced that they are literally second-class citizens fit only for cooking and cleaning and having babies, and that they shouldn't dare to expect more out of life than a good man to take care of them. I want them to realize that women are every bit as intelligent and capable of achieving greatness as men are — and that we're entitled to the same dreams of success."

"I see," River said, identifying with her problem more than he cared to admit. Certainly he had seen firsthand how impossible it could be to rise above the circumstances of birth, especially when someone had been born under the "wrong" circumstances.

"And it wouldn't have to stop there!" she went on, her enthusiasm growing. "I wouldn't just be helping women by doing this. Once my name is known, people will want to read other things I write — on whatever subject."

A glimmer of where this was leading crept into River's thoughts. "What are you saying?"

Aidan's brown eyes sparkled earnestly. "I'm saying, Mr. River Blue Eagle, that since neither of us seems to be getting anywhere alone, we should join forces and attack our obstacles together. In other words, you help me get what I want, and I'll help you get what you want."

She studied the expression on River's face as her words registered in his mind. "Well? What do you think?"

"Go on," he said thoughtfully.

Encouraged, Aidan drew herself up to her full height and went into her pitch full force. "As I see it, you want to find

53

support for your cause—raising the standard of living of the Indians on reservations—and you're here because you *hope* Theodore Roosevelt will be able to do something—when he gets through with his 'little war' in Cuba. Instead of waiting around on the *chance* that one man *might* help you, doesn't it make more sense to take your cause directly to the public by using the best means of raising public consciousness mankind ever devised—the newspapers?"

"No one is interested in printing stories about Indians anymore."

"Maybe not this week, but there's always tomorrow. And that's the beauty of my plan. What better way to arouse interest than to have the banner of your cause taken up by a famous journalist?"

"A famous journalist?" he asked skeptically.

Aidan nodded, her smile wide and optimistic. "A famous journalist who just *happens* to be deeply in your debt because she owes her entire success to you, and you alone! Because of *you,* she was the only American newspaper*woman* to report on the war in Cuba firsthand—maybe the first female ever to write about any war from the front lines."

Chapter Four

Amazed that Aidan's idea actually made perfect sense to him, River stared incredulously at her. Of course, it was out of the question for him to even consider taking her up on it. Still . . .

"Well?" Aidan asked impatiently. "Do we have an agreement?" She jabbed her right hand out at him.

River looked down at the petite hand extended between them. He was tempted to take it, tempted to make the bargain that could quite possibly solve both their problems — but at what cost?

Raising his eyes to her, he shook his head. "Believe me, Aidan . . ." he started, then stopped.

The optimistic smile on Aidan's face dissolved into a look of hurt. "You're not going to let me go, are you? Why, River? Is the idea of my company so terrible that you would turn down an opportunity to help your people just to avoid it?"

River threaded his fingers into his thick black hair. "You know that's not the reason," he finally said. "It's just that . . ."

"I'm a woman," she said, completing his sentence for him, her tone scathing.

"No," he protested unconvincingly.

A scornful sound, not quite a chuckle, not quite a sob,

escaped from Aidan's lips. "Really? But if I were a man you would have snapped up my offer, wouldn't you?"

Though it shamed him to admit she was right, River couldn't deny it. "It's not the same thing."

"Oh? And how is it different? Why, if I were Clay Donovan's son instead of his daughter and I offered you the same chance, would you have accepted my offer instead of giving me an unconditional rejection?"

"Aidan . . ."

"Go on, River! Say it! Tell me why I can't go to Cuba!"

"All right, dammit!" he shouted. "You can't go because war is no place for a woman! And like it or not, that's what you are. A woman! A fake mustache and men's clothing won't change that. You're a woman, and you can't be a man!"

Aidan lifted her chin slightly, struggling to hold back the tears that threatened to crash through the tenuous check she had on her emotions. "I really thought—" Her voice cracked. She cleared her throat and began again. "I thought you, of all people, would understand. I don't want to be a man any more than you want to deny your Indian blood. I simply want to be myself, an intelligent, capable human being. I want the opportunity to be recognized for my own contributions and abilities—not for my sex. I just want to be judged as an equal."

She turned away from him and picked up her bedroll from the divan. "But I guess I was just asking too much, wasn't I?" She crossed to the door and wrapped her fingers around the knob. "I won't bother you anymore. I'll wait on the end platform for the train to stop so I can catch the next one back to San Antonio."

Without thinking, River dug into his pocket for the key. Then, just in time, he caught himself and let go of it. Damn! She'd almost done it again. Drawing his hand from his pocket, he chuckled. "Have you ever given any thought to taking up the theater?"

56

Aidan gaped at him. "The theater? What does that have to do with anything?"

"I have to admit, you had me going there—right up to the end," he said, shaking his head at his own gullibility.

"I had you going? What are you. . . ?" Suddenly, what he was suggesting hit her, and her temper flared to new heights. "You mean you think everything I said was an act!"

He nodded. "And a damned good one! If I hadn't seen you in action one time too many, I would have fallen for it."

Her mouth opened and shut several times, the only sound she could get out was a strangled, gasping sputter as she groped for the word to express her indignation.

"Well, you're right!" she finally spit out. "Everything I said was an act! Because, quite frankly, I'd die before I'd ever reveal my true feelings to bigoted, egotistical chauvinist who is so consumed by his own cause that he can only see wrongs and suffering when they pertain to him."

She turned back to the door and grabbed the knob. "Good-bye, River Blue Eagle. It'll be interesting when you take off your blinders and discover the world is filled with injustice, and that no one—not even you—can do anything about it alone."

Not trusting herself to say any more without crying, Aidan twisted the doorknob, but it didn't click open. Damn! She'd forgotten it was locked. "Unlock this right now, and let me out of here!" she ground out through her teeth, unable to look at him.

"So you can get lost in the crowd, and hide out until we're on the boat for Cuba and it's too late for me to stop you?"

She flashed him a fiery, brown-eyed glare. "So I don't scream and let everyone on the train know you've got a woman in your compartment."

"You're not going to do that," he said with a knowing look.

"Oh? And how're you going to stop me—with a gag?"

"It's a thought, but it won't be necessary. No one could hear you over the noise of the train."

"We'll just see about that!" She opened her mouth and sucked in a deep breath in preparation for a scream.

"And . . ." he went on, his mouth lifting in a taunting grin, "you don't want anyone to know you're a girl any more than I do—not if you're still intending to find a way to go to Cuba as a Rough Rider. That is what you're planning to do the minute you get out of here, isn't it?"

Doing her best to look outraged, Aidan denied his accusation. "I told you I was going to back to San Antonio."

"And I told you I knew you were lying."

Her lips formed a grim line, and she shot him a look of pure loathing. "It won't do you any good, you know. You can tie me up, gag me, and personally put me on the train back to San Antonio; but one way or another, I'm going to get to Cuba to report on this war! And nothing you can do is going to stop me."

"I'm beginning to see that," River muttered, his intense blue eyes moving over her tiny frame, from battered cavalry hat to booted toe. Funny, even in the unattractive enlisted man's uniform, she was pretty. Well, maybe pretty was pushing it. Cute? Yes, that was it. Cute. Aidan Donovan, who had more fire and courage than ten men twice her size, looked *cute* dressed as a Rough Rider.

A twinge of regret rippled through him as his gaze settled on the sensitive area between her stubbornly set mouth and pretty nose. A bright pink now, it looked sore, and he knew it was his fault. He should have known the spirit gum would take a layer or two of skin with it when he tore the false mustache off her upper lip.

"All right," he said, wheeling away from her and crossing to the lavatory. "You win."

"And if I get caught again, I'll just— What did you say?" Aidan asked, not believing what she thought she had heard.

He turned to face her again, his expression hard. "I said, 'You win.' I'll help you get to Cuba."

Aidan's eyes grew round with disbelief. "Do you mean it?" she shrieked. Leaping across the space that separated them, she threw her arms around his neck. "You're really not going to send me back to San Antonio?"

Determined to ignore the flutter of happiness that surged in his chest at the knowledge that she wasn't going to leave, River resisted the urge to smile and clasp Aidan to him. Instead, catching her by the upper arms, he removed himself from her embrace. "Not if you agree to my conditions."

"What conditions?" she asked, her wary eyes focused on his.

"The first one was your idea. I help you get your story, and you give me your word that the minute we get back to the States you'll start working on exposing the truth about the situation on the reservations."

Aidan smiled broadly. "Consider it done!" She extended her right hand to shake his.

"Wait a minute," River said, not taking her hand. "Don't be too hasty. You may not like my other conditions."

The smile on Aidan's face slipped. "What other conditions?"

"The second one shouldn't be too difficult either. If I'm going to have to look at you every day, you've got to promise me you won't put that mustache back on, and that you'll wash that hair oil out of your hair."

"But I have to wear them, or someone will realize I'm not a man," she protested, hoping he had a good argument for that, because she would do almost anything to be rid of the oily hair and mustache—except give up her story.

"You'll just be a boy instead. Boys don't have mustaches. Besides, anyone with good eyesight could spot it as a fake. And as far as your hair, you should be okay as long as you keep your hat on when you go out."

"And if Mr. Roosevelt notices anything, I'll just tell him I shaved my mustache off," she said happily. Then she sobered slightly. "Wait a minute! You said other *conditions*. What else do I have to agree to?"

"I want your word that from this moment on, you will stay where I can keep an eye on you every minute."

"You can't expect me to agree to that! I need a partner, not a jailer!"

River shrugged indifferently. "Then get your gear together, because it looks like the train's getting ready to stop."

At that moment, the high-pitched squeal of brakes cut through the air. Aidan glanced out the window, spotting a few scattered buildings and carriages. Her expression trapped, she shot a frantic glance at River, then back out the window. *"Every* minute?"

He tilted his dark head to the side and gave her a regretful smile that oozed with insincerity. "That's the offer, Aidan. I expect to know where you are and what you're doing every minute you're with the Rough Riders. Take it or leave it."

The train lurched to a stop, and she stumbled, catching herself against the wall to keep from falling.

"Time's up." Now he was the one to offer his hand. "Do we have a deal?"

Aidan's glance went from River's hand to the people gathered on the platform outside the train window. Of course, she could go through with her alternative plan—willingly get off the train, then, as soon as River was gone, find a way to sneak back on . . . or board the next one coming through. On the other hand, why should she risk being exposed when River was willing to remain silent about her disguise in exchange for a simple promise? Besides, who was to say his idea of "every minute" was exactly the same as hers.

Her mouth spread in a wide, surrendering grin, and she

grasped his outstretched hand. "I guess we've got a deal."

A frisson of misgiving flashed through River as his fingers wrapped around her tiny hand. What was he doing? Could he still be under the effects of the whiskey he'd consumed the night before at the last-night-before-going-off-to-war celebration he'd attended with some of the other officers? He'd heard often enough that Indians and firewater don't mix. And that would certainly explain how he'd let himself get trapped into this ridiculous bargain.

River opened his mouth to tell Aidan he had changed his mind, but the realization that she would find a way to get to Cuba with or without his help stopped him, forcing him to think. What if he turned her out and she got killed? How would he explain to her parents that he could have protected her and hadn't? For that matter, what would he tell his own parents? At least if she was with him, he could keep the trouble she got into at a minimum. It would be hell, but he was sure it could done — by the right man. And the exposé she'd promised to write could actually be the catalyst that might finally free the Indian from the white man's oppression.

So, no matter how appealing backing out of the deal was, he couldn't afford to renege — not on the grounds that he didn't trust her, and not because keeping her in line would be a superhuman feat. There was just too much at stake to take the chance. He had to try.

He tightened his grip on her hand, gave it a single downward shake, then dropped it. "Good," he spit out before spinning away from her. "After you get that oil washed out of your hair, I'll be back to get you." He jabbed the key into the lock of the door and turned it.

Indignant, Aidan made a dash for the door. "Where are you going? I'll go too. I can wash my hair later."

"Sorry," he said, his expression anything but contrite. "That's not our deal."

"But my story needs to cover everything from the very

61

beginning of the trip. The mood. The—"

"The hair first. You have three days to get the *mood* of the trip to Florida," he said, opening the door and stepping into the hallway. "And be sure you get the rest of that spirit gum off your upper lip." With a pleased grin, he pulled the door toward him.

Acting automatically, she grabbed for the door, stabbing her foot toward the narrowing opening. But she was too late. The door clicked shut and the toe of her boot slammed into the doorframe.

"This isn't part of our bargain!" she protested, watching the door in horror as she heard the scrape of the key turning in the lock.

"I'll be back in thirty minutes," he said from the other side. "Be ready."

"I'll be ready, all right." She eyed the compartment window thoughtfully. It still wasn't too late to get off the train and lose herself in the multitude of soldiers who would be reboarding momentarily.

"And Aidan," River crowed knowingly from the other side of the door, "I know you won't do anything stupid—like trying to use the window for a door."

Her mouth dropped open in disbelief, and her head swiveled back around.

"Don't take too long," the amused voice added. Then she heard retreating footsteps, her astonished gaze flying from the window to the door.

At that moment the train released a loud burst of steam and lurched forward, then stopped. Leaping across the compartment, she grabbed for the window frame. Aware of the frantic rush of men hurrying to reboard the train, she pushed up on the window. Nothing happened. It was locked! Damn!

Refusing to be daunted, she grabbed at the bow-shaped knob at the top edge of the divided window and twisted angrily. As though it had joined forces with River, the lock refused to give.

The engineer released another cloud of steam, and before her desperate eyes, the depot, the civilians, and the few remaining soldiers disappeared from view, as if they'd been swallowed by the billowy mist outside. Panicked, she angrily jiggled the window lock—to no avail.

The train, joining the obvious conspiracy against her, gave an unexpected jerk forward. Unprepared for the jolt, Aidan lost her balance and toppled over onto her side. Before she could right herself, the train pulled slowly out of the station. Crawling frantically back onto her knees, she stared out the window, her expression forlorn, as her chance of escape quickly disappeared into the distance with the train's mounting speed.

Turning back to the compartment, she studied the locked door. "You may have won for the moment, but don't get too cocky. You haven't beaten me yet, Mr. Blue Eagle. You've made this a war, and if you think you're going to win it by keeping me a prisoner and muscling me into submission, you're in for a rude awakening, my friend."

A look of spiteful determination on her face, Aidan whisked off her hat and threw it down, then dragged her pack onto her lap so she could rummage in it for the bottle of shampoo she'd brought from home. Once she found what she was looking for, she stomped toward the sink and turned on the water, her vengeful glare leveled at the door.

River stood outside the compartment in which he'd left Aidan forty-five minutes before. Giving his watch a quick check to be sure he'd given her enough time to understand that he, not she, was in control, he shoved it back into his pocket. Of course, he had to admit that if he hadn't tried to open the window earlier and found it stuck, he wouldn't be so confident she would be waiting for him.

"Madder than a wet hen, no doubt," he said to himself,

63

his expression anxious as he inserted the key. After all, Aidan Donovan wasn't exactly the type of woman who would take kindly to having her freedom denied her. In fact, she brought to mind that one wild pony in every cowboy's past, the one he couldn't break.

Shaking his head as if doubting his own sanity, he chuckled to himself. *And I'm crazy enough to think I'm going to do it! Who am I fooling? I'll be lucky if I can just keep her from getting herself killed—and myself from losing my mind.*

Halfway expecting to be attacked physically when he stepped back into the compartment, River opened the door warily. When nothing happened, he widened the opening and poked his head inside, hurriedly glancing over the room.

Empty! She was gone!

His gaze immediately went to the window. "What the hell?" It was still shut! Confused, he stomped into the compartment, slamming the door behind him. "How'd—"

"Oh, you're back." Aidan stepped through the doorway that led to the private "convenience" room that was part of their quarters. "Has thirty minutes passed already?"

Taken back by her casual welcome, River was momentarily dumbfounded. "I . . . uh . . . thought . . ." His gaze flew to her hair.

Still slightly damp, it had been towel-dried into a disheveled array of soft springy curls that complimented her face in a way no perfect coiffure ever could.

Uncomfortably aware of a tightening in his loins, it hit him for the second time that morning that Aidan was pretty. But this time, he didn't qualify the thought and decide she was just cute.

Panic stormed through him. He couldn't avoid the truth anymore. Even in the loose-fitting Rough Rider's uniform, Aidan Donovan wasn't the kid he'd told himself she was.

She was actually a beautiful woman. A beautiful woman

he had committed himself to be with night and day for the next several months. And for the next three nights in these cramped quarters. His alarm grew to magnanimous proportions.

Aidan was really furious with River Blue Eagle. Not only had he locked her up like a naughty child, but he'd deliberately—and she knew it had been deliberate—left her waiting longer than he had led her to expect, obviously meaning to put her completely in her place.

Well, she had no intention of giving him the satisfaction of knowing how angry she was. Let him think he had won. Let him believe his typically masculine use of brawn could automatically make him the winner. Let him assume he had outsmarted her and that she was going to go along with his plan to shadow her every move from here on out. It would do him no good whatsoever. In the end, she would triumph, because no man alive had a chance in a battle of wits with a smart woman.

"What are you staring at?" she asked, her smile guileless, though she silently continued to consider potential "war" tactics. "Didn't I get all the oil out of my hair?" She raked her fingers through her short locks, then patted her upper lip. "Or do I still have spirit gum on my lip?"

"No," River said, shaking his head, his expression confused. "You look . . . Your hair is— What the hell are you up to now, Aidan? I thought you were going to be—"

"Mad?" she asked, then laughed as gaily as she could. "Oh, I was at first. After all, treating me like a convict wasn't a very nice thing to do. But I realized you were only doing it because you didn't trust me." She gave him a sheepishly contrite grin. "Then I admitted to myself that I couldn't blame you for that. I haven't exactly done anything to earn your trust, have I? But that's all going to change. From now on, I—"

"Why do I get the feeling I'm being conned?" River asked, his eyes narrowing suspiciously.

A flash of irritation ignited in Aidan's eyes, but quickly disappeared. River Blue Eagle was going to be a more formidable foe than she'd at first assumed. Rising to the challenge, she picked up her hat and smiled. "That's because you still don't trust me. But you will. I'm going to see to that." She dropped the hat over her auburn curls and added, "Shall we go?"

Not certain he'd done the right thing in telling her to get rid of the mustache and the Macassar oil, River shrugged. Even in the hat, she still looked awfully female to him.

Stepping forward, he grabbed the brim of her hat and drew it down on her head, hoping to hide her face so she wouldn't look so good to him. "Yes, we'd better . . ." The words dried up in his mouth as he became helplessly ensnared by the brown eyes looking up at him. "I mean, if you're going to write your story . . ."

Aidan dragged her tongue along her bottom lip to moisten a mouth suddenly gone dry, unable to free herself from the hypnotizing blue eyes that held her enthralled. Yes, this was definitely going to be one of the hardest tasks she had ever undertaken—possibly even *the* hardest. In fact, with him standing so close to her, she couldn't quite remember why she had declared war on him in the first place. How was she supposed to function under the spell of eyes that had the power to turn bones to jelly? Eyes that blue should be declared deadly weapons, for they were obviously as dangerous as any knife or gun.

"The story?" she asked, her voice a rough croak. His incapacitating gaze dropped to her lips, and her willpower sank to the pit of her belly. Inadvertently, she leaned toward him.

"You wanted to write about the trip to Florida," he explained, his voice huskier than before.

"Oh, the *story!*" she said with a half-smile and an exaggerated nod. "Sure." It was hard to muster enthusiasm when her stomach was doing flip-flops, her heart was racing like a runaway horse, and her eyes were riveted on River's mouth. "I have a story to write." She sounded distracted. She found it odd that she'd never noticed what a nice mouth River had. Well-defined, perfectly shaped lips. The kind of lips that would drive a woman into a mindless bundle of longing should she ever be kissed by them.

Seeming to be unable to stop his upper body from slanting closer to her, River kept his gaze on her mouth. "If we don't go, you won't get much of a story."

Aidan slowly shook her head. "Not much of a story," she repeated, certain she was actually melting. It was becoming difficult to stand without support. Her lips parted slightly, her eyes blinked sleepily, and inadvertently she swayed.

As she caught herself by placing her hands on his chest, River grabbed her upper arms. Both blue and brown eyes grew round with surprise when electricity jolted through them at the physical contact; and for an instant they simply stared at each other.

River was the first to recover. "Are you all right?"

Dumbfounded by the magnetic pull of the wall of his chest, Aidan held her hands flat against it and managed a silent nod. The wild thumping of his heart against her palms matched her own pulse, and fire seared through her, turning her mouth dry.

He cleared his throat and licked his lips. "Then, I guess we'd better go." He didn't loosen his grip on her arms.

Not meaning to mimic him, she cleared her throat and licked her lips, too, then gave him a weak smile. "We need to go." She didn't even try to take her hands from his chest because she knew they would refuse to move as long as he retained his compelling grasp on her arms.

"I mean," he went on hesitantly, "it would be a shame, after you've gone to all this trouble to be here, to miss anything."

"A shame," she agreed.

Somewhere in the far recesses of her brain, where the

barest shred of sanity remained intact, a voice told her she had better get away from River and out of this room before it was too late. If he even suspected the effect he was having on her, she would lose the "war" before it had really begun.

She knew all that, yet in her passion-drugged state, it suddenly wasn't all that important to beat River. Certainly not as important, or urgent, as the unbearable throbbing she felt deep within.

He lowered his head so that his face was only inches away from hers. "So I guess we should go," he said, his eyes focused on her mouth. Before we—"

"Do something foolish," she finished for him, still unable to back out of his intoxicating embrace.

"It would be a mistake to allow this to become anything other than business."

Aidan moved her head up and down in agreement. "We have to keep it platonic."

"Platonic," he repeated, his mouth continuing to descend toward hers. "Right. The only way this arrangement can work is if we keep it platonic."

"After all." She rose up on her toes, unbearably aware of the warmth of his breath wafting across her face. "It would ruin everything if we . . ."

He nodded his head. "Everything."

Helpless to resist any longer, River released a fierce growl. Ripping the hat off her head, he tossed it aside—along with the last of his restraint. He brought his mouth down hard on hers and wrapped his arms around her slim shoulders. No longer able to think he clutched large handfuls of her uniform into his fists and roughly hauled her against his chest, the last of his willpower destroyed.

Chapter Five

Aidan and River were hit at the same time by the possible ramifications of what was happening. They reared back simultaneously and looked at each other, frightened dark eyes staring into surprised light ones.

"Why did you do that?" Aidan gasped, her breathing ragged as she fought the desire to let her hands glide around to his back so she could get even closer to him. "You don't even like me."

Stunned by her comment, River raised a questioning eyebrow, his hands still locked behind her back. "I don't? What gave you that idea?"

Aidan's heart skipped a beat, and she smiled slightly. "You mean you do?"

"Of course I do. I like you a lot. I always have—since we were kids."

"But I thought . . . I mean, if you like me, why are you so—"

"Just because I like *you* doesn't mean I like the things you do—or the way you do them," he said truthfully. "For instance, if you had an inkling of common sense, you—"

"Common sense!" Aidan yelled, his words bringing her back to reality. She pushed hard on his chest and wheeled out of his embrace. "You, of all people, have the audacity to accuse *me* of not having common sense? I'm not the one

69

who tried to turn a perfectly legitimate business arrangement a . . . a . . ." She groped for a word. ". . . sordid . . ."

"Me? I didn't see you fighting it. In fact, if a woman was ever begging to be kissed, it was—"

"Begging! You think I was begging you to kiss me? What conceit!" She tried to muster a derisive snicker, but couldn't quite manage it. He was too close to the truth. She had wanted him to kiss her, so much so that for one insane moment she probably would have been willing to give up just about anything—even her story—for that kiss. Well, she might admit that to herself, but River Blue Eagle was never going to know it. And though she might have to draw on every ounce of strength she possessed, she certainly wasn't going to allow it to happen again.

River's face grew dark with anger, his narrowed eyes seeming more black than blue. "Are you saying I forced my kiss on you?"

Unable to look at him, Aidan skirted around giving him a direct answer to his question. "Believe me," she said, retrieving her hat from the floor and putting it back on her head, "if I'd known you were planning to take improper advantage of our arrangement, I never would have agreed to it." She stomped to the door and waited. "But now that I'm aware of the kind of thoughts you're entertaining, I'll definitely be on my guard!" She opened the door—he hadn't locked it—and marched out into the passageway, leaving him staring at her back.

Fuming, River stormed after her, slamming the door to their compartment behind him. "Believe me, lady," he hissed as he caught up with her and captured her arm, "you've got nothing to worry about. Only a fool would deliberately walk into a raging wildfire."

Just as she opened her mouth to blast him with an angry retort, the door to the next car burst open. "Ah, there you are!" Theodore Roosevelt boomed, his myopic eyes darting cheerfully from River to Aidan. Stepping between the pair, he clapped them both on the back and steered them toward the door he'd just come through. "I thought we might amble through the day coaches to check on how the rest of the men are faring."

"That sounds like a good idea, sir," Aidan said in her deepest voice. Her eyes beamed a silent warning to River. She wanted to be sure he knew that this interruption was only a delay and that he hadn't had the last word, not by any means.

"And who knows, boy? We might even pick up some human-interest stories along the way."

"Yes, sir!" Aidan said, his word just what she needed to restore her excitement about being there. For the past hour or so, she'd let herself get so involved with River that she'd practically forgotten her real purpose. Well, that wasn't going to happen again. From this moment on, she wasn't going to think of anything but her story. As far as she was concerned, River Blue Eagle didn't exist! "I'm really anxious to get started."

"That's the way we like to hear our men talk, isn't it, Lieutenant?"

"Yes, sir," River answered, his irritation with Aidan barely disguised. He held the door open so the others might step through. "That's what we like to hear."

"By the way, A.D.," Roosevelt said over his shoulder as he entered the next coach ahead of Aidan. "I'm glad to see you decided to get rid of that false mustache."

She stopped in the doorway, her face hot with embarrassment. "You knew?"

Roosevelt released his unique laugh. "It's been a while since I had peach fuzz on my face, but not so long that I don't remember that a boy's got to be a lot older than you are before he can sprout a full mustache."

"Aren't you mad because I tried to fool you into thinking I was older?" she asked, her admiration for Roosevelt's

71

powers of observation and his understanding evident in her expression.

Laughing, Roosevelt shook his head and slapped her on the back. "We've all done some foolish things in our lives, especially when we were young. It's part of growing up. Besides, there's no limit on age when it comes to enthusiasm and a desire to fight for your country, is there, son? Just stay near Lieutenant Blue Eagle and follow his orders—I assume he's the man we should thank for getting rid of the mustache—and write your stories. You'll do fine! No matter how young you are, I'm expecting big things from you. If you're anything like your father, this is just the beginning for you." Spotting someone he wanted to speak to, Roosevelt waved and moved ahead of Aidan and River.

Pleased by Roosevelt's words, Aidan smiled at River, who stood just to her left and slightly behind her. When he didn't return her smile, her relaxed expression disintegrated into a frown. "I hope you don't intend to glower over me like some black cloud the whole trip. You heard what he said. I'll be fine."

"And you heard him tell you to stay with me and follow my orders."

"I'm sure he didn't mean that literally!"

"Well, I do! The first time you so much as take one step out of my sight, I'm putting you back on a train bound for San Antonio. And that's not just an order from a superior officer, *Private* Donovan. It's a promise."

All through the hot day, as the changing countryside whisked past the windows, Aidan concentrated on keeping up with the energetic Roosevelt who wandered among passengers, officers, and enlisted men alike. No one was beneath the notice of the outgoing, dynamic man, and he stopped to talk to them all. He had even turned over his own comfortable sleeping arrangements to a young trooper who'd been taken ill shortly after their departure, and at stops along the way, he purchased buckets of coffee and had it served to the men in the day coaches. He even bought hay and oats, out of his own funds, to be sent on for the horses in case of an emergency.

In every town where the train stopped, the Rough Riders were given a wild reception by the local folk who turned out in their Sunday best to greet them. Amid excited shouts of encouragement and gratitude, American flags were held high, while children perched on their fathers' shoulders to better see the brave troopers going off to war. It was a heady experience for the soldiers. They were already being treated as heroes, and they hadn't even gotten to Cuba yet!

By the time Aidan and River worked their way back to their compartment in the sleeping car, all she could think of was getting off her feet. "How can he keep up that pace?" she asked, her eyes half-closed as she staggered blindly toward the sofa.

Before she could cover half the distance to the couch, which she knew to be at least four feet, she bumped into something and tumbled forward onto her face. "What the—?" she exclaimed. Lifting her head, she was amazed to find herself sprawled across a narrow bed.

Evidently, in their absence, the porter had come in and prepared the compartment for the night by lighting a lamp and making up the bed. But now, instead of four feet of space to move about in, there was just an aisle, not more than twenty-four inches wide, to allow access to the sink and convenience closet.

"I'm glad you don't object to the sleeping arrangements," River said snidely as he sidled into the compartment, his long frame making it seem even smaller.

Suddenly realizing exactly what the *sleeping arrangements* were, Aidan flipped over onto her back and bolted to a sitting position. "Surely, you're not planning on both of us sleeping in this bed are you?"

"Unless *one* of us prefers the floor," he said, enjoying himself for the first time since Aidan had forced her way

73

back into his life that morning. With exaggerated casualness, he removed his hat and hung it on one of several wall hooks at the foot of the bed. Sitting down on the bed, he gave it a couple of testing bounces, then began to unlace the leather gaiters that covered his boots. "Me, I prefer a bed. It must be my white blood." He kicked his boots under the bed and reached for the buttons on his jacket. "I'll be glad to get this off."

"Wait a minute!" Aidan scrambled to her feet. "We can't sleep in the same bed. It's not ri— I mean, what would people—" She stopped herself, realizing she'd put herself in a position where neither of those arguments held any weight. Daring a glance at the bed, she pointed. "Look at it. There's not enough room for two people in it."

River ran a casual eye over the sofa bed. "It'll be close, all right," he said, taking particular delight in her discomfort. He shrugged off his shirt and hung it up. "Do you want the inside by the window or the outside by the aisle?"

Staring aghast at his bared chest, Aidan was momentarily at a loss for words. Her panicked gaze went from side to side, searching for a solution to this unexpected predicament. "Can't we discuss this?" she finally asked.

"Discuss all you want. I'm going to bed." He stood up, stretched his arms high in the air, yawned, then dropped his hands to the top button of his fly.

"What are you doing?" she choked, her expression horrified.

Ignoring her, he quickly stripped off his trousers. "Don't worry," he chortled tauntingly, retaliation for all she'd put him through that day. "I won't sleep in the nude—tonight. I'll leave the breechcloth on." He pulled back the cover and slipped between the cool muslin sheets. "Good night, *A.D.*" Without further ado, he closed his eyes. "Put out the light when you're through."

Aidan stared at River, not certain what to do. Maybe she should go back to one of the day coaches and try to find a seat. Yes, she would do that—because staying here was obviously out of the question. She took a step toward the hook on which he'd hung his pants, pretty sure she'd seen him put the door key in a pocket.

Then an unpleasant thought occurred to her, and she hesitated. The other cars were all crowded beyond capacity. How could she find a place to sleep at this late hour? Men were probably already stretched out in the aisles.

At least with River, she had a private toilet and lavatory. She had to admit, that alone was sufficient argument to convince her to stay. Besides, even if River was an overbearing, egotistical bully, he was a gentleman. He'd said she needn't worry, so she wouldn't. "I'd like to sleep on the outside, if you don't mind," she said, deciding that falling out of bed during the night was preferable to being trapped between the wall and the nearly naked River Blue Eagle.

River mumbled something unintelligible and heaved a deep sigh, but he didn't move.

Annoyed, Aidan planted her hands on her hips and bent forward. "River, you're not fooling me. You can't be asleep yet. Now stop pretending and roll over. I want to sleep on the outside."

Rolling onto his side with a sleepy grunt, River presented his back to her and resettled himself solidly on the outside half of the bed.

Aiden let out a frustrated groan. "Keep going," she coaxed when he stopped; instinctively putting her hand on his shoulder to help him.

The minute her fingers wrapped around the hard, *naked* muscle of River's upper arm, she knew she'd made a serious mistake. As if a jolt of electricity had struck her hand, it flew back, slamming into the wall immediately behind her.

"Owwwwww," she yowled. Her eyes instantly watering, she covered her throbbing fingers with her other hand, then fell back against the wall, rocking her upper body. This was

75

definitely not the way she had planned for this venture to go.

Almost as suddenly as the pain had hit her, it subsided. Her unforgiving expression making it obvious she blamed River for her injury, she rested against the wall and watched him.

At that moment, he drew in a deep breath, then released it in a long, shuddering snort before rolling over onto his back again—still on the side of the bed she wanted.

Tempted to slug him, she pushed away from the wall and angrily balled her fists. "Dammit, move over," she ground out. Drawing back a fist, she froze, her eyes suddenly focusing on the broad male chest that had been exposed when he'd pulled the sheet down to his waist during his last turn.

Held captive by the sight of the naked expanse of tanned flesh that stretched over River's shoulders and torso, she was hypnotized by each curve and bulge gleaming in the golden glow of the gaslight on the wall. Remembering the reaction she'd had when her hand had grazed his shoulder, she stopped to reconsider her decision.

Realizing she'd been holding her breath, her body tense with anticipation as she wondered what it would be like to touch the strength contained in that bronzed, living statue lying before her, she unflexed her fists and released a long sigh.

To block out the visions her mind was creating, she squeezed her eyes shut. If just looking at River Blue Eagle had such an effect on her senses, what would happen if she ever gave in to her curiosity and . . . ?

Aidan shook her head in disgust, vowing she would never give in. No matter how much her body wanted it, she would not allow herself the luxury of knowing what it would feel like to really touch him. That shock when she'd touched his shoulder had been a warning, one she'd better take very seriously, because the next time it might come too late.

Finally admitting to herself that River wasn't going to move unless she used physical force, and knowing that she didn't dare touch him, she surrendered to the idea of sleeping on the inside—this one time.

Besides, she could tell by the way he was breathing, slowly, his chest expanding and relaxing in a tempting dance of glistening flesh and muscle, that he was oblivious, not only to his own perfectly sculpted body, but to her as well.

Anyway, soundly as he is sleeping, and as exhausted as I am, what could happen?

After long deliberation, Aidan finally decided that sleeping in her clothes and crawling over him at the foot of the bed would be the safest approach. She gingerly placed a knee on the mattress by his feet, then hesitated.

It was so hot in the tiny compartment. Maybe she could just take off the first layer of her clothing. After all, she had on a blouse and camisole underneath the wool shirt and three pairs of cotton drawers under the trousers. She certainly wouldn't be nude if she at least removed the heavy uniform. And she certainly would be more comfortable.

Standing back up, she turned down the gaslight and hurriedly stripped off the uncomfortable men's clothing, including the extra camisole and blouse she had wound around her waist to disguise her curves—and so no one could discover them in her pack. Feeling better immediately, she unbuttoned her blouse and ran a damp washcloth over her face and neck. Her stamina reviving by the instant, she brushed her teeth.

She took one last glance to be sure River was still asleep, then extinguished the lamp and crawled onto the bed. Moving as subtly as the train's bumpy movements would allow, she eased her way over River's feet and legs and slipped beneath the sheet.

Exhaustion finally catching up with her, she pressed herself against the wall beneath the window, as far from River as she could get, and sank into the blessed oblivion of sleep.

It was as if she were floating in space. Everything was so peaceful as though her body didn't exist at all. No arms, no legs, no sights, no sounds, nothing but her thoughts. And she felt so warm and protected, the way a baby must feel in its mother's womb. She wanted to stay in this blessed state forever.

Slowly at first, reality began to seep into her lethargy with the sounds of train wheels on the track. Then, as the clacking grew more evident, she became aware of warm sunlight burning into her back, its light streaming through the window and changing the view behind her closed eyelids from black to gray to pink.

"Just a few more minutes," she begged, rolling onto her stomach. Annoyed to realize she had turned over onto a bunched-up blanket that felt more like a log than a cover, she rose up and tried to shove the lumpy cover aside, her eyes still glued shut. Somewhere in the back of her mind, it occurred to her that a blanket couldn't be so bunched up that it didn't give, but she decided it wasn't worth trying to figure out why the contrary bedcovering she was sprawled on wasn't soft. She let her head drop again.

"Good morning," a deep voice said very close to her ear.

"Mmmph," she murmured. Taking in a deep, annoyed breath, she turned her face into the pillow beneath her head.

The spicy mixture of bay rum and male flesh assaulted her at the same moment she realized her pillow was so solid it was bending her nose sideways.

A sudden suspicion clutched at her, setting off a clangorous alarm in her head. What if . . . ?

Surely what she was thinking wasn't true. Doing her best

78

to laugh at her imagination, she lifted her head so that her nose could resume it's normal position and opened one eye slightly. At once she was awake.

Oh, please don't let that be a male chest her chin was propped on. Don't let the hard, lumpy blanket beneath her be a man's body.

Panic building to unstable proportions inside her, she pried open the other eye just the tiniest bit.

"Oh, God!" she cried, total awareness jolting through her as she lifted her head from its resting place with a nerve-twisting jolt. "What . . . ?"

"Did you sleep well?" River asked, looking into her astonished face, with an irritatingly self-satisfied smile as he wrapped his arms around her waist.

"What am I doing on top of . . . ?" Aidan choked, so stunned she just lay where she was.

He ignored her unfinished question. "I did. At least, until you woke me up by . . ." He wiggled his eyebrows and grinned. "Now I'm beginning to think we wasted a lot of time sleeping." His gaze dropped to her chest. "You look much better in this than in that wool shirt."

Unable to keep her eyes from shifting in the direction his had taken, Aidan looked down. New horror ignited in her brain. The blouse she had worn to bed was gone!

Somewhere in the back of her mind, she recalled being hot and removing the protective shirt. Her eyes went to the upper corner of the bed for confirmation. There it was, wadded up and right where she had evidently thrown it. Thank God, she hadn't taken the camisole off too—though she might as well have, for all the good it was doing. Damp with perspiration and clinging to her small breasts, the skimpy undergarment concealed very little.

Meeting the amused glint in River's blue eyes, Aidan flushed and hunched her shoulders to hide her breasts as she struggled to roll away from him. "Let go of me!"

"You're not changing your mind, are you?" he asked, a

79

baiting lilt in his voice.

Aidan's eyes grew wide with surprise and she froze. Surely he didn't think she . . . Her horrified gaze flew to his face. *Oh, Lord. Of course, he thinks it. What else would he think?* "Are you suggesting that I intended this to happen?"

His mouth stretched in a knowing grin, and he arched his eyebrows. "What?"

"I mean, if you hadn't forced me to sleep on the inside, I never would have—"

"What?" he asked again, his smile challenging.

"Uh . . . uh . . ." Her face reddened even more. "Uh . . . you know. Look, I know what you think this is," she tried to explain, straining against his hold on her, "but believe me, you're wrong."

He ran his hands down past her waist and back again. "It doesn't feel wrong. In fact, it feels just . . ."

Right! Aidan realized with alarm. *Oh, Lord, help me. It feels so right!* In fact, lying on top of River, her body pressed to his from breast to knee, felt more right than anything she'd ever experienced. And nothing had ever felt as right as his hands burning over her back and bottom. Unless it was the way her own slim hips fit so perfectly in the cradle of his thighs. Or the way instinct told her to press harder against the masculine bulge at the juncture of those thi—

"No!" she cried, giving him a sudden shove and rolling off him and the bed.

Backing into the corner of the compartment, her eyes bright with a mixture of desire and fear, she tried to cover herself with her hands. "I don't care how right you think it feels. It had better not happen again or I'll . . . I'll . . ."

River rolled over onto his side and propped his chin on his elbow. "What, Aidan?" he asked with a slow challenging smile. "What will you do? I had the definite impression you would do anything to get this story. Now you say there

80

are limits?"

She scanned the magnificent length of River's tanned body, from his mussed black hair to his feet, which were the only parts of him still under the sheet one of them must have tossed off during the night. Something deep inside her twisted and tightened, and it was all she could do to ignore what her body was begging for.

Making an effort to sound indignant and cool, she haughtily lifted her chin and said, "Of course, there are limits. No story in the world could turn me into a . . . a . . . One of those women! And if this is some attempt on your part to add conditions to our bargain, or to blackmail me, you can forget it! You gave me your word you'd help me get my story if I would write the Indian reservation exposé, and I intend to see that you hold up your end of the bargain."

Tired of the game he had initiated to teach her a lesson, River sat up and swung his feet onto the floor. He wearily threaded his fingers through his hair. "Relax, Aidan. I'm not going to take advantage of our proximity to have my way with you or turn you into a 'soiled dove.' I'm just making a point. It's time you get it through your head that no matter how positive you are that you have all the answers, you're no longer in your safe little world where your mama and daddy can buy you anything you want and get you out of any trouble you might get into. You're in the real world now, and you haven't even begun to understand the reality of it, or how dangerous it is—especially for a spoiled little white girl who's never faced anything more perilous than deciding which fork to eat with."

Instead of frightening Aidan into admitting how dependent she was on him, which was what he obviously meant to do, his insults filled her with an extra burst of rebellion. "We'll just see about that, Mr. Blue Eagle."

"I'm sure we will," he answered with a resigned sigh. He gave a bored shrug and stood up. "Do you want the bath-

81

room first, or should I go on in?"

Heat crept up Aidan's neck to color her face a bright pink. No matter how sophisticated she liked to picture herself, she couldn't imagine doing anything so private with a man just on the other side of a thin wall — where he could hear everything! "Go on," she mumbled, unable to look at him. Turning her face toward the side wall, she pretended to be busy with the uniform shirt she snatched off its hook. "I'm in no hurry."

Smiling to himself, River shuffled sleepily into the tiny lavatory and closed the door behind him.

The instant he was out of sight, Aidan scrambled across the bed to retrieve her cotton shirt.

Just then the door to the bathroom opened and River stuck his dark head out. "By the way, Aidan, about what happened earlier . . ."

Clutching the blouse to her bosom, Aidan looked up, a ray of hope in her dark eyes. Maybe he was going to apologize. "What about it?"

"I didn't say it felt right. 'Right' was your word. Not mine."

Chapter Six

Tampa, June 3, 1898. A bleak, colorless desert, teeming with confusion and disorder was the scene that greeted the last section of the First Volunteer Cavalry as it stepped off the train in Florida today.

Lesser men would have been discouraged by this unappealing welcome. However, even after spending five days and four nights crammed into the dirty, overcrowded train that brought them from Texas, the reverse is true of the Rough Riders. Under the fearless and inspiring command of the former Secretary of the Navy, Lieutenant Colonel Theodore Roosevelt, these spirited cavalrymen remain undaunted by the turmoil in which they find themselves.

Their first disheartening discovery upon arrival was indeed the most difficult for these brave men to accept. It was immediately learned that since the end of April, as many as thirty trains a day have poured soldiers and supplies into the Tampa Bay area, which was selected as the central location from which to orchestrate the invasion, because of its proximity to Cuba, and because it has both rail and port facilities. Unfortunately, almost none of the soldiers or supplies have gotten past this congested point.

Everywhere we look, men are milling about, wait-ing—and praying—that their orders to ship out will come before the war is over!

To make matters worse, more than a thousand freight cars line the railroad sidings, waiting to be unloaded. Some are said to be standing as far away as Columbia, South Carolina. A goodly portion of the troops are forced to drill in civilian clothing, all the while knowing that somewhere between Tampa and Columbia are fifteen freight cars containing more than enough uniforms for them all. Rifles, ammuni-tion, and food are held up too, but without bills of lading, which are said to be late in arriving, if they arrive at all, locating specific items to unload is para-mount to finding a particular grain of sand in a West Texas dust storm!

The one bright point in this circus of bedlam is the Tampa Bay Hotel. Completely out of place in a dreary city composed of bare wooden buildings swept clean of paint by the sand, this ornate, dark red brick structure towers five stories in the air. Boasting nearly five hundred rooms, the building takes up over six acres of the hotel's sixty-acre grounds. It is so large that its porches are as wide as many of the sand-covered streets of Tampa, and a walk from the ro-tunda to the dining room is reported to be all one needs to work up an appetite!

Topped with glistening silver domes and minarets decorated with crescent moons, this impressive build-ing is fireproof, having been constructed with con-crete floors supported by steel cables and old railroad tracks.

Inside, the hotel is fitted with ebony and gold fur-niture, elegant tapestries, imported carpets, oil paint-ings once owned by royalty, enormous porcelain vases, and beautiful European statues. The furnish-

ings alone are reported to have cost over one million dollars.

Yet for six dollars a day, guests of the Tampa Bay Hotel can not only enjoy a luxurious room — with adjoining private bath — but they will be indulged and entertained in opulent and exciting surroundings.

A T-shaped casino, elaborate club rooms, a grand auditorium, a swimming pool situated under a removable floor, and a golf course are provided for their amusement. Or they might choose to take a romantic stroll over the lush grounds that abound in fragrant-smelling blossoms, exotic plants and majestic peacocks . . .

"Let's go," River announced irritably from behind Aidan. "A tourist canceled his reservation, so we got his room."

Slamming her journal shut and stabbing her pencil into her pocket, Aidan twisted around to face him from where she sat on the steps with their bedrolls. "Room? But I thought—"

"Don't say it," River commanded. "We're lucky to get a room at all. The President himself couldn't have gotten two rooms in this ugly monstrosity." Hefting his pack, he turned about and stomped back to the entry of the Tampa Bay Hotel.

Snatching up her own gear, Aidan leaped to her feet and ran after him. "Surely, you could have offered the desk clerk a . . ."

River came to a dead stop and turned slowly to glower down at her, his scowl fearsome.

Sliding to a halt, Aidan did her best to scowl back at him.

"Just where do you think we are, Aidan? These are the only accommodations available, and they are crammed with officers and tourists and rich enlisted men, with two or three people to a room. I could only get *one* room." He held a long index finger within a half-inch of the tip of her nose. "I repeat, one! Consequently, no matter how much it offends your delicate sense of privacy to share it with me, and no matter how much I dread the idea, there's nothing I can do about it. So if I were you, I'd keep my mouth shut and start hoping they don't decide to put a third man in with us!"

He pivoted away from her again, making no effort to shorten his long, angry stride so she could keep up. Quite frankly, he'd reached the end of his patience with the spoiled Miss Aidan Donovan. It was bad enough that he'd spent the last three nights trying to sleep sitting up in a filthy day coach, rather than chance another encounter in the cramped bed of the train compartment. But he had no intention of allowing her to deprive him of a decent night's sleep tonight. Hopefully, there was a sofa in their room, or at least a bed big enough for two people to sleep without lying on top of each other!

Painful memory curled tightly in his groin at the thought. *Figuratively speaking*, he pointed out to himself, but too late to undo the harm done by the thought. Already, his mind was pulsing with the vision of her slim body against his. She'd been so light that he'd been no more aware of her weight than he'd have been of a light sheet draped over him. Yet, even now, he could feel the impression of her body stamped into his flesh.

Able to see that River was at a point where he could easily be on the verge of refusing to honor their bargain, Aidan wisely desisted from further arguments. She would just have to make do with one room until other arrangements could be made.

They didn't speak as River strode across the ornately decorated lobby of the hotel, Aidan hustling in a half-run/half-walk to keep up with him. Once they were inside the elevator, the tension between them swelled to near tangible proportions as they silently stood side by side their attention on the floor-indicator arrow moving upward as they were whisked up to the fourth floor.

"Well, here we are," River finally said a few minutes later. Making a sweeping gesture with his arm, he stepped aside to allow her to enter their room. "Are you staying, or do you prefer the ground where the 'real men' will be sleeping tonight?"

Assuming her most condescending expression, Aidan crossed the threshold and closed the door behind her. "I've already told you I need to be here so I'm at the center of what's happening," she explained impatiently, her glance skimming restlessly over the room. She immediately registered the fact that there was no sofa, only one large four-poster bed. Well, she wasn't going to let River know it made any difference. From now on, she was going to forget his sex — and hers — and think of him as just another soldier, like she was.

River nodded his head with a knowing grin. "Oh, yes. How could I forget? I can't imagine why I keep having this peculiar suspicion that you're not as prepared to give up life's little luxuries as you claim to be. Still, I'm anxious to see how you manipulate your way out of sharing your bedroll with the snakes and insects of the Cuban jungle."

A shiver squirmed up Aidan's spine, shaking her shoulders before she could gain control. She ran her hand around the back of her neck and wearily rotated her head in an attempt to cover up her automatic reaction to the unpleasant thought he'd deliberately planted in her mind.

"Don't forget, I'm from Texas. I'll do just fine. A few snakes and bugs don't bother me. I'm prepared to be treated like any other soldier. The only reason I wanted to stay here instead of at the campgrounds with the others is — as I explained to Lieutenant Colonel Roosevelt — most of the press is quartered here so I will be better able to keep apprised of the latest news."

Smiling cynically at her vain effort to hide her vulnerability, River shrugged and tossed his bedroll and hat onto the bed. "Then I guess since creature comforts are of no importance to you, you won't mind if I use the bathtub first, will you? After all that time on the train, I'm in the mood for a nice, *long* soak."

Alarm igniting in her eyes, Aidan looked toward the open bathroom door, homing in on the claw-footed end of what appeared to be the kind of tub a person could lie down in. That had definitely been the other reason she'd wanted to stay at the Tampa Bay Hotel. On the train she'd been able to take sponge baths twice a day, but they hadn't been satisfying. Right now, what she needed more than anything in the world was a real bath. But she would cut out her tongue before she would admit that to River. Oh, how she'd like to smack the condescending smirk off his face!

Swallowing the protest that rose to her lips, she smiled and shook her head. "Of course not," she said stiffly, doing her best not to think about how anxious she was to lie back in a tub full of warm water. "Take all the time you want. I'm in no hurry."

Smiling to himself, River shrugged off his jacket and shirt, then hung them over the back of the chair with slow, deliberate actions. Funny, now that he was getting the hang of reading the stubborn Miss Aidan Donovan and could tell when she wasn't being entirely honest, he was actually starting to enjoy the game they were playing.

A self-accusing frown formed on his brow. What kind of thought was that to have? There was no time in his life for that kind of thinking. He was here with Aidan for one reason, and only one reason! There was a good possibility that she could actually help him achieve his goal. Games, fun, and enjoyment were not part of the bargain.

His back to her, he balanced on one foot, then the other, to take off his boots and trousers. Stripped down to his breechcloth, he stepped into the bathroom, slamming the door behind him with a purposeful bang.

"What ever happened to ladies first?" Aidan asked under her breath, directing a nasty look at the closed door.

She swung around and hauled her blanket roll onto the bed. Untying it, she flipped it open, her face screwed into an expression of distaste as she reviewed the contents. Spare union suits, more woolen uniform shirts, socks, trousers, journals, pencils, sketchpads, hairbrush, comb, toothbrush, soap.

Suddenly, she wished she had indulged herself and brought along at least one dress—and a dressing gown. At least, when she was in the room she could have been comfortable.

The screech of a faucet cutting off a stream of rushing water knifed into her thoughts, and she shot an irritated glance at the bathroom door. A deep, masculine groan of pleasure accompanied the thump and splash of a body being lowered into water—a large, naked male body.

A mysterious coil of longing curled deep in her belly.

"God, this feels good!" River's voice echoed from behind the bathroom door.

Thinking how she'd like to throw a bucket of ice water over him, she stuck out her tongue. But she did her best to sound gay when she called out, "Good."

Determined to ignore her vision of a long, bronzed male form lazing back in steamy water, she dragged her attention away from the bathroom door.

"It feels *sooo* good," she mimicked, her head wagging back and forth, as she snatched up an armload of clothing and stomped toward the bureau to drop her things into the top drawer.

Going back to the bed for a second load, she caught sight of herself in the full-length oval mirror in the corner, and her anger with River dissolved into horror.

No wonder he had no desire to extend her any of the

courtesies a gentleman would automatically show a lady! What man would? Just look at her!

Her hair, so drenched with perspiration it looked dark brown, was pressed flat around the circumference of her head, where her hat had rested all day. And the curls that had not been shaped by the hatband stood out in wet clumps on top of her head, giving it a leg-o'-mutton shape that might have been funny if it hadn't been such a blow to her vanity to look so ugly. She sniffed in disgust. She even smelled bad!

As she gawked at herself in the mirror, a bead of perspiration trickled out of her hair at the temple, to wind brazenly past her ear, along her jaw, down her neck, and disappear into her neckerchief. Mortified to see the muddy trail the perspiration had created on her grimy cheek, she fumbled frantically to untie her bandana. Tilting the drinking-water pitcher, she soaked the colored cloth, then scrubbed angrily at her face and neck.

Suddenly, she couldn't stand to wait until River got out of the tub. She had to do something now or she would go crazy. Giving the possible consequences only the briefest consideration, she tore off her boots, uniform, and waist padding.

Immediately, she felt better. But the relief was only temporary and not sufficient. Her blouse and camisole and drawers were all plastered to her in a translucent gauze that felt as warm as a heavy shirt. She had to get them off, too! She gave the bathroom door a cursory glance to be sure River was still in the tub.

As if in response to her question, the sounds of splashing water reached her. Satisfied that she was safe, she ripped off her cotton blouse and flung it onto the floor with the uniform. Without pausing, she peeled the remainder of her clammy clothing downward, as if she were shedding an extra layer of skin.

"Ohhh," she groaned, relief oozing over her as the afternoon breeze coming through the screened window grazed her bared flesh.

"Okay, the bathroom's all — "

Aidan's startled gaze vaulted to the mirror, her round-eyed stare focusing on the stunned male face reflected over her shoulder.

For an instant, which seemed like several minutes, neither River nor Aidan moved, as if they'd been simultaneously turned to stone by a magic spell. Then, released from the "spell" at the same moment, they spoke at once.

"Sorry, I . . ." Unable to force himself to stop staring at the petite feminine form the mirror allowed him to view from every angle, River took a stumbling step backward.

"Don't you know . . ." Aidan's gaze automatically dropped to where a *very* small towel was wrapped *very* low, on River's *very* lean hips. She reached out and groped blindly for something to cover her nudity.

". . . thought you . . ." His awed stare moved helplessly to the pink tips of her small, upturned breasts. As though he'd physically touched them, they contracted into hard points, and his own body reacted with a tightening of its own!

". . . to knock before . . ." Oh, Lord! The skimpy towel stretched across the front of his belly wasn't flat anymore! It was molded to the changing contours of his body and was doing nothing to disguise his maleness. Seized by the familiar combination of pain and pleasure that throbbed deep in the center of her whenever she thought of River's body, Aidan instinctively clenched the inner muscles of her thighs together.

". . . were still dressed," he explained, taking another backward step, his dark skin assuming a red tinge.

". . . before you enter a r-r-room?" she stammered, finally catching hold of the bedspread and dragging the corner of it up in front of her.

The ridiculousness of her question and the strain of the

entire situation hit River all at once. Unable to stop himself, he felt a grin threatening to creep across his lips. "I guess no one ever told me I had to knock when I was coming *out* of the bathroom."

He closed the door, but not before she saw the glimmer of amusement in his eyes. Rage and humiliation discharged violently inside her. He was making fun of her! What she had thought was desire in his eyes hadn't been desire at all. It had been laughter. He had been laughing at her! Laughing at her body, her hair, her dirty face. Laughing at the way the heat and sand had made her skin all splotchy, and no doubt laughing most of all at her obvious reaction to him.

As if to rub the proverbial salt into her wounded ego, a series of quick raps sounded from the bathroom door. "Is it safe to come out now?" River called in a singsong voice.

Panic stormed through Aidan. Paying no heed to the remaining items on the bed as they fell to the floor, she dragged the spread completely off the bed and wrapped it around herself.

Again, he tapped on the door. "Aidan? Can I come out now? Are you decent?"

"Yes, she snapped, then scurried over to the window so she wouldn't have to look at him when he came out.

Cracking the door open, he poked his head out. Upon spotting her safely wrapped in her bedspread cocoon, back to him, he ventured the rest of the way into the room. "I forgot to take anything to wear with me," he explained, and padded over to the window side of the bed, where his bedroll had been pitched to the floor when she'd taken up the spread.

Directly behind Aidan, he stooped to retrieve the pack, then paused. As he looked up the compact length of her body, his expression suddenly became sympathetic. Bundled in the bedspread, her shoulders slightly hunched, she looked so vulnerable. Even though what had happened hadn't been his fault, he felt a need to apologize.

"Listen, I'm sorry. It really was an accident. I didn't mean to embarrass you. Why don't we just forget it? From now on, I promise I'll remember to knock."

His sincere tone struck a chord in her, and all the doubt and uncertainty she'd struggled to hide since she'd left San Antonio suddenly came tumbling to the surface. Her eyes filled with tears, and raising a hand that still gripped the spread, she rubbed at her eyes. "You laughed at me." She sniffled, not questioning why she was more hurt by that fact than embarrassed because he'd seen her without clothing. "I can't forget that."

"I didn't laugh at you!" he responded, and stood up, looking puzzled.

"Oh, not out loud. But I saw it in your eyes, and I saw the grin on your face. I'll bet you had a real good laugh once you closed the bathroom door."

"You're wrong. I wasn't laughing at you."

But Aidan didn't acknowledge his denial. "I can just imagine what you were thinking: What's that scrawny—"

"Petite." He corrected, now a step closer to her back.

"—girl so worried about? Does she actually think her skinny—"

"Slender."

"—body could turn a man into a raging, passion-starved animal?"

"It does," he said softly, his breath soughing over her cheek as from behind, he wrapped his fingers around her upper arms.

A spark of electricity ignited in Aidan, but she refused to acknowledge it. Whatever he'd just said, she was convinced it couldn't have been what she'd thought she'd heard.

She went on speaking for him. "What man would be attracted to a woman with about as many curves as a twelve-year-old boy?"

He turned her to face him. "It just so happens, I know

93

one man who thinks your curves are perfect."

The temperature inside the blanket increased drastically. Aidan raised her eyes to study his face. "You do?" she asked breathlessly, wanting to believe him more than she'd ever wanted anything in her entire life.

River smiled, and his hands slid over her shoulders to slip inside the blanket and encircle her neck. "I do." He ran his fingers up into the flattened hair at her temples and ruffled it so that it became a curly frame to her face. "As a matter of fact, he likes everything about your curves, from that mop-top head of red hair to your littlest toe."

"Really?" His hands in her hair were doing strange and wonderful things to her equilibrium.

"Really," he confirmed, dipping his head to brush his lips over her forehead. "Aren't you hot all bundled up like this?" he asked against her throbbing temple as his mouth drifted down her cheek.

"Uh-uh," Aidan admitted with a weak nod as her eyes fluttered closed. "Very hot."

He kissed a trail of moist fire down her jaw to her neck. "Maybe you'd be more comfortable if we did this." Sliding his hands down either side of her neck, he swept them outward toward her arms, taking the bedspread off her shoulders. "Is that better?"

"Better," she sighed. The tightening spring in her belly was becoming unbearable and was sapping her strength and rationality. "Ohhh," she moaned, sagging toward him.

Letting his mouth run over her shoulder, he slid the spread down her arms to the inside bend of her elbows. Then, bringing his hands to where she clutched the cover protectively to her bosom, he worked his fingers in between her tight fists and separated them. Before she could protest, he drew her hands, still gripping the blanket, around to his back and stepped into the blanket with her.

He looped his arms over hers, interlaced his fingers at the small of her back, and hauled her hard against him. No longer able to deny the pent-up desire he'd been refusing to acknowledge for days now, he worked the bedspread lower on her back.

"God, you feel good." He rubbed his chest against the sharp points of her breasts.

Forgetting all the reasons why this shouldn't happen, he moved his hands downward under the blanket to her bottom. Digging his fingers into firm, smooth mounds, he brought her against the throbbing rigidity of his sex. "Just the way I knew you would feel."

Erotic thoughts of the wonderful, mysterious new knowledge she was on the verge of receiving danced wildly in Aidan's brain, pounding in rhythm with the primitive thrum of passion that originated in the very core of her. She dropped her hold on the blanket and splayed her fingers over the corded muscles of River's back, tightening her embrace.

Wedging a strong thigh between her legs, he lifted her upward. Rounding his upper torso to adjust his height to her small stature, he burrowed his face in the curve of her shoulder. Running a hand down the back side of one of her thighs to her knee, he lifted her leg and wrapped it around his hips. Sensually moving his own leg against the hot moistness of her sex, he arched her backward and grazed his lips over a small breast, then took its erect peak deep into his mouth.

His tongue and lips on her nipple, sucking, tugging, squeezing, sent a jagged streak of electricity throughout her body. "Ohhh."

Her body limp, she protested when he took his mouth away from her breast by trying to draw his head back to her. A moment passed before she realized he was resisting. Sluggishly, she opened her eyes and took in his miserable expression. "What is it?"

Easing her back to a firm standing position, River shook his head. "I'm sorry, Aidan. I never should have . . . I didn't mean for it to go this far . . ."

"You didn't? I don't understand."

"I can't— I mean, if we give in to this, it can only make our relationship more impossible than it already is."

Stunned, Aidan shook her head, then nodded, her hurt eyes miraculously dry.

Pushing out of his embrace, she grabbed up the bedspread and threw it around her shoulders. "Of course, you're right. I don't know what came over me. It must be the heat." She hurried toward the bathroom. "It must have brought on a temporary loss of sanity!"

Slamming the bathroom door, she fell back against it and buried her face in her hands. How could she have been so stupid? What had possessed her? She'd made a fool of herself. How could she ever look at River again? But the worst hurt of all was that he'd seen how she felt. It was the knowledge that when she'd revealed her intense desire for him, he hadn't wanted her. She had thrown herself at him, body and soul, had practically attacked him. And he had still rejected her!

"I'm going out," a deep voice announced from the other side of the door, interrupting her self-pitying thoughts. "Don't wait up. I'll probably be late getting back."

His words sent new hurt storming through her. But disgust and anger at that reaction rose to combat the ache in her heart.

Fighting the urge to crawl into a corner and hide, Aidan released a last shuddering breath and pushed herself away from the door to stand without support. Never again would she allow a man to get close enough to hurt her like this.

Chapter Seven

The banging of a door broke into Aidan's lethargic depression. Jackknifing up from her reclining position in the tub, she clutched a washcloth to her bosom and stared at the closed bathroom door.

Her first thought was that River had returned, but of course it couldn't be him. He had said he wouldn't be back until very late, and that had been less than an hour ago—if the tepid temperature of her bathwater was any indication. Obviously, someone had watched him leave and had thought the room was empty and prime for robbing.

She sliced a panicked glance around the small bathroom for something to protect herself. Spying a short, three-legged wooden stool, she eased herself up out of the water, all the while aware of the heavy footsteps stomping about the other room, evidently looking for something to steal. She knew it was just a matter of time until the intruder checked the bathroom.

Climbing quietly out of the tub, Aidan grabbed the stool and scurried to the door. Each hand grasping a leg of the stool in a knuckle-whitening grip, she raised her makeshift weapon above her head. Poised for attack, she waited.

The footsteps approached the bathroom. Not daring to breathe, Aidan tensed, listening, her stare leveled on the doorknob. Above the roar of her frantic heartbeat, she heard the intruder pause on the other side of the door.

Then the doorknob started to turn, and from that instant on, everything seemed to happen at once. The door opened; a large male form loomed into view; she sucked in a deep breath and brought the stool down toward the crown of his dark head; he spun around, blocking the descent of the stool with his forearms.

"What the hell?" River jerked the stool away from her and tossed it aside.

Her eyes round with shock, Aidan pushed at this chest and darted past him into the bedroom. "What're you doing sneaking up on me like that? Don't Indians ever knock?"

He followed her into the bedroom, his stride lazy. "I wasn't sneaking. For your information, it was so quiet, I thought you might be gone, or drowned in the tub."

"Thought or hoped?" she asked, snatching a uniform shirt off the back of a chair and wrapping it around her shoulders to cover her nakedness. "Is that why you came back? To see if your little attempt to degrade and embarrass me worked and sent me running home to my parents?"

"What?"

Her back to him, she poked her arms into the shirt sleeves. "Well, I've got news for you, Mr. Danny — River Blue Eagle — Edwards! Humiliating treatment and bullying are not going to make me change my mind about going to Cuba! So you might as well give up. We made a bargain, and you're going to live up to your end of it or . . . or . . ."

"Or what?" he asked, closer to her back than she had anticipated, so close she could detect the scent of whiskey on his breath.

"Or . . . or . . . you're going to be very sorry!"

"I guess that's the chance I'll have to take, because that's why I came back — to tell you I've decided you can't go to Cuba."

Aidan's head snapped up, her hands pausing on the buttons of the shirt. "What did you say?"

98

"I said, you're not going to Cuba."

She spun around to face him, her lip curled in a resentful sneer. Fighting her tears, she jutted out her chin. "Dare I ask what brought this on? I was under the assumption that living up to one's word was a point of pride with you people. I guess whites aren't the only ones 'guilty of speaking with forked tongues,' are they?"

"You don't think much of me, do you, Aidan?"

Taken off guard by the hurt in his voice, she shook her head. "That's not true. I—"

He shoved his face up to hers, his blue eyes bright with accusation. "Yes, it is. You think I'm a lying, mannerless, stupid, low-life Indian, who should be honored to do a spoiled little white girl's bidding, don't you?"

"No!" Aidan protested. She couldn't look at him. "I don't think that at all."

"Dammit, Aidan!" He grabbed her hair at the nape and arched her neck back, forcing her frightened eyes to meet his. "You don't care about anyone but yourself. Have you given any thought to what you're doing to me? Do you even care?"

"What I'm doing to *you?*" Her voice broke. "I'm not the one who's done everything possible to embarrass, humiliate, and hurt you! I'm not the one whose moods swing back and forth like a pendulum." Tears slipped from her eyes, but she made no effort to wipe them away. "And it's not me who can't decide from one minute to the next what I want!"

"What I want *is* the problem," he said, his voice husky with pain.

"You want to improve conditions on the reservations. And we agreed that I'm going to help you do it, in exchange for taking me to Cuba. How is that suddenly the problem?"

His face contorted with frustration, he grasped her upper arms and shook her. "Dammit, Aidan. That's not the issue here!"

Eyes still glistening with tears rose to study his unhappy frown. "Then, what —"

"This, dammit." His mouth slanted over hers in a hard, punishing kiss, as if he could stamp out the torturous desire that grew in him.

At first, Aidan's instinct for self-protection gave her the strength to brace her hands against his chest and try to push away from him. But as quickly as the will to resist possessed her, it was gone, leaving her with a longing so intense she didn't question it. All she knew was that this was what she wanted. More than she'd ever wanted anything in her life.

Kneading her hands over the muscles of his chest and shoulders, she wound her arms around River's neck and drew herself up on tiptoe, returning his kiss with equal fervor.

Intelligence and rational thinking shouted at him to get the hell out before things got more out of hand. But this time, the warning was just a faint whisper at the back of his mind, made inaudible by the pounding of the blood in his head. Mounting passion rendered him helpless to think of a reason why he shouldn't make his fantasies of Aidan lying naked beneath him a reality.

Crushing her to his chest, he filled her mouth with his tongue, claiming it as his body screamed to claim all of her. In and out his tongue thrust, in perfect rhythm with the movement of his hips against hers.

A moment of rationality hit him, and he caught her hair at the crown with the fingers of one hand, pulling her head back so he could see her eyes. The raw desire reflected there told him there was no need for words, but he spoke anyway. "Now do you understand what it is I want, Aidan?"

She nodded her head. "It's what I want too." Her voice was a husky whisper.

"Oh, God," he ground out, burying his face in the curve of her neck and shoulder. He dropped his hold on her hair and drew her tiny frame more tightly into his arms, desire blotting out the last argument as to why he couldn't have her. Moving like a man half-crazed, he ripped open the bulky shirt she had just put on.

Eager to feel the smooth flesh of his chest beneath her fingers, Aidan inserted her hands between their bodies and fumbled with the buttons on his shirt.

Keeping his mouth sealed to hers, he stood on one foot, then the other to remove his boots. When she had his shirt open, he tore it off, hurling it to the floor.

Frantic to know and see and feel all of him, Aidan loosened his belt buckle, then undid the top button of his trousers.

In her anxiousness, the edge of her hand brushed the hard bulge in his pants, causing him to cry out with pleasure.

A rush, second thoughts filled her mind. Suddenly, she was afraid.

Drawing her lips away from his, she raised her questioning gaze to his blue ones. Her bottom lip trembling, she smiled uncertainly.

"What is it?" he asked, his breathing ragged.

"I-I'm . . ." She stopped, searching for words. "I don't . . . I think I'm afraid."

His expression softened, "Ah, no," he cooed sympathetically. "Don't be afraid, Little Fire." Ashamed that he'd almost given in to his own desires in spite of what he knew was right, he fought to regain his normal breathing. He pulled the front of her shirt together, then brought her cheek to rest on his chest. "You never need to be afraid of me."

She drew back her head and looked at him, his tender expression tugging at her heart. He had been every bit as driven by passion as she was by hers, yet he was willing to stop.

With an embarrassed smile, she reached up and pressed

101

her open palms to his cheeks. "You don't understand. I could never be afraid of you. It's me. It's just that . . ." Her eyes shifted nervously to the side. "I mean, I've never . . ." She glanced up into his face again, then down at his chest. "I'm afraid I'm going to disappoint you," she finally managed to admit.

His mouth spread in an astonished grin, and he released a long relieved sigh. "Disappoint me?" Shaking his head in denial, he hunched his long frame and wrapped his arms around her tiny waist in an embrace so tight his elbows crossed at the small of her back.

"Ah, Little Fire," he laughed, scooping her up into his arms. "How could you disappoint me? Don't you know I've ached for you since the moment I saw you in the entryway of your parents' living room on that first night?"

Her heartbeat doubled. "You have? Then, why . . ." She broke off her question, and her mouth stretched in a wide grin. Why he had pushed her away suddenly didn't matter anymore, nor did all the reasons why they shouldn't be together. She looped her arms around his neck and opened her mouth hungrily over his. Nothing mattered but the fact that River wanted her as much as she wanted him.

His stride purposeful, he carried her to the bed and lowered her onto the mattress. Smoothing her wool shirt aside, he cupped each of her breasts with his hands and settled himself over her.

Massaging her breasts with desperate, hungry caresses, he rotated his hips against hers as his tongue sparred aggressively with hers in a primitive mating dance.

Propping himself above her on one arm, he cupped her jaw in his hand and kissed her mouth, gently, reverently. Then, raising up so he could watch her face, he swept his hand down the front of her, over her breast, along her ribs, past her waist and belly to the gently rocking heart of her desire.

"Oh," she cried out, her eyes widening with surprise. She

brought her head up off the mattress. "What are you doing?"

"You mean this?" he asked, continuing to watch her as he caressed her gently.

"Yes." Her eyes fluttering shut, she dropped back an inch toward the bed.

"Or this?" he teased, trailing a forefinger down the channel leading to the wellspring of her body.

Her head fell back another inch. As though she'd been given a strong drug, she fought to open her eyes again. But the lids were simply too heavy.

She made a last token effort to gain control of her limp muscles. But it was useless. It was as if every fiber of her being had evaporated. Everything she was, everything she wanted to be, was now combined and concentrated into that one surviving pinpoint of existence.

Giving up her fight, she melted back onto the bed. "Yeeeees," she ground out, arching her neck and rocking her head from side to side as the tension in her body suddenly exploded in a mind-shattering eruption.

Frantic urgency thrumming in her blood, Aidan slipped her hands down River's back, into his trousers, and under his breechcloth to grip the firm mounds of his bare buttocks and urge him even closer.

Dragging his mouth from hers, he trailed a line of hot kisses down her neck to a breast. Molding its soft flesh with his hand, he brought the erect tip to his lips. His tongue curled possessively around the eager peak, adoring it with starving, sucking motions.

Streamers of electricity rocketed through Aidan. She was alive with desire, ravenous for more of him—all of him. Blind impulses controlled her now. Wedging her hands between their melded bellies, she fumbled with clumsy fingers to unbutton the fly of his trousers.

When she had succeeded in undoing his pants, she struggled to work the waistband down over his smooth buttocks.

His mouth now fastened to her other breast, he lifted his hips and roughly shoved trousers and loincloth down his thighs.

River winced as his masculine flesh leaped free of the hindering clothing, desire to be buried within the moist heat of her femininity guiding him as urgent motions of her hips beckoned him.

Summoning all the control he could muster, River lifted his head and looked down into her face. "Are you sure this is what you want?"

Opening her eyes just enough to see him through a screen of thick lashes, Aidan smiled and tightened her embrace, "I'm sure," she panted.

She felt the muscles in his back relax, and she realized how tense he'd been waiting for her answer. "I've never been more sure of anything in my life," she added.

Unable to put off his own release for another moment, River pressed the tip of his strength against her still-trembling flesh. Poised on the brink of discovery, he hesitated for the barest fragment of an instant.

The intimate contact made Aidan's senses reel, and her hips bucked upward.

Reckless with his own frantic need, River plunged deep into her. But when he saw the look of shock that came to her face, he immediately stopped, his own features revealing regret. "Oh, Little Fire," he whispered. "Did I hurt you?" He lifted his hips to relieve her tiny body of his weight.

Already the pain was subsiding, and Aidan was certain the agony she saw in River's eyes was worse than the momentary pang she'd experienced. She smiled and tightened her embrace. "You didn't hurt me. I was just surprised."

Relief washed over him and he relaxed his hips on hers, but he didn't move. "Are you sure?"

Touched by his gentle concern, Aidan felt tears spring into her eyes. "I'm sure," she said, clasping his worried face between her palms and lifting her head to kiss his mouth.

Instinctively, the snug sheath of her femininity clenched around him and her lower body rocked upward in an open invitation. "Very, very sure."

River's reaction was immediate, and his manhood swelled to steel hardness. "Oh, God, Fire," he groaned, ramming hard into her, no longer able to contemplate any pain other than his own. Supporting his weight on his forearms, he sank his tongue into her mouth, matching the rhythm of its probing strokes with the urgent thrusts of his lower body.

She sucked hard on his tongue as the hot, tight glove of her femininity molded itself to the length of his passion. Desperate for more of him, she wrapped her legs around his perspiration-misted thighs and squeezed. Her hands roved hungrily over his back, her fingers digging greedily into cords of tense muscles.

Gasping for air, she tore her mouth from his, only to sink her teeth into his shoulder as the volcano of passion at the heart of her erupted for the second time, sending her spiraling into ecstasy.

"Sweet Fire," he rasped, his lips stretched across bared teeth in a strained grimace. Throwing his head back, he released a tortured groan and spewed his passion deep inside her in hard, convulsive stabs.

"Are you all right?" he groaned out in a ragged voice as he collapsed on her, his vitality drained.

Her breathing rough and uneven, Aidan could only nod her head and smile. Her hands slid up from the small of his back to clasp his shoulders.

His chest rising and falling as though he'd just run a race for his life, he rolled his forehead from side to side against the sheet beside her head to remove the sweat from his brow. "I thought Hell was the only place a man could experience this kind of fire. Not Heaven! he panted into the mattress, unable to find the power to roll away from her, though he knew he must be a deadweight on her.

Her heartbeat slowing to a less erratic rhythm, Aidan grinned lazily and turned her face to him. "And I always dreamed of soaring with an eagle," she said, her lips moving over his ear. "But those dreams can't compare to the reality."

Finally able to feel some of the strength returning to his limbs, River raised his head and smiled down into her dark, blazing eyes. "Well, you sure singed this eagle's feathers, Little Fire. I may have 'soared' my last time."

Emboldened by her success, Aidan poked out her lower lip and frowned with insincere sympathy. "Oh, that would be sad," she said, lifting her bottom a bit and rotating her hips against his. "Are you sure?"

River tilted his head and eyed her with amused surprise. Then he broke out laughing and shook his head. "I was right. You *are* a devil."

Suddenly Aidan's teasing expression grew serious. "Do you realize that's the first time I've heard you laugh since we were children?"

Tensing as though he'd been caught desecrating an ancient burial place, River stopped the happiness on his face dissolved into guilt. "That's ridiculous. I laugh," he said rolling away from her to a sitting position on the side of the bed. "It's just that there hasn't been anything particularly humorous about our recent situation."

Aidan's heart twisted in her chest. When would she learn to think before she spoke? In the space of a few minutes she'd made him forget whatever it was that caused him to be sad, only to toss a shroud of depression over him again with a few careless words.

She could see him drawing away from her as if they hadn't just shared the most intimate experience of her life, and she didn't know how to stop him. Desperate not to let him reerect the wall between them, she scooted to her knees behind him.

Laying her cheek against his slumping back, she wrapped her arms around his waist and held him tightly. "What is it, River? What happened to make you feel you have no right to laugh? What turned the carefree boy, Danny Edwards, into—"

"Dammit, Aidan, is that all life is to you?" he growled, bolting out of her embrace to a standing position. "Just one big something to laugh about?" He snatched his breechcloth up from the floor and slapped it around his hips.

Stunned by the sudden attack, Aidan's first instinct was to lash back. But she was stopped by something she heard in his gruff voice—not exactly a sob, but definitely a crack that made him sound very vulnerable and tore at her heart.

"No, I don't think life is just 'one big something to laugh about,' " she answered, her tone gentle, compassionate. Wrapping a sheet around herself and clutching it to her bosom, she rose from the bed and went to him. "Don't you know that when you hurt so much you can't think of anything but your pain, laughter can do more than any medicine ever could? It's not wrong to laugh, River. It's good for you. Its the best medicine in the world. You shouldn't feel guilty about it."

River turned to face her, any sign of vulnerability carefully hidden behind a half-smile that didn't hide the pain in his eyes. "Are you hungry? I'm starved. Dinner is served at six sharp. If we go now, we can be first in line." He whisked his trousers up off the floor and walked away from her.

"River!" Aidan said, her voice high with exasperation. "Don't do this to me. Don't shut me out. Tell me what hurt you so deeply. Let me help you."

"I can see why you're a writer," he said with a forced smile. "You have quite an imagination." He came back to her and pressed a paternal kiss to her forehead. "But the simple fact is the only pain I'm feeling right now is in my empty belly. Now be a good girl and get dressed so we can

107

go eat."

Aidan opened her mouth to protest, then clamped it shut again. Did he have to slap her in the face to make it clear that he didn't want to discuss his problems with her? Obviously, he had only wanted one thing from her, and now that he'd relieved that hunger, he had no further use for her. Only a stupid, immature, infatuated fool would have let herself believe that sharing his bed would make him want to share his thoughts and feelings, maybe even love her!

Humiliation brought tears to her eyes. She realized now that she had actually convinced herself the lust River had felt for her was love.

"You go on," she said, rushing into the bathroom. She closed the door behind her. "I'm not hungry."

Ashamed of the way he had behaved, River crossed over to the bathroom. Raising his hand to knock, he hesitated. What good would it do to talk to her about it? She couldn't possibly understand what he felt. She truly believed she had the power to overcome any obstacle, no matter how great. What did she know about cruelty and violence and death and hopelessness?

A sad smile skittered across his face, and he chuckled silently. Aidan Donovan thought she had the power to do anything she wanted—even relieve his burden.

Maybe she does, a voice deep inside him whispered. *For a while she made you forget. She made you happy. You even laughed.*

He dropped his hand to his side and turned away from the door, bent on ignoring the niggling thoughts.

Without speaking, he hurriedly finished dressing and left the room.

In the bathroom, tears streaming down her cheeks, Aidan washed away the pink stain of her lost innocence. She could already see faint bruises beginning to form on the tender flesh on the insides of her thighs, and the delicate tissues of her most private part were painfully sensitive. But she wasn't crying because of physical discomfort she was experiencing, or even for her lost virginity.

Her tears were for the knowledge that she was in love with a man who had encased his heart in stone — stone that represented the first obstacle she'd ever encountered that she could see no possible way to overcome.

Her spirits lifted ever so slightly by her second bath and an indulgent half-hour of self-pity, Aidan nervously paced the room. She really was hungry. Maybe she should have gone with River after all. Of course, she could ring for a maid and have some dinner brought up.

But it was more than hunger that made her regret her decision to stay in the room. The slanting rays of the afternoon sun were turning it into a sweltering oven. She had to get out.

Giving the clock on the bureau a hopeful glance, Aidan let out sigh of relief. There was still an hour before dinner was to be served. She made a dash for the bureau and opened the drawer. Taking out fresh underclothes, she quickly donned them.

She reached for her uniform shirt, then stopped, her head reeling with second thoughts. At least in the room, she could stay in her underclothes. But if she went out, she had no choice but to wear the sweltering uniform shirt.

A knock at the door interrupted her quandary and she looked up. She ran over and pressed her ear to the wood. "Who is it?" she asked, using her A.D. voice.

"Maid," a youthful-sounding woman answered. "The lieutenant, he say you weel want to order dinner to be brought up to your room."

An idea flowered in Aidan's head. "Are you by yourself?"

After a moment of silence, the maid answered. "Pardon?"

"Are you by yourself?" Aidan repeated impatiently. "Is there anyone out there besides you?"

Another pause, then a hesitant, "There is nobody here but me."

Aidan wrenched open the door and grabbed the unsuspecting maid's arm. "Quick, get in here before anyone sees you," she ordered, dragging the young girl clad in a black dress and white apron into the room.

Closing the door behind her, Aidan waited a scant second, then turned to face the frightened maid, her expression distraught. "Please! I'm desperate. You've got to help me."

Chapter Eight

Doing his best to stifle a yawn, River covered his mouth and chin with an open hand, and turned his head to the side. The major and the captain he was facing continued their animated conversation with Colonel Roosevelt, each doing his best to impress his own accomplishments upon the famous man. No one was particularly concerned with a bored aide—which was just fine with River.

Taking advantage of his companion's inattention, he casually viewed his surroundings. Strung with electric lights that swayed in the breeze, the long hotel porch echoed with sounds of celebration. Everywhere he looked officers were laughing with or cheerfully greeting fellows they had not seen in years, perhaps since West Point or at some distant post.

Sprinkled among the blue- and khaki-uniformed men were the wives, daughters and sweethearts who had come to Tampa to see their loved ones off to war. Their flowing skirts and ruffled bodices dotted the porch and the lawn with splashes of color, as the beautifully dressed females added their higher voices and gay laughter to the sounds filling the warm evening air.

River watched as a young couple glided arm in arm across the lawn, their heads together in whispered con-

111

versation, and he felt a pang of loneliness. Refusing to acknowledge why the pair had aroused such an emotion in him, he deliberately forced his attention back to the veranda.

Not far away, he spotted a group of very young, dark-haired women chatting and giggling. From the occasional phrase that floated to his ears from the lively group, it was easy to conclude they were speaking Spanish. No doubt, these young ladies were daughters of the rich Cubans, newly arrived in Tampa, who often brought their families to the hotel in the evening for dancing and socializing.

His gaze idly skimmed over the handsomely gowned girls, lit briefly on one who stood slightly apart from the others, then settled on the regimental band now gathered on the lawn to play waltzes and patriotic tunes for the guests' entertainment.

Suddenly, something slightly familiar about the girl who wasn't quite in the cluster of Cubans, brought his attention back to them. But she was gone. Evidently she had blended into the group or moved on.

Stretching to make himself even taller, River strained to see if he could spot her again. Not that he had any intention of following through on his curiosity about her. There was just something about the way she had been looking directly at him, as though she were some-one he should know — which was crazy, since he didn't know any Cuban families.

Well, she was gone now. So whatever it was that had struck that familiar chord would remain unknown. He turned back to the officer discussing the Cuban campaign and concentrated on what the man was saying.

"What do you think, sir? Is there any truth to the rumor that they're going to land us on the southern coast of Cuba and make us march across the island to Havana?" the major asked Roosevelt.

"We'll lose half our men to yellow fever if they do," the captain put in.

Roosevelt shook his head and brayed loudly. "Come now, gentlemen. You know how rumors get out of hand. There's no use trying to second-guess decisions that haven't even been made yet, is there? As far as the First Volunteer Cavalry is concerned, we're just glad to be here, and we're ready to go wherever they send us— yellow fever or not. Isn't that right, Lieutenant?" He slapped River on the back.

"Wha— Oh, yes sir. I agree totally," River stammered, forcing a smile in the other officers' direction, though he realized his mind had wandered again and he had no idea what he had just agreed to.

"I think our young *unmarried* friend has found something else to interest him," Roosevelt teased good-naturedly, letting out his unique laugh and nodding his head toward the Cuban *señoritas*.

The major and captain both twisted their heads in the direction Roosevelt had indicated. Smiling, the major turned back to River. "I don't blame you, Lieutenant. Why don't you go introduce yourself? If I'm not mistaken, the one over by that pillar is trying to catch your eye."

"Oh, I doubt that, sir," River said with an embarrassed shrug, but he couldn't stop his gaze from veering to that very pillar.

His eyes suddenly widened in surprise. It was her! The dark-haired Cuban girl he'd been curious about!

The instant their eyes met, she lifted a small gloved hand in close to her bodice and wiggled her fingers in a little wave.

113

Frowning, River looked over his shoulder, expecting to find someone behind him returning the greeting. But no one was there. Curious, he glanced back at the girl. But the breeze swayed the strings of electric lights so, he couldn't make out her features. Still, he couldn't shake the feeling there was something vaguely familiar about her.

"Go on, boy," Roosevelt boomed. "Go meet her."

Pivoting in a one-quarter turn toward his commander, River forced his attention back to the officers. "Oh, no sir. I'd rather not," he protested.

"Well, it looks like this little lady believes in going to the mountain, if the mountain won't come to her," Roosevelt commented out of the side of his mouth, inclining his head toward River, but keeping his eyes focused on a spot just beyond the younger man's right shoulder.

Another pushy female. That was all River needed to make his evening complete. As if the one in his room wasn't enough to drive him crazy. "I'm sure you're mistaken, sir." He refused to turn his head to look.

"I don't think so." Roosevelt chuckled, lifting his eyebrows as he pointedly looked over River's shoulder.

Obviously annoyed, River finally glanced back and was startled to find the object of his curiosity not two feet away, her smile beaming with friendliness.

Recognition hit him with the force of a Florida hurricane, and his mouth tightened into a grim, threatening line. His eyes narrowing angrily, he leaned toward her, but she cut him off.

"Rivah, tha-ah yuh ah," she sang out in a heavy southern drawl. "I been lookin' all ovah for yuh, sugah." She glided up beside him and slipped a small hand into the crook of his arm, then favored the other three officers with a sweet smile. "This must be the famous Mistah Rooseva-lt." She extended a gloved hand to the surprised officer and smiled. "Rivah and mah li'l cousin, A.D."—She dragged out the D, her voice rising as though she were asking a question."—have tol' me so much about yuh. It's a real honah to meet yuh, suh. I'm A-un-juh-la Donovan from Atlanta. I've come to Tampa ta see A.D. off ta the wah."

"It's a pleasure, Miss Donovan," Roosevelt answered, taking her hand. "I must say the family resemblance is remarkable, except for the dark hair, of course. And the accent. Speaking of your cousin, where is he?"

Aidan glanced up at River, her expression playfully scolding. She appeared to be undaunted by the grim stare raining down on her. "Shame on you, Rivah. Didn't you tell Mistah Roosevelt 'bout po' li'l A.D.?" She turned back to the other officers, seeming not to notice that the scowl on River's face grew even darker. "My po' li'l cousin's in his room with a belly ache. I s'pose he ate somethin' that didn't agree with him."

"I'm sorry to hear that," Roosevelt said, obviously captivated by "Angela Donovan." "Perhaps, I should send a doctor to check on him. It would be a shame if he doesn't get to see something of Tampa while we're here."

"That won't be necessary, sir!" River interrupted, his statement one degree away from a snarl. Subtly—and firmly—he freed his elbow from Aidan's grip and took hold of her upper arm, digginggg his strong fingers into the soft flesh beneath her sleeve. " 'Angela' and I were just going to do that. If you gentlemen will excuse us please . . ." Without waiting for an acknowledgment, he gave Aidan a less than gentle shove away from the group.

115

"Nice meetin' yuh, suh," she sang over her shoulder, waving her free hand. "I hope tuh be seein' y'all agin."

The muscles in his cheeks bunched into hard knots, River picked up his pace, forcing her to run to keep up with him. "What do you think you're doing?" he hissed out of the corner of his mouth once they were out of Roosevelt's earshot. "And where'd you get those clothes and that wig?"

"I didn't *steal* them, if that's what you mean. I got one of the hotel maids to buy them for me. Slow down," she demanded, her smile and Southern drawl gone as she double-stepped to keep up with him. "Dammit! I said, slow down!"

"I'll slow down when I get you up to the room and out of that ridiculous getup," River growled, his long strides lengthening.

"All right! That's it!" Aidan said, diggin in her heels. "I've had all I'm going to take from you. I'm sick of having you run my life. Let go of me, or I'm going to scream! And I won't stop until everyone on this porch knows the truth about A. D. Donovan—and that you knew *he* was a *she* all along!"

River hesitated a scant second. His anger and frustration were so great he was tempted to take the risk. He didn't for a minute believe she'd follow through on her threat. She was too stubborn to deliberately do anything to jeopardize her own situation, unless she was ready to give up covering the war—and only a fool could imagine that happening.

Her seething look locked in head-on combat with his, Aidan's mouth stretched into a smug, triumphant grin as she raised her eyebrows expectantly. "Your move, Lieutenant. But unless I'm mistaken, isn't this what chess players call a 'stalemate'? Looks like any move you make will put you in 'check'.'"

A secretive smile curled River's lips, and he released her arm. Lifting his shoulders indifferently, he held his hands out at his side, palms up. "Have it your way, *A-un-juh-la*. I thought you would be interested in getting a lead on a story that's supposed to break in the morning. But since you don't want my help . . ." His mysterious grin deepened and he shrugged. "It's no skin off my nose." With long, lazy steps, he brushed past her. "Have a nice evening."

Her expression indignant, Aidan watched his broad, retreating back as he stepped off the porch and ambled across the lawn. *He wouldn't know a good story if it stood up and hit him in that cocky smirk of his. He's just trying to get even with me for "Angela."*

She pirouetted toward the hotel lobby.

Besides, even if he did have a story, she didn't need his help. She was perfectly capable of finding her own stories.

She reached the entrance to the hotel and stopped. On the other hand, what if he really had a lead and she lost it because of stubbornness?

Aidan looked back over her shoulder, her expression suddenly indecisive. His retreating form was growing smaller. *No. He's just doing this to irritate me. I know he doesn't have a story.*

She turned away from him and reached for the door. *Still . . .*

Swinging about, she lifted her skirts and dashed across the porch.

Her eyes on the man who was quickly being swallowed up by the shadow of the manicured hedge edging the lawn, Aidan bounded across the grass, unconcerned that her unladylike gallop was totally incongruous with her dress.

Oblivious to the turned heads she was causing, she drew up alongside River, her chest rising and falling rapidly. "All right," she panted. "You win."

"Why, where did you come from?" he asked with an artificial smile, his tone absolutely oozing with bogus surprise. "What happened? You're all out of breath. Are you all right?"

"You can drop the front, River," she said with a disgusted sneer. "You knew I'd come. Now, what's this big story?"

His bottom lip jutted out in a childish pout. "Story? Aw, gee. And I thought it was my company that made you willing to make a spectacle of yourself and chase after me." He turned and continued on toward the outer edges of the lawn.

"I knew it!" she shrilled, running after him. "You don't have a story!"

He spun about to face her, his expression hard, and she stopped dead in her tracks.

"Then why are you here, Aidan?" He took a menacing step toward her.

Unable to keep herself from withering slightly under his scathing glare, Aidan cleared her throat. "I . . . uh . . . had to be sure."

"Sure of what?" He advanced a pace in her direction, his eyes glittering like steel in the moonlight. "Did you have to make sure your little threat to 'expose' me hadn't backfired on you? Is that why you came? Or was it something else you wanted?"

"Backfire? What are you talking about?"

"Come now, Aidan, how long did you think it would take me to figure out what you were up to? Do you really think I'm so dumb I wouldn't eventually realize all those 'accidental' little shows you put on for my benefit weren't accidental at all? You thought teasing me with your body would distract me so I wouldn't come to my senses and refuse to take you to Cuba with me. But when I told you I had changed my mind anyway, you had to follow through, so you could *blackmail* me into taking you. I am curious about one thing though. Was what happened in our room earlier part of your initial plan to force me into a corner if it was necessary? Or was it a last-minute improvisation?"

Tears welled in Aidan's eyes, and her bottom lip trembled. "A-are you a-accusing me of . . ." She swung out her hand, bringing it down on his cheek.

One corner of his mouth twitched up in a humorless smile as he caught her wrist in strong fingers and wrenched her arm behind her back. "Spare me the theatrics, *A-un-juh-la,*" he drawled, his face close to hers, his features twisted with disgust. "We've already established what a convincing actress you are, haven't we?"

Her heart racing with new fear, Aidan struggled against his grip, shoving at his chest with her free hand. "You're hurting me."

"You should have considered that before," he retorted. Catching her free hand in his fist, he dragged it behind her and hauled her hard against him.

"I'll scream."

"No, you won't." His mouth descended on hers.

Her frightened eyes focused on his sneering lips, then shifted to the side. "I will," she said, her threat a breathless whimper.

"Then go ahead. But you ought to know one thing first. If you do *anything* to injure my reputation, you'll be announcing to the whole world what happened in our room this afternoon. Do you know what they call a

119

woman who uses her body to get what she wants, Aidan?" A cruel, taunting smile curved his lips. "I'm sure your parents do."

Astounded and hurt by this threat, Aidan narrowed her eyes. "You wouldn't dare!"

His mouth stretched into a vindictive line. "Try me."

"But you'd lose too!"

"Not as much as you will. Since people are inclined to forgive men's indiscretions, I'm sure they'll understand how I could have been taken in by a . . . well you know the type of woman I mean. On the other hand, no one's going to sympathize with a hard, calculating female who deliberately set out to take advantage of a man."

When she didn't reply to his last statement, he couldn't resist one final jibe. "And that, my dear Miss Donovan, is *checkmate!*"

Hurt and disillusioned, Aidan acknowledged defeat. "All right. I give up. I'll leave for Texas on the morning train." Twisting her torso, she strained to free herself from his grip.

"I don't think so."

She looked up in surprise. "What do you mean? You've won. What more do you want?"

Licking his lips purposefully, River glanced down at her breasts. Thrust forward by the way he held her arms behind her, they pillowed out of her low-cut bodice.

Aidan's eyes widened in indignation. "First you seduce me. Then you threaten to tell the entire world about it! And now you expect me to . . . to— Well, you can forget it! Now let me go."

"You know I can't do that, Aidan."

Confused by the husky sorrow she heard in his voice, she ceased to struggle, her expression puzzled. A peculiar excitement curled through her belly. Maybe he did

120

care for her. Maybe he hadn't meant all those ugly things he'd said. Maybe he'd just lashed out because she hurt him. "Why not?"

Because you're in my blood, the voice in his head responded. *And now that I've had you, I can't stand the thought of being without you.*

River quickly masked his longing behind a bitter chuckle. "Remember, Aidan. I know what you're willing to do in order to get what you want. You have no intention of leaving Tampa, and I'd be very surprised if you haven't already tricked some unsuspecting soldier into helping you. I wonder if he'll be as patient as I was about collecting his fee. But it doesn't matter because you're not going to get a chance to find out."

As if she'd been hit in the face, Aidan flinched. Then the fire that had temporarily left her returned. Her eyes narrowed vengefully.

"As if the threat of being publicly exposed as a liar, a blackmailer, and a prostitute weren't enough, now you're accusing me of being stupid. Tell me, River, if, as you seem to think, I really am too dumb to know when to concede, what makes you think there's anything you can do to stop me? Do you intend to have me thrown in jail as a spy for Spain?"

"Believe me, it's a possibility I haven't totally disregarded," he responded sarcastically. "But I have something else in mind. I'm taking you to Cuba with me so you can write your story and make a name for yourself."

"You're what?"

"No matter what I think of some of your methods, I have to admit that your plan to arouse sympathy for the plight of the People on the reservations makes sense. As long as someone is going to reap the benefits of an alliance with you, it might as well be me. At least I

121

already know what to expect."

"Why you bastard! I wouldn't go along with you if you were the last man on earth. If that was the only way I could get a story, I'd never write another word."

River lifted his shoulders and gave her a mocking smile. "Don't flatter yourself, Aidan. The 'benefit' I was talking about is the exposé you're going to write about the reservations." A taunting grin slithered across his face. "Of course, I'm not averse to including 'additional benefits' in our deal—if that's what you want."

"Over my dead body."

"Do we have an understanding?"

"What if I say no?"

He dropped his hold on her wrists and held his hands out to his sides. "Then, you'll leave me no choice but to do an 'exposé' of my own." He hesitated, giving her time to weigh the meaning of his words. "Well, what's it to be? Are you going to be smart or stupid?"

Massaging her numb wrists, Aidan eyed River resentfully. Pride tempted her to tell him to go ahead and make his ugly accusations public. But intelligence—the one good quality that outweighed her stubbornness—wouldn't let her do that. Not only could she not chance publicly disgracing her parents, she was simply too smart to let pride take this story from her after all she'd given up to get it. Yes, she would go with River to Cuba—she'd even write his Indian story for him—but if she lived to be a hundred, she would find a way to get even with him for what he was doing.

She smiled, her dark eyes gleaming vindictively. "As you've pointed out, I have no choice." She held out her right hand. "Shall we shake hands on it?"

Ashamed of the tactics he'd used to gain control over the unpredictable Aidan Donovan, River hesitated. *She brought it on herself,* he told himself. *None of this would have been necessary if she could be trusted not to pull stunts like the one she staged tonight.*

He glanced at her face and laughed inwardly. *Even now, I can see the wheels turning in your head, Little Fire. And the only way to handle you is to get the upper hand and hang on to it. I just pray I'm up to it.*

He grasped her extended hand and hauled her toward him. Squeezing her cheek with his other hand, he brought his face down to within an inch of hers. "So help me, Aidan, if you ever again so much as think about moving a muscle without my knowledge, you're going to regret the day you left San Antonio."

The threat in his voice silenced any retort she might have been inclined to make. That and the sorrow she saw in his "old-man's" eyes. For a fleeting instant, she believed he regretted all the cruel things he'd said, and she was hit by a sudden desire to reach up and wipe the sadness from his face.

Don't be ridiculous, she said to herself when she realized the unexpected turn her thoughts had taken. *That's gloating satisfaction you see. Not sorrow. He knows he's beaten me and he's enjoying every minute of it!*

She inhaled deeply, determined not to be fooled by what she imagined she saw — by what she *wished* she saw. But the familiar scent of his hot, masculine flesh assaulted her, and her thoughts flashed back to those glorious moments when she'd held his shuddering body as he'd spilled his seed into her.

Didn't it mean anything to you at all? she silently wondered, searching his expression for a sign that he hadn't been pretending. *Was I so naive that I fooled myself into believing you cared for me, when all along I was giving myself to a man who could have satisfied his desires with any woman?*

Blinking back the tears that threatened to spill from her eyes, Aidan did her best to sound strong. "You've made your point, River. Can we go now? Colonel Roosevelt expects us at the camp before dawn, and I suddenly find myself very tired."

Chapter Nine

*Tampa—June 6, 1898. The visionary Henry Brad-
ley Plant may have built the magnificent Tampa
Bay Hotel to accommodate thousands, but he was
totally short-sighted when he planned the port—as
was the War Department when they picked it as the
Army's point of departure for Cuba.*

*Not only are the wharf's facilities insufficient to
handle the vast supplies needed by a 25,000-man
army, but only eight vessels at a time can lie in the
narrow, twenty-one-foot-deep channel. Though additional railroad tracks have been laid to transport
supplies to the wharf, the congestion only grows
worse. There is barely enough space at the pier for
two ships at a time, and the loading must be done
by stevedores who lug food and supplies over at
least fifty feet of sand and up a steep ramp onto
the ships.*

*If this inefficient operation is not enough to
convince the most casual observer that grave orga-
nizational errors have been made at every turn,
read on, for at every turn the confusion is further
compounded. In most instances, invoices aren't*

available, so it is impossible to assemble complete cargoes at one time. Often, in this madhouse of day-and-night activity, it is necessary for a transport to move away from and return to the wharf several times before it is loaded.

Now, to top off the frustration, the Rough Riders have had a bombshell dropped on them this very morning. Because of the lack of transports, General Shafter has given orders that the Riders go to Cuba dismounted, and that only eight troops of seventy men each out of the regiment's twelve will ship out. The thought of going to war on foot is a disappointing blow for men who have spent their lives on horseback, as have most of the Rough Riders have; but it is nothing compared to the despair the men who will be left behind are feeling. Some of the most hardened of them burst into tears at hearing the news that they were to remain in Tampa.

As though controlled by some outside force, Aidan's spine tensed against the trunk of the palmetto tree on which she leaned, her journal propped on her bent knees. Her pencil stopped moving across paper for the first time in an hour, and she glanced out from under the brim of her hat at the slim-hipped officer who sauntered toward her.

Of course, it hadn't been necessary for her to look up to know it was River who was approaching. This wasn't the first time she had "felt" his presence before she'd actually had reason to know he was nearby. In fact, it had happened so many times since they'd had their confrontation on Friday night that it was beginning to annoy her. How was she supposed to write if, after she finally managed to put him out of her mind and lose herself in her work for a few minutes, he popped back into her thoughts when he was just in the general vicinity, whether she saw him or not?

Aidan swallowed back the lump in her throat, and snapped her notebook shut. "Must you keep checking on me?" She looked up at him from her position on the fern-covered ground at the edge of the Rough Riders' camp, two miles from the hotel. "I told you I wouldn't budge from this spot. And as you can see, I haven't."

"I'm not checking on you," River returned, his tone equally disgruntled. "I came to tell you we've been dismissed for a few hours so we can make any last-minute preparations before shipping out tomorrow!"

"Tomorrow?" Forgetting her anger, Aidan sprang up from the ground, her grin jubilant. "You don't mean it! I thought we were going to be stuck here for weeks!"

Determined not to be drawn in by her infectious enthusiasm, River realized it was almost impossible to avoid it when she hit him full blast with that smile of hers. He would just not look at her, he decided, he deliberately glanced back over his shoulder at the frantic activity behind him, as men scurried in every direction in preparation for breaking camp.

"Don't get too excited," he droned with forced nonchalance. "It's probably just a false alarm. But Colonel Roosevelt wants me to take you into Tampa just in case, to be sure you've got everything you need—pencils, paper, film, things like that. He said to tell you to be prepared to do lots of writing."

Irritated by his attitude, Aidan stooped to retrieve her pack. "For your information, Lieutenant, I have everything I need. All I have to do is get my bedroll from the hotel and I'm ready to go."

"Yeah, well, if the colonel says get more supplies, then you'll get more. You ready to go?" He started off.

Thinking about how heavy her pack already was with writing supplies she'd brought from San Antonio, Aidan panicked at the thought of adding poundage to it. "This is ridiculous. Why do I have to get more supplies if I already have plenty?" she asked, running to catch up with River's long-legged stride.

River stopped and turned to her, his expression hard, his eyes boring into hers. "It's time you realized that you're in the army. And in the army, when a superior gives an order, you don't ask why. You just say, Yes sir, and do it! Have you got that?"

"Bu—" Aidan bit off her protest. "Yes, sir," she forced out through clenched teeth. "I've got that—*sir!*"

The corner of River's mouth twitched as he fought the grin that threatened to be his undoing. He covered it with his fist and cleared his throat. He agreed that it was ridiculous to take more supplies than she needed—or could carry. But it wouldn't do to let her know that, not if he expected to keep her under control. If he let his guard down and revealed his reluctant admiration for her spirit, she would take advantage. Not to mention what would happen if he ever gave in to the desire to make love to her that still gnawed at him night and day. It was, in fact, worse now than it had been before he'd tasted the ecstasy of her that one time.

"That's better." He pivoted away from her before he reached the point he couldn't resist temptation and would toss good sense to the wind. "Let's get this over with."

Aboard the United States Transport Yucatan, *off the eastern coast of Cuba—June 21, 1898. At last we have received the news that we land tomorrow. Amid shouts of joy, strong men weep with relief at the promise of release from this floating prison on*

*which we have been packed for close to two weeks,
many of us violently ill from the constant motion
of the sea. In fact, capture by the Spanish promises
to be a veritable luxury when compared to the
tortures the United States Army has heaped upon
its own men since Colonel Wood and Colonel
Roosevelt literally fought to get a place on a transport out of Tampa Bay.*

Aidan tucked her pencil behind her ear and stood up,
not really in the mood to write. Ambling over to the rail
of the *Yucatan,* she stared out at the dull, sage green
hills of the Cuban coastline. Instead of jungle as she'd
expected, what she saw reminded her of the approaches
to the Rocky Mountains. On the closest point of land,
she could even see a settlement that looked like an
American mining town. When she had asked about it, a
Cuban on board had told her it was owned by the
Carnegie Corporation of Pittsburgh and that it produced
some of the finest iron ore in the world.

Behind the town the Cuban had called Daiquirí, there
rose a sharp, green spur of the Sierra Cobra mountains.
But it was not that peak that aroused Aidan's curiosity.
It was the second peak to its right that held her attention, for on it, she could make out a Spanish flag
waving over a military blockhouse!

A strange combination of apprehension and excitement rocked through her as she zeroed in on the blockhouse, then let her gaze dip into the deep gorges
surrounding the peak on which it sat. Tomorrow they
would discover whatever secret dangers those shadowy
crevices and green mountains held.

"They say there are Spaniards behind every rock and
bush in those defiles," River said, silently coming up
behind her.

Startled, Aidan jumped forward, then spun to face him, her heart racing. "Do you do that on purpose?"

"Do what?" he asked, his tone quite innocent as he stepped up beside her at the rail.

"Sneak up on me like that! It's really annoying!"

"I wasn't sneaking up on you."

Certain he'd had every intention of startling her but unable to prove it, Aidan let out a disgruntled harumph and looked back at the land. "Well, deliberate or not, I wish you'd stop it. Can't you stomp your boots or clear your throat or something?"

"Admit it, Aidan, you're not jumpy because of the way I approach you. You're having second thoughts about going, aren't you?"

Aidan's eyes widened in astonishment and she forced a laugh. "What makes you think I'm having second thoughts? For your information, I can't wait to go ashore."

His brow furrowed, and River shook his head in disgust. "See those fires all over those mountains? That's the Spanish army signaling its units that we've arrived. And letting us know they're ready for us."

As if to support his point, there was a sharp retort and a flash of light exploded on shore.

Aidan tensed, her gaze immediately going to the gulch where the explosion had occurred.

"See?" he went on. "They're telling us that this isn't a game. They want us to know that it's real and they're going to do everything in their power to kill us."

"I'm not afraid of the Spanish," she said, not sounding as confident as she had moments before.

"If you had any sense, you would be." He drew in a deep breath and clutched her upper arms, spinning her around to face him. "Can't you see what a dangerous situation this is? Look, I'm willing to forget our bargain

130

if you'll go back to the States when the transports return for the rest of the men."

Aidan studied him suspiciously. "Who's having second thoughts now, River? Maybe you're the one who's scared. You've hardly spoken to me for two weeks except to give me orders. Why this sudden concern for me now? Are you afraid I'm actually going to succeed?" She didn't wait for his answer. "That's it, isn't it? You would even sacrifice your precious exposé of the reservations just to have the satisfaction of seeing me surrender, wouldn't you? Well, you're wasting your breath. I haven't suffered your insults and threats and blackmail, not to mention the tortures of the damned on this floating hell, just to be scared off by a little cannon fire. We made a bargain, and you're not going to get out of it!"

Not trusting himself to discuss it further, River pushed away from the rail and strode away from her.

Daiquiri, Cuba—June 22, 1898. Their muscles cramped and aching from long hours of sitting about and waiting to go ashore, the Rough Riders spent the night camped on a dusty, brush-covered flat a few hundred yards inland. A few energetic souls, with the help of some Cubans, threw together thatched huts made of palm leaves. However, most of the Rough Riders were too exhausted to do more than stretch their tent halves out on the ground and cover them with blankets.

The landing met with no resistance from the Spaniards, who obviously fled during the night. Even the flag on the blockhouse, once visible from the ship, has been taken down.

Two welcome things the Spaniards left behind are decent water, a rejuvenating change from the tepid swill we've been forced to drink since board-

131

ing the Yucatan *fifteen days ago, and plenty of
coconuts, which, after we learned how to crack
them open, are providing a marvelous addition to
our tasteless diet of hardtack and beans.*

Today, we begin our long walk to Santiago. . . .

"All right, men," Theodore Roosevelt shouted, leading
one of the horses he'd brought from San Antonio. The
other had been drowned in the landing operation. "We're
moving out."

All at once, the Rough Riders sprang into action,
gathering their gear and restuffing their haversacks with
personal items and rations of bacon, hard bread, beans,
potatoes, onions, canned tomatoes, coffee, sugar, vine-
gar, candles, soap, salt, and pepper, as well as the newly
acquired coconuts. Still adjusting their shoulder packs
and checking their canteens, they fell into line.

Her white blanket roll, packed with extra clothing
draped over her left shoulder secured at her right hip,
Aidan adjusted the loaded haversack on her left hip.
Full of chewing gum, eating utensils, oranges, and whatever extra rations she'd been able to scrounge up, its
weight was already making the strap cut relentlessly into
her right shoulder, over which her canteen and camera
case were also slung.

Gritting her teeth to keep from groaning under the
weight of the gear every "man" was expected to carry,
she stooped to retrieve the additional backpack she had
been "allowed" for writing supplies, since she was to be
the one Rough Rider not toting a carbine and cartridge
belt holding one hundred twenty-five rounds of ammuni-
tion.

Sitting back on her haunches amidst the hubbub of
clearing camp, Aidan shrugged her arms under the
straps of the extra pack, and started to stand back up.

Just then a soldier shoved past, bumping her lightly on the arm. The slight nudge of the faceless soldier was all it took to send her sprawling onto her bottom.

"Sorry, kid," the soldier yelled, then melted from view.

"Need some help?" River asked, his amused smirk all too evident.

Aidan looked up from the brush-strewn ground and twisted her face into an angry mask to disguise the tears that threatened to spill down her sweat-drenched face. "No, I don't," she snapped. Folding her calves under her, she grabbed at a tree trunk and tried to haul herself to a standing position.

River shook his head and slipped his hands under her arms, whisking her, pack and all, off the ground with no more exertion than it would have taken to lift an unencumbered child who had fallen.

Dangling for a split second in his grip, her boots a few inches above the ground, Aidan clutched instinctively at his upper arms, and her confused gaze flew to his face—just in time to see a flicker of something she couldn't quite identify skitter across its angular surface.

Puzzled, she frowned, vaguely aware of the bunching muscles under her fingers. That look he had given her—what had it meant? If she didn't know better, she might easily have fooled herself into believing it was tenderness, maybe even caring. But of course that was naïve, wishful thinking on her part. She knew better than anyone that River didn't care for any one—only for what they could do for his precious Indians on the reservations. "You can put me down now," she said, her voice huskier than normal and lacking the scathing tone she had intended.

"Are you sure you can walk with that load?" River asked, lowering her feet to the earth, but retaining his hold on her.

The heat of his hands burned into the sides of her breasts, sending arrows of fire streaking directly to the core of her, adding to the weakness she was already feeling due to the Cuban temperature and weight of her packs.

Knowing she had to be free if she was to stay on her feet, Aidan pushed at River's hard chest. "Yes, I'm sure," she spit out, staggering as she took her first step without the benefit of his support.

Shaking his head, River snatched the extra pack off her back and slipped it over his own shoulder. "Now, try it."

Relief immediately washed over her, but pride wouldn't allow her to simply accept the kindness. "I don't expect you to carry my gear," she protested haughtily. "I can carry it myself. I got it this far."

River nodded his head and prodded her in the direction of their position on the march. "And we were the last Rough Riders to make it into camp."

Upon remembering the struggle she'd had getting her gear the slight distance inland, Aidan twisted her mouth into a disgusted line. "Well, all right, you can carry it. But only until I get used to the heat. Then I'll carry it myself."

Even without her extra pack, the march west to Siboney, a town on the route to Santiago, was the most torturous thing Aidan had ever endured. The gear she toted slid and shifted as she trudged up and down the slopes, straps cutting into and chafing the tender flesh of her shoulders until she was certain she had to be bleeding. And the packs often caught on brush and trees, sending her stumbling more than once.

The fact that all the Rough Riders were having a difficult time managing their packs, terrain, and the ungodly heat, did little to ease Aidan's feelings of inadequacy. It was River Blue Eagle who kept her going—not because he was there with a helping hand every time she tripped or staggered. It was that cocky look on his handsome face that made her prefer death to accepting help every time he offered it. He was just waiting for her to fall down and not be able to go on without leaning on him. But she wasn't about to give him the satisfaction. Until her last heartbeat, she would keep going.

She glanced back over her laden shoulder, her resentment intensifying. *Look at him. He's not even sweating. The rest of us were wringing wet before we covered the first mile, and he has only a few beads of sweat on his upper lip and forehead.*

Walking single file now, though they had started out in a column of fours, the Rough Riders, truly earning their newest nickname, "Wood's Weary Walkers," began to shed their blankets along the winding mountain trail. Then came the canned meat, to be followed by coats and underclothes, until many had only their guns and ammunition.

Aidan was tempted to do the same, but she knew River would see it as a sign of weakness, even though the men were suffering as much as she was. Besides, she really didn't think she could face Cuba without a change of clothing or a blanket to put between her body and the ground when night came. No, she would keep moving.

The air pungent with the smells of foliage, damp earth, and perspiration-soaked bodies, the soldiers tramped through sand and mud and thickets filled with rough brambles and trailing vines, pausing to rest more and more frequently as they climbed the steeper inclines. But at last they arrived in Siboney, and were relieved to learn it had been deserted by the Spaniards during the previous night.

Revived by the sight of houses set in a gap between

the hills, Aidan picked up her step, determined to make it to the journey's end. Colonel Wood led the column through the village, and had them set up camp in a coconut grove just beyond the town. When at last they were ordered to make camp, Aidan broke into a wide grin and cheered as loudly as the rest of the Rough Riders. She had made it. She had proven she could do it.

Turning to glance at River, she arched her eyebrows and angled her head to the side, her grin smug. "Well, Lieutenant, what do you say now?"

Ignoring her question, River pivoted to the left and shrugged out of his gear, dropping it onto the ground in a heap. "I'll start our supper fire," he said, strolling to the edge of the woods and picking up a piece of wood. "You put up the tent."

Refusing to allow his indifference to deflate her revived spirit, Aidan watched his retreating back. Not until she was convinced that he had no intention of returning right away, did she allow herself the luxury of removing her own packs.

Wincing, she eased the cutting straps off her aching shoulders. "Ohhh," she groaned as her frail frame was relieved of the agonizing weight. Now, if she could just strip down to her chemise and drawers, or better still, sink naked into a bathtub filled with cool, perfumed water.

Chiding herself for even having such a thought, she stared enviously at the bare back of a soldier who had shed his shirt. She spun around, turning away from the rest of the camp. She just wouldn't look at them.

Her movements angry and pronounced, Aidan quickly divested herself of the remainder of her gear, then squatted down beside the discarded baggage. As if she were tearing at his smug, superior face, she ripped into River's pack, retrieving the tent-half he'd been issued.

She would show him. She didn't need his approval. What he thought made no difference to her. She was in Cuba, and she was going to get her story. Nothing else mattered.

After today, he could look at her in that snide way of his all he wanted, but it wouldn't phase her. Whether or not he admitted it, she had proven herself, and nothing he could say or do would make her doubt her ability again.

She would concentrate on putting up their tent and on how good her blanket was going to feel under her weary body—rather than draped over her shoulder! And she wouldn't allow herself to wonder or care about what he was thinking, not ever again.

Drawing on a reserve of energy fueled by anger and determination, Aidan deftly buttoned their two tent flaps together, then draped them across the rope she had stretched between two trees. Just as she tied the bottom edge of the canvas to the last stake she'd hammered into the soft ground, the sky literally opened up and dumped thousands of gallons of rain on the unprepared camp. Cookfires were instantly doused, and soldiers frantically scrambled for protection from the tropical storm.

Desperate to get their gear, especially her journals and cameras to safety, Aidan gave no thought to staying dry herself. Running the few feet to their things, she grabbed up two packs, sloshed over the wet ground to the tent, and pitched them under the flaps. Then she started for a second load. She stopped short when she saw River, already laden with everything else, splashing toward her.

"Quick, get inside," he ordered, his large body hunching over the unwieldy burden in his arms.

Reacting automatically, Aidan dove under the water-repellent flaps, just ahead of him.

137

Diving in after her, River released a war whoop as his long body slipped under the canvas. "Looks like it might rain."

Aidan stared at him incredulously. "Are my ears deceiving me? Or did you just make a joke?"

His expression immediately soured, and he peered out from under the tent flap at the stream of water flooding past. "Lucky you set up on this rise or we'd be sitting in a pond right now."

Though she was tempted to throw him and his belongings out into the deluge, Aidan began rearanging the packs to be certain her own things were still dry. To hell with his. "Luck had nothing to do with it, Lieutenant. Anyone with a lick of sense puts up a tent on the highest ground around." She took off her hat and slapped it against her thigh, then set it on a pack.

River stared at her, a surprised half-grin on his face. "You mean you put it here on purpose?"

"Look, I'm getting a bit tired of your inferences that I'm a helpless idiot."

All at once, his eyes dropped to her soaked shirt, and a chill shuddered through her, more from the memories the glance evoked than from the cold.

"You'd better get into some dry clothes before you catch cold."

Searching his face for any hint of derision, she was surprised to find none. In fact, with his wet, black hair hanging in a fringe over his forehead, he looked like the boy she remembered from her youth. Her heart skipped a beat, and for a scant second her breath was trapped in her lungs. "Wh-what about you?" she finally asked. "You're wet too."

"I'll just take off my shirt," he said, his hands already going to the buttons of a shirt opened to mid-chest because of the heat. "But you'd better change while this

138

heavy rain gives you some privacy. Otherwise, it might be dark before you can put on something dry."

Aidan peered out each end of the tent cover and had to agree with him. Except for the tree trunks on which their rope was secured and the heavy sheets of rain that fell, she could see nothing. "I suppose you're right," she admitted, carefully pulling her blanket roll onto her lap and untying it.

Retrieving a dry white blouse and a uniform shirt, she shifted around so that her back was to River and she faced the slanted tent wall. Working as quickly as her stiff fingers would allow, she removed her sodden clothing and started to put the dry garments over her wet camisole.

"Wait a minute!"

Startled, Aidan clutched the dry blouse to her bosom and glanced over her shoulder at River, who was leaning toward her, his blue eyes angry and intent. "You could at least have the decency to turn your head."

"How long's that been like that?" he asked, reaching for her shoulder. "Why didn't you tell me?"

Aidan glanced down at the strip of red flesh that ran from front to back on her shoulder. In a few places the skin had been rubbed away and the raw tissue was oozing a clear fluid. "And give you another excuse to leave me behind?" she asked defiantly. She shrugged into her white blouse, determined to get the wound out of sight as quickly as possible.

"Take that thing off," he ordered, pulling the blouse down to her elbows before she could touch the abrasion with it. "You need something on that."

"Don't be silly. I'm fine."

Holding her by the arm so she couldn't put the blouse all the way on, he dug in his haversack with his free hand. He brought out a small tin, pulled the lid off with his teeth, then placed the tin on the ground. He dipped the corner of a clean handkerchief into the waxy salve it contained and, without giving her a choice, dabbed the strong-smelling medicine on her shoulder.

His hands were gentle, and before Aidan knew it, he had applied a thick coating of the soothing remedy to her chafed skin and had covered the affected area with a white gauze bandage. "There, that ought to feel better," he said softly, drawing the blouse up her arm.

Bewildered by this tender treatment, Aidan didn't argue. "It does. Thank you."

"How about your feet?"

"My feet?" she asked, buttoning the white shirt.

"Do you have any blisters that should be looked at?" He grabbed one of her feet and quickly unlaced her boot.

Knowing she should be refusing his kindness, but too tired to resist, she watched patiently as he doctored her heels, where wet socks and ill-fitting boots had rubbed angry blisters. "You really should have told me about these. We could have stopped and put something on them earlier."

After you mocked me for not keeping up, she thought. But she couldn't bring herself to say it, not when he was being so sweet.

"Where'd you learn your doctoring skills?" she asked, deliberately changing the subject.

"My Aunt Prairie Moon taught me the summer before the soldiers . . ." He stopped speaking, and placed her foot back on the ground. "How does that feel?"

Aidan studied him, wondering what he'd been about to say, but the sad expression on his face told her to keep her silence. "I think I'll live after all." She laughed and drew a dry sock over her bandaged heel.

"Aidan?" he said, his voice so low she could barely

hear it over the falling rain and the rush of water sweeping past their snug little cocoon inside the tent.

She looked up from the boot she was lacing. "Yes?"

"You did all right today."

Her heart thumped loudly at the compliment. "But you had to carry one of my packs, and I kept falling down."

He nodded his head, the corners of his mouth twitching into a reluctant smile. "But you did okay."

Chapter Ten

*El Pozo Hill, Cuba, on the outskirts of Santiago—
June 30, 1898—The Rough Riders were shaken out
of their blankets at three* A.M. *on June twenty-
fourth, many shivering from sleeping in clothing wet
from yesterday's rain. Though all were excited and
eager to be underway, the camp was a scene of general chaos, so it was nearly six before Young's
column headed along the valley road toward Santiago, with another fifteen minutes or so passing before the Rough Riders moved out in columns of
four.*

*Though the land was rough and the pace set by
Colonel Wood grueling, no man complained, despite
aching legs. In fact, not one Rough Rider would
have given up his place on this march, for Colonel
Wood had assured them they would smell gunpow-
der before the day's end. And he was right.*

*Forced to condense the four-man column to single
file before Siboney was out of sight, the Riders
tramped relentlessly along the trail. Our khaki uniform shirts, only slightly less sweltering than the
heavy wool blues, were wringing wet with perspiration before we were out of camp, but we continued
to hack our way along a path walled by such dense*

142

underbrush that one Westerner likened it to tangled barbed wire. Land crabs are all along the trail, but swarms of flies, gnats and beetles are the worst menace, adding the sounds of men's curses and skin being slapped to the slosh and slurp of boots sinking into, then being drawn out of the spongy, rain-soaked earth.

Before the Riders had gone two miles, the pace through the teeming jungle began to tell on even the strongest of men. Along the way, we began to see discarded gear, and even an occasional trooper who had dropped to the side.

When we reached Las Guasimas, a village approximately four miles from Siboney, the air of excitement heightened perceptibly, for the 22nd Infantry had reported earlier that the Spaniards were there. We were ordered to maintain total quiet, but the order was unnecessary for we all held our breath as we searched the jungle ahead of us and on our flanks for evidence of the enemy.

At 8:15 A.M., little more than two hours after we had left Siboney, an explosion reverberated through the heavy growth, causing us to drop as one to a crouch or flat sprawl in the waist-high grass, our eyes searching intently for the source of the cannon fire. Only later did we learn it had originated with Wheeler's Hotchkiss guns fired in the hope of flushing out the Spaniards.

An answering volley immediately came from behind the bushes and the trenches along the path ahead of us. However, we quickly realized the Spaniards were using Mauser rifles with smokeless powder, making it impossible to spot their exact positions.

On both sides, the firing became heavy, the strange popping of the Spanish guns contrasting

143

with the heavier roar of the American Krag-Jorgen-sen carbines. Above the general uproar, we could hear the two Spanish machine guns, but the Riders could only retaliate with rifle fire, for their rapid-firing Colts and dynamite gun had not yet arrived from Siboney.

When the battle was finally over, many Spaniards lay dead, and eight brave Americans had left this world, including Sergeant Hamilton Fish, Jr. of New York City, who was the war's first casualty, though some men had already died of malaria.

Since that eventful day, the hours have been spent waiting, and our meager diet has consisted of coffee and hardtack three times a day. Our rations remain short, and what we have must be watched closely because the Cubans, who are not willing to do their own fighting, steal our supplies the instant they are not under the watchful eyes of guards. Besides the shortness of food, most of the men are so desperate for tobacco that some have taken to smoking dried horse droppings, grass, roots, and even tea! To add to our torture, every afternoon without fail we are drenched by about an hour of angry tropical rain, and must spend the next few hours trying to dry out while standing in three or four inches of water, then combating the hordes of mosquitoes that descend on us at dusk.

Today, Lieutenant Colonel Roosevelt finally gave the orders to break camp and prepare to march, and the spirit of the troops improved drastically. Already the muddy trail to Santiago was clogged with moving columns, and the Riders were anxious to join the others. But because progress was so slow, it was four this afternoon before Roosevelt gave the order for the Rough Riders to join the march toward Santiago.

144

One thing that keeps the path clogged is a huge observation balloon that floats just above the trees. Attached by a cable to a reel on an army field wagon, it draws attention wherever it goes, and all movement comes to a standstill when it is sited above the curious foot soldiers.

Said to require 17,000 cubic feet of oxygen to inflate and to carry a load of 400 pounds or more, this magnificent giant arrived from France on the steamship Teutonic *in May, along with Maurice Mallet, the world's greatest balloon expert. What understanding and advantage would be afforded a correspondent fortunate enough to view the war from the lofty heights of that glorious, bloated, yellow war machine.*

Tonight, the last night before the battle for Santiago begins, we lie on our ponchos, waiting, wondering, praying. Anticipation and apprehension are so great that sleep is impossible for many. Our clothes are wet and cling miserably to our skin due to the latest afternoon deluge; and throughout the camp, there hangs an overwhelming cloak of uncertainty because even the bravest and most optimistic men know this night may well be their last on earth. Tomorrow many fine and courageous soldiers will know the agony of a Mauser bullet, and many will not survive. Yet, no Rough Rider complains. Not one would turn back or give up his chance to fight for the United States, even if it means his own death. Here are Americans at their finest.

Aidan blew out the candle that had allowed her to see well enough to make this latest entry in her journal. She sat back, staring at the men reclining all around her. What she would give to be at the front of the battle when it started.

Suddenly an idea came to her. Why couldn't she? All she had to do was get in that balloon observation basket before it was launched in the morning. Surely there would be something she could hide under until the craft was aloft and leading the army into the attack. No one had to know she was on board—until it was too late to take her back, of course.

Suffering an unexpected pang of guilt, Aidan glanced down at River, who had an uncanny ability to sleep under any conditions. She smiled, thinking how he'd really treated her quite decently the past week. It was obvious that he was starting to trust her. He'd even given her a few compliments, and he'd stopped watching her so closely. Could she really betray him by sneaking out of camp during the night?

I won't really be betraying him, she told herself, her eyes taking in the long, relaxed length of him. *It's going to help his cause, too. Besides, with me out of the way, he'll be free to do more for Lieutenant Colonel Roosevelt.*

Easing her boots back under her, she hurriedly grabbed up her canteen and haversack, stuffed extra paper, pencils, and her camera inside, and made a dash across camp.

Aidan held her breath when she heard the order to untie the balloon's ground moorings. With a clunk and a lurch, each straining rope was released from its stake, and the balloon jerked upward. From her hiding place beneath the musty tarpaulin, she could only see up into the yellow air-filled dome of oiled pongee silk. But it didn't matter. She was on her way now and was going to have a view of the battle no other correspondent would have.

It had been quite easy to talk her way past the balloon's guards. Most of them had been tired, but they had been willing to answer questions about the intriguing war machine. Pad and pencil in hand, she had merely worked her

146

way closer and closer to the observation basket, interviewing soldiers until she'd found a blind spot. Then, when no one was looking, it had been simple to scramble into the basket and get herself settled under the canvas only moments before the balloon's pilot and the man she heard someone with a French accent refer to as Sergeant Dawson came on board. Now all she had to do was wait until it would be impractical for them to land before she exposed herself.

Aidan's eyelids grew heavy, the effects of the preceding day's march and a night without sleep taking their toll. Within minutes of the balloon's takeoff, she drifted off, rocked by the breeze as gently as a baby in its mother's arms.

When River awoke to the 4:00 A.M. reveille, it was a moment before he realized Aidan wasn't beside him, as she had been every morning since they had left Florida. Evidently, she had taken the opportunity to slip off into the jungle to take care of her personal needs in privacy. Unworried, he went on to tend to hiw own duties, not returning to their gear until the Riders were ready to depart.

However, when he saw that their packs were undisturbed, the first twinges of concern rocked through him. His eyes swept anxiously over the men in the surrounding area. What if she had left camp for privacy and had been found to be a female by some woman-hungry soldier? Worse still, what if she'd been taken prisoner by the Spaniards? Or hit and robbed by one of the gangs of Cubans who were always lurking around the fringes of the camp waiting to steal anything they could?

Panic roared in his ears. "Has anybody seen Donovan?" he asked loudly. Growing more worried by the instant, he gazed into the surrounding jungle.

"I saw him going toward where Lieutenant Colonel Roosevelt was bedded down, sir," a young infantryman answered.

"You did?" he shouted, his relief obvious. He clutched desperately at the soldier's arms and looked urgently into his face. "What time was that?"

"About one o'clock, maybe a little later."

"One o'clock? Are you sure?" The alarm coursing through him reached frantic proportions. "Did you see he—him—come back?"

"No, sir. I didn't. I guess I finally fell asleep about that time."

"Has anyone else seen Donovan?" River shouted. The only response he received was a shaking of heads as men loaded heavy packs onto their backs and ambled away from the area.

Just then, Roosevelt strode over to River, buoyant with excitement. "Well, my boy, this is it. Many of these men will be heroes before the day is out."

River answered the commander's enthusiastic greeting with an anguished look. "Sir, I can't find A. D. Donovan. He's always the first to be ready to leave camp, and no one has seen him since about one this morning."

Roosevelt tossed back his head and released his loud horse laugh. "Gave you the slip, did he? I'm not surprised. Those correspondents will do just about anything to be up at the front lines, won't they?"

River's dark brows drew together as a new worry hit him. The soldier had said he'd seen her going toward where Roosevelt was sleeping. "I don't understand, sir. Do you know where Ai—A. D. is?"

Roosevelt looked to the west just as the morning sun caught and was reflected off a huge yellow globe rising from the valley below like a magical bubble. "Unless he missed his ride, there he goes now," he said, pointing toward the observation balloon that was to guide the troops

148

into Santiago.

River's mouth dropped open "You mean sh—he's in that balloon? How?"

Taking off his glasses and wiping them with a clean handkerchief, Roosevelt nodded his strong head. "That's exactly what I mean. He came to me after most of the men were bedded down and told me he'd been given permission to go along with the balloon's observation crew today, if I would dismiss him—which of course I did. You've got to admire that boy's ingenuity, don't you? Here Cuba is crawling with veteran correspondents like Frederic Remington and Richard Harding Davis, even those two moving-picture makers from the Vitagraph Company, and a mere boy steals a plum like this right out from under their noses!"

River stared angrily at the rising balloon, the muscles in his jaw knotting as he fought back the curse that swelled in his throat.

Aidan stretched sleepily and threw back the heavy cover, her eyes closed against the blinding glare of the sun.

"What the hell're you doing here, boy?" a deep voice growled near her ear.

Instantly alert, Aidan's eyes snapped open, and she found herself staring into the angry green eyes of a man she'd never seen before. Bolting from her hiding place, she saluted and launched into an explanation. "War correspondent A. D. Donovan, attached to the First Volunteer Cavalry under the command of Lieutenant Colonel Theodore Roosevelt, reporting for duty, sir."

"On whose orders?" the man asked, the anger in his eyes sending second thoughts to pummeling at Aidan's temples.

"On the colonel's orders, sir," she responded, having difficulty keeping her voice deep. She hoped he wouldn't

149

ask which colonel.

"You're lying, boy," the man said accusingly, his eyes hard with suspicion. "No colonel or anyone else told you to stow away in this basket. You saw the balloon as a chance to get the jump on your reporter pals, so you sneaked on board during the night and hid. You thought when we discovered you it would be too late to do anything about your being aboard, didn't you?" A grin crept across the sergeant's face and gloating, he picked up a canvas packet from the floor of the basket. "But you were wrong, son. Dead wrong."

Sweat broke out on Aidan's upper lip. "Are you going to make me go back, sir?"

"In a manner of speaking," he said, handing Aidan the canvas bundle. "Put this on."

"But, sir, to land now will cost you too much time. Can't I just go on with you since I'm here? I don't take up much room!" She spoke quickly as, with the sergeant's rough assistance, she slipped her arms under the straps of the back pack he had presented to her. "What exactly is this, sir?"

"A parachute," he answered, slipping a strap between Aidan's legs from behind and securing it to the strap that stretched across her chest from arm to arm.

Horrified at realizing what the man intended to do, Aidan glanced over the side, her heart pounding. She looked down at a sea of green jungle, and her stomach began to churn violently. "Surely you don't mean to—"

"We're not that high up," the sergeant said, watching the ground for a clearing in the foliage. "You'll be fine. Just pull this cord—" He handed her the end of a short rope. "—when I yell 'now,' and you'll float down easy as you please. You should land just a short distance from the road."

Aidan looked down, her eyes wide with terror. "But, sir. . ."

"Get ready. I see a clearing ahead." He prodded Aidan to get up on a box.

She resisted. "What if the parachute doesn't open?" she asked.

The man shrugged. "Maybe that'll teach you newspaper reporters to stay out of places where you're not invited. Now, get going. Every second you waste takes us closer to enemy lines, and we need to get rid of all excess weight so we can gain some altitude before we get to them. Besides, if we get any closer, they'll see your parachute and start shooting at you."

"But I don't weigh that much," she wailed, her eyes wide with fright.

It was too late for argument. The officer gave her a rough shove and yelled, "Now!"

The tops of the trees rose to meet her at an alarming rate, and Aidan stared, paralyzed with fear.

"Now, goddammit!" the voice above her yelled. "Open the damned chute *now!*"

Reacting instinctively, Aidan yanked on the rope in her hand. With a roar, the silk parachute billowed out of the pack on her back and filled with air. A neck-snapping, muscle-wrenching jolt followed instantaneously, and her death-defying tumble toward the ground was slowed.

A feeling of euphoria washed over Aidan. She was floating, dangling in the air like a child's kite. Never had she felt so free, so at one with the universe. She wished it could last forever.

Then, just as suddenly as the state of bliss had descended on her, a new terror rose in her sights. Helplessly, she watched as the wind carried her past the clearing where the balloon commander had intended that she land, and back over the dense jungle.

The crack of breaking tree limbs and the piercing screeches of frightened birds joined her screams as she crashed through the green treetops to land in a dank, moist tangle of vegetation and mud.

At 11:15, after wading across the knee-deep San Juan River, the Riders were climbing the far bank when a barrage of bullets rained down from the ridge ahead of them.

Frustration and anger his constant companions since dawn, River dropped to his belly, his gaze darting over his shoulder to the balloon that he knew was fast approaching the river. Immediately, his breath caught in his throat. Something was wrong. The balloon was closer than it should be.

It was supposed to stay out of range while drawing the Spaniard's fire until the Riders got into position, but it was coming too fast. Too fast and too low.

Before he could give voice to his fear, the balloon heaved and doubled in half as if a huge fist had slammed into it.

Too astounded to do anything but gape, River stared as the massive yellow ball quivered and then sank into the midst of American soldiers now under fire.

Bullets and exploding shrapnel whizzed and whirled around his head, but River could think of only one thing. He had to get to Aidan. Giving no heed to his own safety or to the fact that he might seem to be retreating from battle, he ran toward the downed balloon.

Arriving at the scene of the crash, he came to an abrupt halt, his eyes taking in the dead and wounded men lying strewn about the field. Where did he begin to look?

Spying the broken balloon basket and a soldier he recognized as part of the balloon's observation crew, River was rocked with relief. If that man had made it to safety, probably Aidan had too. "Sergeant," he yelled, grabbing the man's arm. "The correspondent you had on board! Where is he? Is he all right?"

His face pale with shock, the sergeant stared vacantly at

River for a moment. Then understanding lit his features. "You mean that stowaway? The little weasel's probably drinking coffee at headquarters by now."

"What are you saying, Sergeant? Talk sense," River ordered, giving the soldier a shake.

"I am, sir. We gave the little rat a parachute and dropped him about half a mile from El Pozo Hill."

"You what? My god, man, do you have any idea what you've done?"

"Probably saved the lucky little bastard's life. If you see him, tell him I said he owes me."

Literally knocking the sergeant aside, River ran back to his unit, his body crouched low to avoid the shrapnel that was growing heavier with each volley.

"Sir, I've just learned that Donovan didn't have permission to be with the balloon and they dropped him over the side with a parachute about a half-mile back in the jungle. I feel responsible for not keeping a closer watch on him, sir, and I'd like your permission to go find him."

Excitement glistening in his eyes at finally being in the battle, Roosevelt nodded. "Go ahead, Lieutenant. But hurry. You don't want to miss this."

As she regained consciousness, Aidan felt a heavy weight inching slowly up her body. Warily peeking through slitted eyelids, she lifted her head and glanced down at her chest.

Her eyes snapped open wide as they focused on two small, berrylike eyes mounted on short stalks, staring back at her.

"Get off me!" she screamed, her arms flailing hysterically at the creature as she bolted up from the marshy ground with the speed of a person in top condition, certainly not one who'd just crashed to earth from the sky.

The land crab, its shell a mixture of colors—red, yellow,

orange, and black—landed on the jungle floor. Its six legs and two huge pincers all moving at once, it sidled into the foliage.

A shudder of revulsion shook Aidan as she watched the jungle scavenger disappear from view. "Yech," she exclaimed, certain she was going to be sick.

Called creeping buzzards by more than one veteran, the land crabs fed on dead flesh. Relatively harmless to the living, they had been prevalent along the trail, but never so bad as the night after the battle at El Pozo. Another shiver shook Aidan as she remembered the eight men who had died in the battle. They had been laid out under a canvas while a burial trench was dug for them, but the smell of death had brought the repulsive scavengers out of the jungle in hordes. A circle of small fires had been set around the bodies, but despite that, all night long, guards had battled the vile creatures off with clubs and bayonets.

When she was reasonably certain the land crab was gone, Aidan looked around to get her bearings, knowing that she was going to have to find her way out if she planned to leave the jungle alive. Surrounded by vines and brambles taller than she was, she glanced upward to the bit of sky visible overhead. She realized she was looking through the path her falling body had cut in the heavy growth. On the broken branches that marked her descent were the remains of her parachute. Shreds of it were caught on thorny limbs all the way from the treetops to the ground.

Slightly recovered from the shock of finding a land crab on the verge of claiming her for his next meal, Aidan forced herself to breathe in slowly as she considered what she should do. Of course, the first necessity was to free herself from the ruined parachute. Working with fingers that were not yet steady, she unbuckled the straps on her chest and shrugged out of the cumbersome pack.

What next? A compass! Yes, a compass. That was what

154

she needed.

Her hands went to the haversack strap that ran diagonally across her chest from shoulder to hip. Thank God, she hadn't taken it off when she'd boarded the balloon, because that sergeant certainly hadn't given her time to gather up any belongings. Her lip curled resentfully as she recalled being thrown out of the balloon basket. "If it's the last thing I do, I'm going to find that low-life sergeant and make him pay for this."

Starting to sit down on a nearby log, she stopped herself and whirled around to give it a cursory check. Finding the log free of other occupants, she lowered her aching body onto it, then slid the haversack around to her lap.

Refusing to acknowledge the bleeding cuts and scratches on her arms and hands, Aidan forced herself to concentrate on getting out of the jungle alive.

If she was right, all she had to do was head north and she would cross the trail the army was hacking through the jungle. Digging into the pack, she removed several items—the army-issue first-aid kit, two cans of tomatoes, and a pad of paper—before she found her compass in an inside pocket.

Her face breaking into a smile, she pulled the lifesaving instrument from the haversack. Then a frightening thought occurred to her. She was just guessing that she was south of the trail. She hadn't really been able to get a bearing before she'd "landed." What if the balloon had been drifting north of the trail, rather than south as it had the day before? If that were the case, the road was in the opposite direction.

Glancing in the direction the compass arrow indicated as north, she narrowed her eyes and listened intently for something, anything, that would prove her first assumption was correct.

To her left, in the distance, she heard the popping of rifle fire, interspersed with the explosions of shells and the bark of cannons. The anticipated battle with the Spanish had obviously begun in the west, but that did not tell her whether the trail was north or south of where she was stranded.

She considered heading west toward the San Juan River, but quickly discarded the idea, opting to go with her first hunch and head north. If she didn't reach the trail in one hour, she would turn back and head south. Satisfied that she'd come up with the best plan under the circumstances, Aidan stood up and pulled out her pocket watch.

Suddenly, her vision clouded, and she fought to focus on the numbers on the face of the timepiece. But it was impossible. Her legs, steady only moments before, seemed to have turned to liquid, and her head throbbed unbearably.

Supporting herself against the trunk of a nearby tree, she sank back down on the log, panicked by thoughts of the dreaded malaria. Folding her upper torso on her lap, she pressed her forehead against her knees, rocking her head from side to side in protest.

As if to confirm her worst suspicions, a violent chill rattled its way through her. "Noooo," she pleaded through chattering teeth. "Not now!"

Berating herself for not being more religious about taking her quinine, she dug into the haversack with shaking fingers, blindly seeking her first-aid kit. But she was too late.

Her last conscious thought as she fell forward onto the jungle floor was of the land crab.

Chapter Eleven

Swinging his machete with a vengeance, River hacked his way through the jumble of vines and false pathways. "Aidan!" he shouted. "Answer me!" His voice was already hoarse, and his lips were dry with panic.

He stopped and removed his hat, wiping a forearm across his sweating brow. After checking his compass to be certain he wasn't going in circles, he concentrated on the sounds of the jungle. But the only answers he received to his frantic calls were the ever-present drone of insects and the rustle of foliage. The breeze, which confined itself to the treetops, did nothing to relieve the heat on the sweltering jungle floor.

River glanced back over his shoulder at the trail he'd blazed through the tangle of vegetation. Already, the teeming jungle seemed to have grown in over it, as if he'd never been there. Second thoughts began to worry him.

He'd left the military road on the word of an English-speaking Cuban native who had said he'd seen what looked like a man hanging from an "Englishman's umbrella" drop into the jungle from the "giant air ball" several hours before. But what if the Cuban had been lying? What if he'd just said what he knew the American soldier wanted to hear so he could get his hands on the sack of rations that had been offered for information?

River cupped his hands to his mouth. "Aaaaaaai-daaaaaaan," he yelled in a final desperate attempt to be heard.

In the fog of semiconsciousness, Aidan heard a voice calling her name. A man's voice. A voice she recognized.

"River," she rasped, fighting her way out of the gray mist that enshrouded her. "I'm here," she croaked through parched lips, her voice a rough whisper.

Struggling to lift her head, she forced her eyelids apart a fraction of an inch, her muddled mind straining to discern the dark face over hers. "River?"

A voice she was sure she didn't recognize answered with a jumble of unfamiliar words. Confusion furrowing her brow, Aidan opened her glazed eyes wider.

Shock and panic abruptly cleared her vision. It wasn't River who was bending over her!

Her heartbeat jolted to hysterical proportions. "Who are you?" She labored to prop her weak body up on her elbows. "What are you doing?"

The Cuban nodded his dark head and gave her a wide grin. Then, without warning, he raised a large knife over her.

"Oh, God!" she screamed, fully conscious now, her stricken eyes round with fear. "Somebody help me!"

The native's smiling face bobbed up and down.

"Aidan!" a voice bellowed from the jungle. "Is that you?"

The Cuban glanced over his shoulder in the direction from which the shout had come. Tugging on her haversack, he sliced downward with the knife.

"River! Help me!" she shrieked, paralyzed by the sight of the blade descending toward her chest. "He's going to kill me!"

"I'm coming, Aidan! I'm coming!"

The Cuban cut through the haversack strap with one sure stroke, then leaped up from the ground, clutching a corner of the bag.

Realizing that it had been her belongings and not her life that had been at stake, Aidan grabbed for the dangling strap of the haversack with a strength denied her until that instant. "No!" she grunted, hanging onto the canvas strip with both hands. "Let go! My camera and journals are in there! Give it to me!"

"Hey!" River burst through the foliage.

For an instant, all three of them—the woman, the thief, and the soldier—froze and stared at each other in shock.

"River!" Aidan cried, inadvertently relaxing her hold on the strap.

Fright and desperation on his dark face, the Cuban studied River warily, waving his knife threateningly above Aidan's vulnerable chest.

River skidded to an abrupt halt and held his hands out at his sides in a position that implied surrender. "Okay, okay," he said, his fear disguised behind a falsely calm expression. "Just take the sack and go. I won't stop you. But if you so much as cut a thread in her shirt, I'll shred your hide into so many pieces even the land crabs won't bother with you," he hissed through tight lips.

Though the Cuban obviously did not understand River's words, there was no doubt the tone he'd used had registered. A flicker of indecision skittered across the man's dark face. He stopped making agitated motions with the knife and frowned at River.

"Go on," River coaxed. "Take it and leave."

The Cuban clutched the bag closer to him and started to turn away.

"No!" Aidan grabbed the Cuban's leg. "My journals and camera are in that!"

Retaining his hold on the bag with one hand, the Cuban shifted his wild-eyed stare from River to Aidan. After the briefest hesitation, the knife he held descended toward her.

"Nooo!" River bellowed, catapulting into action. His body parallel to the ground, he flew at the struggling pair, wedging his large torso between Aidan and the Cuban as the deadly knife completed its descent.

White-hot pain exploded through River's shoulder and upper arm as the knife sliced into his flesh, but anger numbed him to the pain. Reaching out, he caught the Cuban's leg and brought the fleeing man down.

His shirt sleeve already glistening with blood, River crawled forward and flopped over the Cuban. Wrapping his fingers around the wrist of the hand that gripped the knife, he twisted.

With a loud howl, the Cuban rose up on all fours. Unprepared for the smaller man's surprising strength, River was flipped over onto his back with a hollow-sounding thud, and the breath in his lungs rushed out in a loud whoosh.

Taking advantage of the larger man's momentary incapacity, the Cuban scrambled to his feet and made a dash for cover, the haversack he'd dropped in the struggle forgotten.

His usual stoic mask a mix of agony and worry, River dragged himself over the ground to Aidan. "Are you all right?" he moaned, gathering her into his arms and covering her face with overwrought kisses. "I thought I'd lost you."

Latching onto his strength as if it were the only thing standing between her and death, Aidan wrapped her arms around River's waist, her fingers digging into his blood-soaked shirt and back. "R-R-River," she sobbed, greedily inhaling the salty, masculine scent of him like a drowning man would gasp for air. "I was so afraid."

Burrowing his fingers into the tangled mop of hair at the crown of her head, he pressed her cheek to his chest. "Shh, *Cikala Peta*—Little Fire," he murmured, burying his face in her hair. "I'm here now. You don't have to be afraid anymore. I'm going to take care of you." He lifted her weak body into his arms and cradled her. "I swear I won't let you be hurt again."

Aidan opened her eyes to find herself staring into the eyes of an old, white-haired woman. Panic racing through her, she struggled to sit up. "Where am I? Who're you?" Her gaze zigzagged from side to side in a frantic search of a body-strewn field of flattened grass. Immediately, her vision blurred and her head began to pound.

"There, there, you need to stay still," the black-capped woman soothed. With a gentle but firm push, she forced Aidan back down onto the poncho on which she'd been placed. "You're at the First Division's Red Cross hospital outside Santiago, and you've had a nasty blow to the back of your head. You need to rest and stay quiet. You'll only make things worse for yourself if you get up too soon."

Hopelessness stormed over Aidan, and she tossed her head from side to side in denial. "You don't understand. I can't stay here. I've got to find River. I've got to explain—"

"If you're referring to Lieutenant Blue Eagle, he's being treated right now. He brought you out of the jungle."

Somewhere in the back of her mind, Aidan recalled being carried a long distance, her face pressed to River's perspiring chest, his strong arms a band of security at her back and the bends of her knees. Then the struggle with the Cuban in the jungle came back to her, and the memory of River's heavily bleeding wound colored her vision red. "But he was hurt," she protested urgently. "How — ?"

"How, indeed?" the woman returned, pressing Aidan's head down on the haversack serving as her pillow. "I've heard it said that love sometimes gives men superhuman powers — not to mention that it causes otherwise sensible people to do things they would never do under ordinary circumstances."

"Love? River doesn't lo — " Aidan's dark eyes rounded in alarm. "You know about me?"

"Young woman, you are fortunate that it was I who examined you," the nurse answered with a stern nod. "Now, suppose you explain to me how you got here, and tell me Lieutenant Blue Eagle's part in your deception."

The possible repercussions of the nurse's discovery thundered through Aidan's aching head. It was inexcusable that River had been injured because of her thoughtless, irresponsible behavior, but now he was in danger of facing a court-martial. He might even have to serve a prison sentence! All because of her!

"Please, nurse, you don't understand. None of this was Riv — Lieutenant Blue Eagle's fault. He didn't know anything about this. He thinks I'm a man just like everyone else does! He just thought he was helping another soldier when he brought me here. That's all."

The old woman busied herself with adjusting the bandage she'd wrapped around Aidan's head. "I suppose you expect me to believe that he would have run three-fourths of a mile through the jungle with a heavily bleeding wound of his own to get you to this field hospital if you'd been just 'another soldier'? Now, young woman, if you want any assistance from me, I'd suggest you start telling the truth. Exactly how did you get here?"

Aidan searched the old woman's kind eyes, and instinctively felt she'd found a kindred spirit, though the nurse

162

looked to be about eighty years old. "You can't let them blame him for any of this. He tried to make me leave, but I refused. And he knew if he sent me back I would just find another way to get to Cuba, so he . . ." Suddenly, Aidan knew why River had brought her with him. "He brought me so he could protect me!" she finished, her expression stunned. "He risked everything of value to him to protect me — even his life — and now I've destroyed him if you report him."

River stared with red-rimmed eyes at the tiny old woman who watched him, her expression compassionate. "Is Aidan all right?" he asked weakly.

"Lieutenant, I'm Clara Barton, and I have rather distressing news about the young correspondent you brought in this afternoon."

The name of the famous Civil War nurse didn't register in River's distraught mind. Nor did he find it peculiar that a woman of her age was tending the wounded and sick at the field hospital. All he heard were two words — "distressing news."

Lifting his head up from the flattened grass on which he lay, he gripped the woman's frail arm. "You don't mean . . . ?"

Nurse Barton smiled and shook her head. "No, your friend isn't dead."

River released his anxious hold on the nurse and lay back down. "Thank God." He rotated the heels of his hands against his forehead, trying to organize his morphine-hazed thoughts. "Is it malaria?" he asked, his words slurred.

"I don't think so. Evidently, she sustained a severe blow to the head. That could be the cause of her intermittent unconsciousness. Just to be safe, we're dosing your friend

163

with quinine. However, I think you know we have a more serious situation on our hands."

Still not grasping what Clara Barton was talking about, River envisioned a more deadly possibility than malaria. "Not yellow fever!"

The nurse's lips curved upward in a slight smile. "It's not quite that serious, Lieutenant Blue Eagle. But it is serious nonetheless."

"What is it?" River demanded, his drugged thoughts colliding with rationality as he tried to imagine what illnesses Aidan could have.

"Upon examining the patient," Miss Barton went on, "I made a most shocking discovery. It seems that . . ." Her old eyes darted around the area to be certain no one but River was listening. Then she leaned closer and lowered her voice to a confidential whisper. ". . . the young man you brought in is not a man at all, but a young woman!"

Overwhelming relief washed over River. "Oh," he said with a relieved sigh as he blew out the breath he'd been holding.

Somewhere in the back of his mind, he realized the error he'd made, and he tried to compensate. "A woman? Are you sure?"

Hands planted on her hips, the aged nurse took a step back, her stern glare leveled down at him. "Spare me the pretended innocence, Lieutenant, and tell me what you suggest I do about the outlandish dilemma in which your poor judgment has placed me."

Trapped, River rolled his head from side to side in surrender, too drugged to even try to construct a lie—a talent he didn't have, even under the best of circumstances and fully alert. "I don't know," he said, the morphine and exhaustion taking their toll.

"Well, suppose you tell me how you allowed yourself to become involved in this scheme."

Sensing a desire to understand in the nurse's tone, he started talking, his words halting and slurred. "Roosevelt . . . hired. . . . to write . . . about Rough Riders."

Clara's eyebrows rose in disapproval. "Surely you're not suggesting Teddy Roosevelt willingly allowed this to happen?"

River shook his head adamantly, his brow wrinkling in frustration. "No! Doesn't know . . . thinks she—"

"Why haven't you told him? Didn't you think it was your responsibility to inform him of the truth, Lieutenant?"

River nodded his head slowly, using the last of his strength to concentrate on making the nurse understand. "When I . . . realized who . . . hired . . . didn't want . . . embarrass him . . . and because . . ."

"Go on," Clara prodded. "Because?"

Berating himself for not being more coherent, River did his best to look into the woman's penetrating eyes. " 'cause he'd . . . send her back."

"And you didn't want her to go back?"

River nodded his head, then frowned and shook his head. "At first . . . But more I knew her . . ." His eyes begged for understanding. "Aidan's a writer. . . . A good writer . . . shouldn't be . . . deprived of chance . . . to prove it because . . . she's . . . woman."

"I see," Clara said, her manner softening slightly. "However, the fact remains that the middle of a battlefield is no place for a young woman."

"No place," River repeated, the last of his concentration melting into nothingness.

"Then we agree that she must return to the United States immediately."

"Mmm," he mumbled, giving a slight nod.

"And of course, Lieutenant Colonel Roosevelt must be told the truth."

Relieved that the lies and deception were at an end, River closed his eyes, unable to stay awake any longer. "I'll tell him everythi. . . ." He couldn't finish the statement.

Clara Barton smiled at the sleeping man. "However, I don't see that it will serve any particular purpose to disclose the exact time you made the discovery. In fact, I believe it will be best for all concerned if Teddy believes you learned the truth from me, rather than firsthand."

Hesitating outside the pup tent, Aidan looked back over the patient-littered field to give Clara Barton a silent thank you. But the woman was already stooping to cover one of the many soldiers who had been brought from surgery and dumped naked on the flattened grass, unprotected from the elements.

"River," Aidan whispered, dropping down on her haunches and peeking inside the tiny tent that was barely large enough to keep the sun and rain off his head and upper body. "Are you awake?"

"Aidan?" he asked, twisting his head around to see out.

"It's me," she answered, struggling not to show alarm when she saw that he'd bled through the bandage wrapped around his chest and shoulder.

His pale features broke into a weak smile. "Are you all right?"

Guilt rocked through her at the sound of his voice. He was wounded — critically, if infection set in — yet he'd asked about her. This was all her fault. If it hadn't been for River, she never would have gotten to Cuba, much less gone undetected for all this time. He had even risked his life to save hers! And how had she repaid him? By piling one problem after another on him. Now he was on the verge of going to prison because of her hare-brained, self-serving actions.

"I didn't mean for any of this to happen, River," she announced, the urgency in her voice desperate. "Can you ever forgive me?"

"Shh," he soothed. He reached up to brush a lock of perspiration-soaked hair off her bandaged forehead with the backs of his fingers. "We'll talk about that later. Right now, you just concentrate on getting back to the States and writing the best articles a newspaper ever ran."

"Articles? Do you think I can ever write again after what I've done to you?"

"Don't talk like that."

"You could be court-martialed if anyone finds out you've known about me all along."

Lacking the strength to lift his head more than a few inches off the ground, River fell back. "They're going to find out I knew anyway, Aidan, so you may as well write your stories. Besides, we have a bargain. You owe me a story about the reservations, written by a 'famous' correspondent, so you have to write the article about Cuba."

"No! Nurse Barton has promised me that she's going to tell them you didn't learn the truth about me until she told you. And I'm certainly not going to tell anyone, so how will it be found out?"

"Because I'm going to tell Lieutenant Colonel Roosevelt as soon as I'm able. I've already sent word to the front that I have to talk to him when he returns."

"You can't do that! Don't you understand how serious this is? You could be court-martialed and sent to prison for bringing me to Cuba!"

"I'm willing to take the risk that it won't go that far," he said, his voice tired.

"Well, I'm not," Aidan vowed angrily. "You're not going to be punished for what I've done."

Her tone agitated, she took his face in her hands and

brought her own close to it. "Promise me that you won't tell him, River. I couldn't bear it if you suffer any more because of what I did."

His smile weak, River removed her hands from his face, but didn't immediately release them. "Don't worry, Little Fire." He caressed the backs of her fingers with his thumbs. "I'll be fine."

Little Fire! He'd called her Little Fire, just as he had when they'd made love. Joy swelled in her chest. Did she dare allow herself to believe he felt something for her after all? Or was it just the morphine talking?

Afraid to trust her own impressions, she searched his face for a sign that the tenderness she'd heard in his voice meant what she wanted it to mean. But already his eyes were closing.

"Promise me, River," she implored, tears spilling down her cheeks. "Please promise you won't let them take you away from me."

"I can't, Little Fire." The words were barely audible, for he was slipping back into drug-induced sleep.

When Aidan realized he was sleeping, she sat back on her calves, her watery gaze on his still body. "Well, River Blue Eagle, you may not be able to make any promises, but I can. And I promise you that I'm going to use every trick I can think of to stop you from taking the blame for any of this."

When River awoke, he was aware of a gentle rocking motion beneath him. Certain he was having delusions, he opened his eyes to see a starless sky. He was vaguely aware that sometime in the last hours, he'd been lifted off the ground onto a stretcher, so he didn't think it odd that he no longer felt rocks and twigs gouging into his back as he had when he'd been on the bare ground. Still, there was that strange swaying motion.

Certain it had to be caused by the pain-killing drugs he'd been given, River twisted his head to the side. Stretching out from him were the shadowy outlines of low cots occupied by other patients. That came as no surprise to him; after all, he was at the field hospital. However, he couldn't help wondering if he'd somehow been moved to a different facility, and how long he'd been here.

The hospital he remembered from that first day of battle, when he'd carried Aidan in from the jungle, was filled with confusion and noise. That day, the wounded, many of them naked, had been lying all over the field, some of them being attended by the handful of medics, most of them receiving no treatment at all. Yet, these men were lying on cots set in a neat row, and they were covered with blankets. But they all seemed to be swaying with the same lulling motion he felt. And instead of screams of agony, there was only an occasional moan.

Determined to rid himself of the odd swinging sensation, he dragged his elbow under him and levered his torso up off his cot. Squinting into the darkness, he tried to get a more exact impression of his surroundings. But he only became more confused. Where was the skyline? Where were the tents?

"Where the hell am I?" he roared, staring at what looked like a low wall that ran along the row of wounded men.

"Shh, you'll wake the others," a voice scolded, as a small, black-clad figure carrying a lantern stepped out of the darkness and came toward him.

Relieved to recognize the black dress and bonnet of the approaching woman, River lowered his voice. "I don't understand. Where are we?"

"We're on the Red Cross hospital ship bound for home," the nurse answered, kneeling beside his cot with the agility of a much younger woman so their conversation wouldn't disturb her other patients.

A suspicious spark of light flickered in River's groggy brain. "Nurse Barton?" he asked uncertainly.

"She's still in Cuba," the nurse whispered. "Won't I do?" She lifted the lantern high so that it illuminated her face.

Puzzled, River frowned. His first impulse was to embrace her. Then the full meaning of her presence hit him and he grew angry. "What's the meaning of this? What am I doing on this ship?"

"Is your opinion of me so low that you really thought I could leave you in Cuba to be court-martialed for something I did, River?"

"And is your opinion of me so low that you thought I would thank you for having me drugged and loaded onto a stretcher so I could sneak away without assuming responsibility for my own actions?"

"It's not like that at all. You didn't sneak out of Cuba. Miss Barton sent you back to the States because you were wounded — just like all the other men on this ship."

"And were they all drugged so that they would appear to be more seriously injured than they were?"

The resentment in his voice hit her like a slap in the face, and the tears she'd labored so valiantly not to shed spilled down her cheeks.

At seeing them, the corner of River's mouth twitched as though he were biting back tears of his own. "How could you do this to me, Aidan?"

"Do this *to* you?" she asked with a shocked sniff. "I thought I did it *for* you. Silly me. I actually thought that if I protected you from exposure and kept you out of prison I could repay you in some small way for all the pain and misery knowing me has caused you. Obviously, I was wrong."

She leaned closer to him, the fire in her teary eyes brilliant in the lantern light. "And as far as my having you drugged so that your injury would seem more serious than it was, the next time you're delirious with pain and have an infection so serious the doctors aren't sure whether they should amputate your arm or let you die intact, I'll be sure to tell them not to give you anything for the pain!"

She pushed away from him to leave.

"Don't go," River rasped, reaching out to catch her arm as she started to rise from the deck.

"Why not?" she asked. "Haven't we said all we have to say?"

"Not quite." He drew her back down beside his cot. "I just want you to know that being with you hasn't been *all* pain and misery."

Surprised by his change of tone, Aidan asked, "It hasn't?"

He shook his head and cupped her face between his palms. "No. As a matter of fact, keeping up with you these past weeks you has made me feel more alive than I've felt in years."

"Does that mean you admit I did the right thing by getting you on this hospital ship?"

His mouth turned up at the corners in a sad grin. "No, I still don't like that you would presume to make such a choice for me. But I want you to know that I don't blame you for anything that's happened to me . . . and that I intend to turn myself in to the authorities as soon as we dock."

"Just like that?" Her mouth dropped open in an astonished grin. "And you accused *me* of being selfish? Believe me, my selfishness is nothing compared to yours. You're willing to destroy your own reputation, embarrass Lieutenant Colonel Roosevelt, and let your parents and the

People down by ruining your relationship with the colonel, all because of some misplaced sense of masculine honor? Well, for your information, River Blue Eagle, that's not honor. That's stupidity!"

Chapter Twelve

When the Red Cross ship docked at Port Tampa, Aidan frowned in dismay as she walked down the gangway behind the last of the stretchers bearing wounded men. She had expected some relatives of the injured to be waiting at the wharf, but she hadn't thought there would be so many.

To her right, there was a flash of light, followed by a puff of smoke. Startled, she looked up to find a photographer aiming his camera in her direction. Another light flashed, then another.

Wondering what newsworthy personage behind her might warrant such a welcome, she glanced over her shoulder. But, except for a few crewmen and one or two straggling Red Cross volunteers, there was no one back there. Deciding this exuberant welcome by the press had come about because these men were the first of the wounded to return to the States, she continued down the gangplank.

"That's her!" a male voice shouted from the wharf. "That's the lady Rough Rider!" another called out. "Look this way, Miss Donovan!" a third yelled. "Miss, Donovan, is it true . . . ?"

Aidan directed an astonished stare at the crowd. They were all looking at *her!* Yelling to *her! She* was the person

173

being photographed.

Comprehension of the situation made her head reel. Somehow the press had found out about her. She scanned the shoving throng of reporters, desperately seeking some explanation of how they'd heard. But no sooner did she look to the left than she heard her name called from her right.

"What was it like, Miss Donovan?" "Did you actually go into the front lines?" "Who helped you?" "How'd you get that wound on your head?" "What did Teddy Roosevelt say when he learned the truth?" "What is Lieutenant Blue Eagle to you?" "Where is he now?" "Is it true he knew all along that you were a woman?"

The last questions struck a chord of fear in Aidan's heart, and it took all the grit she could muster not to turn around and run back up the gangway. But, for the same reason she wouldn't run, she would come up with the strength she needed to fight. River! She had to protect River!

Inhaling deeply, she straightened her spine and drew herself up to her full height. Forcing her mouth into a large smile, she stopped halfway down the gangway and held up her hands for silence.

The roar of the crowd was immediately reduced to a hum as newspapermen, pads and pens poised in readiness, waited for her comment. The only sounds now were the restless shifting of feet and the clicks and poofs of the cameras as photographers continued to take pictures.

Inwardly thrilled that the desire to hear what she might have to say had quieted this crowd, Aidan sucked in a stabilizing breath.

"I don't know where you gentlemen got your information," she began with a laugh. "But your facts seem to be *slightly* confused."

Several people looked toward a slender young man who

174

stood on the edge of the crowd. Recognizing him as one of the wounded men from the Red Cross ship, Aidan's heartbeat pounded wildly in her ears. Somehow, he must have overheard her talking to River. Still, it was just his word against hers, unless River . . . Well, at least she didn't have to worry about him right this moment. He and the other seriously wounded men had been the first to debark, and had been taken directly to the Red Cross hospital for treatment.

"Are you saying you didn't disguise yourself as a man and go to Cuba with the Rough Riders?" a voice shouted from the back of the crowd.

Tearing her attention away from the young man who'd been on the ship, who watched her, a superior grin on his face, she stretched her mouth into a mischievous smile. "Oh, yes. I certainly did that. And I plan to write the full story for publication. However, I resent the implication that I had to rely on *anyone* other than myself to carry out my charade. No one had any idea I was a female until I was wounded, and then it was Nurse Clara Barton— who was clever enough to see through my disguise— which no *man* had done." She directed another charming grin at the newspapermen. "Which is the reason I refuse to share the credit for my accomplishment with anyone."

"Do you expect us to believe you had no help whatsoever?" the man Aidan had recognized shouted. "What about Roosevelt's aide, that Indian, Lieutenant Blue Eagle? Isn't it true he assisted you in this deception from the beginning?"

"I know you!" Aidan announced, her face a mask of pleasantness and friendliness, despite the hostility she felt. "Aren't you the correspondent who tripped and sprained his arm when your ship docked in Cuba?"

"Sprained?" another newspaperman bellowed, his accusing eyes on the reporter's sling. "You told me you were shot in the attack on San Juan Hill!"

Narrowing his eyes at Aidan, the wounded reporter yelled, "Don't you see what she's doing? It's obvious she's trying to make me out to be the liar here to cover for herself. But she's the one who's lying. I heard her discussing the whole thing with Roosevelt's aide!"

Pasting a tolerant, slightly amused smile on her face, Aidan shook her head. "This young man could easily have *seen* me speaking to the lieutenant, but if he'd gotten close enough to overhear our conversation, he would have heard me thanking Lieutenant Blue Eagle for saving my life the day the Rough Riders took San Juan Hill, even though he was seriously wounded doing so. Not only did I owe him my gratitude for risking his life to save me, but I thought he deserved an explanation as to why I had deceived him and everyone else — which was the fact that I wanted to prove to the world that women are as capable of covering newsworthy events as men are. And I did. Though it evidently threatens this young man's masculinity to admit that a woman can accomplish anything more challenging than keeping house and raising children."

Her expression grew stern, her tone determined. "But whatever his reason for trying to discredit me, I want to assure you I don't intend to allow this man, or anyone else, to minimize my accomplishment by suggesting I couldn't have done it without a *man's* help!"

She smiled again, making eye-to-eye contact with many of the reporters standing before her as she swept her gaze over them one last time. "Now, if you will excuse me, I have a suite waiting for me at the Tampa Bay Hotel, and I'm anxious to notify my family that I'm safely back in the United States."

She directed a final "sympathetic" smile at the reporter who'd very nearly destroyed River's reputation. There might still be a few diehards whom she hadn't convinced, but judging by the disgusted looks her attacker was receiving, and by the respectful smiles directed at her, she had succeeded in ending what could have been a very nasty scandal. A twinge of shame pinched at her conscience at having discredited the man, but it was him or River. And she intended to protect River's reputation at any cost!

"Just one more question," a man working his way toward her through the crowd called out.

"Yes?" she asked, certain her face was going to crack if she couldn't drop the phony, confident smile she had affected. "What is it?"

The man who approached took off his flat-brimmed straw hat and offered her a business card. "William Hearst, owner of the New York *Journal*. I'd like to talk to you about publishing your story in my paper. I hope you aren't already committed. This is just the kind of sensational account the *Journal* likes to give to its readers."

Aidan's calm facade slipped as she recognized the famous newspaperman's name. And he actually wanted to publish her story! Could this really be happening? "But you haven't seen it yet."

"I pride myself on being a good judge of what the public likes to read."

There was a hush as Aidan looked from the business card in her hand to the smiling Hearst. Of course she wanted to accept. This was the opportunity of a lifetime, something she had worked and prayed for all her life. Still, something held her back. "I'll have to let you know, Mr. Hearst," she finally said. "Quite frankly, your offer has surprised me, and I'm simply too exhausted to commit myself to anything right now." She looked around at the reporters, who obviously waited for her answer as eagerly as Hearst did. "Besides," she said, the artificial smile still painfully in place, "I'd prefer to discuss this in more private surroundings. May I contact you later today?"

"Of course," Hearst said with a charming smile. "I'm at the Tampa Bay also. But don't wait too long. Today's big story will be tomorrow's old news!"

Locking herself inside the lavish two-room hotel suite, Aidan heaved a relieved breath and sagged back against the door. Alone at last!

Frantic to get out of the austere black clothing she'd borrowed from Nurse Barton, she didn't wait until she got to the bedroom before she started shedding her clothes. Tearing the black bonnet from her head, she tossed it into a chair and began unbuttoning her bodice.

Directing an idle glance at the trunks standing in the corner to confirm that they were the ones she'd had her sister send from San Antonio to be held in storage for her, Aidan smiled as she thought about her parents' reaction to the wire she had sent them. Of course, at first they must have been furious. But after the shock wore off and they realized that she had done what no other woman had ever accomplished, they would be proud of her. As they always were. She had no doubt.

Slipping her arms out of the snug long sleeves, she bent her head to unfasten the hooks at her waist, and without ceremony, she peeled the dress and petticoats down her slim body and then stepped out of them. While crossing the sitting room on her way to the bedroom, she hurriedly added a camisole, drawers, shoes and stockings to the trail of clothing she left behind her, until she was finally naked. Completely naked for the first time in weeks— though it seemed like years.

Always one to delight in the freedom of being totally

unencumbered by clothing, Aidan threw back her head and laughed out loud. Stretching her arms above her head, she arched her back languorously and rocked her torso from side to side. The only thing that could make her feel any better than she was already feeling was the bath awaiting her.

Concentrating on sinking up to her chin in clean, fragrant water, she padded across the sleeping alcove and burst into the bathroom. Immediately focusing on the gleaming white porcelain tub at the center of the room, she ran to it. Giving the plug an energetic jab into the drainhole, she opened both water spigots full blast.

Unwilling to wait until the tub filled, she stepped in and lay back in the inch or so of water that had already collected. Even that little bit was more than she'd had to bathe in for so long, she was sure she was in heaven.

Forty-five minutes later, toweling her hair dry, she stepped from the bathroom, still enjoying the freedom of her nudity.

"Hello," a deep voice crooned from the corner.

Startled, Aidan snatched the towel from her head and protectively clutched it to her bosom. "River! What are you doing here? You're supposed to be at the hospital!"

His smile hiding none of the discomfort he was obviously feeling, he shrugged his good shoulder. "I left." Wincing, he pressed a hand to his wound.

"What's wrong!" she exclaimed, securing the towel around her as she ran across the room to him. Her eyes round with worry, she knelt beside him pushed his hand from the wound. She hurriedly unbuttoned his shirt and drew it off his injured shoulder. "Let me see," she ordered, guiding him forward so she could see his back. "It's bleeding!" she scolded, immediately going to work to remove the bandage from his chest. "Why is your bandage wet?"

179

Lifting his good arm so she could unwind the gauze, he gave her a sheepish grin. "You aren't the only one who couldn't wait to soak in the tub."

"You took a bath? Why? You're not supposed to get your stitches wet!" Peeking under the blood-tinged covering on the wound, she moaned aloud. It was worse than she had realized, and gut wrenched with pain at the sight of the angry jagged gash that marred the tan flesh of River's back from his shoulder to his upper arm.

"I was dirty."

"But you've opened it up! Why didn't you stay at the hospital and let a nurse give you a bath?"

He glanced over his shoulder at her, looking vulnerable. "Because the only nurse I wanted was here at the hotel."

Aidan's hands stilled on the bandage she'd been using to blot at the oozing wound, and she looked up, her expression a mixture of questions and joy as what he had said absorbed into her understanding.

"You mean . . . me?"

River nodded, his blue eyes focused on her lips. "All I could think of was being with you," he confessed. "This is all I need to heal my wounds—not some stranger who smells like starch and carbolic fussing over me."

Staring into his eyes, her own damp with emotion, Aidan shook her head. "But you need a real nurse, someone who knows what to do."

"You're the only nurse I need, Little Fire, the only one I want. Don't send me away."

Deep inside her, in her very soul, a warm, nurturing throbbing began and spread throughout her body, until it exploded in her breast in a starburst of love. "No," she whispered, pressing her lips to his shoulder near the ugly knife wound. "I won't send you away. I'll take care of you."

He cupped her jaw in a gentle hand and lifted her tear-stained face to his as he shifted in the chair so she was directly in front of him. Separating his thighs, he drew her to him. "It's not just my shoulder that needs your care. My whole body aches to be healed by your fire."

An uncertain smile wavered on her face, and she clasped his face between her hands. For the first time, River was exposing his vulnerability to her, admitting that he needed her; and the sweet pangs of desire squeezed at her insides.

"It's what I need too, River," she whispered, her lips so close to his she could taste his breath as it entered her mouth. She brushed his lips with a kiss.

"Sweet, sweet Little Fire," he moaned. His hands rough with urgency, he tore the towel from between their bodies and slanted his lips over hers in a deep searing kiss. Exploring her mouth hungrily, he tightened his embrace, bringing her up hard against his bared chest.

Her nipples puckered and hardened with desire at this intimate contact with his warm flesh, and their reaction spiraled down her body to settle in the deepest recesses of her passion. Immediately, hot moistness formed at the juncture of her thighs and she wanted — no needed — to have him touch her there.

Hunger guiding her, she slid her hands down his smooth chest and wound them around to his back. It was then the reality of what they were doing hit her, and she drew back from him, her expression worried. "Your shoulder, I need to bandage it."

His blue eyes dark with desire, River leaned toward her. "I need this more." He buried his face in the curve of her neck and shoulder. "I need you to heal more than my shoulder, Little Fire. My very soul craves to be wrapped in you. Please don't deny me your fire."

His bone-dissolving kisses made it impossible for her not to loll her head to the side, and his impassioned plea drove all practical thoughts from her mind. She wanted to heal his wounds, both physical and emotional — and in the process heal herself.

Sighing in surrender, she burrowed her grasping fingers in his black hair and drew his head to her breast.

His hands rode down her back to cup the mounds of her buttocks. Kneading, lifting, separating the firm flesh with strong fingers, his hands mimicked the manipulations of his mouth at her breast. Wrapping his tongue and lips around one hard nipple, he tugged gently, then harder on the swelling tip, taking it deeper into his mouth until all of the thrusting area around the aureole was in the heat of his mouth. Suckling, squeezing, circling, biting, he nursed her long and voraciously before moving his lips to her other breast.

Forming a band around the backs of her thighs with his hands, he then found the pulsing threshold to her femininity. His mouth trailing wet, biting kisses down her torso to her belly, he lifted her off her knees to stand before him. "I want to kiss all of you," he moaned against her softly rounded flesh, his hands gently bringing her hips forward.

Mounting tension knifed painfully inside her, softening any shock his obvious intention would have evoked only moments before. Urgency and need ruled her now. She tangled her fingers in his hair and clung to him for support, arching her hips forward in an instinctive invitation.

His breath against her sensitized skin sent waves of passion spiralling through her. All of her desire gathered into a boiling point at the center of her body as he kissed and caressed her, carrying her to a point of fullfillment.

"Oooooooooh." She sagged in his embrace as the building tension exploded inside her in shuddering spasms.

Releasing his intimate hold on her, but keeping her from falling, River trailed his lips up her body as he rose.

Desperate for him to fill the emptiness the removal of his hands and mouth had created, Aidan grappled frantically with the buttons on his fly, freeing them with record haste. Covering his chest with kisses, she peeled his trousers and breechcloth down over his hips.

Wrapping her arms around his waist, she kneaded and caressed the hard muscles of his buttocks, bringing him toward her, revelling in the hard column of his manhood as it pressed and prodded against the softer flesh of her stomach.

Kissing, pressing, massaging, pulling, she backed toward the bed, coaxing him to follow.

She lay back on the mattress, carrying him with her. Her legs opened, and he slid into the quivering heat of her, like a released arrow seeking its target.

Groaning his relief, he rolled them as one onto their sides so they were facing each other and his weight was supported by his good shoulder. Catching her upper leg behind the knee, he bent it up to her chest, and thrust his hips into the space created by their position. Harder and harder he slammed into her. Deeper and deeper. Until, crying out his erotic anguish, he pumped his strength deep inside her with a final desperate fury.

With a long, shuddering groan, his whole body relaxed, and he turned his head away from her. "Are you okay?" he panted, his chest heaving as he labored to catch his breath.

Her own breathing still ragged, Aidan smiled and nodded her head. "I'm fine. What about you? Is your shoulder hurting?"

He rolled his head back to her, his eyelids drooping drowsily, a satisfied, drunken grin stretching his mouth. "What shoulder?" Tightening his arms around her, he kissed her nose, then bent to nuzzle her neck.

"Oh, no you don't" she warned, squirming to remove

183

herself from the tangle of their intertwined limbs. "I'm going to take care of that shoulder, and you're not going to distract me again."

"Wanna bet?" He reached for her breast.

Scurrying out of reach just in time, Aidan did her best to sound stern. "All right, River, that's it. Either you behave, or I'm going to send you back to the hospital and let them worry about you."

His mouth turned down at the corners, he jutted his lower lip out in a pretended pout. "You'd do that to me? After you promised not to?"

Whipping a blanket around her nakedness, she glowered down at him. "You don't intend to hold me responsible for something I said in a moment of . . . ?" She hesitated.

"Passion?" he finished for her, with a knowing smile.

She folded her arms across her chest in a gesture of mock irritation. "For your information, what I was going to say was *com*passion." With a sassy pirouette, she spun away from him and went into the sitting room. "I'm going to have some gauze and carbolic sent up."

"Are you going to tell them it's for the naked man you have in your bed?" he called after her. "Or for just some passing stranger who brought out your '*com*passion'?"

Aidan paused, one hand on the telephone. River was right. No one could know he was in her suite. Then she remembered her own injury and laughed over her shoulder. "I'll just tell them I need the supplies for my head," she announced playfully. Lifting the receiver from its holder, she put it to her ear.

She gave the telephone handle a couple of energetic cranks, then waited, her mouth directly in front of and close to the speaker. "Operator," she said loudly, "this is Miss Donovan in room three-oh-six. Will you please have a maid bring me a generous supply of gauze and carbolic for my head injury as soon as possible?" She listened for a few seconds. "No, a visit from the doctor won't be necessary. Thank you anyway." She was silent for a moment more, then said. "Yes, thank you, that's all. Oh, just a minute. I'd like to have dinner sent up to my room. I'm dying for an enormous steak, vegetables, potatoes, and a piece of pie. No, I'll be dining alone . . . Thank you."

She hung up the earpiece and turned back to the sleeping alcove. "In the meantime, I suppose you'd better tell me where your room is so I can find a way to sneak your things up here."

Aidan stopped in the archway between the two rooms. River had crawled under the covers and was lying on his side—sound asleep. A warm, contented feeling enveloped her at the sight of him in her bed. It was as though he belonged there, as though he had always belonged there.

Seeing a chance to examine his shoulder without interference from him, she tiptoed over and crawled onto the bed. Black stitches crisscrossing it like so many railroad ties, the gash had a nasty look to it, but at least it wasn't bleeding. Maybe it had been good to expose it to the air for a while.

Still, there's going to be an ugly scar, she thought, her heart twisting painfully in her chest. Again a wave of guilt rocked her. If she hadn't been so determined to get to the front, he wouldn't have suffered, wouldn't have had his bronzed, statue-perfect body defaced by that Cuban's knife.

Aidan plumped a pillow against the headboard and leaned back against it, pondering the curious change in the way she felt about things. Was this what love did to a person? Was it love that caused her to feel his pain, to wish she could take it on herself? Did love make her find joy just watching him sleep? Was it love that made her

185

want to take care of him and protect him from anything that threatened him? And was it love that made her feel as if she would stop breathing, her heart stop beating, if she were never to see him again?

Aidan shook her head and grinned down at the sleeping man beside her. *If it's not love, I don't think I could survive the real thing.*

A quiet knock on the door startled her out of her musings. "I'm coming," she called, leaping off the bed and running to the door before the knocking could awaken River.

Securing the cover around her nakedness, she cracked the door open a bit and peeked out into the hall. Relieved to see the maid holding a tray containing the first-aid supplies and the meal she'd ordered, she shot a nervous glance over her shoulder to be certain the bed couldn't be seen from the doorway. Satisfied that as long as River was quiet his presence would go undetected, she opened the door wider and let the laden girl in. "Just put it here." She indicated the table, listening nervously for any sound that would give away the fact that she was not alone. "Mmm, smells good," she declared in a falsely gay whisper, snatching up her purse and digging in it for money as she prodded the maid back to the door. "Thank you so much," she said, dropping a coin into the woman's palm. With a literal shove she pushed the astonished girl out into the hall and closed the door in her face.

Heaving a sigh, Aidan sagged back against the door frame and grinned. "So far, so good," she said, padding quietly back into the bedroom. Pleased that all the activity hadn't awakened River, she went back into the bathroom, intent on taking a second bath.

By the time River awakened an hour later, Aidan was fully clothed in a bright yellow- and green-striped day dress. She had fluffed her hair into a downy halo of auburn curls, and her cheeks had been pinched to bring out their color.

He opened his eyes slowly, his mouth stretching in a sleepy grin. "I must be dreaming. I could swear you're the famous Rough Rider, correspondent, and balloon traveler, A. D. Donovan. But that's impossible. You're wearing a dress."

"What do you think?" Aidan asked, rising from the chair beside the bed and slowly circling for him to view her gown.

He propped himself up on an elbow and yawned. "I think you're beautiful, but to tell you the truth I liked you better the way you were earlier. I think the French call it *au naturel!*"

"I think the dress is more suitable for my dinner engagement. Besides, I doubt the Tampa Bay Hotel dining room is quite ready for Aidan Donovan, *au naturel!*"

He stopped yawning, sleepiness instantly deserting him. "What dinner engagement?" he asked suspiciously, lifting the cover and swinging his feet off the bed.

"That's what I want to talk to you about," she said, going to sit on the edge of the bed with as much calm as she could muster. "Something I didn't count on happened when we docked today. It could have been disastrous, but I think I managed to turn it around so that it will work *for* us instead of *against* us—if you'll do your part."

"Will you just say what this something is?" He already knew by her tone that he wasn't going to be happy with her explanation.

"You have to promise me you'll listen to my whole plan before you say anything."

"Aaaaaai-dan," he dragged out her name, the way he did when he was losing patience.

"Promise?"

"All right, I promise. Now, get on with it."

187

"Well, remember I told you I didn't feel right about writing my story because of what it could do to you—"

He interrupted. "And I told you to go on and write it since I was going to—"

She pressed a finger to his lips. "Shh. Let me finish."

When she was through recounting what had happened on the wharf earlier, she shrugged her shoulders, though inwardly she cringed. "So, the way it stands now, we don't really have a choice. If you tell everyone you helped me, you'll not only needlessly ruin your own reputation, but you'll brand me as a reporter who can't be trusted to tell the truth. And that will be the end of any chance we might have to interest Mr. Hearst or anyone else in our reservation exposé."

River studied her, his hurt gaze boring into hers. "Congratulations, Aidan. Once again, you've manipulated everything and everyone to suit your purposes."

Stung by the anger in his voice, she stared at him. "No! You're wrong. I didn't arrange any of this. It just happened."

"Did it, Aidan?" He stood up and crossed to the bathroom. Turning back to her at the door, he said, "With you, nothing ever 'just happens.'"

Chapter Thirteen

"Then we are agreed," William Hearst said, removing the cap from his fountain pen and offering the pen to Aidan.

Hesitating only an instant, she grinned and accepted the pen. Agreed? Of course she agreed. Two thousand dollars for a story she would have given away to get the kind of coverage William Hearst was going to give her? Who wouldn't agree?

"We're agreed," she said, scribbling her name in large scrawling letters at the bottom of the contract. "I'll have the story done by noon day after tomorrow, and you'll run several preliminary stories, so you can 'tantalize' the readers with the 'thrill' of reading my 'eye-witness' account of what it was like to be the only woman in the Rough Riders." She shoved the signed contract across the table to Hearst.

"Now that we have that taken care of," Hearst said, glancing at her signature, then folding the contract and tucking it into his breast pocket, "I'd like to talk to you about the possibility of your doing another investigative story for the *Journal*."

Aidan's heart leaped with excitement. Could this really be happening to her? Did William Hearst actually want to talk to her about doing another story? He'd already fulfilled all her dreams by promising to make her the most famous woman reporter in the United States. It was too much to believe.

She pinched herself under the table, then clenched her fists with restraint as she struggled to keep up her professional façade. When what she wanted to do was leap into the air shouting, *Thank you! Thank you! Thank you. Of course, I'll do another story for you!*

"I'm glad you brought that up, Mr. Hearst," she said, with so much aplomb that she amazed herself. "I've been talking to Lieutenant Blue Eagle, the man who saved my life, about doing an exposé on the atrocious conditions on the Indian reservations in the United States. Do you realize—"

"That's all well and good," Hearst interrupted, putting a hand on her arm to stop her. "However, I don't think the American public is particularly interested in reading about Indians right now. They want something more meaty, more titillating with their morning coffee. They like to learn about the seamier sides of life. They want something they can gasp over and shake their heads in horror about, as they sit safely ensconced in their own homes and enjoy their newspapers. Intrigue, scandal, violence, corruption. Those are the things they want."

"But the Indians—"

Hearst cut her off with a humoring smile. "Trust me, my dear. The Indians hold no appeal for our readers."

"If I could prove all those things you want are part of the reservation system right now—intrigue, scandal, violence, corruption—then would you consider my idea?"

Hearst rocked his head from side to side noncommittally. "Perhaps we can discuss it again, at a later date, but today I have a more daring and exciting project in mind. The minute I saw you at the wharf, I knew it was just perfect for you."

Her interest piqued in spite of her annoyance because Hearst wouldn't even listen to her proposition, she asked, "What is that?"

Hearst leaned forward, his expression secretive. "I'm sure you've read rumors that in San Francisco's Chinatown, innocent young white women are being lured into opium dens by white slavers. Then, supposedly, once they are addicted to the drugs, the slavers use these unfortunate young women for their own evil purposes."

Aidan lowered her voice. "Are you proposing I do a story on the white slavery in San Francisco?"

"I want more from you than just a story, Aidan—may I call you Aidan? Any reporter can write that. What I want from you is something like what you did in Cuba. I want you to infiltrate the opium dens and white slave organizations of San Francisco, then write an actual accounting of what it was like to be there."

Her eyes gleaming with excitement, Aidan shook her head. "This sounds a little too dangerous, even to me, Mr. Hearst."

"That's what makes it so perfect for the *Journal* and for a fearless young woman like yourself. Of course, I don't intend to send you into this alone. We'll take every precaution to guarantee your safety. I will hire two or three Pinkerton detectives to accompany you everywhere. Though they'll be in disguise and you may not always be able to spot them, they will be instructed not to let you out of their sight. Then, if you run into a situation you can't handle—which I doubt will happen if the way you dealt with that mob of reporters today is any indication—they will immediately come to your assistance."

Aidan couldn't quite bring herself to say no to his offer, even though her conscience and sense of honor told her to refuse. If there were just some way she could do the Chinatown thing without going back on her word to

191

River . . . "I'll have to think about it, Mr. Hearst. Though it sounds like a fascinating idea, I just don't see how I can manage it. I've already given my word to Lieutenant Blue Eagle that I will write the reservation story."

"This one pays four thousand dollars plus your expenses. What are the Indians paying you?"

"Your offer is very tempting, Mr. Hearst, but even if I didn't owe my life to Lieutenant Blue Eagle, I can't go back on my word."

Hearst sat back in his chair and studied her. Propping his elbows on the chair arms, he steepled his fingers over his middle and tapped them together thoughtfully. "Tell you what," he finally said, "if you'll agree to do the Chinatown piece first, the *Journal* will buy your Indian story and run it on the front page—whether it's the kind of thing we usually print or not."

Amazed, and flattered, that Hearst would commit himself to printing a story he wasn't particularly interested in just to get her to work for him, Aidan had to muster all her self-control to keep from extending her hand to him in acceptance of his offer.

But she couldn't agree to it, not without talking to River first, to make certain he understood. She didn't care to repeat the scene they had earlier in her suite.

She dropped her hand back into her lap. "Though I'm inclined to accept your generous offer, I need some time to think about it, Mr. Hearst. May I give you my answer when I hand in my Cuba story day after tomorrow?"

Sensing he had pushed Aidan Donovan as far as he could, Hearst backed off. She was obviously a young woman who did things her own way, and in her own time. To pressure her for a decision would only defeat his purpose. "Certainly, day after tomorrow will be fine—but only if you'll stop calling me Mr. Hearst. My name is William."

Satisfied, Aidan smiled and said, "Then, if we have no further business, William, I'd better return to my room and get to work. Hopefully, the typewriting machine I ordered has already been delivered, and I can start right away."

"I'm back," Aidan announced excitedly as she let herself into her suite a few minutes later. "Wait until you hear what happened! Hearst bought my Cuba story, *and* he's going to print our . . . River?"

She stopped short, registering the fact that the sitting room was awash with the gray of twilight, lit only by the last feeble rays of the evening sun. A feeling of dread rocked her. He was gone.

He just went back to sleep, she told herself optimistically, though she knew in her heart that he had left her. Tossing her purse onto a chair, she ran toward the bedroom.

Steadying herself against one side of the archway, she stared in disappointment at the empty bed that filled the room. Hurt and disappointment gathered in her stinging eyes. He hadn't even waited to hear how her appointment had gone.

Well, he's not going to get away with it! she silently vowed, pride surfacing to overwhelm the pain his absence had brought. She crossed the room and lifted the earpiece off the telephone wall box. *If he thinks he can come in here and use me and then disappear without a word just because he doesn't like the way I handled a sticky situation, then he is going to be very surprised!*

"Hello, operator! I understand Lieutenant River Blue Eagle is here in the hotel. Can you give me his room number? . . . No! Don't ring it! Just give me the room number!" Hearing the harsh impatience in her voice, she

193

felt a wave of guilt. Consciously softening her tone, she added, "Please . . . Two-oh-three? . . . Thank you, operator."

She gave the ear cone an energetic slam into its holder and whirled around to face the room again. It was time someone taught River Blue Eagle he couldn't always have things his way.

"Walk out on me, will he? Just wait until I get my hands on him!" she declared. Then she stomped across to the door, grasped the brass knob, stopping short.

Wait a minute. Just telling him off wasn't enough! Not nearly enough. He might be used to treating women like toys and having them let him call all the shots—even when his pride made him too stupid to know what was good for him. Well, it was about time he learned that she wasn't other women, and that she was perfectly capable of making an intelligent decision without his "wise" counsel!

River lay on his bed, idly staring into the darkness. Damn Aidan Donovan. She was going to drive him crazy. She always had an answer for everything, an answer that made everything go her way, no matter what anyone else felt.

A light tap on the door brought him out of his reverie. His heart leaping, he jackknifed up off the bed and hurried to the door. "Who is it?" he asked, sure it was Aidan coming to apologize and ask for his forgiveness—which of course he would give.

"Eet ees the maid, *señor*," a female voice responded with a heavy Cuban accent. "I have come to turn down the *señor*'s bed for the night."

Disappointment burst forth in River's chest, and his shoulders slumped. Well, what had he expected? Aidan had what she wanted now: her story and fame. She didn't need him anymore. She even had the added bonus of knowing she'd "protected" him, despite the fact that she'd placed him in the position of being forced to lie. In fact, now that he thought about it, he wouldn't be surprised in the least if she didn't try to get out of writing the exposé now that she had everything she wanted from him.

"Señor?" the small voice repeated from the other side of the door. "Are ju steel there?"

"Yeah, I'm here," he replied with disgust. "Thanks anyway, but I can do it myself." He started back toward the bedroom.

There was an urgent knocking. "Señor! I must prepare all the beds on theese floor, or the boss señor, he weel be mucho angry weeth Lolita! He weel beat me!"

Certain the maid was exaggerating, but in no mood to argue, River turned back. "All right," he grumbled, plucking the door open. "But be quick about it."

"Gracias, señor. I weel be queek like the leezard een the hot skeeleet," the dark-haired girl promised. Bustling through the doorway, head bent, she scurried across the sitting room and disappeared into the sleeping alcove. "Sí, queek, queek, queek!"

River flopped down on an upholstered chair, his mood dejected and disgruntled. Aidan. What was he going to do about her? For a while there, he'd almost believed she cared for him, really cared for him. She'd touched something deep inside him when she'd offered to give up her story so she could protect his reputation. And when he'd gone to her room, she'd been so warm and receptive that he'd almost convinced himself there might be more to their relationship than just a mutual need for each other's help.

Then she had told him about Hearst's offer, and he had seen the light in her eyes and known what a fool he'd been. Protecting him hadn't been her intention. She'd just wanted to keep his part in her deception quiet to make her story more fantastic, her fame greater!

"*Señor*, come queek!" the maid squealed from the bedroom, her voice high with distress.

Bounding to his feet, River strode to the archway, concern pounding in his veins. "What's wrong?" he asked, hesitating in the opening as he tried to locate her in the darkened room. "Why didn't you turn on the light?"

Spotting a petite figure silhouetted in front of the window, he stopped short, his eyes widening in shock. "What are you doing?" Paralyzed, he stared at the woman's back as she wriggled out of her clothing. "Put that back on!" he ordered, turning to leave the bedroom.

"The *señorita*, she say ju like—"

River tensed. "What *señorita*?" he asked suspiciously.

"The *mucho*, beautiful *señorita*, with the hair of red."

"Aidan Donovan sent you here?"

"*Sí, señor. Señorita* Aidan say ju weel be pleased weeth Lolita eef she ees *au naturel*."

"Did she now?" he asked, his voice hardening with anger. This time, Aidan had gone too far. "Well, she was wrong. Now get dressed and go tell the *señorita* to send her surprises to someone else."

"Are ju sure ju want Lolita to go, *señor*?" she asked, wrapping her arms around his waist and fumbling with his belt buckle. "The *señorita*, she say ju—"

He jumped as though he'd been burned when her breasts pressed against his bare back. "I don't care what she said!" he choked, swatting her hands away from his belt.

"But, *señor* . . ."

"Can't you get it through your head? I'm not interested." He whirled around to face her. "What the . . .?" His gaze swept down the length of the petite brunette, then shot back to her face.

A smug, cat-with-the-canary grin stretched lazily over "Lolita's" face. "Do ju really theenk the beautiful *señorita* weel let the handsome *señor* get away because they have the teeny, weeny little argument?"

"Aaaaai-daaaan," he ground out, battling to suppress the relieved smile that threatened to break on his face. His struggle evident, he shook his head in defeat. "What the hell am I going to do with you?"

Stepping closer to him, she curled her arms around his waist. "I have a couple of suggestions, *señor,*" she whispered. Raising herself on tiptoe, she trailed her lips from shoulder to shoulder, across the expanse of flesh at the base of his throat. "Do you want to hear them?" She lowered her heels, and traversed the breadth of his muscular chest with her kiss. Meanwhile her hands sought his belt buckle and quickly finished the work "Lolita" had begun. "Or are ju steel mad weeth me?"

Releasing a frustrated laugh, River ripped the black wig from Aidan's head and tossed it aside. Then his mouth covered hers with bruising force, staking his claim on her with his tongue. Releasing a surrendering groan into her mouth, he hauled her naked torso against his thrusting hips.

Her hands working frantically to release the buttons of his trousers, Aidan freed her mouth to kiss his chest, then slid to her knees as she dragged the trousers down his lean hips, along the columns of his muscular thighs and calves, and off his bare feet, her lips leaving a trail of fire down the length of him.

Curling into a ball at his feet, she bent her head and kissed an ankle. She flicked her tongue over the bony knob, circling it once, then nibbled her way upward to his knee.

Sitting back on her calves, she looked up the towering

length of him. "Ees the *señor* steel angry weeth the *seño-rita?*"

"Damn you, Aidan," he rasped, dropping to the floor and shoving her over onto her back. "I ought to lock you in your room and only let you out on a leash."

Her feet and legs trapped under her, held her hips high in the air. Instinctively, she spread her thighs farther apart to make room between them for his slim hips. Inserting her hands between their bodies, she wrapped her fingers around the probing column of his manhood. "Does that mean you're going to keep me after all?" she asked, her voice husky as she moistened the tip of him at the pulsing entrance to her body.

"Oh, my god," he moaned, heaving his loins forward in urgent demand.

She tightened her grip on his engorged shaft, blocking its plunge into the haven it sought.

"Let me in, Aidan."

"Not until you answer my question, River." Her tone was no longer teasing or coy. "I have to know if it's me you want."

"My god," he panted in her ear, "how can you ask that? Can't you tell how much I want you? Can't you feel how I burn for you?" He strained against her hands, but she didn't yield.

"Yes, I can feel that your body wants mine," she said with a sad smile. "And mine yearns to be filled with you, but it's not enough, River."

He reared his head back and stared down at her, his blue eyes dark with confusion. There was no longer a playful gleam in her dark eyes. All he saw was a hunger that matched his, and a determination not to give in to that hunger.

"There has to be more, River. I want to hear you tell me there is more to us than only a mutual physical need."

He could feel himself withering in her hand. He rolled off her and flopped a forearm up over his eyes. "What do you want from me, Aidan?"

"I want everything, River—or nothing." She slid over onto her side and faced him, draping an arm over his waist as she straightened her legs. "Right now my body is screaming out its need for you, but it's not enough. I need to know I'm more to you than just a convenient release for your passion."

"Of course, you mean more to me than that," he declared, wrapping an arm around her shoulders and facing her. "I care about you."

"If you really care about me, River, you have to care about all of me, not just the parts of me that are easy for you to tolerate. You have to care about the parts of me that aren't so easy for you to accept too. What about the playful side of me, the intelligent side, the aggressive side, the independent side, the stubborn side, the arrogant side, the ambitious side? And don't forget the side you called manipulative, the side that gives me the ability to think fast enough to turn a bad situation into a good one, like when I protected your reputation from those reporters in spite of your blind male pride. Do you care about all those other sides of me? Because they're who I am, River. I'm an independent, thinking individual who knows what she wants, not the helpless little girl you seem to want me to be, who will be content to let the man she lo—*cares for* run her life for her. I can't be what I'm not, River. Not even for you."

River didn't speak for a long time after she finished, so long in fact that she wondered if he had fallen asleep. *I guess that's your answer,* she sobbed inwardly. Hurt and disappointment cutting through her, she rolled away from him.

As she sat up, a warm hand reached out and touched

199

her shoulder. She started, snapping her head around, her gaze meeting blue eyes filled with such pain she was rocked by guilt. *I didn't mean it*, she wanted to cry out. *I'll change, I'll be whatever you want me to be. Just don't let me walk out that door!*

"It's those 'sides' to you that make me . . . care. It's just that they . . ."

"What, River?" she asked, covering his hand with hers. "Tell me."

He released an embarrassed laugh. "I've never known anyone like you, Aidan. And . . . you scare me."

"Scare you? Why?" Her expression disbelieving, she twisted around to see him better. "You're not afraid of anything."

He blew out a derisive snort. "That's me all right. River-Not-Afraid-of-Anything. Except there's a slight catch to that premise, Little Fire. I'm afraid of lots of things. For one, I'm afraid down deep in my gut that anything I can do to help my people will be too little and too late. But since you came back into my life, I've realized there are two things that scare me even more than that. One is wanting you to the point of not being able to think of anything else, and the other is that I won't be able to hold you." He gave her a self-conscious grin.

"Oh, River, my sweet sweet love. Don't you know how hard it's going to be to get rid of me? Why do you think I came here tonight? When I returned to my room after dinner with Mr. Hearst and found you gone, I was afraid you had left me for good, but I knew I couldn't give you up without a fight." She leaned over him and kissed his mouth. "I want to share everything with you, River. Our successes as well as our failures, our weaknesses as well as our strengths, our minds as well as our . . . passions. Together we can have it all. Together we can do it all!"

Tightening his embrace around her tiny waist, he drew

her over him so that she was straddling him. Catching her under the arms, he lifted her higher, bringing a thrusting nipple to his mouth and hungrily latching on to it.

Threading her fingers into the thick hair at his temples, she clutched his head to her breast, certain that she would never love him any more than she did at that very moment.

Leaving the first wet peak, he moved his lips to the neglected crest, laving and worshiping all the flesh between. "I love your breasts," he moaned against her, as he sucked the satiny tip into his mouth.

When not an inch of her chest was unanointed by his passion, he gripped her waist and slid her higher up on his body, trailing wet kisses down her torso to the soft, downy juncture of her desire.

Delving his tongue into that treasure of femininity, he sent flames raging through her every fiber. Borne on the heat of his intimate kiss, Aidan soared toward the sun. Then, just as she felt herself become one with white-hot brilliance, it shattered inside her, all around her, splintering her very being into billions of tiny lights to be scattered throughout eternity.

Her fall to earth sent her writhing down his lean, muscled torso in a frantic quest to replenish herself with his power. Driven by a need so great that her actions were frenzied, almost desperate, she lifted her hips off him for only an instant, then, dropping her weight downward, impaled herself on him, groaning with satisfaction.

For several seconds, neither of them moved; they just luxuriated in the contentment of being united. Then, slowly, Aidan lifted upward, almost removing the tight sheath of her body from him before plunging downward again, only to withdraw and plunge again . . . and again . . . and again. She rode him, her head thrown back in delirious rapture, her fingers clawing into the straining muscles of his chest.

Then, she was flipped over onto her back, and the rider became the ridden as River slammed his full length into her, unable to hold back.

"Yes, yes, yes!" she chanted, as together they were hurled into infinity, where there was nothing but the two of them and their ecstasy. Clinging to each other, they finally fell back to earth, his hips still undulating against her.

His breathing heavy and labored, he collapsed onto her, no longer capable of supporting himself on his good arm, which had held the bulk of his weight off her through the last moments of their lovemaking.

Wrapping her arms and legs around him, she squeezed him to her, wishing they could stay like this forever.

"I'm sorry about the way I acted when you told me what happened to you at the wharf," he said suddenly, his voice still rough. "I know you did it for me."

Love swelled painfully in her breast. Tears springing to her eyes, she tightened her embrace on him. "I did it for us, River. I did it for us."

Chapter Fourteen

Aidan concentrated on knotting the bandage she'd wrapped around River's chest to hold the dressing in place on his wound—though he didn't think he needed a bandage at all. "There!" she said, giving his arm a pat. "Now, don't get it wet again!"

"How did your appointment with Hearst go?" River asked, doing his best to disguise the wish that they could put off this conversation even longer. "I assume he's going to buy your story and make you famous."

Excitement sparkling in her dark eyes, Aidan nodded. Her expression pleased, she arranged herself on River's lap and looped her arms around his neck. "But that's not the best part. The best part is that I got him to agree to print my exposé on the reservations on the *front* page of the New York *Journal*! Can you believe it? It's even better than we planned. Do you realize how many people are going to read that story, River? I thought the most we could hope for would be to sell it to several regional papers, I didn't dream a newspaper with the readership of the *Journal* would want it. No one can raise the public's awareness to a cause as well as William Hearst. Look what he did for the Cubans! I can see it now! Before we're through, the whole country is going to be up in arms over the injustices on the reservations."

River smiled unenthusiastically. He still wasn't convinced Cuba was anything to brag about, except for the many newspapers coverage of the war had sold . . . certainly not because of the lives that had been needlessly lost. Still, he couldn't argue against having the power of the New York *Journal* behind the People's cause. So why was he plagued by this nagging feeling that he didn't want the reservation story in a Hearst newspaper? "You make it sound as though you're intending to set off another war, Aidan. We don't want that, just equal rights and treatment."

Still not recognizing his mood, Aidan giggled and kissed him. "You know I was speaking figuratively. I just meant that the public will be so angry when they learn the truth, the politicians will be forced to do something about the reservations — or lose in the next elections."

He forced a smile, angry with himself for not sharing her enthusiasm about something they had both wanted and planned from the beginning of their relationship. "I know that. It's just that Hearst is known for resorting to sensationalism when it comes to selling papers, and I'd hate to see the People's plight turned into another of his promotions — like Cuba."

Aidan stared at him, her disappointment evident. "I thought you'd be happy."

Remorse rippled through him. *Face it, she's done something you couldn't have done in a million years, and you can't stand it. That's what's bothering you!* He tightened his embrace.

"I am happy, Little Fire. And I'm really proud of you." He kissed her lightly on the mouth, then pressed his cheek to hers, unable to look at her without revealing the unexplainable apprehension her announcement had aroused in him. "So, when can you be ready to leave for South Dakota? Right away, I hope."

204

Aidan tensed perceptibly, and drew back her head so she could look at him. "There's just one small hitch we need to work out first," she said, her expression uncertain and wary.

"Oh?"

River's response sounded so guarded that Aidan dreaded going any further. Maybe she shouldn't. Everything was proceeding so smoothly. They'd worked through a lot of their differences and had come to a new understanding. Did she want to jeopardize that? Was the Chinatown article worth risking losing River? Maybe she should just forget about Hearst's offer and find another newspaper to publish the reservation piece. It shouldn't be that hard to do. Surely, after the Cuba articles ran, she would be one of the most sought-after reporters in the country, and there would be someone willing to print anything she wrote. *But where else can we get the kind of coverage William Randolph Hearst can give the Indians? Assuming someone else can be talked into buying such a story.*

"What's the hitch, Aidan?" River asked harshly. "What *little* detail have we 'got to work out'?"

Slipping out of his lap, she wandered to the window and looked down onto the beach. She wiped her damp palms over the front of the maid's uniform she wore, and turned to face River. "For one thing, I can't do the reservation story until I've finished the Cuba piece," she explained hesitantly.

"That's not a problem. How long can it take to write? A week? Two?"

"Actually, it's practically written. I told Mr. Hearst I'd have it done day after tomorrow. It's just that he wants—" Aidan looked over at River, her gaze devouring him as he sat on the edge of the bed, his broad shoulders relaxed, his black hair falling over his forehead. She noticed that it

205

was much longer than it had been two months earlier when she'd first seen him after so many years. She particularly liked the endearing, rumpled little-boy quality it gave him when it was uncombed. She wanted to run to him and tell him to forget everything she'd said and just hold her, but she knew she couldn't. He was entitled to know of Mr. Hearst's offer.

"It's just that he wants me to do another story—before the Indian exposé." There, she said it.

"I see. And of course you told him you would do it," he said resignedly, lying back on the bed.

"No!" she cried, running over to him. "I said I had promised to do a story for the People, and that I thought it would be perfect for the *Journal*. But he said it wasn't the kind of thing his readers want with their morning coffee. I told him I could make it into the kind of story *Journal* readers will like, but he refused to listen to me, River. So, I told him I didn't see how I could do another piece, since I was committed to the Indian story."

A baffled, pleased grin shaping his mouth, River raised his head and searched her face. "You did?" he asked, propping himself up on his elbows.

"But then he made an offer I don't see how I can turn down."

River flopped back onto the bed. "Somehow that doesn't surprise me, Aidan. It isn't exactly the first time a white backed out of a bargain with an Indian because something better came along." He sounded tired and bored with the entire conversation. "Tell me, what was this great offer?"

Her patience stretched to the point of breaking, she spoke through her teeth. "For your information, Mr. Wronged Indian, I don't intend to back out of anything. In fact, Mr. Hearst only agreed to print the exposé because he knew I wouldn't write his story otherwise. His only condition was that I do the story he has in mind first."

"And that's when you told him you'd accept?"

"Dammit, River! Why are you being this way? No, I didn't accept! I told him I'd have to let him know. I wanted to talk it over with you first!"

He sat up and leveled a hard, accusing glare at her. "Why bother, Aidan? You know you're going to do what you want."

"I don't know anything of the sort. I wanted *us* to make the decision together."

He blew out a derisive snort. "Are you saying if I tell you not to accept his offer, you won't?"

Aidan doubled her fists and clenched her teeth, stretching her mouth in a baffled grimace, and stamped her feet in a rapid series of frustrated steps. "Urrr. Haven't you heard anything I've said?" she shouted. "Why can't you get it through your thick skull that I don't need you or anyone else to *tell* me what to do? I had hoped we could discuss this in a rational, intelligent, adult manner—you know, weigh the pros and cons of the situation. We have to think about the possibility that no one else may want to publish the piece, so we have to decide whether we want to accept the guaranteed 'bird in the hand' or gamble on the 'two in the bush'. And before we make our final decision, we ought to consider any options we have to fall back on if we tell Hearst no. But whatever the final decision is, I thought *we* could determine what *we* should do *together.*"

She shook her head in disgust. "But I should have known that would be impossible. From the very beginning, you've insisted on making every issue a power struggle. You see me as an ambitious, selfish, glory-hungry white out to take advantage of a poor Indian, and you think I don't give a damn how many people I tread on, as long as I get what I want."

Aidan scooped the black wig off the floor, where it had been tossed earlier, and tucked it under her arm. Stomping over to the door, she wrenched it open, then turned back to face him. "But you're the one who is selfish, River. You refuse to see anything from any viewpoint but your own. Well, I'm up to here with it—" She held her fingers under her nose. "—and I'm not going to put up with it or you anymore. If you ever decide you're not the only person in the world who matters, maybe you can look me up. In the meantime, I'm going to spend a few days with my family; then I'm going to San Francisco for Mr. Hearst. At least, *he* has the word 'compromise' in *his* vocabulary!"

She stomped out into the hallway and marched angrily toward the elevator. Then she had another thought. Whirling around, she strode back to River's room, arriving there just as he was starting to close the door. "And another thing, Mr. Blue Eagle, I'm going to write the reservation story when I get through in California—so you can just wipe that martyred, I-knew-you'd-back-out-of-our-agreement look off your face!"

"I'll believe it when I see it."

"Well, you will! Even if I have to hand-deliver it to you and shove it up your . . . up your *nose!*"

This time, when she left, Aidan didn't turn back. And she didn't cry—not until she was safely locked in her own suite.

Aidan stepped off the train in San Francisco and glanced around for the Pinkerton detective who was to meet her at the station. Supposedly, he knew what she looked like, which train she would be on, and the car she'd be in. He would find her, but so far she'd seen no one coming in her direction.

Touched by momentary indecision, she pulled an envelope from her purse and removed the letter it contained. Quickly rereading her instructions, she looked around, seeking the clock she'd been told to stand beside if the detective didn't contact her right away.

Relieved to realize she was in the right place, she picked up her valise and began working her way through the crowd. Stationing herself where she thought she would be most visible, she lifted her lapel watch and checked the time. If the tardy detective didn't arrive within thirty minutes, she would hail a cab and get to the hotel by herself.

Impatiently, she again scanned the milling crowd to see if she could spot anyone who appeared to be looking for her. But everyone in the busy station seemed bent on a definite purpose, and no one even so much as glanced her way.

Then, as though something were drawing her head around, she looked back over her shoulder. There, several feet away, was an Oriental man. He was watching her, a smile on his dark face—a smile that looked predatory to Aidan. A shaft of panic speared through her.

She nervously studied her hands, then directed her attention to the side in an effort to ignore the man, but curiosity persisted and forced her eyes back to him. Dressed in western clothes, he wore a white summer suit and hat, and she couldn't help noticing that he was taller than most Chinese she had seen. *Probably half-white*, she told herself, trying desperately to ignore the apprehension swelling in her chest.

Determined not to think about him anymore, she forced her glance away from him, checked her watch, then began to pace a few feet on either side of where she had placed her satchel. Where was that detective? It certainly was a good thing she had the address and telephone number of the Pinkerton Agency, or she would really have been dismayed. However, her faith in the Pinkertons ability to protect her when she went into Chinatown was beginning to slip.

She made a circle around her bag, coming up short against the Oriental man in the white suit. "Oh! Excuse me," she stammered, her gaze meeting piercing, black, almond-shaped eyes. "I wasn't watching where I was going."

"It is I who must beg your pardon," he said with a friendly smile. He tipped his hat, exposing jet black hair, combed straight back from his flat round face. "You seem to be searching for someone. Perhaps I am the person you seek."

Aidan couldn't help noticing that the man's accent was more Bostonian than Chinese, or that he appeared to be no more than about twenty-five and wore his hair cut short, not in the traditional braid down his back all the Chinese men she had seen wore. These characteristics, coupled with his height and manner of dress combined with his decidedly Asian features, to create an incongruous and frightening picture in her mind. In fact, she could almost feel the man's dark eyes cataloguing every detail about her, as though he had some sinister motive.

"No, thank you. I'm certain my friend will be along shortly," she answered, pivoting away and taking several steps.

Growing more and more uneasy under the man's blatant examination, she silently scolded herself for giving free rein to her wild imagination. Did she actually think the white slavers she was here to investigate lurked around the train station and accosted their victims in broad daylight? He was probably just a polite man who wanted to help her, nothing more. Nevertheless, she didn't intend to look back to see if he was still there, watching her, that

210

ominous gleam in his black eyes. She didn't have to. She could feel his gaze boring into her back.

She checked her watch again. Twenty minutes late. Where was that Pinkerton man? Well, she wasn't going to wait any longer. She was going to go to the hotel. Let the irresponsible detective worry about her when he arrived and she was gone. It would serve him right. She whipped back around, bent on retrieving her suitcase.

The tall Chinese man grinned and tipped his hat at her. What was she to do now? He hadn't budged from the spot right in front of her bag. To get to it, she had to pass him. Well, she wasn't going to be frightened by a smiling man who didn't have sense enough to realize she wasn't interested in anything he had to offer.

Jutting her chin haughtily, she took a step toward him.

"Miss Donovan?" a man's breathless voice asked from behind her.

Relief washing through her, Aidan couldn't resist giving the man in the white suit a look that said, *I told you I was expecting someone*, before she twirled around to greet the overdue detective—and to give him a piece of her mind.

"It's about ti—" Aidan's mouth dropped open in surprise. Before her stood an elderly, unshaven man dressed in tattered clothing that smelled as though he'd slept in a whiskey barrel. "—time." She got the word out in spite of her shock. "*Who* are *you*?"

The man, who was at least two inches shorter than she was, slapped a crisp clean business card into her hand and grinned. "Murph Peterson of the Pinkerton Detective Agency. Sorry to be late, but I've been on surveillance all night. I had to wait until my relief arrived, and of course he picked today to be late. We're on the verge of closing a big case for the railroad, and I couldn't chance leaving before he got there." He directed an annoyed frown past

211

her. "Of course, if I'd known Roger was going to be here, I wouldn't have had to come at all."

Bristling at Peterson's obvious displeasure at having been called away from something more important than guarding her, Aidan kept her tone cool. "I apologize for inconveniencing you, Mr. Peterson, however, as you can see, there is no one named Roger here. Now, if you don't mind, I'd like to . . ."

She realized Peterson wasn't listening to her; his attention was concentrated on some point behind her.

"I take it you haven't met my partner," he said, his grizzled face twisting in disgust. "Get over here, Smith! Why didn't you introduce yourself to Miss Donovan?"

"You only said to keep an eye on her until you got here," a deep, amused voice replied.

There was something vaguely familiar about that cultured accent. Aidan twisted around to face the newcomer, hoping that at least Smith was clean. "You!" she gasped, her eyes round with shock.

The tall Chinese man grinned mischievously. "Miss Donovan," he said, tipping his white hat.

"You're with Pinkerton? Why didn't you . . .?"

"If you recall, I tried, but you weren't exactly receptive to my effort," he explained, hefting her suitcase.

"But I thought—"

"I know," he said, offering her his arm. "Shall we, Miss Donovan? Now that we've been properly introduced."

Aidan couldn't help liking Roger, even though he had deliberately encouraged her misconception of him. She took his arm. "Why do I have the feeling I've just stepped into the devil's parlor?" she asked, glancing between the "derelict" and the "white slaver." "And what kind of name is Roger Smith for you? Shouldn't it be Chen or Ho or Li or something like that?"

Roger grinned. "Blame it on my English father, Miss

Donovan. But if it will make you more comfortable, feel free to call me Tuan the Dragon, the name I am known by in Chinatown."

"Tuan the *Dragon*?" Aidan was intrigued by this cocky young man with the naughty grin, however, she found it easy to believe that beneath his arrogant, teasing exterior, there did, indeed, lurk a deadly dragon that criminals would be wise to stay clear of.

"For the dragon he has tattooed on his right shoulder," Murph explained gruffly, hurrying them toward the street.

"I'll be glad to show it to you sometime," Roger said, wiggling his eyebrows up and down meaningfully. "Just say the word."

Laughing in spite of herself, Aidan shook her head. "You really are a devil, Mr. Smith, and I can already tell I'd better keep my eye on you."

"Don't pay him any heed, Miss Donovan," Murph advised. "Roger's one dragon who's all smoke and no fire when it comes to the ladies. His wife, Sing-Li, keeps his fangs clipped down to the nub—which is probably why she's given him four sons in as many years."

Aidan flashed a reproving once-over at the younger man. "You ought to be ashamed of yourself."

Roger shrugged and gave her a properly contrite, though somewhat saccharine, look. "What can I say? You can't blame a fellow for wanting to keep in practice, can you?"

Aidan threw back her head and laughed, the loneliness she'd known during the past weeks momentarily lifting. It felt good to just relax and have some fun. Since she'd last seen River, she'd been so depressed she'd wondered if she would ever feel like laughing again. Even when her story had appeared on the front page of the *Journal*, she had known no joy. Nor had her spirits risen when she had stopped over in San Antonio to see her parents, despite the fact that she'd finally been able to share her secret with them.

All that time her mind had dwelled on River and how much she missed him. Him and his stubborn, stubborn pride. A hundred times she'd thought about sending wiring William Randolph Hearst and telling him the deal was off, but each time she'd stopped herself, swearing she wouldn't go crawling back to River. He knew where she was going. If he wanted her, he could darned well come for her. For once, he would do the compromising! But the instant she'd made that vow, another wave of hopelessness would sweep over her because she knew he would never come to her.

By the time the unlikely threesome stepped out of the Southern Pacific station, Aidan felt as though she'd always known the two men. But the instant the carriage Roger hailed pulled up to the curb, both men seemed to change personalities.

His eyes becoming greedy little slits, Murph held out a grimy hand, palm up, to Roger. "My money, Mr. Dragon," he said.

Confused, Aidan looked from Murph to Roger, who had gone through a metamorphosis of his own. No longer the easygoing man she had taken an immediate liking to, he was now an evil, sinister being that would set the most courageous of hearts to beating frantically. "What's the—"

"Don't worry, my dear. This doesn't concern you," Roger crooned in a voice that fairly oozed with threatening undertones. He tightened his grip on the underside of her arm. His fingers digging almost painfully into her flesh, he plucked a few coins from his pocket and pitched them to Murph, sending the older man scrambling to the sidewalk to gather up his pay. "Here's your money, old man. You know how to get in touch with me if you come across other merchandise that might interest me. Now get lost. The smell of you makes me sick."

"Why would you talk to—"

"Imperial Hotel, driver," Roger ordered, cutting Aidan's words off and prodding her into the waiting carriage with an ungentlemanly shove. Leaping in beside her, he wrapped his arm around her shoulders and firmly drew her into his clutch, a triumphant smirk on his face.

After darting a quick, indecisive glance at Roger, the driver directed his gaze straight ahead. "Imperial Hotel," he repeated, cracking the whip above the rump of his horse.

Her eyes wide with indignation, Aidan pushed at Roger's hard chest. "Get your hands off me!"

"Struggling will do you no good, my dear!" he said.

Bewildered, frightened, and angry all at the same time, Aidan wrenched herself away from him. "What's the meaning of this? Where are we going? I thought—"

Roger cupped her chin in his hard grip and dragged her face to within inches of his. "You'll keep quiet, if you know what's good for you," he advised through his teeth, his words so low that she doubted she'd heard what he'd said. "You've just been publicly bought and paid for."

"Bought an—" Her words were cut off by the tightening of his hold on her cheeks.

"Unless you want to be killed before the night's over, I suggest you let me do the talking from now on," he said in that same deadly whisper. "Do you understand?"

Her brown eyes almost black with fear, Aidan nodded. What had she gotten herself into? Had one of the crime families of Chinatown learned of her purpose and sent a man to pose as the Pinkerton detective who was supposed to meet her? Or worse still, were the Pinkerton detectives receiving money from the opium and white slavery lords of Chinatown for protecting their evil operations?

Well, whatever was going on, she had no intention of becoming one of their victims.

She shot an apprehensive glance at the driver, then eyed Tuan the Dragon — she could no longer think of him by any other name. "If you think I'm going to . . ."

Then Tuan — or Roger, or whatever his name was — had done the most curious thing. He gave her an understanding wink and grinned ever so slightly. He pressed his cheek to hers. "We were told you were the consummate actress, Miss Donovan," he said, barely moving his lips. "Well, you'd better get into character — and stay there — until we can speak without witnesses. Otherwise, you could end up without your story, and we both could wind up floating in the bay. *No one* can be trusted. Now do you understand how important it is that you do as I say?"

An act! He was just playing a part. Her fear and panic combined into anger. "Yes, I understand," she replied, her tone scathing but low, "but it would have been nice if you'd let me in on what you were doing."

"There was no time. Everyone has ears."

The instant the hotel came into view, Aidan's heart leaped. She'd planned to stay in a hotel in the white section of the city, not right in the middle of Chinatown, where they obviously were. Could she have misinterpreted Roger's words and expression. He was capable of switching personalities so smoothly, she didn't know what to believe. He might have momentarily slipped back into his "Roger" persona to guarantee her compliance until he had her in the heart of the Chinese quarter where she would be entirely at his mercy.

She looked up and down the twisting cobbled street where the carriage had stopped. Everywhere she looked there was color — bright oranges, reds, yellows, blues, purples and greens, giving an exciting, festive air to everything. In front of and between the oddly tiered buildings

216

with upward curving roofs hung hundreds of flags and signs on which strange, unfamiliar symbols and pictures were painted. Evidently these announced the exotic products being sold in the stalls on the sidewalk below.

Roger stepped out of the cab, gave a generous number of coins to the driver, then offered his hand up to Aidan.

She looked hesitantly down at it, then to the driver, who deliberately kept his gaze directed straight ahead, though she had an uncanny feeling that he was very aware of everything that was happening between her and Roger.

Maybe this time she had gone too far in her pursuit of a story. Perhaps she should call off the whole thing—now, while she was physically free of Roger for a moment. She could tell the driver to take her back to the train station. Maybe this was just too big a chance to take.

If she trusted Roger to be who he'd first claimed to be and was wrong, she might never see her family or River again, much less write this story. On the other hand, if she was right, this story would prove to the world that the fame she had earned as a Rough Rider was justified and not just a fluke. Even more important, if she stayed, she'd be able to get the Lakotas the newspaper coverage and aid she'd promised River, proving to him once and for all she didn't welch on an agreement.

Sucking in a deep, stabilizing breath, Aidan took Roger's hand and stepped from the carriage, knowing that she was trusting him with far more than her hand. Her very life could be at stake.

Chapter Fifteen

"Now, suppose you tell me what this is all about!" Aidan demanded, after the carriage pulled away from the curb.

"Inside," he answered, placing his hand at the small of her back to guide her into the hotel.

She dug in her heels and shook her head. "Not on your life, Mr. Smith—or whatever your name is. I refuse to budge another step until you explain to me what you're doing! And if you persist in keeping me in the dark, then I'm going to scream. Do *you* understand?" she asked, throwing his words back at him.

Roger looked from left to right, as if gauging his next words. "All right, let's take a stroll. Though, I must tell you, if you persist in balking every time I give you an order, we don't have a chance in hell of pulling this off."

Retaining his hold on Aidan, he handed her luggage to the doorman, then gave him some hasty instructions. When he turned back to her, he offered his arm in a more gentlemanly manner, and started walking up the sidewalk. "First of all, you've got to understand that there's more at stake here than just Hearst's newspaper story. There's no room in our operation for anyone who can't—or won't—follow orders on a split second's notice."

"And *you'd* better understand, I can follow orders as well as anyone," Aidan interrupted haughtily. "*If* I trust the person who is giving them—and *if* I'm kept fully apprised. However, so far you haven't convinced me that I

218

should trust you, Mr. Smith, and until you do, I have no intention of —"

"From now on, you must refer to me only as Tuan," he hissed, his alert gaze zigzagging from left to right as he studied the crowd to see if anyone had heard her.

Immediately assuming he'd seen something that related to her situation, Aidan scrutinized the area around her, halfway expecting to spot her first real lead. But she didn't notice anything out of the ordinary—at least not on the main street running through the middle of Chinatown.

Really looking at her surroundings for the first time, Aidan had the distinct feeling she'd fallen down the rabbit hole in Lewis Carroll's *Alice in Wonderland*. This place was like nothing she'd ever seen. An explosion of bright colors and oddly shaped buildings, the busy avenue throbbed with life. Everywhere she looked, Chinese men, each with a long black queue hanging down his back, were scurrying along the crowded sidewalk. They moved in and out of the gaudy pagodas and temples that rose up above them, stopping to visit with friends and barter with the merchants in the shops and stalls that claimed every available space on both sides of the street.

Above the ordinary sounds of the street she heard a cacophony of laughter and voices speaking in a dozen different dialects, as the people went about their daily activities.

Through all this colorful bustle of activity, white tourists casually strolled, laughing and talking, their eyes wide with wonder, as they absorbed the sights and sounds and smells of the street, stopping frequently to make purchases in shops displaying jade and ivory carvings, rose and coral crystal, bronze and porcelain, and exotic brocades and embroideries.

"What is it? Did you see something?" she whispered,

leaning closer to him, carefully examining the painted balconies above the street, fascinated by the wind bells and flowered lanterns she saw hanging there.

"Perhaps," Roger said thoughtfully, his gaze on an alleyway leading off the other side of the street. "But whether I did or not, you've got to remember you're out of your element here, Miss Donovan. Everywhere you go, eyes may be watching you, ears may be listening to what you say. That's why I had to 'pay' Murph for bringing you to me."

"Couldn't you have let me know what you were doing?" she asked, still not convinced his intentions were as honorable as he pretended.

"There was no time. When we realized who the cab driver was, we had to act fast or you would have been exposed."

"Who was the driver?"

"He's one of the On Leong Tong's informers."

"What or who is the On Leong Tong?"

"One of Chinatown's most powerful societies—rather like a huge gang. Their people are everywhere, and they pay them for information. Policemen let them know when one of their opium palaces is scheduled to be raided, and men like the driver keep their eyes open for young, attractive women who are traveling alone. When he picks up such a fare, it's a simple matter to report where she's staying to the lords of the tong, who in turn send one of their people to lure her into their clutches. Now do you understand why we came here instead of going to *your* hotel?"

Aidan nodded her head, amazed. "And why you wanted him to believe I was your property."

Roger shrugged. "Not that it will stop them from trying to steal you from me if you are seen alone."

A panicked look skittered across her face. "What's to

stop them from trying when you're with me."

Roger patted her hand, which was resting on his arm. "Don't worry. I'm known here for my skills at hand-to-hand fighting and with the knife. No one will bother you as long as you're with me. Besides, Murph and another man will always be nearby, watching out for you and backing me up, though you won't know where they are most of the time."

Somewhat mollified by Roger's explanation of his behavior, her reporter's curiosity began to be piqued. "Does the On Leong Society control all the crime in Chinatown?"

"No. The fighting tongs have their own areas of expertise," he declared bitterly. "The On Leong Tong deals mainly in slave girls, while the Wa Ting Shan Tong runs the brothels. The Hip Shing Tong handles the gambling clubs. And other tongs have taken over some neighborhoods where the peaceful associations aren't very strong. Of course, the most powerful tongs demand a percentage of any profits the small neighborhoods produce—in exchange for protection from the other tongs. So, in effect, three tongs pretty much control all the crime in Chinatown."

"Doesn't it bother you to be working against your own people?" she asked, her journalist's mind teeming with questions.

Roger looked at her, his black eyes revealing just a fleeting glimpse of sadness. Then it was replaced by a devilish sparkle. "Men who feed on the helplessness and weakness of others aren't my people. Or my wife's. Or those of most of the Chinese living here. Our people are gentle, hardworking men and women who would like to see an end to the tongs. Now," he said, obviously ready to change the subject, "have I told you enough to get you to go back to the hotel?"

Aidan smiled. "Almost. But you still haven't told me how you plan to sneak me into a situation where I can get my story."

Roger shook his head, and continued walking. "After I show off my new acquisition—you—around town, dangle the merchandise under their noses so to speak, we'll put you into an auction and 'sell' you to the highest bidder."

She came to an abrupt halt. "You'll what?"

"Don't worry. Mr. Hearst has given our man adequate funds to guarantee he won't be outbid. Besides, Murph and I will be with you every minute, so you should be perfectly safe."

"*Should* be?" Her face twisted into a decidedly uneasy frown. "I'm beginning to like this idea less and less."

"I told them this would be too dangerous for a woman, but my superiors said Mr. Hearst insisted you would face any danger to get this story. I guess he has an exaggerated opinion of your bravery and ability."

Aidan's mouth curved upward into a scolding grin. "You think you've got me figured out, don't you, Mr. Smith?"

"Tuan," he corrected her with that impish smile he could turn off and on at will. "And I have no idea what you're talking about."

Turning him around, she started walking toward the hotel. "But under *no* circumstances am I going to spend the night in a hotel room with you."

Roger gave her hand a brotherly pat. "That's where Sing-Li draws the line, too. I told her it was strictly business, but she swore she'd give *me* the business if I wasn't home at night."

"Well, good for her! I'd heard that Chinese men give all the orders in their families, and that obeying them is a woman's only purpose in life."

"Oh, I give the orders, all right." He gave her a wink.

222

"It's just that Sing-Li gives them back to me—in no uncertain terms. I guess that's what I get for marrying a girl born in the United States instead of bringing one over from the old country!"

"Then you were both born here?"

Roger nodded absently, his attention suddenly focused ahead of him.

Becoming accustomed to his changing of roles, Aidan looked up just as a black and red satin-clad Chinese man stepped down from an elaborate rickshaw in front of the hotel.

Watching him, Roger spoke out of the corner of his mouth, his lips barely moving. "Better get ready to go into our act. It looks like the driver's already gotten word to the tong that I've acquired some excellent new 'merchandise.' They've sent Chu Wong to barter."

"How do you know?" Aidan asked, lowering her voice.

"Because he's one of the On Leong Tong's most influential slave dealers. Are you ready to meet him?"

Alarm shot through Aidan. It was one thing to talk about this, but to actually go through with it was another thing. "How am I supposed to act?" she asked, slowing Roger's step with a nervous tug on his arm. "What do I say?"

"Just follow my lead. You're a young woman on holiday alone. We met in the train station, and I offered to show you Chinatown. You're not yet aware of my *true* intentions," he explained. Then he smiled and shook his head understandingly. "You know, it's still not too late to change your mind and go back home. Let Hearst get someone else for this if he wants the story so much."

Aidan drew in a deep, fortifying breath, then gave him an uncertain smile. "And miss all this excitement? You just lead the way, Mr. Dragon. I'm ready."

"Good girl," he said, squeezing her hand reassuringly.

"By the way, how do you feel about going by the name Barbara—until we wind this up?"

"Whatever you say."

Roger arched his eyebrows. "Oh?"

"Within limits!"

River stepped out of the train depot in Buffalo Gap, South Dakota, and raised his hands over his head in a long, lazy stretch. He inhaled deeply, filling his lungs to capacity, then released a long, relieved sigh. Already, it was starting to feel like home. The air was cleaner, and he was sure he could smell the fresh scent of the open plains, despite the fumes of the train and 'civilization.' Of course, the real aroma he longed for was still several hours away by stagecoach. But for now this was fine. Just fine.

He'd been gone too long. First, all those lonely years at school in the East, getting the education that was supposed to help him work for the People; then the frustrating months in Washington with Roosevelt, attempting to make contacts who would help; and finally the wasted weeks in Texas and Florida and Cuba, being a part of the Rough Riders. And what progress had he made in all that time? None!

But now he was back, and if he had his way, he wouldn't ever leave again. He had work to do here, and here he was going to stay.

"At least she was right about that," he said aloud. His elated mood immediately deteriorated, as it had every time Aidan had entered his mind since she'd left him in Florida.

Damn her! Where was she? What was she doing? Was she safe? Or had she gotten herself into trouble? A knot of dread clenched his belly. He'd read a number of news-

ACCEPT YOUR FREE GIFT AND EXPERIENCE MORE OF THE PASSION AND ADVENTURE YOU LIKE IN A HISTORICAL ROMANCE

Zebra Romances are the finest novels of their kind and are written with the adult woman in mind. All of our books are written by authors who really know how to weave tales of romantic adventure in the historical settings you love.

Because our readers tell us these books sell out very fast in the stores, Zebra has made arrangements for you to receive at home the four newest titles published each month. You'll never miss a title and home delivery is so convenient. With your first shipment we'll even send you a FREE Zebra Historical Romance as our gift just for trying our home subscription service. No obligation.

BIG SAVINGS AND FREE HOME DELIVERY

Each month, the Zebra Home Subscription Service will send you the four newest titles as soon as they are published. (We ship these books to our subscribers even before we send them to the stores.) You may preview them *Free* for 10 days. If you like them as much as we think you will, you'll pay just $3.50 each and *save $1.80 each month* off the cover price. *AND you'll also get FREE HOME DELIVERY.* There is never a charge for shipping, handling or postage and there is no minimum you must buy. If you decide not to keep any shipment, simply return it within 10 days, no questions asked, and owe nothing.

MAIL IN THE COUPON BELOW TODAY

To get your Free ZEBRA HISTORICAL ROMANCE fill out the coupon below and send it in today. As soon as we receive the coupon, we'll send your first month's books to preview Free for 10 days along with your **FREE NOVEL.**

─ FREE ─
BOOK CERTIFICATE

ZEBRA HOME SUBSCRIPTION SERVICE, INC.

YES! Please start my subscription to Zebra Historical Romances and send me my free Zebra Novel along with my first month's Romances. I understand that I may preview these four new Zebra Historical Romances Free for 10 days. If I'm not satisfied with them I may return the four books within 10 days and owe nothing. Otherwise I will pay just $3.50 each; a total of $14.00 (a $15.80 value—I save $1.80). Then each month I will receive the 4 newest titles as soon as they come off the press for the same 10 day Free preview and low price. I may return any shipment and I may cancel this arrangement at any time. There is no minimum number of books to buy and there are no shipping, handling or postage charges. Regardless of what I do, the FREE book is mine to keep.

Name _____
                    (Please Print)

Address _____ Apt. # _____

City _____ State _____ Zip _____

Telephone ( ) _____

Signature _____
                    (if under 18, parent or guardian must sign)

Terms and offer subject to change without notice.

4-89

paper articles about what could happen to young women traveling alone in San Francisco, and the feeling that Aidan needed him had begun to plague him. It would be just like her to wander about the city without an escort, deliberately leaving herself open to all sorts of dangers in her quest for that story. He could even imagine her getting it into her head that she was perfectly capable of taking care of herself on the streets at night. Well, from now on, she was William Randolph Hearst's problem, not his.

Determined to stop thinking about Aidan, River stomped off the sidewalk and crossed the street, directing his steps toward the Wells Fargo stagecoach office. Let her find out the hard way that she doesn't know everything. He was through worrying about her.

But the instant he had that thought, a drawing he'd seen in a newspaper the day before flashed across his mind, and he stopped in the middle of the street. It had depicted a lovely young girl languishing on a divan, surrounded by leering, evil-looking Chinese men, one of them holding a long, smoking pipe to her lips. The caption beneath it had read: "HOW MANY MORE OF OUR INNOCENT YOUNG WOMEN MUST BE DRAGGED INTO WHITE SLAVERY BY THE EVILS OF THE CHINAMAN'S OPIUM BEFORE SOMETHING IS DONE TO SAVE THEM?"

At the time, he had tried to dismiss the entire thing as nothing but sensationalistic journalism. After all, it had been in a Hearst paper. But try as he had, he just couldn't shake the memory of that girl in the picture. Time after time, her face had come back to nag at his thoughts. Only now it wasn't a stranger's eyes that stared forlornly out at him from the page. Now, he saw Aidan on that divan. Her brown eyes. Her frightened face. Aidan helpless. Aidan lifting that pipe to her lips. Aidan being held

225

prisoner by men intending to use her for evil purposes. Aidan. Aidan. Aidan.

"Damn her!" He wiped his hands over his eyes as if he could erase the visions once and for all.

An automobile horn blared loudly at River, startling him out of his reverie. "Get out of the street!" a man yelled as River looked up and stared dazedly at the approaching machine. "Hey, Indian! Why don't you go back to the reservation where you belong?" the driver laughed as he maneuvered the shiny new vehicle around River. "You people aren't ready for modern progress."

Not moving, River stared after the retreating automobile, breathing in the stink of its exhaust fumes. Not even this close to home was he able to escape reminders of how much the whites had taken from the People. Now the air that had seemed so sweet only moments before was sour and bitter. It reeked with the stench of the white man's "progress." Even here, in his beloved home state, there was no escaping it.

Shaking his head, he continued toward the Wells Fargo stagecoach office. If only Aidan had remained true to her word and had written the story she'd promised, maybe that would have helped to show people like the automobile driver what "progress" was doing, and had already done, to the land and to the People. Of course, she'd vowed she was still going to write the exposé, but he didn't believe her. He knew her too well. Once she was through in San Francisco, something else would strike her fancy, and she'd be off on the scent of a new story.

He wrenched open the door to the stagecoach office, then stopped. Dammit! Who was he fooling? He had no one but himself to blame if she never did the exposé. They'd had an agreement, and he'd just let her walk away before she'd fulfilled her end of it.

Dropping his hold on the handle, he turned back to the

street, letting the door slam shut behind him. *I may not have been thinking clearly in Florida, but I am now. Aidan Donovan owes me that exposé, and she's not going to get out of writing it!*

His expression hardened with angry determination, River strode down the sidewalk and burst into the telegraph office two doors away. "I want to send two wires, one to Pine Ridge, South Dakota, and the other to San Antonio, Texas."

"Are you sure you remember everything I told you?" Roger asked Aidan anxiously as he held open the door for her to step inside the Celestial Flower Mah-Jongg house.

She gave him a shaky smile and nodded her head. "Just don't let me out of your sight."

"Not for a second," he promised, tucking her hand securely in the bend of his elbow and covering it with one of his own.

"Then let's go, because I don't mind telling you, I'm ready to put this story behind me."

Roger spoke in Chinese to a young boy who shuffled up to take his hat.

"Ah!" The servant grinned broadly, bending forward in several quick successive bows, obviously having been told to expect them. Turning on his soft slippers, he started toward the back of the dark, smoke-filled room, obviously expecting them to follow.

"This is it," Roger said out of the corner of his mouth, his glance moving lazily from side to side as he surveyed the curious occupants of the room, in the same manner of a king looking over his subjects.

It really was amazing; he could become a completely different person by just changing his mannerisms. His performance bolstered Aidan's confidence. She again noticed that there was something positively deadly about his Tuan persona, and she was definitely glad he was on her side.

Taking care to let her eyelids droop as though she could barely keep them open, as Roger had instructed her to do so she would look slightly drugged, Aidan glanced idly around the crowded room to see if she could spot Murph—who was supposed to be here, disguised as a Chinese man.

Throughout the club, men of all sizes and ages sat hunched over tables, four to a group, their attention on the small rectangular mah-jongg tiles in racks before them. But try as she might, Aidan couldn't spot Murph. Of course, his disguise would be a very good one, even in a room as dimly lit as this, so it was unlikely that she'd be able to identify him. Still, she would feel a lot better if she just knew for certain he was there.

Suddenly, the back of a man's head caught her attention. It wasn't Murph. He was too tall and lean to be Murph. But he wasn't Chinese either. Not only was he dressed in Western clothing instead of the loose-fitting tunic the other gamblers wore, his short-cut hair was not black.

Wondering if the man was an extra Pinkerton, she nudged Roger, indicating the man in the corner by raising her eyebrows questioningly toward him.

Following the direction of her gaze, Roger shook his head. "Someone out slumming for the evening," he whispered out of the corner of his mouth.

That made sense. She'd seen whites going into all the clubs they'd passed on the way to the Celestial Flower. Still, she couldn't escape the odd feeling that this man's presence wasn't coincidental.

Before she could give the matter more thought, they had reached a door at the back of the club. Roger gave

228

her hand an encouraging squeeze as the servant tapped lightly on the wood. A small window in the door opened to expose dark slanted eyes, which glanced suspiciously over her, then Roger, before disappearing as the window slammed shut.

The sounds of locks being released clanged in Aidan's head, and she instinctively glanced back over her shoulder in a last try to locate Murph. If she could just see for herself that he was there . . . Her cursory gaze went directly to the mysterious Caucasian man.

He was watching her!

Before she could clearly discern his features, however, he quickly ducked his head. But it hadn't been her imagination. He had been watching her! And in that brief instant when their eyes had accidentally met, she'd had the oddest feeling that she recognized him, from another time, another place. Maybe it was the way his eyes had flashed with hatred before he had looked away. But who?

Laughing inwardly, she told herself, *Next thing you know, you're going to start seeing ghosts and dragons jumping out of the woodwork!*

"Ah, Tuan, my friend, it is good to see you," a man said in English. "Come in, come in."

Aidan immediately turned her heavy-lidded eyes on the short, very obese Oriental man with a long drooping mustache that reached past his chin—all of them. She forced a sleepy smile.

Roger greeted the heavy man in an equally friendly manner, though both men watched each other warily. "Gim Hsu, may I present Miss Barbara Grisham from Dallas, Texas. I have been showing her the sights of Chinatown, and of course I wouldn't let her get away without seeing the dream rooms of the Celestial Flower, and perhaps experiencing a special dream of her own."

"Ah." Gim nodded his round head eagerly. "In that

case, I will take you to our most exotic room, so that your dream experience will truly be one you will remember when you return to Texas."

As Aidan nodded drowsily to Gim, a shudder of panic tripped up her spine. *This is crazy,* she thought, tightening her grip on Roger's arm. *What if I go into that room and never came out again?* For all she knew, this evil-looking Chinese man had already had his henchmen do away with Murph, and he was now waiting for the chance to overcome Roger.

"Perhaps it would be better if I just observe this evening, Mr. Hsu," she said, slurring her words as Roger had instructed. Her eyelids lowered sleepily. "I'm feeling rather lightheaded already. It must have been something I ate," she said innocently, pretending not to notice the sly grins Roger and Gim exchanged.

"Of course," Gim responded ingratiatingly. "I understand. Our *unique* foods sometimes affect people that way. But I assure you, it will pass." Turning his back, he slowly lumbered ahead of them, opening the first door on his left. "The Celestial Flower has dreams for all. In this room, friends can gather to dream together."

Peeking inside the dim room, Aidan saw four men, all lying back on divans, their eyes closed. They held the bowls of their very long-stemmed pipes over small lamps, taking frequent drags on the mouthpieces.

Her alert mind began cataloguing every detail of the opium den so she could record what she'd seen when she got back to her room: the sickly sweet smell of the opium, the hazy air, the ornately carved pipes. "Do only men use your facilities?"

"Oh, no," Gim said, quietly closing the door of the dream room and continuing down the hallway. "We have a special room where ladies can dream in private. Perhaps you would like to see?"

His voice was absolutely oily with friendliness, and a feeling of hatred and nausea rocked through Aidan. "Oh, may I?"

"We call this our Celestial Maiden Room," he explained, opening the door wide enough for Aidan to see in, and to recognize the heavy scent of the opium smoke that filled the room.

Within, in various stages of semiconsciousness, half a dozen young Chinese women reclined on upholstered sofas. She was certain these were the "slave" girls Roger had told her Gim Hsu kept on hand for the convenience of the men who frequented his gambling club. Bought in China for a hundred dollars, they were smuggled into San Francisco to be used in brothels or sold to new masters for several times that amount.

Aidan's heart filled with compassion and guilt as her gaze slid over the dozing girls. The oldest couldn't be more than sixteen years old, and here they were, addicted to opium and being used to pleasure old men.

Now, more than ever, Aidan was sure she had chosen to do the right thing when she'd come to California. These girls might not be white as Hearst had expected, but they were human beings; someone had to speak out in their defense, expose the awful truth about their miserable existences.

My God! How can this be happening in this day and time? Slavery has been illegal for almost thirty-five years. Even River would be moved by the sight of them. She immediately wished he had come with her, as she had every minute of every day since they'd separated in Florida. Maybe seeing something like this would help him understand that Indians weren't the only oppressed people in the United States who needed help.

"How do they sleep so peacefully?" she asked Tuan. "It's as though their dreams have carried them to heaven.

231

Do you think it would be possible for me to speak with them to learn how I can have this beautiful sleep?"

"None of my 'daughters' speak English, my dear," Gim Hsu interrupted, his voice a seductive croon. He drew his tongue over his thick lips and ran his gaze over Aidan's body. "But, if you wish, I will be most honored to guide you into your heavenly dream myself."

Swallowing back the revulsion Hsu's perusal caused to rise in her throat, Aidan looked at Roger questioningly, concentrating on making her expression curious but hesitant. "I don't know. . . ."

"Perhaps, Miss Grisham would be more comfortable if I were to act as her guide the first time," he said to Gim, his tone leaving no doubt about who she belonged to.

His fat face bobbing up and down, Gim covered his disappointment with an insincere smile, but he didn't bother to hide the vengeful look in his black eyes. "Since this is a special occasion, it will please me greatly if you will grace the room I ordinarily reserve for my own private use."

"Your generosity is most appreciated," Roger responded, his smile every bit as artificial as Hsu's — and just as frightening.

Aware that her hesitation was no longer an act, Aidan allowed Roger to guide her to the last of the doors that opened off the narrow hallway. When she stepped into the room, she was astonished by its lavish decor: gold brocade covering the walls, an elaborate Oriental rug, ornate tables and lamps, plush upholstered chairs and chaise lounges. At the center of all the opulence was a large bed, large enough for several people, and covered in red.

"I pray my humble offering pleases you, Miss Grisham," Gim crooned. "And now I leave you to your pleasant dreams."

The instant she heard the door click shut behind Gim

Hsu, Aidan's lips split into a triumphant grin and she spun around to face Roger. "We—"

He frowned harshly and gave an almost indiscernible shake of his head. "There's nothing to fear, Barbara," he soothed, advancing on her. Clutching her shoulders he walked her to the bed. Bending his head to "kiss" her ear, he whispered, "Remember what I told you about eyes. They're all around us. Now is the time to do some acting, because if they see anything that looks suspicious, they won't hesitate to kill both of us. Do you understand?" he asked, lowering her to the bed.

"Now just lie back and let me take you into the land of flower dreams," he said, lifting a golden, long-stemmed pipe from the table beside the bed. He lifted a small dish of something that looked like wet clay and held it out to her. "This, my dear Barbara, is what dreams are made of."

Fascinated, Aidan watched as Roger inserted a long needle into the clay, then used the needle to poke and pack it around the bottom and inside rim of the pipe. Placing two fingers over the bowl of the pipe to keep the soft material in place, he withdrew the needle. He then inserted the bowl of the pipe into the flame of the tiny lamp on the bedside table. When steam began to rise from the pipe, he took a deep drag on the mouthpiece and sat down beside Aidan on the bed, holding the pipe stem to her mouth. "Now you."

Freezing, she shot him a quick look of panic. She didn't think she could do it!

"Trust me, Barbara," he said, urging her to take the pipe. "You know, I would never hurt you."

Praying she was doing the right thing, Aidan took a deep breath, then leaned forward and placed her lips on the tip of the pipe stem.

Chapter Sixteen

River lurched awake, his heart pounding frantically. Looking around the dimly lit coach of the train and seeing only sleeping passengers, he shook his head with disgust. A dream! It was just a dream!

Snatching a handkerchief from his pocket, he wiped the sweat from his forehead and forced himself to sit back in his seat. Unable to close his eyes for fear the nightmare would return, he stared out the window at the darkness, though he couldn't see any of the Wyoming landscape. Not that he would have noticed it anyway.

If he could just get some sleep. It might make the seemingly endless trip to San Francisco pass more quickly. Then maybe he'd be able to shake the desperate feeling that Aidan needed him, and that he wasn't going to get to her in time to save her—which he'd finally admitted to himself was his reason for going to San Francisco. She needed him . . . and he needed her.

His eyelids drifted downward. If only he didn't have to spend endless hours doing nothing but staring out the train window. If only . . . His eyes popped open. If only the nightmare would go away . . .

"Doesn't it bother you to have Roger doing this kind of

work?" Aidan asked as she tucked an errant strand of red hair beneath the black, braided wig she wore.

"I suppose I would worry less if he owned a laundry, but because my husband's work is the most important thing to him, after his family, it is also most important to me," Roger's petite, soft-spoken wife, Sing-Li, answered. She grinned impishly as she stood back to check Aidan's servant-girl disguise. "Of course, if he did not bring you to stay in our house so that he could protect you and I might know you, it is possible I would be jealous of all the time he is spending with another woman."

Aidan smiled and kissed Sing-Li on the cheek. "I'm glad he brought me here too. I've loved being here. In fact, I'm the one who is jealous. You have everything. A man you love, one who loves you more than anything in the world, and your four beautiful little boys." Tears welled in her eyes. "Do you know how fortunate you are?"

"Yes," Sing-Li replied, her round face twisting with compassion. "But you are fortunate too. You are a very talented writer, and you are free to travel all over the world."

Aidan nodded. "Yes, I'm fortunate." She was unable to hide the note of sadness in her tone. "I have everything I ever wanted—at least, everything I thought I wanted. It's just that . . ."

"Just that?"

Aidan looked at Sing-Li, her expression forlorn. "It's just that I now realize it's not enough. What good is all I've done if there's no one to share it with?"

She spun away from Sing-Li and took an embarrassed swipe at her watery eyes. "I must sound awfully greedy to you. But from the moment I first came into your home and saw the love you and Roger share, I knew I'd been seeking the wrong thing. Fame and success won't bring me the kind of happiness you and Roger have."

"Does the man you love not love you in return?"

Startled, Aidan whirled around to face Sing-Li. "What makes you think there's a man?"

"It is not so easy to hide a sad heart from those who care about you. Perhaps, it will help if you tell me about him."

"There's really not much to say," Aidan declared morosely, forcing back tears that lumped in her throat. "I thought he loved me. I really did. But I was wrong. He only cared about what I could do for him."

"Are you so sure?"

Aidan nodded, her lips turned downward in a bitter line. "Oh, I'm sure all right. I tried to work things out before I came to California, but he wouldn't listen. He just let me walk away without even trying to stop me. I ask you, is that the way a man who loves you acts?"

"Sometimes men in love do very foolish things. Such as letting the one they love go because of stubborn pride. I think you must give him another chance. Does he know where you are?"

"Just that I'm in San Francisco, but not what I'm working on or where I'm staying," Aidan said, the tenuous bubble of optimism Sing-Li's words had created now bursting.

"If he does not know where you are, he cannot come to you. Therefore, you must go to him and tell him how you feel."

"I can't, Sing-Li. I can't go to him. He doesn't have any use for me. He thinks I used him to get what I wanted."

"Are you ladies through in there?" Roger called through the door. "Aidan and I must be leaving so we can get to the Imperial in time for her to change her clothing before we go out."

"I'm ready," Aidan replied, wiping the last of her tears

236

on the coal scuttle-shaped sleeve of her gray tunic. Giving her appearance a last-minute check, she smoothed the hair of her wig back over her ears to the braid that began at her nape and hung down her back past her waist. Of course, she didn't really look Chinese, but with her head bowed, and by copying a servant girl's timid little running steps, she had been able to travel back and forth along the streets of Chinatown between the Imperial Hotel and Roger's house for over a week without being noticed. Convinced her disguise was intact, Aidan opened the door and smiled. Flattening her palms together, she bowed low and said, "Most honorable master, your humble servant is ready."

"Then let's be on our way. If everything goes as planned tonight, this will be the last time you'll have to go into an opium den." He bent low and kissed his wife's forehead. "Don't wait up for us. We may be late."

"You be careful," Sing-Li ordered, a worried look skittering across her brow. "Both of you. And I *will* wait up until I know you are both home safe."

Aidan gave the petite woman a hug. "Thanks for everything, Sing-Li. Now, Mr. Dragon, please let's go so we can get this over with. After spending a week pretending to be smoking opium every night, I'm beginning to feel as if it's all been real. By the way, what *do* you put in the pipe?"

"Take my word for it, you don't want to know," Roger said with a wry grin. "Just remember, it's nothing that will harm you."

Giving him a doubtful glance, Aidan left the room, laughing. "Well, we'll let it drop for now, but when this is all over, you *are* going to tell me."

Plopping a straw, cone-shaped hat on over her wig, she lowered her head so that her chin was practically on her collarbone; then with tiny, quick steps, she shuffled out the front door.

Once outside, Aidan peeked out from under the brim of the hat. Spying Murph, disguised as a Chinese vegetable peddler, she relaxed, relieved to see that her "bodyguard" had again arrived in time to insure a safe walk down the eight blocks to the back entrance of the Imperial Hotel. Glancing from left to right, she started out, Sing-Li's advice ringing in her ears. *You must go to him.*

River let the door to the Willow Boarding House for Ladies swing shut behind him, his brow furrowing deeply. His worst nightmares had just multiplied tenfold. Aidan had never arrived at the Willow.

He rechecked the name and address Clay Donovan had wired him after he'd been contacted. Not that they were going to be different than they'd been before he had gone inside. Still . . . He looked back over his shoulder at the numbers above the door—just to be sure.

"Damn!" He crumpled the telegram and stuffed it into his pocket. *Where the hell do I go from here?*

"Well, well, well." The masculine voice came from his right. "I knew if I was patient, you'd eventually show up out here. What took you so long, Lieutenant?"

River looked up to see a slender man sauntering toward him. "Are you speaking to me?"

The stranger gave him a cocky grin. "You've got that right, Lieutenant Blue Eagle."

"I'm afraid you have me at a disadvantage. Have we met?"

"Not exactly, but I know all about you. You're the man who helped Miss High-'n'-Mighty Aidan Donovan sneak into the Rough Riders—and then make a fool of me."

Instinct told River who this was. Unless he was mistaken, this pushy man was the reporter who had publicly

238

confronted Aidan at the Tampa pier, and had tried to make a name for himself by taking the thunder out of her story and stealing it for himself. "Somehow, I have the feeling you didn't need Miss Donovan's help to accomplish that feat." River turned and started across the street. He didn't have time to waste on scum.

"Aren't you interested in knowing where she is, *and* what she's been up to since she got to San Francisco," the reporter called after him.

River froze in his tracks. His fists clenching open and shut, he slowly turned and faced the man. "If you have something to say, I'd suggest you say it—and fast."

The reporter's mouth twisted into a goading smirk. "I thought that would get your attention." Obviously taking pleasure in making River wait, he dipped his fingers into his breast pocket and pulled out a cigarette. Taking his time in lighting it, he drew in smoke, then lazily exhaled.

"Not so fast, Lieutenant. You and your girlfriend cost me a shot at working for the *Journal*, so I figure you owe me. How much is it worth to you to know where she is and what she's been doing this past week?"

River's mouth stretched in a sinister grimace, and he took a slow, stalking step toward the man. "If you mean to get money from me you're wasting your time. I don't buy information or anything else from slime like you."

Instinctively moving back as River joined him on the sidewalk, the reporter did his best to look unintimidated. "Have it your way. I just figured you'd be interested in knowing she's sunk to a new low. First an Indian, now a Chinaman." He shook his head in pretended amazement. "Next thing you know, she'll be sleeping with a Ni—"

River grabbed him by his shirtfront and lifted him off his feet, bringing the reporter's startled face up to his own. "I'm warning you, if you know where Aidan Donovan is, you'd better tell me!" he snarled through

239

bared teeth. "Or I'm going to spread that filthy mouth of yours all over this sidewalk."

"All right, all right," the reporter choked, his eyes bulging with panic. "I'll tell you."

River lowered him to the sidewalk, but retained a grip on his shirtfront. "Start talking."

Breathing easier now, the out-of-work newspaperman regained a bit of his gall. "I don't want your money. I just want a story from you. Now that she's two-timing you with someone else, I figured you'd be more than anxious to give me the dope on how she really got into the Rough Riders."

River tightened his hold on the shirt and jerked upward. "Where is she?"

"What about my story?"

"Unless you want to write your own obituary for tomorrow's paper, I suggest you tell me what you know before I really get mad."

River's features hardened, and even the obtuse reporter could see that he was balanced precariously on the edge of reason. And it suddenly came to the man that he had more to gain than he'd imagined. By siccing the Indian on that Donovan bitch, he could definitely land the kind of story William Randolph Hearst would pay well to have. A double murder resulting from a sordid love triangle—a white woman and an Indian and a Chinaman. Such a story would make him more famous than a Donovan's story about how Aidan sneaked into the Rough Riders. Of course, he still needed that one too, to reestablish his credibility.

"Okay, okay," the reporter said, holding out his hands in surrender. "I'll tell you all I know, but I hope you'll remember where you got your information when you get ready to spill your guts about her."

River's lips opened to expose clenched white teeth. "I'm

warning you!"

"She was met at the train station by a tall, smooth-looking Chinaman when she arrived in San Francisco last week. Obviously, he was expecting her, because she got into a cab with him right away."

"Where did you get this information?"

"I was on the same train. I followed her from the East. She cost me my job with her Cuba story, so I figured I'd let her lead me to a big story. Besides, I knew you'd be here too, and give me the proof I need to show her for the liar she is."

River released his hold on the shirt. "Go on."

His manner a little more confident now, the reporter smoothed the front of his shirt and straightened his necktie. "From the train station, they went right to the Imperial Hotel, where they have *one* suite. They've been there together ever since — when they aren't out on the town, visiting every gambling hall and opium den in Chinatown. The word is that your girl friend — or should I say ex-girl friend — has developed quite a liking for the *poppy* dreams!"

"Do you know who he is?" River asked sharply.

"On the street, they say he's a slave trader from New York who's starting up a lucrative new business — importing white girls from the East Coast to be sold as slave girls here and in the Orient." The reporter spoke in a taunting singsong voice, obviously enjoying River's reaction to this information. "In other words, he's a pimp who deals only in high-priced, very white 'merchandise.' They call him Tuan the Dragon."

"Where did you get your information?" River demanded.

"There's always someone who'll talk for the right price. They say he uses his charm to lure high-class girls to Chinatown. Then, when he has them there, he addicts

241

them to opium to ensure that they'll do anything he tells them to do. Such a woman will do anything for the next 'flower dream'—including whoring for him."

River stared dumbfounded at the sleazy reporter then his face contorted with vicious ire.

The man took a step back, confident that he was turning a mad dog loose on Aidan Donovan. All he had to do now was wait and watch. He'd let the Indian and the bitch write his story for him. "I'm staying at the Wynn House on California Street," he said, handing River a business card. "When you're ready to talk, get in touch with me."

River studied the card for an instant and then looked up, his expression hard and deadly. "I thought you understood, Mr. —" he glanced down at the card again. "—Scott Percy, I don't have anything to discuss with you." He stepped off the curb and started across the street.

The reporter raced after him and grabbed his arm. "What are you going to do now?"

Stopping, River studied the shorter man, then cast a meaningful look at the fingers on his coat sleeve. Flicking Percy's hand off his arm as though it were vile-smelling dung, he looked purposefully into the reporter's eyes. "First, I'm going to check into a hotel. Then I'm going to catch up on my sleep. And I'd advise you to do likewise—unless you're ready to kiss your career goodbye."

"What does that m-mean?" Scott stammered, instinctively shrinking back.

"That means if I ever see your face again, I'll wipe up the sidewalks of San Francisco with it."

"Aren't you going to confront her?" Percy yelled. "She used you! Don't you want to help me show the whole country what a lying little slut Aidan Donovan is?"

For the second time, River turned to face the reporter. "Evidently you only understand one kind of talk, Percy."

Folding the fingers of one hand into a tight fist and coiling back his arm, he grasped the smaller man's lapels. "This is the only story you're going to get from me," he said, bringing his punch crashing into the reporter's astonished face.

Leaning heavily on Roger's arm, her eyes half-closed, Aidan staggered along the sidewalk. "Is everything set for tomorrow night?"

Roger nodded his head, a huge smile coming to his face as his eyes shifted carefully over the people around them. "We've brought in special agents to raid the opium dens and get the slave girls out. They're just waiting for me to give them the word."

"Are you sure all these men can be trusted?" she asked. "I'd hate to have someone let what we're doing slip out."

"They can be trusted. But to be sure no one gets talkative, they won't be told any details until the last minute. They don't even know who'll be paying their generous bonus if everything goes off without a hitch."

"Good, the faster we get this over, the better I'll feel. I'm ready to go home." Carrying her opium-addict pretense to the limit, Aidan deliberately tripped and stumbled forward. "Oops!" she giggled drunkenly.

Roger laughed loudly. "To what do we owe this sudden hurry to get back to San Antonio?" he whispered, scooping her limp body into his arms. Seemingly unaware of the attention they were attracting, he carried her through the Imperial Hotel door the Chinese doorman held open. "Another story?" he asked against her ear.

"Actually, I'm not going to Texas. I'm going to South Dakota," she announced.

"South Dakota? What's in South Dakota besides plains and Indians?"

243

Smiling, she looped an arm around his neck and rested her head against his chest, continuing to play her part convincingly. "My future . . . if I haven't waited too long."

"Sounds like a man."

She grinned sleepily. "One of those Indians you mentioned. Sing-Li helped me realize that if I'm not willing to fight for him, I deserve to lose him."

"Ears," he hissed, bringing their whispered conversation to an immediate halt. He carried her into the elevator, his demeanor becoming superior and cocky for the benefit of the operator.

Pretending to pass out, Aidan hid the swell of happiness growing in her chest. She was going home to be with River. And no matter what it took, she would make things right between them.

From the shadows across the street, River stared, dumbstruck, at the wide, ornate entrance to the Imperial Hotel. Paralyzed by what he'd just seen, he swallowed back the sick feeling that rose in his throat. He'd been so sure Scott Percy had lied in order to dupe him into refuting Aidan's story about Cuba, but only a fool would continue to deny the truth after what he'd just witnessed.

He shook his head and squeezed his eyes shut. There had to be some mistake. It couldn't have been Aidan he'd seen clinging to the Chinese man in the white suit. It must have been another woman who'd been so drugged it had been necessary for her to be carried into the Imperial Hotel in that man's arms.

Aidan addicted to opium? Aidan in the clutches of a white slave trader? How could he believe it? But how could he not?

River opened his eyes, his denial hardening into cruel

reality. His worst nightmare had come true.

"Why, Aidan?" he whispered to himself. *How could you be so gullible as to fall into his trap?*

"Gullible?" he repeated, the word striking a discordant note when used to describe Aidan. Manipulative, foolhardy, independent, overly sure of her own capabilities. Yes. But gullible? When had she ever been tricked into doing something she didn't want to do?

He straightened his slouching posture, his blue eyes narrowing angrily as they fixed on the entrance of the Imperial. On the other hand, how many times had she deliberately wangled her way into a life-threatening situation in order to get a story? And with no more than her inflated belief in herself to back her up?

"Damn!" Realization exploded in his tired brain, with all the illumination of a thousand Chinese firecrackers. *Aidan Donovan hasn't been lured into anything! She's here because she wants to be. This is some crazy stunt she's pulling to get a story. And if I know her, she's in deeper than she planned, and hasn't got an idea in hell how she's going to get out once she's the information she needs.*

Charged with an odd mixture of anger and relief, River launched himself forward, his target the Imperial Hotel. Once he had brushed past the low-bowing doorman, he hesitated only an instant before striding purposefully over to the desk. "A tall man in a white suit, carrying a white woman, came in here a few minutes ago. I need his room number."

"So solly, sir, but not supposed to give out that information," the Chinese clerk answered in halting English.

Controlling his first impulse to haul the desk clerk over the counter and beat the room number out of him, River whipped his billfold out of his breast pocket and said, "He dropped something I'd like to return to him."

245

"You reave with me. Chu will give," the clerk answered, his hand extended toward River.

River shook his head and grinned. "I'd better do this myself," he said, removing a large bill from the wallet and sliding it across the counter to the clerk.

Glancing from left to right, the clerk whisked the bill off the counter and into the sleeve of his tunic, so quickly that even River blinked. "Foh-oh-tlee," he whispered, pivoting away from River in obvious dismissal.

During the elevator ride up to the fourth floor, River planned what he would do to Aidan when he got her out of this latest mess. All too soon, he was standing outside room "foh-oh-tlee."

Rage guiding him now, he pounded squarely on the door.

"Yes?" a deep male voice called from within.

River responded by lifting his foot and kicking the lock with the heel of his boot, sending the door crashing open.

"What the hell's—"

Immediately recognizing the man in the white suit as the one who'd carried Aidan into the hotel, River flew across the room and plowed his fist into the "pimp's" astonished face.

His adversary was almost as tall as River, but not so obviously muscular. "You bastard! Where is she?" He flung the slimmer man over onto his back, landing on top of him.

"She's not here," Roger grunted, wedging his feet between himself and his attacker and heaving the heavier man off him. Rolling onto River and straddling him, Roger whipped a knife from the scabbard he wore hidden beneath his coat at the small of his back. "Now suppose you tell me who sent you here." He grasped a forelock of River's hair at the same time he pressed the point of the knife to the pulse in the side of his neck. "And why?"

"Nobody sent me, you rotten pimp." River sneered, rage and contempt making him foolhardy. Bringing a hand upward, he knocked the knife away from his neck, oblivious to the trail of blood the point left from his jawline to his ear. At the same time, he bucked his hips off the floor and wrapped long, muscular legs around Roger's neck. Calves crossed at the Oriental's Adam's apple, River exerted just enough pressure on Roger's windpipe to convince him that he meant business. "Now, where is she?"

"I tell you, she's not here," Roger croaked, rasping from lack of oxygen, his almond-shaped eyes almost round because of the pressure.

River tightened his leg lock slightly. "Where is she?"

Grabbing at the calves pressing on his neck, Roger leaned back against River's bent thighs and brought his own feet together under his opponent's chin. Digging his heels into River's throat, he straightened his own legs, forcing River to clutch at his ankles.

"Roger, what's all the noi— River!"

Both men looked toward the source of the impatient female voice.

"Aidan," Roger choked out.

"Aidan?" River asked at the same time, his vision blurring, his ears ringing.

"Get help," they grunted in unison.

Chapter Seventeen

Shock, confusion, and elation streaked through Aidan, paralyzing her in the doorway to the connecting room, where she'd been changing into her servant-girl disguise for the walk back to Roger's house.

"Aidan, the knife." Roger strained against the grip of River's legs and, at the same time, dug his heels more forcibly into River's chin. "Give me the knife."

Roger's labored words slammed into Aidan's consciousness, and her mobility was restored. "Stop it!" she screamed, rushing to the grappling men. "There's been a horrible mistake!"

"Get the police," River ground out between teeth forced together by the pressure of Roger's feet.

Grabbing at Roger's ankles with one hand, Aidan fought to pull River's legs from around Roger's throat with the other. "River, let him go!" she wailed. "He can't breathe! Roger, please stop! He's a friend! River! You're going to kill him."

Gradually, her desperate pleas penetrated the rage that held the two men deadlocked in bizarre combat. Though neither was willing to give up his advantage completely, each man relaxed the pressure on his opponent, and both men greedily sucked in air.

"You're right," River gasped, his chest rising and falling

laboriously. "Killing's too good for this low life bastard! I ought to show him how my grandfathers took care of their enemies in South Dakota!"

"South Dakota?" Roger panted, directing puzzled black eyes at Aidan. "*Your* South Dakota?"

Her expression embarrassed, Aidan nodded. "I'm afraid so," she responded with a sick grin.

"What the hell's going on?" River again tightened his hold on Roger. "For God's sake, Aidan! Don't you realize what you've gotten yourself into this time? This guy's a pimp! And he's planning to *sell* you into white slavery!"

"River, stop! He's not what he seems. It's just an act."

Digging his heels into River's throat in self-defense, Roger rasped, "Didn't you hear what she said, South Dakota? It's all an act. You and I are on the same side. Now ease up, before I have to snap your neck."

"You and what army, pimp?" River grimaced, but he didn't ease up. Instead, he clamped his legs more tightly against Roger's neck.

Her panic rising, Aidan grabbed a brass vase from a nearby table and raised it over her head. "River, I'm warning you! Let him go!"

"Like hell I will!"

"Call your Indian off, Aidan!" Roger wheezed, though the threat was still obvious in his tone. "Or I'll kill him!" To emphasize the point, he created a vise with his feet and twisted River's neck.

Knowing Roger could do as he'd threatened with no more effort than it would take to break a matchstick, Aidan no longer had the luxury of time. "Oooh." She brought the vase crashing down on River's head.

River's eyes bulged in surprise, then snapped closed as he lapsed into unconsciousness, the muscles of his body relaxing.

Leaving Roger to disentangle himself, Aidan dropped

249

to her knees beside River, tears coursing down her cheeks. "Look what you made me do!" She lifted his head onto her lap. "Why wouldn't you listen to me?"

"That's one strong Indian." Roger coughed as he crawled away from River. "What the hell's he doing here?"

"I don't know—" Realization struck Aidan, and her face broke into an ecstatic, tearful smile. "Oh, River!" she cried, hugging his head to her breast. "You came for me. That must mean you do love me!"

Then, with a force equal to having the Imperial Hotel tumble onto her, Aidan was struck by the hurt in River's eyes just before she'd knocked him out. Her heart contracted painfully. She knew exactly what he'd thought in that brief instant before he'd lost consciousness. He had come to save her, and she had attacked him. It didn't matter that he'd been the one who needed saving. In his eyes, she had betrayed him.

"Oh, Roger, what have I done?" she wept smoothing River's dark hair back from his forehead. "He'll never forgive me now!"

Dragging himself up to the sofa, Roger shook his head. Still panting to catch his breath, he leaned forward, placing his elbows on his knees. "We've got a lot worse problems than whether or not he'll forgive you for keeping him from getting his neck broken."

"Oooh," River moaned. His head rocked back and forth in Aidan's lap.

"He's coming to!" she announced excitedly. "River, are you all right? I'm so sorry! Can you ever forgive me?"

Opening his eyes, he stared up into her tear-streaked face. "Aidan?" He was confused. The face was hers, but the hair and clothing were definitely Chinese. "What happened? Why are you wearing those clothes?"

"Oh, River, I'm so sorry!" she cried. "I didn't want to hurt you. You've got to believe me. I couldn't let him

250

break your neck! Why wouldn't you listen?"

Recollection dawned in River's blue eyes, darkening them to a stormy gray. "You knocked me out!" he accused, rolling free of her embrace and sitting up. "I came here to get you out of this mess you've gotten into, and you attacked me!"

"In case you've forgotten," Aidan hissed, "Roger was on the verge of killing you to save his own life. I didn't know what else to do to get you to release your hold on his neck. Can't you see? I did it to keep him from killing you!"

"Don't you get tired of lying, Aidan? If you were so anxious to save *me*, why isn't he the one who's got the lump on his head?" He jabbed his humb in Roger's direction.

Now she was really getting mad. Who did he think he was anyway? "Because *he* didn't break into *your* room and attack *you!*" she said, poking her forefinger into River's chest. "And because *you* wouldn't listen when we tried to tell you who Roger was. And because . . ." She swallowed and bit her bottom lip in an attempt to control the tears that threatened to erupt again. "Because I . . ."

The tremble of her bottom lip vibrated faster and faster, and she looked up at him, her expression lost and helpless. "Because I couldn't bear the thought of losing you."

Unable to resist her tears, River caught Aidan's face in his hands and studied her questioningly, his gaze probing deeply into hers. "You couldn't?"

"Look," Roger interrupted standing up to face them, but keeping his distance from River, "I'm sure someday we'll laugh about this, but in the meantime I think we ought to get going. Sing-Li will be calling out the National Guard if we're not home soon."

"Sing-Li?" River asked, a light beginning to dawn in his

251

mind. He looked questioningly at Aidan.

"His wife," she answered with a sniff. "And the mother of his *four* children," she added with a spiteful huff.

"Aidan has been staying in our home while she's been in San Francisco — for her safety as much as for propriety. That's the reason for the servant-girl disguise, so she can go to and from my house without being noticed."

River glanced around the hotel suite and nodded. "And all this is just for—"

"Show," Aidan finished for him. "Did you really think I would go into something this dangerous without assistance?" She paused, her mouth curving up in a sheepish grin as she realized the absurdity of what she'd just asked. "Don't answer that."

River shrugged his shoulders. "How was I supposed to know you finally got some common sense?" He turned to Roger and held out his hand. "I owe you an apology. I hope you won't harbor any hard feelings . . . uh . . . Did I hear Aidan call you Roger?" he asked, just now becoming aware of the incongruity of the Chinese man's name.

Roger stepped forward and took River's hand. "Roger Smith," he said, his tone still cool. "White father, Chinese mother. I'm with the Pinkerton Agency. Mr. Hearst hired us to help Aidan, and to protect her while she's in San Francisco."

"River Blue Eagle. White mother, Indian father," River responded, mimicking Roger's serious delivery.

Neither completely trusting the other, the two men eyed each other warily. Roger was the first to flash a hesitant smile. "Look, I know we got off to a bad start, but you're welcome to stay at my house too — if you don't mind sleeping on a mat on the floor."

"Thanks," River answered tersely. Then he made an effort to return Roger's offer of friendliness. "A mat would be fine, but I've already checked into a hotel near the train station. I think we'd better stay there tonight."

"We?" Aidan and Roger both said.

"Aidan and I." River studied them carefully, then turned to Aidan. He arched his eyebrows, his expression testing. "Unless there's a reason you don't want to come with me?"

"No!" she exclaimed, determined not to let anything prevent her from getting River back. She'd walked away from him once. She didn't intend to do it again. "It's just that . . . my things are at their house!"

"We can pick them up before we go to the hotel. There's a train leaving early in the morning, and I'd like us to be on it—before either one of us makes any more mistakes."

Roger and Aidan looked at each other, then at River.

"Just like that? Without even asking what she thinks about it?" Roger exclaimed.

"Aidan has obligations in South Dakota, which she's put off long enough," River stated, looking directly at Aidan, the harsh light in his eyes probing. It was obvious he still believed there was something Roger and Aidan weren't telling him about their relationship. "Isn't that true, Aidan?"

"Yes, but—"

River interrupted. "Then I ask you again: Is there any reason you prefer to stay with him rather than come with me tomorrow to fulfill your obligation?"

"Maybe she already has plans for tomorrow!" Roger suggested, amazed that Aidan was allowing River to dictate to her.

"Plans?" River asked suspiciously.

Aidan had no doubt that River would turn around and walk out of her life for good if she told him she couldn't go with him until her job was finished. He would feel she was chosing a story over him—again. And she couldn't let that happen. Torn between being thrilled that River had come for her, yet angered by his authoritative tone, she knew she couldn't tell him the truth because he would leave. She directed a subtle shake of her head at Roger.

Yet as happy as she was that River had come for her, and as sincere as she had been when she had vowed never to let her work come between them if she could just have a second chance with him, she knew she couldn't leave San Francisco in the morning. No matter how much she wanted to be with River, she would never be able to live with herself if she left before the slave girls she'd seen in the opium parlors were safely at the Presbyterian Mission on Sacramento Street.

There had to be a way to keep River in San Francisco one more day. She just needed to think of it.

"It's nothing urgent," she assured River, taking his arm and Roger's, and steering both men toward the door of the suite, which stood ajar. "We can talk about it later, but right now we really must go. Sing-Li will be terribly worried, and I'm surprised Murph hasn't come storming up here to see what's taking us so long."

As they opened the door the rest of the way to leave, a dark form scurried into the stairwell at the end of the hallway. A shudder of apprehension shimmied up Aidan's spine and she shot a questioning gaze toward Roger.

"Just one of the hotel's houseboys," he said reassuringly, his eyes leveled on the stairwell. "Or a guest who doesn't care for elevators!"

Aidan smiled and nodded. "You're probably right. No doubt, the strain of the last hour has made me a little more jumpy than usual.

"It doesn't make sense for you to come all the way to San Francisco and not see any of it," Aidan argued as she preceded River into his hotel room. "You haven't been anywhere! Wouldn't you like to see the bay—it's supposed to be beautiful—or Nob Hill where all the rich people live? And what about taking a ride on a trolley car? I've always dreamed of riding on one. It would really be a shame to come so close and miss—"

"I didn't come out here to sightsee," he said sharply, as he handed a coin to the bellboy who'd brought up her bags.

Spinning around to face him, Aidan watched as he closed and locked the door. "Why *did* you come, River?"

River's hand paused on the lock, then dropped to his side, but he made no move to face her. "I told you. You owe me the reservation story." His voice was suspiciously hoarse. "I came to collect what's owed me."

She studied his back, his broad shoulders, his dark head; and her heart filled with longing. His hair now reached past his collar, though the sides had been trimmed so they just covered the tops of his ears. She suddenly realized how much she loved him and how much she'd risked when she'd left him in Tampa. If only she weren't too late to make him believe in her again. "Is that the only reason?"

He sucked in a deep breath and turned around, leveling an intense gaze on her. She had changed out of her servant-girl clothing and wig when she'd picked up her suitcase at Roger's house. "What other reason do I need? Isn't collecting that debt reason enough to come?"

The side of Aidan's bottom lip folded inward and she chewed on it thoughtfully, not trusting herself to speak for several seconds. "I suppose so. It's just that we both know I already told you I was going to do the story just as soon as I was through out here—and that it's already sold. When you came here anyway, I guess I fooled myself into thinking you'd come for some other reason. Per-

255

haps because you'd realized I meant more to you than just a way to help the Lakotas . . . that you actually . . . cared for me." She couldn't bring herself to say the word that had really come to her mind: *love*.

River cleared his throat uneasily.

"Crazy, huh?" She moved slowly toward him, her glistening eyes pleading. "I should have known better. But I was just so happy to see you, I must have gotten carried away." She stopped directly in front of him and looked up into his face, no longer attempting to hide her feelings from him.

The muscle in River's jaw bunched, but he didn't speak.

"Tell me, River, is there the slightest chance that it wasn't just wishful thinking on my part? Is there any possibility that you've missed me as much as I've missed you?"

A deep, guttural moan soughed through his lips, and his eyes darkened with frustration. "Dammit, Aidan, just for once, can't you tell me the truth? You and I both know you don't want to stay in San Francisco another day so I can see the bay, or ride the trolleys. Do you think you can get what you want by playing on my emotions? Why don't you just admit it and get it over with? You want to stay to finish Hearst's story. Isn't that it?"

Feeling as if she'd just been stabbed in the chest, Aidan wrapped her arms around her waist as though she could hug away the pain. She'd been a fool to think all she had to do was let him know how she felt, and he would take her in his arms and tell her he loved her!

"Well, isn't it?"

Her spine stiffened and she lifted her chin defiantly. "Yes, damn you! I want to stay another day to finish my story! I can't put anything or any*one* before it."

Deep inside him, where only Aidan could reach, the

vulnerable, defenseless part of his soul, trembled, then shriveled, curling into itself in agony. On the surface, however, his expression barely changed, and only an instant passed before he managed to hide his hurt behind cold blue eyes. "Can't or *won't*, Aidan?"

"All right—won't! There! Are you satisfied? I *won't* leave San Francisco until I'm through with this story."

He nodded his head. "That's what it always boils down to with you, isn't it? But that's the trouble with placing all your values on something as elusive as fame. Every morning when you wake up, you have to go out and fight for your place in the limelight all over again, because yesterday's news is just that, yesterday's news."

Unable to hold back her tears, Aidan raised her fists and pounded on River's chest. "Damn you! Don't you think I know that? Do you think I haven't learned that fame won't bring me happiness?"

Catching her wrists with both hands, he stopped her attack and held her fists against his chest. "Then why, Aidan? Tell me why you want to stay?"

"What good will it do? You'll only accuse me of lying," she protested. Her anger had dwindled to soft sobs and an occasional sniff.

"Try me," he rasped, that vulnerable knot in his heart releasing the bonds on his control ever so slightly.

Studying his face for a long silent moment, Aidan reached a decision. "All right," she finally said, shrugging her shoulders indifferently. "I have to stay because there are people depending on me to complete this story."

River's mouth curled in a sardonic sneer. "Hearst."

"Hearst is one of them. I gave him my word I'd do it, and despite how little trust you have in my word, I do live up to bargains I make." Ignoring the disbelieving smirk that twisted his lips, she went on. "Then there are the Indians who live on the reservations. You conveniently forget they are going to gain from this story, because once I write it, they'll have the influence of a powerful newspaper like the New York *Journal* behind their cause. But I have an even more immediate responsibility to about twenty-four young girls in several of the opium dens of Chinatown. Their very lives are riding on what happens tomorrow night. And until I can end my story with the fact that they are free and safe, I can't—excuse me, *won't*—leave San Francisco. Not even if my staying means you and I will never be together, though that will tear my heart out."

His grip on her wrists loosened, but he didn't speak. He just watched her.

Uncomfortable under his distrustful study of her face, she jutted out her chin. "I told you that you wouldn't believe me. But it doesn't matter, I'm—"

"Shhh." His movements slow and deliberate, he inserted his thumbs into her fists and opened them, all the while holding her gaze captive to his intense stare. Flattening her open fingers against his chest, he slid her hands upward, over his shoulders, overlapping them behind his neck. "I don't want to talk anymore."

Afraid to believe that his change of mood meant he was no longer angry, Aidan couldn't find the strength to test him. If this moment were only a dream, she couldn't bear to break the spell. She clutched at his thick hair with desperate urgency, as if she could hold onto the magic if she didn't relax her grasp.

Sliding his hands down her arms, along her rib cage, River gripped Aidan at the waist and propped his shoulders back against the door. His relaxed position thrusting his hips forward, he dropped his grip to her buttocks and pulled her to him. "Did you mean what you said? Would you really care if you never saw me again?"

She nodded and dragged her tongue around the rim of

her lips in a vain effort to moisten a mouth gone suddenly dry. His lips were only inches from hers, his breath hot and tangy with the scent of the whiskey he'd drunk at Roger's house while she'd changed clothes. It blew across her face in a warm enveloping mist, sending an incapacitating heat curling through her. She leaned heavily on him, her knees weak, and rose up on her toes to more fully press herself to the hardness of his groin.

"I've felt dead inside since I left you in Florida," she admitted. "I've just been going through the motions of living. But when I saw you tonight and thought you had come because you'd missed me too, I felt as though I'd been brought back to life — as though God had given me another chance. And I can't bear to think of losing you again, River."

"Damn you, Aidan Donovan." He brought his lips down to within a scant quarter-inch of her mouth. "Don't you know yet that you can't lose me? You're mine, and God help me, I'll never let you leave me again."

Her heart singing with joy, Aidan brought her lips to his, her mouth open and pleading. He wanted her! Wanted her with him! She was his! And he was hers!

Urgently, she drew his head down, fire raging through her as he kissed her. But it wasn't enough. She wanted more — she wanted to engrave herself on him, to merge her soul with his, to brand his very flesh with the stamp of hers.

Her hands going to his chest, she tore his jacket off his shoulders, then pulled at his tie, loosening it with desperate, agitated movements — all the while kissing him, her tongue probing deep and hard into his mouth. Grabbing handfuls of his shirt, she wrenched its tails out of his waistband, then reached for the button at the throat. Her shaking fingers fumbled to release it, but they couldn't. Desperate to feel his hard muscular chest, she lost all

259

patience.

Inserting her fingers inside the shirt, she ripped it open, oblivious to the pinging of buttons that fell to the wooden floor, with small clicks. "I want to love you, River," she panted, tearing her mouth from his to kiss the satiny flesh stretched tight over the tensed muscles of his chest. "All of you."

Her mouth fastened on a flat male nipple and sucked hard on it, while her tongue caressed the raised nub at its center.

His hips rocked upward against her small body, and he let out a helpless groan. His ability to think was being completely shattered by her fingers and mouth, as she touched and kissed her way over his ribs and waist and belly. Incapable of resisting, River rolled his head from side to side against the door on which he leaned.

Her own frantic need ruling her now, Aidan stepped back just enough to allow her hands access to his belt buckle. Instinct making her fingers sure, she undid it, then released the buttons of the fly on his trousers, all the while acutely aware of the hardness pressing against her hands from beneath the fabric. Finally, falling to her knees before him, she whisked trousers and breechcloth down his lean hips and long thighs in one compelling motion.

"Ahhh," he breathed out in agonized relief as his swollen maleness leapt free, jutting and thrusting toward her.

Her fingers closed around him, and she thrilled in the moans of pleasure her exploration inspired.

Leaning forward, she kissed his taut belly, delighting in the way his body flinched and contracted at the touch of her lips.

"I want to put my mark on all of you," she whispered, looking up the length of him to the passion-glazed blue eyes staring down at her. Leaning forward again, she brought the tip of his manhood to her lips and kissed it lightly.

"Oh, God." River groaned, the sound rising from deep in his chest, as his hips gave an involuntary lurch forward in instinctive response to the hot moistness of her mouth. "I can't let you . . ." His words drifted off as, Aidan drew him deeper into the warmth of her mouth.

His chest rose and fell irregularly, as his breathing grew more rapid. Not certain he could withstand the exquisite agony much longer, he pulled her up the length of him and hastily began to tug her skirts upward. When he encountered the frustrating obstacle of her underdrawers, he growled impatiently. Grabbing their waistband, he ripped the drawers apart with one frenzied movement, and lifted her onto him.

Aidan clung to his neck and wrapped her legs around his lean hips to ride his passion to fulfillment.

His hands cupping her buttocks, he guided her up and down until she screamed for release. Then he filled her with one final thrust and together they cried out their simultaneous release.

His breathing labored, he slid down the door to the floor, carrying her light body with him, neither ready to give up possession of the other quite yet.

Chapter Eighteen

Aidan rolled onto her side and draped an arm around River's slim waist. "Are you asleep?" she whispered, molding her body to his back and pressing her lips to the smooth flesh of his shoulder.

"I was," he replied groggily, lifting the sheet off their naked bodies to accommodate himself as he shifted onto his back. He wrapped an arm around her and drew her to his side. Yawning loudly, he flopped his free arm over his closed eyes. "What are you doing awake? It's not even daylight yet. I thought you 'spoiled' white girls slept until noon."

Knowing he was teasing her, Aidan playfully bit the bulging pectoral muscle beneath her cheek. "Sleeping just seems like a waste of time today. I thought we might . . ."

He lifted his hand off one eye and peered at her purposefully. "Might what?" he asked in a silky tone. His smile leering, he turned to face her and crushed her lithe body to his from breasts to knees, entangling his calves and feet with hers. He kissed the tousled curls on her head and rocked his hips suggestively against hers. "What exactly did you have in mind?"

She breathed in the scent of him, wondering how she had survived this past month without him, and how she would go on living if he left her. But she couldn't let her desire to stay with him stop her from doing what she hadn't been able to bring herself to do the night before. She grinned and squeezed his waist. "That would be nice, but I had a different idea."

"Oh?" His muscles tensed, and his caressing hand stilled on her hip. "What is that?"

"You don't have to sound so serious," she said with a smile, though dreading the moment when she had to tell him that last night hadn't changed anything. "I just thought it would be romantic to get up and watch the sun rise over the bay," she suggested in a delaying tactic.

River relaxed, his warm breath ruffling the curls framing her face. "I can think of something a lot more romantic than that."

Propping her chin on his chest, she did her best to keep her expression light and playful as she looked into his blue eyes. Lord, she loved him like this. If only she didn't have to ruin it. But she might as well get it over with.

"We have the rest of our lives to do that, but this might be our last chance to see the bay at dawn. Besides, we need to talk, and if we stay here and indulge in *your* romantic idea, I'm afraid we won't get much talking done."

He released his hold on her, and eyed her suspiciously. "What exactly do you want to talk about?"

"Don't look at me like that. We just need to talk about what we're going to do today."

He withdrew his arm from around her shoulders and rolled away from her to sit up on the edge of the bed. "I thought we'd already decided that."

Feeling empty and lost without his arms around her, Aidan fought the temptation to reach out and bring him back to her. She wished she could tell him she didn't

263

really want to talk either. But for once in her life, she couldn't let selfishness rule her. If only the price weren't going to be so high!

"No, River. *You* decided. It's the same as before. You issue orders and I'm supposed to obey them, without any consideration for my thoughts or obligations."

"Then what were all those regrets about leaving me and coming to San Francisco? More of your lies?"

"No!" She scrambled up to her knees and scooted over to where he sat. "It was all true. I do regret it. I told myself I was doing it for you and the Lakotas, because it was the only way I could get Hearst to print their story. But I know now that was only an excuse to do what I wanted without feeling guilty about it, rather than following through on what I was obligated to do. Unfortunately, this new knowledge of myself doesn't change the fact that I did come. And now that I've seen those young girls in the opium dens, I can't leave until I've helped them, even though what I really want is to go with you."

River breathed in deeply. "How long is this supposed to take?"

Encouraged by this concession, and by the fact that he hadn't said no outright, Aidan quickly answered. "Just one more day. Everything will come to a head tonight. I can leave in the morning. Oh, River, please say you'll wait for me! Don't make me choose between going with you and helping those unfortunate girls!"

"What exactly will 'come to a head tonight' that can't take place without you here?" he asked, obviously clinging to his resistance.

But Aidan refused to be discouraged by his disbelieving tone. At least they were still talking, and that was more than she'd dared to hope for. "Roger and I are going to create a diversion in the suite at the Imperial, one that will occupy the heads of the tongs that own the opium dens and brothels in Chinatown. Then, while we're keeping them busy, specially selected teams of Pinkerton agents will go into the opium dens, take the girls out, and spirit them away to the Presbyterian Mission, where they will be safe and will be helped to start new lives."

"And what exactly is this diversion you're going to cause? Why do you have to be there?"

Aidan cringed within. This was the sticky part. River would never agree to it. She was tempted to lie, or at least to evade the truth, but since telling the truth had kept him listening, she decided to keep it up. "I'm the bait."

His shoulders stiffened, and he stopped breathing. "Bait?" he asked in a wary drawl.

Aidan winced. "For want of another word," she replied.

He turned to face her, his expression fierce. "Suppose you find that 'other' word anyway."

Wrapping the sheet around herself, Aidan stood up and walked to the window, unable to look at River. She regretted not having come up with a convincing story to tell him. "They think they're coming to the suite for a special auction . . ."

"Go on," he urged, his tone indicating he'd already surmised the direction in which she was heading. "What will they be bidding on at this 'special auction'?"

Turning to face him, Aidan hunched her shoulders defensively and ducked her head, then peered up through her eyelashes at him. "Me." She choked out the word, her voice barely audible.

River closed his eyes for a moment, then opened them wide. "What did you say?" he hissed through clamped teeth.

Panicked by the shocked look in his eyes, Aidan hurriedly went on. "It's not as bad as it sounds. I won't be in any real danger. There will be a Pinkerton man there, and he'll outbid all the others."

"Like hell he will!" River bolted off the bed and stormed over to her. "If you think I'm going to allow you to put yourself in that kind of danger, you're crazier than I thought you were. You've gotten yourself into some dumb messes in the past, but I refuse to let you take part in this."

Aidan's eyes blazed angrily, fire igniting in their depths and turning them almost red. "Allow?" she gasped. "Refuse? Why you egotistical, overbearing oaf! Who do you think you are? I don't need your *permission* to do anything. I was hoping for your support, but I don't even need that!"

Letting the sheet drop to the floor, she snatched up the dress she had placed over the chair the night before and pulled it down over her head.

"What do you think you're doing?"

"I'm getting dressed! What does it look like?" She slipped on fresh drawers. "Unless you think I should go out in nothing but a sheet."

"You're not going anywhere until it's time to get on that train headed east."

Stepping into a petticoat and wriggling to get it up to her waist, she laughed derisively. "And how are you going to keep me here?"

"Oh, you'll stay all right." One hand shot out with the speed of a striking snake and grabbed her upper arm. The other snatched the drapery tie off one of the curtains. His fingers digging into her flesh, he dragged her to the bed.

"What do you think you're doing?" Aidan demanded, her physical resistance meaningless against his superior strength.

266

"Making sure you stay put until I get back." Sliding his hand down her arm, he held her wrist and shoved her down onto the rumpled bed.

As she realized what he was planning, Aidan panicked. "You can't tie me up!"

"I can," he muttered, deftly wrapping the cord around her wrist, then securing it to the bedpost above her head, "and I am. It's about time you learned how to follow orders. You're fortunate I'm more patient than my grandfathers were. They would have done this the first time one of their women defied them — and administered a beating."

The instant he released his hold on her, Aidan attacked the knot with her free hand. But before she could make any headway, he was back with the other curtain tie. Wrenching her unbound wrist upward, he quickly tied it to the other bedpost.

"You can't leave me like this!" she protested, anger and fear wrestling within her for control. But she could see the truth in his angry eyes.

"I won't be gone long." He slung his breechcloth around his hips, then picked up his trousers and angrily jabbed a foot into one leg.

"I'll scream!" she threatened.

"That's a good point." His eyes angrier than she'd ever seen them, he picked up her camisole and ripped it in half. Kneeling on the bed, he stuffed the smaller half into her mouth and hurriedly tied it in place with the other half. "That ought to keep you quiet until I get back."

"Mmm, mmm, mmm," she squealed, tossing her head back and forth in an effort to remove the gag, and straining against the ropes on her wrists. *I'll never forgive you for this, River,* she thought, the fury in her eyes sending the message to him as clearly as if it had been uttered aloud.

He stood beside the bed and studied her face. Unable to resist, he reached down and trailed the backs of his knuckles down her cheek. "I don't like this any more than you do, Little Fire. But you've left me no choice. When your fire rages uncontrolled, it's too destructive for me to take another chance on trusting that you'll use good sense."

Turning away from her piercing stare, River finished dressing and went to the door. He clutched the knob, then paused. "I know you're angry now, but this is for your own good. I'll be back as soon as I explain to Smith why you won't be in on the big plans tonight. I'm sure he can take care of it without your help." He stormed out into the hall, slamming the door shut behind him.

Certain he wouldn't really leave her tied up, and that he was just doing this to "teach her a lesson," Aidan watched the door. Waiting. Listening.

The scrape of a key being inserted into the lock sent a new burst of fear and anger trembling through her. If he was coming right back in, why would he lock the door? *Just to make sure I'm good and scared,* she told herself, determined not to listen to the inner voice that said River Blue Eagle had no intention of coming back for a while.

The key was turned in the lock. *He is coming back. He is,* she silently repeated over and over, her conviction weakening with every second that ticked by while the door remained closed.

Finally, the door rattled and shook as if it were being opened, and relief swept over her. *I knew it. I knew he'd come back! So help me, if I live to be a hundred, I'll never forgive him for this!*

Aidan held her breath and stared expectantly at the door, willing it to open. Why didn't he just come in?

Why was he torturing her like this?

Then the truth of what the rattling had meant dawned on her and squeezed painfully at her insides. He hadn't been coming back. He'd just decided to test the lock! As if to confirm her suspicion, the clomp of retreating footsteps pulsated in her ears, dashing her last hopes. He wasn't coming back into the room until he had done what he intended.

Panic dissolved into anger, anger so strong it left no room for fear. If it took every ounce of strength she possessed, she was going to free herself—and to make River Blue Eagle pay for the way he had treated her.

The desire for vengeance keeping her thinking level, she rolled her head back and thoughtfully eyed the rope at her left wrist. Twisting her hand in the rope bracelet, she tested its fit. Disappointed that there was no space whatsoever between the rope and her flesh, she shifted her gaze to the knot on her other wrist.

Aha! she exclaimed silently as she spotted a scant one-fourth of an inch of leeway. *I'll show that arrogant boor* she vowed. *Tie me up and leave me, will he?*

Her double-jointed thumbs had always allowed her to squeeze her small hands in and out of things others couldn't slip through, and with that quarter-inch of slack he'd foolishly left her, she could do it now! She smiled at the thought of River coming back and finding her gone.

Frowning in concentration and holding her breath, she folded her thumb to the inside of her palm, keeping it straight. She squeezed her remaining fingers together and twisted the entire hand from side to side, slowly, carefully easing down on the rope without straining against it. The rope slid to within half an inch of her bottom thumb knuckle.

Almost there! she encouraged herself, her gaze fixed on the satin curtain tie. *Just a little bit more.* She lifted

269

her shoulder up a bit to give the rope more slack, all the while twisting her hand ever so subtly.

Aidan was concentrating so completely on the rope that she didn't notice the stealthy turning of the door-knob until whoever wanted entrance to her room met with the lock's resistance. Then the door began to shake and rattle, as it had when River had tested it.

I knew it! I knew he couldn't leave me like this!

Just as it occurred to her to wonder why he wasn't using his key, the door crashed open. It's frame was immediately filled by a huge Oriental man . . . who looked like one of the bodyguards she'd seen at the Dream Garden opium den.

The large man's round, shaven head pivoted from left to right, his slanted eyes darting over the room. When he had determined it to be safe to enter, the bodyguard stepped into the room and moved to the side to allow a second man to enter. This one Aidan recognized as Chu Wong, the slave dealer for the On Leong Tong.

Pointing in Aidan's direction, the slaver spoke in rapid Chinese to his servant, who immediately responded by rushing to Aidan and untying her wrists.

Her hands freed, Aidan reached for the gag and pulled it down around her neck, spitting out the wad of material as she did. "Thank God. I don't think I could have stood another minute of that," she babbled gratefully, so relieved to be free that she didn't stop to wonder why this tong official had come to River's hotel—or how he'd found her. "Thank you."

The Chinaman raised his scant eyebrows. "I'm most pleased to be of service, Miss *Donovan*."

As though she'd been struck in the face, Aidan froze. "Miss Donovan?"

An evil smile snaked across the slaver's features, transforming his eyes to mere slits. "Oh, come now, my dear.

Surely, you did not believe your true identity would go undetected indefinitely. Though I must admit if your friend hadn't come to me and told me what you were up to, it might have taken us a while longer to see through your disguise."

"Friend?" Fear and shock warred inside Aidan as the full meaning of Chu Wong's statement seared into her. *No!* she protested silently. *It's not true! It can't be!*

Only a handful of people knew the truth about who she was and why she was here: Roger, Sing-Li, Murph, River, and Mr. Hearst. None of them would betray her. None of them!

Yet, no matter how she fought it, she couldn't deny that someone had told Chu Wong the truth about her. Her heart clenched painfully. There was no escaping it. Someone she had trusted had actually revealed her identity to the tong.

Veering her gaze from left to right in a hasty search for a way to escape, Aidan knew she had to keep up her act, if she were to have even the smallest chance of getting out of this situation. "There's been a mistake. I don't know anyone named Miss Donovan. My name is Barbara Grisham." Doing her best to appear nonchalant, she stood up and started to inch toward the door.

Chu shot her a tolerant grin. "I must admit, your talent for playacting is admirable, Miss Donovan, but it is wasted on me. Perhaps it will be more appreciated in your new home." He glanced at his servant and tipped his head in Aidan's direction.

Fear knotting in her throat, Aidan shrank back from the approaching giant. "N-n-new home? Tell him to get away from me."

"There, there, Miss Donovan. There's no need to be afraid. No one will hurt you—as long as you please the prince who has sent a great deal of gold from the old

271

country to pay me for a white concubine."

"You're crazy!" Aidan shrieked. Ducking low, she made a dash past the servant who blocked her path. "Help me!" she screamed, reaching for the doorknob. "Somebody help me!"

"Scream all you like, Miss Donovan! No one will hear you. My men have already cleared this floor of its occupants."

"I don't believe you!" she shrilled, wrenching the door open. "Help!"

Chu shrugged. "It was really very simple. Once your male companion left, all they had to do was knock on each door and tell the guests there was a fire in the hotel. The entire floor was emptied in a matter of minutes— with the exception of your room of course."

"You're lying!" She shot a frantic glance up and down the hallway, and her stomach tightened into a cramp of despair. Every door stood open wide, as though the people occupying the rooms had left in a great hurry. They were all gone. There was no one to help her. She was truly alone.

She twitched in a sudden spasm as the bodyguard pressed his strong fingers against twin points at the sides of her neck. There was an instant of light-headedness when she had only one thought: *River will think I left him of my own free will and he'll never know how much I love him.* Then there was nothing.

Angrily, River stormed across the crowded lobby of the Imperial, damning himself for not having the strength of his forefathers when it came to keeping his woman under control. He hadn't even gotten three blocks from the hotel before he'd ordered the driver to turn back.

But though he'd weakened in his resolve to let her stew

for a while, he didn't intend to let her go through with her latest hare-brained scheme. They would go to Roger Smith together, and explain that a replacement for Aidan must be found. Then they would board the first train out of San Francisco and be on their way to South Dakota.

"You can't use the elevator!" a voice shouted as River punched the button that rang for the operator. "There's a fire on the fourth floor!"

The words slammed into River's ribs. "What did you say?" Guilt and fear raged through him.

"There's a fire on the fourth floor," the man repeated. "The elevator's not running until it's safe."

"Oh, my god!" River, frantically searched the lobby for the stairway. "Aidan's on that floor!"

The informative guest shook his head. "No one's up there. The whole floor's been evacuated. The firemen are on their way."

Driven by the cold, hard knot of terror in his chest, River broke into a run. Ignoring the warnings shouted after him, he burst into the stairway and bolted up the first flight. Stretching his long legs to their full capacity, he took the steps three at a time, slowing only slightly to catch his breath as he rounded the landings between floors.

Never in his life had he known such fear, such total helplessness. What if he was already too late? What if he had killed her? *No!* a voice screamed in his head. *She's not dead! I'm not too late!*

Oblivious to any danger to himself, River exploded through the doorway at the top of the stairs. He was prepared to walk through a blazing inferno to get to Aidan, and would not turn back until he had her safe in his arms.

The empty hallway stretched before him, halting his forward momentum as no flames could have done. In fact, that was the problem. There were no flames.

A tremor of new apprehension ricocheted through him. It was one thing not to see a fire, but why didn't he smell smoke?

Just then, a woman cried out and a door swung open at the far end of the hall. River recognized Aidan's curly red hair as her head poked out into the corridor. He was too far away to make out her features in the dimly lit hallway, but he knew it was her. Relief and confusion shot through him, and he instinctively lunged toward her.

As he opened his mouth to call out to her, a large, seemingly disembodied hand was thrust into view, clasping her neck from behind. To his horror, her head pitched forward and her knees folded beneath her as though her muscles and bones had turned to liquid.

"Aidan!" he shouted, breaking into a frantic run.

At the sound of his voice, a muscular giant of a man dressed in pajama-like servant's clothing appeared in the doorway above Aidan's limp body.

Black, almond-shaped eyes glistened purposefully, and a pleased grin slithered across the Oriental's mouth. White teeth bared, he lowered his bald head and hurled himself at River.

Still breathless from the rush he'd made up the four flights of stairs, River didn't have the strength to withstand the force of the hulking man's weight as it crashed into his midsection. With a loud whoosh of air, River's lungs deflated. He fell forward, unable to breathe, catching his balance by grasping the bodyguard's mammoth shoulders.

Taking advantage of River's inability to recover from the blow to his diaphragm, the Oriental lifted his head in a forward thrust.

The force of the bald head caught River under the chin, snapping his head back with a violent cracking sound. As though his head were being ripped from his shoulders, blinding pain vibrated the length of his spine, and starbursts of light detonated in his brain, then dissolved into total blackness.

Her limbs heavy, Aidan twisted onto her side and struggled to open her eyes. Surprised to find herself surrounded by darkness, she inhaled deeply, inadvertently drawing the dank, musty odor of stale air and old bedding into her nostrils. Wrinkling her nose in distaste, she levered herself up on an elbow to look around.

Suddenly, she became aware of a gentle rocking sensation. She sat up straighter and cocked her head to the side, listening for a clue to her whereabouts. When she heard the low, moaning creek of timbers moving in a swaying, lulling rhythm, everything that had happened earlier came cascading back into her mind.

She was in the hold of a ship! A Chinese ship. A ship bound for China!

Chapter Nineteen

Still dazed from the blow to his chin, River stumbled into the lobby as the first of the firemen burst through the front entrance to the hotel, hollering and shouting orders at the people standing about.

"Somebody get the police!" River yelled over the pandemonium, his words slurred. "It was a hoax to kidnap a woman! There's no fire!"

A hum of questions came from the hotel guests crowding the lobby, most of them still wearing their bedclothes. "No fire?" "Is he drunk?" "Kidnap?" "Is that blood on his mouth?" "Maybe he's crazy."

Giving his men the signal to go on up to the fourth floor, the fire chief rushed over to meet River. "Are you saying this was a false alarm?"

Panting, River nodded and collapsed against a brocaded pillar. "Get the police," he panted. "The fire was just a ruse for them to kidnap Aidan."

"Aidan?" the chief asked, obviously not certain he should pay serious attention to what this young man was saying until he got a report from the men who were checking on the fire. "Who's Aidan?"

"That would no doubt be Aidan Donovan, sir," a smooth male voice offered from behind the fire chief.

Both the fireman and River looked up in surprise. "Percy!" River accused. "What are you doing here?"

"Who are you? Who is Aidan Donovan? And what do

276

you know about all this?" the chief asked.

"Scott Percy at your service, sir. I'm with the New York *Journal*."

"Since when?" River blurted out, a germ of suspicion sprouting in his mind as he began to recover from the beating he had taken.

Ignoring River's question, Percy continued. "Miss Donovan is also with the *Journal*. You may have read her article last month, about how she disguised herself as a man and went to Cuba with the Rough Riders. She was in San Francisco to do a story on—"

"Was?" River pushed himself away from the wall and twisted his fingers into Percy's shirt front. "What the hell do you know about this? Where is she?"

Scott gave the fire chief an embarrassed grin. "Did I say was? Of course, I meant *is*. Miss Donovan *is* still in San Francisco—as far as I know." His smile widened as he looked at River, his expression deliberately taunting. "Unless she has departed the city since I saw her yesterday. But you would know more about that than I would, wouldn't you, Lieutenant?"

"It's all clear," a fireman called out. "Another false alarm."

"Now will you get the police?" River asked impatiently.

Spurred into action by the fireman's report, the chief ignored River, but held up his hands to silence the waiting crowd. "The danger's over, folks," he announced. "You can go back to your rooms now." He turned back to River and Scott. "As for you two, you stay here. I'm sure the police will want to talk to both of you about this."

"Of course, I'll stay, if you think it will help solve this mystery," Percy said, "although I don't know what I can tell the police that I haven't told you. If Lieutenant Blue Eagle doesn't know where Miss Donovan is, I doubt

277

whether I can shed any light on her whereabouts. After all, he was the last person to see her. He was with her all night." Scott Percy directed a vindictive smile in River's direction, then looked at the fire chief. "Just let me place a quick telephone call to cancel my breakfast appointment, and I will be at your disposal."

"I'll go with you, Percy," River said purposefully. Using every effort not to conceal the fear clutching at his vitals, he grabbed Scott's arm and fell into step with him. "I have a very strong feeling that if we work together, we can determine Miss Donovan's whereabouts pretty quickly. Don't you have that feeling, Percy, old friend?"

The newspaperman shrugged his shoulders, his gaze shifting uncomfortably between the fire chief and River. "That's a good idea, *old friend*. I, too, have the distinct hunch that if we pool our information, we may both get what we are searching for."

"Just don't go too far," the fire chief called after them, his attention already focused on regrouping his crew and getting them back to the firehouse. "Nobody leaves before I find out who turned in that false alarm."

Once they were out of the fire chief's hearing range, River dragged the writer into an alcove. "All right, Percy, where the hell is she?"

Scott Percy assumed a pseudo-innocent look that would not have fooled a child. "How would I know? Is it my fault you can't keep up with your sweetheart? I haven't seen her since yesterday afternoon—before I met you outside the Willow Boarding House."

Clamping the smaller man's chin in a strong grip, River slammed him into a corner and brought his own face close to Percy's. "If you haven't seen her, how'd you know she was with me last night?"

Percy's eyes widened in surprise at his own slip. Then he gave River a sly grin. "I didn't. But you just confirmed my suspicions. May I quote you on that?"

River tightened his grip on Percy's jaw and pressed the heel of his hand against the reporter's windpipe.

The smug expression slithered off the other man's face, to be replaced by a desperate look. "I can't breathe," he wheezed.

River ignored his plea. "Can you imagine the agony of being staked out naked on top of a giant anthill, with the hot summer sun beating down on your sickly white skin, with hour after hour, until you are praying for death, Mr. Percy?" River snarled through gritted teeth. "Well, I suggest you try—so you'll have an idea of what I'm going to do to you if I ever read one word—in any newspaper—about where Aidan spent last night. Do I make myself clear?"

Nervous sweat trickling down his brow, Scott Percy nodded feebly.

"Good." River eased the pressure on the reporter's throat. "Now, suppose we begin again. Who's got Aidan and where is she?"

"I tell you, I don't know. She's probably with that Chinaman boyfriend of hers. I told you about him."

Again pressing his hand against the writer's neck, River slid Percy up the wall so that his feet were dangling above the floor. "I'm losing patience. The next word out of your mouth had better be what I want to hear—or you're a dead man."

"All right, all right," Percy choked out. "Put me down and I'll tell you what I know."

Lowering the reporter so that his toes touched the floor, River nodded his head. "Go on."

"When I found out this whole thing with the Chinaman was an act so she could get a story, I saw my chance to get even with her for what she did to me in Florida—*and* to get the story of a lifetime for myself.

279

Since I knew Chu Wong of the On Leong Tong was interested in her, I went to him and told him who she was and what she was up to."

Rage and frustration exploded in River's chest. "You rotten bastard! You set her up to be kidnapped and killed?" His fist doubled, he slammed it into Percy's midsection.

The reporter grunted. "No! You don't understand! It wasn't like that at all!"

"Oh? How was it?"

"I didn't intend for them to hurt her! I just wanted them to teach her a lesson—scare her a little. You've got to believe that."

"You've got three seconds to tell me where she is." River ground the words out, his self-control snapping. He wasn't sure he'd be able to stop himself from killing Scott Percy after he got the information he wanted. What Percy had already confessed to was more than enough justification. "Time's up!" River announced, squeezing Percy's neck, this time with no thought of stopping until the man was dead.

"I'll tell you!" the reporter rasped weakly. "I'll tell you everything. Please don't kill me," he begged, oblivious to the tears and sweat streaming down his cheeks.

River hesitated, but he didn't ease the pressure on the reporter's windpipe. "Where is she?"

"I think they took her to the docks," Percy admitted hoarsely, his words punctuated by desperate gasps for air. "Wong said something about sending her to China for some prince over there."

Horror and fear shook River. "And you set it up?" He brought his knee upward, the top of his rock-hard thigh crashing into the vulnerable masculine flesh of his victim. "Which ship is she on?"

"Unnnnh!" Percy retched, his impulse to double over

thwarted by River's tight grip on his chin, which kept his head forced back against the wall. "That's all I know. I swear it! Please let me go."

River paused, tempted beyond all endurance to kill the man. He searched Percy's bulging, watery eyes, and decided the reporter had told him all he knew. Then he loosened his hold. "Consider yourself fortunate that I don't have the time to kill you properly, Percy. But if I find out you've lied to me, you'll wish I had." Drawing back his fist, he plowed it into the sniveling writer's face, then let him slide down the wall as though he were dissolving into the floor. "Next time, I'll have all the time in the world to do it right! Make no mistake about that," he told the unconscious heap at his feet.

Aidan leveled a black look at the bowl of rice and vegetables set before her. "I told you, I'm not hungry." She picked up the bowl and flung it at the young servant who'd just brought it into the small cabin. "I want to talk to Chu Wong!"

Ducking as the bowl flew past his head, but unable to protect himself from being splattered with rice and broth and vegetables, the servant shook his head sadly. "Ti so solly, missy. Master Wong say he not see you tirr we sair."

"Sail?" Aidan repeated, her anxiousness to talk to the man responsible for her plight suddenly losing precedence. "You mean we haven't— Does that mean we're still in San Francisco?"

The servant's eyes filled with fear as he realized he'd told his master's captive something she was not supposed to know. His hands clasped together, he nervously bowed his slight body up and down, then started backing toward the door. "Engrish velly bad, missy. Ship reave San

Flancisco. We at sea."

Her pity for the servant genuine, Aidan smiled consolingly. "Don't worry, Ti," she said, moving toward him and catching his arm before he could make good his escape. "I won't tell anyone you told me—not if you'll help me get off this ship before it sails."

Terror widened the servant's dark almond-shaped eyes until they seemed round. Wagging his head from left to right in frantic denial, he shook free of her hold and turned toward the door. "No, no," he protested. "Master kirr Ti. No can help, missy."

Aidan knew Ti was right; he would be punished severely if he helped her escape. A spasm of guilt clawed at her insides, but she had no choice. "Chu won't be able to hurt you if you come with me!" she said in an urgent whisper, certain she'd found the perfect solution to the war between her conscience and her instinct for survival. "We can both get away."

A flash of longing ignited in the servant's dark eyes, then dimmed with fear. "No. Too dangelous. Ti stay on ship. Master find and kirr."

Understanding his fright, but encouraged by that flicker of hope she'd seen, Aidan crossed to Ti, who was no taller than she, and touched his arm. "No! He won't. I promise. I have friends—important friends—who will pay you much money for my return, and they will protect you from Chu. They'll even help you move to a place where he'll never find you."

Ti took a breath and turned back to face her, as if he meant to accept. Then, as before, the light left his eyes and his shoulders slumped.

Refusing to give up, Aidan closed in on him. "Think about it, Ti," she whispered, her voice luring. "You'd have enough money to live on for a long time. My friends could even help you start your own business—if that's what you want. You'll never have to follow a master's orders again, because you'll be free. You could even employ people to work for you, and you'd be the one giving the orders."

Ti didn't speak, but he continued to shake his head.

Knowledge that time was running out throbbed in the back of Aidan's mind. The ship could be setting sail any minute, and if she didn't convince Ti to help her right away, she was going to be forced to do something more drastic. Her gaze darted to the heavy vase she'd noticed earlier on the table beside the door. As much as she hated the idea, if he couldn't be persuaded to help her, she would have no choice but to use force.

She tried again, her calm tone belying the urgent pounding in her chest. "I don't think you understand what I'm offering you." Keeping her intense gaze leveled on Ti's face, she angled her body to the side and eased back a step in the direction of the table and vase. "This could be the only chance you'll ever have to escape." She took another step back. "Come with me, Ti! Don't say no to a future as a free man!"

Ti stopped shaking his head and gave her a helpless shrug. "Fleedom is my dleam since a smarr boy when my palents serr me to Chu for money to feed bluthahs and sistahs. But Ti not want to die."

"Neither do I, Ti! And I'll do everything in my power to see that neither of us do." Aidan's slow, deliberate movement backward came to an abrupt halt as her bottom collided with the table. Unable to stop herself, she drew in a surprised breath. This was it. A flicker of panic rose in her eyes as she glanced at Ti, certain he'd seen her reaction to the table. Then relief washed over her as she realized he was too lost in his own plight to notice.

Seeing how desperately Ti wanted to go with her cut

into Aidan's heart, but she didn't know what else to do. She'd offered him a way out, and if he was too blind to take it, she had no choice but to leave him behind. She could delay her escape no longer. Much as she hated to knock Ti out, she would, because one way or the other she was getting off this ship before it sailed.

Stealthily slipping a hand behind her back, she grazed the table top with her fingers. "But no matter how afraid I am of dying, I'd rather die than spend the rest of my life as a slave." She lightly patted the table behind her. "Don't you see? No matter how grave or dangerous the consequences, freedom is worth any price."

Her hand stilled at the sudden feel of the smooth, cool vase, and a shaft of panic speared through her. The moment was at hand—literally! She shot Ti a look of regret. Could she do it? Could she crash the vase against the skull of this frightened young man?

Freedom is worth any price, a strong voice repeated in her head. *Any price.* She closed her fingers around the narrow indentation above the vase's pedestal.

"One last time, Ti. Will you pay the price and take the risk?" She secured her grip on the vase.

Ti shook his head. "I not want . . ."

Aidan's heart sank. Until that very second, she hadn't given up hope. But now . . . She started to lift the vase. "I'm sorry, Ti," she whispered, her vision blurred by a sheen of tears. "I'm so, so—"

". . . to be srave. Ti want to be flee man. Ti want to take lisk for fleedom!"

River and Roger crouched between the stacks of crates piled on the unlit wharf, worriedly taking in the rush of activity only a few feet away aboard the square-sailed Chinese junk that was obviously being readied to sail.

"She's here," River whispered, almost to himself. "Aidan's on that ship. I can feel it."

"I agree," Roger muttered huskily. "They're in too big a hurry to leave port for me to believe they're not carrying some sort of contraband—like a white woman."

River bolted to his feet. "To hell with those policemen you called for! I'm going after her without them."

"Get back here!" Roger roughly forced River down beside him. "You can't just storm up there and tell them you want her. You'd be dead so fast you wouldn't know what hit you."

Realizing Roger was right, River made no further effort to leave. "I can't just sit here waiting for assistance that may not come. They could be torturing her. Every second she's their prisoner, there's a bigger chance we won't find her alive."

"You don't need to worry yourself about that, my friend," Roger said with a sad smile. "They won't kill her—or torture her. They want to keep her comfortable and in good health . . . so she will bring the highest price when they get her to China."

"You sound like you've seen this happen before," River said, his distraught gaze never leaving the open deck of the junk.

"More than once Pinkertons have been hired to locate missing young white women, only to have the search lead to Chu—and end there."

Rage burned in River. "If you know about him, why hasn't he been arrested?"

"We've never been able to prove anything against him. We always just miss catching him red-handed—which is another reason I can't let you rush up there like a one-man army. If Chu suspects we're on to him, he'll kill Aidan—and any other young women on board—in order to destroy the evidence we have against him."

285

Fear and frustration discharging in his brain, River, pounded his fist against a wooden crate. "Well, we've got to do something! I can't take much more of this waiting."

"I think one of us should sneak on board to make certain she's there while the other waits for the police."

River started to rise. "Good thinking. I'll go."

"Wait a minute!" Roger hissed, catching his arm. "I said *sneak*. How far do you think you'd get before you were spotted? With your height and your eyes, you'd stand out like a Chinaman at a Baptist prayer meeting. You stay here and wait for help. I'll go."

Knowing Roger was right didn't make it any easier for River to agree to stay behind, but he hunkered back down on his haunches. "All right . . . for now. But if you're not back fast, I'm— Wait a minute!" He nodded toward the gangplank as two stealthy figures appeared at its top. "What do you make of that?"

As Roger shifted his gaze in the direction River was indicating, two small, coolie-hatted forms started down the gangway toward the wharf. "Just a couple of servants going out to pick up some last-minute provisions," he replied nonchalantly, turning his attention back to River. "I want your word you won't move until I get back."

"Yeah, sure," River answered. But for some peculiar reason he was unable to accept Roger's explanation. Something about the Chinese servants just didn't seem right—though he couldn't put his finger on what it was. Both were clad in the loose-fitting trousers and shirts he'd seen a thousand times since he'd come to San Francisco. Nothing odd about that. And they both kept their covered heads bowed, as the lower class people did all over Chinatown, and they both used short shuffling steps to scurry down the gangplank. Still, something didn't sit right with River. It was if he'd seen one of them before.

Before he could contemplate further the cause of that odd feeling of familiarity, the servants came to an abrupt standstill halfway down the gangplank, their heads swiveling from side to side in indecision.

Automatically, River's gaze shifted to the foot of the gangplank. There, two very large Orientals, long ugly knives in hand, advanced on the hapless servants.

"Oh, oh!" one of the trapped servants cried. "I sure hope you can swim." Giving his companion a shove into the dark water below, he followed him off the gangplank.

Immediately recognizing Aidan's voice, River bolted up from his crouch, the revolver he'd hidden in his belt drawn and cocked. "Hold it right there!" he shouted to the two guards standing on the gangplank and peering into the water to locate their escaped quarry.

Startled, the two Orientals looked up, their slanted eyes darting over the stacked cargo littering the dark wharf in search of the source of the threat.

"Drop your knives in the water and come down here," River ordered.

The guards gave each other puzzled looks and then turned back toward River, but they didn't surrender their knives.

Realizing they didn't understand him, River called back to Roger, "Tell them I'll blow their goddamn heads off if they don't drop the knives."

Speaking in rapid Chinese, Roger conveyed River's message, his tone immediately convincing the two thugs that they were dead men if they didn't follow orders.

As their knives sliced into the water, a team of San Francisco policemen swarmed over the pier, leaping onto the junk, shouting orders and arresting every sailor or bodyguard they encountered.

His mind whirling with horrible thoughts of what

could have happened to Aidan, River dropped his revolver and ran to the edge of the pier, tearing off his coat and hat and tossing them aside as he went. Frantically, he searched the narrow, inky space between the wharf and the Chinese junk that rocked and bumped against the pilings with the sloshing rhythm of the sea, tugging off his heavy boots as he did so. What if Aidan couldn't swim? Surely she could. She had to be able to swim well enough to stay afloat until he got there.

Leaping into the inky void into which Aidan had disappeared only moments before, he refused to consider the very real danger that she could already be dead. As cool, salty blackness closed over his head he told himself not to think about the possibility that she might have been crushed against one of the supporting timbers if, in her hurry to escape, she had gotten caught between a submerged piling and the hull of the junk. Struggling to the surface of the foul sea water, he tried to blank out a vision of Aidan at the bottom of the bay, enmeshed in a tangle of seaweed, dead fish and the trash that littered the water.

His breathing labored, more from terror than from exertion, River struggled for air as his head bobbed to the surface. His black hair, slicked down over his eyes, was obscuring his vision, so he grabbed hold of a piling and shook it back. "Aidan!" he shouted, his eyes frantically moving over the collection of debris surrounding him. "Can you hear me?"

"River . . ." a small, weak cry came from beneath the wharf.

His heart leaped with relief. She was alive! "Yes, Little Fire, it's me. Where are you?"

When there was no response, River's panic grew to new proportions. Maybe he'd imagined the cry. Maybe he was too late. Maybe she was injured and had already held herself afloat as long as she could.

"No!" he said aloud. It was Aidan he'd heard and she was still alive. "Aidan, for God's sake, answer me! Tell me where you are!"

He moved deeper into the pitch black darkness beneath the wharf, his eyes burning from the saltiness and the filth of the water. "Aidan! I'm coming." Straining to hear above the crash of waves breaking against the pier supports, he swam in what he thought was the direction of that one weak cry for help. "Dammit, Aidan, I can't see! You've got to answer so I can follow the sound of your voice." Still, he received no reply.

River swam back and forth through the floating waste under the pier. Over and over, he called out her name, his tone sometimes pleading, sometimes angry, each cry more desperate. Every time a large fish or a clump of submerged seaweed curled around and past his body, his breath formed a strangling lump in his throat, as he felt beneath the water to be certain he hadn't collided into a dead body—Aidan's.

"Aiiiiii-dannnnn!" he yelled, clinging to a post to catch his breath. "Please answer me!"

"Ri-ver," a weak voice answered, sounding more like a whisper than a cry.

Not certain he wasn't imagining things, River snapped his head around. "Aidan?" he asked testingly. "Is that you?"

"River, help me. I can't hold on much long—"

"Oh, my god!" He lunged toward the piling he thought Aidan had called him from, praying that God would give her the strength to last just a few minutes more. "Hang on, Little Fire!" he cried. "I'm coming! Don't give up on me now."

Chapter Twenty

Aidan came awake with a start. What was that deafening rumble she heard? Not only did it block out all other sound, but it seemed to be vibrating throughout her entire body. Her eyes snapped open.

Panic engulfed her as she became aware of the darkness of her surroundings. Memories of a watery shelter beneath the pier assaulted her, and she immediately wondered if she was still there. No, she hurriedly decided. If she were still in the water, she would be cold and wet, not warm and dry. Besides, didn't she remember strong arms lifting her limp body out of the water? Or was that just a dream? She squeezed her eyes shut, mustering what memories she could: the two enormous Chinese guards coming toward her, jumping with Ti into the black void of the bay, excruciating pain when something had cracked into the side of her head, and the . . . What?

Terror seared through her. Could the arms that had pulled her from the water have belonged to one of the Chinese guards? Was she again a prisoner on the Chinese junk? *No!* Her mind screamed. *It can't be!* Yet that would account for the rocking sensation she was experiencing, wouldn't it?

But this sounds and feels more like a train on land

than a ship at sea.

Relief flooded through her. That was it. It had to be! She was on a train! Not a Chinese junk, but a train. A glorious train!

Without warning, the words to an old spiritual she'd heard years before suddenly echoed in her mind. *This train is bound for Glory, this train . . .*

"Oh, god! No!" She bolted upright as the full meaning of the words slammed into her consciousness. "I can't be dead!"

"Aidan?" a sleepy masculine voice asked. "What is it?"

Snapping her head around in the direction of the voice, Aidan stared with eyes that were just beginning to make out shapes in the darkness. "River?" she asked, afraid to trust the joy that swept over her. "Is it you?"

River raised up beside her and wrapped his arms around her shoulders. "Of course, it's me. Who else would it be?"

"Oh, it is you!" she cried, finally breaking free of the mental fog that had held her prisoner for the past few minutes. Burying her face against the taut muscles of his chest, she clung to him. "I thought . . . I was sure I'd . . ." Already struggling to remember the fast-fading, half-awake thoughts she'd been having, she shook her head helplessly. "Where are we?"

"Shh. Everything's okay now. We're on a train bound for Cheyenne."

"You pulled me out of the water, didn't you?"

River nodded and lay back down, carrying her with him. "Yeah, it was me," he said, his voice rife with guilt and self-disgust, as he remembered that she wouldn't have needed saving if he hadn't been so stupid as to lock her in the hotel room.

The security of his embrace melted over Aidan like a beautiful dream, erasing all recrimination from her mind.

291

All she could think of was how good it felt to be secure in his arms. "I knew it, you know. I knew you would come."

"Yeah, well, I almost didn't get there in time." Thoughts of what would have happened if he hadn't gone back hit him, as they had repeatedly over the past twelve hours. Ferociously, he tightened his hold on her. "So help me, Fire, I'll never let anyone hurt you like that again. I swear I'll. . ."

"Ti!" Aidan exclaimed, raising her head and staring urgently into River's pained eyes. "What happened to Ti?"

"Who?"

Alarm rocked through Aidan as she pictured the frightened young Asian's trusting face. She'd promised to help him, and instead she'd . . . No! She wouldn't let herself think that. "The Chinese servant who helped me escape!" she insisted urgently. "You saved him, too, didn't you? He's all right, isn't he?"

River shook his head, and a terrible coldness came over Aidan. "You mean he . . . ?"

Seeing what she thought in her eyes, River hurried to explain. "No. *I* didn't save him, but, your friend's all right."

Her brow furrowed in confusion. "I don't understand. Is he alive or not?"

"He's not only alive, but at this minute he's on his way to start a new and 'flee' life in New York City with Roger and his family—who have decided to relocate for 'health reasons,' since the San Francisco tongs are now aware of his double identity and are looking for him."

"How did Ti get out of the water? I have the feeling that he couldn't swim—or did I just dream that?"

"From what Ti said, he told you he didn't swim as the two of you went into the water. Then you both must've been bumped by the hull of the junk as it battered the wharf, because that's all he remembered. He lost consciousness. Fortunately, in spite of a really nasty blow to your head, you managed to swim to safety back under the pier, dragging him along. When Ti came to, he said you had his arms looped around a piling and were holding him there. You didn't let go of him until the instant before I found you, and by then he was recovered enough to pull your head out of the water before you went under."

Aidan was silent for a long time, straining to make some sense out of what River had told her. Finally, she had to concede that the memory of those grueling minutes in the water might be forever lost to her. She shook her head. "I guess I'm just too mean to die, huh?"

River forced a chuckle and settled her head on his chest, smoothing her hair with his hand. "Or too stubborn to let someone else write your story!"

Her head popped up again. "That's right! My story! What are we doing on this train? I can't go to South Dakota yet. I've got to get back to San Francisco to make sure the raid on the brothels in the opium dens goes as planned."

He patted her head and tried to bring it back down to his shoulder. "Your business in San Francisco is finished, Aidan. The raid was a huge success. All you've got to do now is write the story, and you can do that between here and South Dakota."

She clapped her hands. "Thank goodness!" she exclaimed. "I knew it would be. How many slave girls did they save? And what about Chu Wong? He didn't get away, did he?"

River let out a long sigh. "I don't suppose there's much chance you'll go back to sleep and let all this wait until morning, is there?"

293

Aidan tilted her head to the side and arched her eyebrows capriciously. "I thought you said it was *me* who got bumped on the head. You know I have to get this all written up and wired to New York before the story breaks and someone else beats me to it. I just hope I haven't lost too much time." She rolled to a sitting position on the bed. "Now, tell me everything!"

Shaking his head in defeat, River swung his feet to the floor and sat up. He raked his fingers through his hair and yawned loudly.

"Riiiii-ver," she said, her voice rising with impatience. "Stop delaying. Tell me what happened!"

"All right, all right, but only if you promise you'll go back to sleep when I'm through. The doctor said you shouldn't try to do too much until the swelling goes down. That's why he gave you a sedative. He wanted you to sleep."

"I promise!" she vowed, her excitement and anticipation evident.

River heaved a defeated sigh. "First of all, while I was fishing you and Ti out from under the pier, Roger and the San Francisco police were raiding Chu's junk. It turns out they've been after him for a long time, but never could catch him committing a crime. This time, thanks to you, they not only caught him off guard, they found all the proof they needed to put him away for a long time. It seems you weren't the only white woman bound for China on that junk."

"You mean there were others?"

River nodded his head. "Besides you, eight frightened young female tourists had been lured on board to be used as prostitutes in China."

"Are they all safe now?"

His head moved up and down. "They were all pretty scared, but other than a few rope burns on their wrists, they're okay. The best part is that every one of them is willing to testify against Chu."

"No wonder I was unable to find any evidence of white women being lured into prostitution in Chinatown! They must've all been sent out of the country."

"On the same junks that were bringing Chinese slave girls here from China. Chu was making a fortune on both sides of the ocean."

"What about the girls in the opium dens? You said the raids went on as planned. How many got out? And where are they now?"

"While we were at the docks with Chu, the Pinkertons stormed into seven brothels and brought out twenty-two girls in all," River replied. "Right now, they're all safely tucked into clean beds at the Presbyterian Mission on Sacramento Street, where they'll be nursed back to health and taught a trade—just the way you envisioned it."

Aidan sat back on her calves, a satisfied smile on her face. "Then it was all worth it, wasn't it?"

River shrugged his shoulders. "I'm not sure I'd go that far, but because of you, thirty young women have been given new leases on life, so I can't really criticize you for what you did. But I'm warning you, if you *ever* again put me through anything like the past couple of days, I'll personally strangle you with my own hands! Is that understood?"

Aidan scooted over to him and wrapped her arms around his neck. "You're not fooling anyone, River Blue Eagle. You loved it. In your whole life, you've never had as much excitement as you've had since the day you found me on that train last May. Admit it," she goaded, trailing a line of fluttery kisses along his collarbone, "I brought fun and adventure into your serious, sensible life, and now you just can't get enough. That's why you keep coming back for more, isn't it? Because you're afraid you're going to miss something."

"Humph!" he grunted, his eyes drifting shut as she covered his throat with kisses. "Your head injury must be causing you to have delusions," he declared with a forced laugh as he lifted her onto his lap. "No amount of excitement wouldn't drag a rational, perfectly sane man into even one of your escapades. Only a crazy man would deliberately—"

Moving her lips along the outer rim of his ear, Aidan settled herself more comfortably in his lap. A tortured groan escaped from his lips. "And we both know you're not crazy, don't we? So, how do you explain it?" she murmured against his ear.

"Explain what?" he asked hoarsely.

"If you're not crazy, and if it's not for the excitement, what keeps dragging *you* into my escapades? Why, no matter how angry you are with me, and no matter how you disagree with what I'm doing, are you always there to help me when I need you most?"

His shoulders tensed beneath her caressing fingertips. "I feel responsible for your safety."

Aidan smiled knowingly and flicked her tongue along the crease between his chin and mouth. "Responsible, huh? And that's the only reason?"

"Well, of course there's our bargain. I do have a duty to my people to keep you alive until you write their story," he added huskily, his hands caressing up and down her back.

"Yes, the story about the Indians . . ." She lowered her mouth to his chest and covered a taut pectoral bulge with kisses. "Duty and responsibility. Both very commendable reasons for a practical and 'sane' man to risk his life to save an impulsive writer when she gets *in over her head*." She giggled mischievously.

"Face it, River. Duty and responsibility don't have anything to do with why you came to California for me."

He shifted uneasily, not quite able to look at her. "What other reasons would I have?"

She nodded, continuing her gentle assault on his flesh with her lips. "You tell me."

Emitting a low primal growl, River flipped her over onto her back and covered her body with his. "Dammit, Aidan, do I have to spell it out for you?" His lips covered hers, his hands tearing at her gown.

The teasing game Aidan had been playing came to an end as her body responded to the weight of his over her. She sensuously lifted her hips to him. "Yes, River," she whispered, breaking off the kiss. "I have to hear you say it."

He reared his head back and stared down into her dark eyes. Finally, he spoke, his tone a mixture of relief and misery. "Because as hard as I've fought it, I . . . I care about you. And no matter how wrong we are for each other, I don't like the idea of a future without you. There! Are you satisfied?"

Tears filled Aidan's eyes, and her mouth spread in a triumphant grin. It wasn't an admission of undying love, but it was close enough—for now. She clasped his cheeks between her palms and held his face above her. "Was that so hard? Was it so terrible to admit that you want to be with me? Don't you know I feel the same way about you? Don't you realize I'm miserable every minute I spend away from you?"

She smiled lovingly at seeing his solemn expression. "And, my serious Indian brave, as for our being wrong for each other, I'm going to prove to you how wrong you are when you say that. Can't you see, there were never two people more perfect together than we are? We're two halves of a whole. We're only wrong when we're apart."

"Now, who's being serious?" he asked, his teasing

words not quite disguising the emotion that made his voice break.

"Serious? You think that's serious? I'll show you serious!" she announced, shoving his large body off her and rolling him onto his back.

Straddling his waist, she caressed his muscular arms, then raised them above his head and held them there as she surrendered her mouth to his.

Flattening her body against his chest, she traced the crease between his lips with her tongue. He started to lower his arms to embrace her, but she stopped him. "Uh-uh," she warned against his mouth, pressing his arms back into the mattress. "Don't move. Just lie still and let me show you how *right* we are together."

When she felt the muscles in his arms relax, she slid down his body, bathing his neck and upper chest with kisses.

Stretching her arms above her head so she might keep her grip on his biceps, she moved lower on his torso and covered a flat male nipple with her mouth, flicking her tongue over its pebble-hard center in a slow, deliberately torturous attack.

"Ohhh." He moved restlessly beneath her. "You'd better stop if you know what's good for you."

Aidan smiled. Already his swollen manhood was probing urgently against her stomach in a plea for relief, but she had no intention of granting his request — yet. "Oh, I know what's good for me . . . and for you. Don't move," she whispered.

Lifting herself off him, she caught his breechcloth at the waist and whisked it from around his lean hips. Making no attempt to disguise her hunger for him, she leaned back and slowly untied the bow at the neck of her gown. With seductive motions, she slipped the gown off one shoulder, then the other. Inch by inch, she peeled the

298

garment down her body, exposing her pale flesh to River's caressing gaze, her own eyes bright with passion.

When they were both nude, Aidan lowered her head to kiss and nibble her way along a sinewy calf, pausing to pay particular attention to the back of his knee before thoroughly mapping his thigh, side to side, knee to groin.

Raising her head, she looked up the length of his lean body. Eyes closed, River was still sprawled as she had positioned him, hands above his head. His hips rose and fell softly in an instinctive invitation to her.

"Not yet," she told him coyly, bending her head to give his neglected leg the same foot-to-hip adoration she'd given the other one.

By the time she had licked and kissed the flesh of the second tanned limb, his hips were rocking aggressively upward.

Tickling the swollen length of his manhood with the pads of her fingertips in a teasing hint of what was to come, Aidan ran her tongue along the crease at the top of his thigh, over and over, each time stopping just short of her ultimate goal.

"Oh, god," he moaned, "you're killing me."

"Should I stop?" she asked, her lips poised a scant quarter-inch from him, her fingers circling him lightly.

The answer she received was the helpless groan he released as he thrust upward with his need. At last taking pity on him, she tightened her hold on the rigid flesh and took it into the loving heat of her mouth.

Knowing he wouldn't be able to control his body's wildly pulsating desire much longer, River brought his arms down and caught her under the arms. He wrenched her away from him and dragged her upward. Settling her over him, he brought her down on him with a satisfied moan.

His fingers gripped her hips and bottom. Time and again, he lifted her almost off him, then brought her back down on his rock-hard passion, each thrust coming faster, going deeper, until every nerve in her body was concentrated on the sensations he'd aroused.

Then it was happening, that glorious rocket ride to the heavens, and all either one of them could do was cry aloud and wish that euphoric state of exaltation would last forever.

"Oh." Her bones feeling as though they had turned to jelly, Aidan collapsed onto his rapidly rising chest. "Do you still think we're wrong for each other?" she asked breathlessly.

"Humph." That one syllable had a decidedly bitter ring to it. "There's no doubt our bodies are compatible. If we could spend the rest of our lives in bed, we'd be fine. It's other aspects of us that will eventually cause one of us to destroy the other. Look what happened yesterday. I came out here to protect you, and I almost got you killed."

"Almost got me ki—?" A flash of memory ignited in Aidan's thoughts, and she wrested herself free of his embrace. "You tied me up and left me alone in that hotel room!"

He didn't try to hold her. "I didn't intend to leave you there more than a couple of minutes—just long enough to teach you a lesson. But you made me so damned mad, I wasn't thinking straight . . . and I left. By the time my temper cooled down and I realized what I'd done, I raced back to the room. But I was too late. Those bastards already had you, and before I could do anything, a Chinaman the size of a locomotive came at me. The next thing I knew, I was coming to in an empty hallway, and you were gone. I wouldn't blame you if you never wanted to set eyes on me again—much less go to South Dakota with me."

River's confession, and his obvious misery, washed away the flare of anger that had erupted when Aidan had remembered the minutes in the hotel room before she'd been kidnapped. "I knew it," she murmured. "I knew you didn't intend to leave me like that. Just like I knew you'd come in time to keep me from drowning."

River looked at her, stunned. "Haven't you heard what I've been saying? I almost got you killed!"

"But you didn't. You saved my life."

"If it hadn't been for me, you wouldn't have had to be saved."

"You don't know that. Chu came to that hotel with one purpose—to get me, If you hadn't left, he probably would have had you killed when he burst into the room. Then who would have fished Ti and me out of the bay? And who would have called the police so they could save those unfortunate women on the ship and put an end to the evil Chu Wong's slave ring?"

"You mean you're willing to forgive and forget what I did?" he asked, his tone disbelieving.

Aidan grinned at the shocked expression on his face. "Forgive, yes, because I know you believed . . ." She paused and shook her head. ". . . in some *demented, misguided* way I'll never understand, that you were doing it for my good. And because even the most sane and practical man is allowed *one* mistake in judgment. But, forget?" She blew out a huff of laughter.

"Not on your life, mister! I'll never forget. And if you ever so much as think about doing something like that to me again, you'd better be sure you're in good running shape—because when I find you, you'll pay in ways even your Indian ancestors would have considered too cruel for their worst enemies!"

"That's a pretty serious threat."

"That wasn't a threat, Mr. Blue Eagle," she said, flopping over him and kissing his nose. "It's a promise. A solemn promise! And you know me well enough to be sure that when I decide to do something, I don't stop until I find a way to do it, no matter what—or who—stands in my way."

"And no matter how your actions go against logic and common sense," he added with a disapproving grunt.

Aidan grinned mischievously. "You talk as though common sense and logic should keep you from following your dreams. But you're wrong. Common sense is to protect you, not tie you down. It's what gives us an intelligent respect and awareness of the obstacles that stand between us and our dreams. It's what keeps us from blindly forging ahead without considering the consequences of our actions. That's where the logic comes in. Logic allows us to figure out ways to overcome those obstacles, no matter how great or small they are."

She sighed wistfully. "Don't you see, River? If we use our common sense and logic to get rid of roadblocks instead of letting them become the actual roadblocks stop us from following our dreams, there's nothing we can't achieve."

"I had no idea you were such a philosopher," River said, his voice touched with admiration. "Not that I necessarily agree with your theory."

"That's because your common sense and logic are still working against you—not to mention a healthy dose of negative thinking. In fact, I wouldn't be the least bit surprised if right this minute your common sense isn't asking you why you're wasting time worrying about the reservation exposé being written, because your logic is telling you that nothing I write will make the whites care about the Indians or do anything to correct the situation on the reservations."

"And you're telling yourself that you can just waltz onto the reservation, write a story about Indians, and create a happy ending with the flick of your pen—like in one of your spoiled little white-girl fairy tales. Don't you think it's time you realized you're not a little girl anymore, Aidan, and life is no fairy tale? Isn't it time for you to come down to earth and see things as they really are and not the way you think they should be?"

His derisive tone twisted in Aidan's chest, and she rose up, her anger fairly crackling between them. "If coming down to earth means having my feet so firmly planted on the ground that I've taken root like you have, I'll never do it. You're too full of reasons why you can't do this and why you can't do that, River. I believe in old adages like, 'Nothing ventured, nothing gained,' and 'If at first you don't succeed, try, try again.' "

"What about 'Better safe than sorry'?" he asked with a derisive snort.

"Not in my vocabulary. I believe 'It's better to have tried and failed, than never to have tried at all.' "

"Isn't that supposed to be 'loved and lost,' not 'tried and failed.' "

Aidan shrugged. "Either way, it means taking a chance on getting hurt, doesn't it?" She flopped over onto her side, her back to him. "It's really too bad. Together, we could have had it all. I could have taught you to fly, and you could have taught me the value of having my feet on the ground. But since you're not willing to let go and take a chance on flying with me, I'll fly alone, because no matter what you do or say, I'll never allow you, or your suffocating logic and common sense, to anchor me so securely to the ground that I'm afraid to take a chance on overcoming the impossible."

Chapter Twenty-one

The Chadron, Nebraska stable owner's gaze traveled over River's expensive clothing, then returned to the stick he was using to remove manure and straw from his own worn boot. "Don't rent my rigs to Injuns, Mesicans 'r Niggers, no matter what kind o' fancy duds they's wearin'," he stated flatly, spitting a stream of tobacco juice at a pair of flies mating on a nearby post.

"I'll pay double your regular charge," River offered, deliberately ignoring the man's baiting. He was too tired to let himself be trapped in a no-win situation by a bigoted old fool. He just wanted transportation to complete the last miles of the trip to the Blue Creek Indian Agency in South Dakota, and the only stage had left town eight hours earlier.

"Don't rent to breeds neither — or their fancy hussies," the man added, giving Aidan a disapproving glance.

Shocked, she looked at River's rigid profile. Well, if he wouldn't say something, she certainly would. How could he let that last statement go unchallenged? She stepped toward the liveryman, her eyes blazing. "Why you fatuous, inconsequential little buffoo—"

River's strong fingers clamped around her upper arm, cutting off the rest of her tirade as surely as if he'd slapped a hand over her mouth. "Then we'll buy it," he ground out through gritted teeth, his grip digging painfully into her flesh. With his free hand, he reached into his breast pocket and retrieved his wallet. "How much?"

Eying the wallet, the man thoughtfully licked his lips, then spit another stream of tobacco juice out the side of his mouth. "Ain't got none for sale."

"The sign out front says, 'Horse and Buggy for Sale,' " River pointed out evenly, though the effort to restrain his temper was obviously taking its toll.

The stableman shifted his gaze toward the sign, then back to River. "The sign's for white folks. Not In—"

His anger nearing the point of explosion, River spun Aidan around and roughly prodded her toward the stable door. "Let's go."

Her expression protesting, she resisted. "Are you going to let him get away with that?"

"Don't guess you'd be in'er'sted in that old buckboard parked out front?" the old man called after them, no doubt deciding he could "relax his standards" just this once.

River stopped in midstep, the muscles of his jaw bunching into a hard knot. "How much?" he asked, turning slowly to face his tormentor, his expression grim.

The man scratched a whiskered chin and rolled his eyes thoughtfully. "I guess I could let it go to a Injun what can read for say . . . fifty dollars."

"Including two mules," River countered, knowing that wasn't the case.

The man laughed raucously and slapped his thigh. "That's a good 'un. An' they say Injuns ain't got no sense o' humor!" Wiping the grin off his mouth as he rubbed the dribble of tobacco juice from his chin with the back of his sleeve, he made his offer. "That's fifty for the buckboard by itself. If ya want the mules too, it'll cost ya extree. That'll be another fifty." He paused to spit, studying River's reaction. When he saw the billfold come out of River's pocket, his mouth split in a victorious sneer. "Each."

Aidan couldn't prevent the indignant gasp that escaped her. "Why that's robbery!"

The old man shrugged. "Take it 'r leave it."

"We'll take it." River glowered at Aidan as he counted out the money. He held it out, just short of the greedy stableman's reach. "I'll need a bill of sale."

"Bill o' sale? What for? You can trust me."

Smiling, River turned to Aidan and shook his head. "And they say white men don't have a sense of humor!"

"That was just a small taste of what an Indian puts up with all his life," River said, giving Aidan a boost onto the weathered and splitting seat of the rickety buckboard on which he had placed their luggage.

"I'll tell you one thing," she declared, freeing her skirt which had snagged on the rough edge of the seat, but paying no heed as the expensive fabric ripped, "I wouldn't have given that disgusting man a penny! I'd have gone somewhere else."

River blew out a derisive snort and climbed up onto the seat beside her. "It wouldn't have been any different anywhere else. We'd have just used up a lot of time and energy, and in the end we still would've paid too much for a wagon that's not fit for much more than firewood — or we'd be walking."

"Humph!" She glanced over her shoulder to be sure their things were securely tied down. "That may be so, but I sure would have felt better if you hadn't stopped me from giving that illiterate boor a piece of my mind. How dare he talk to you like that? Why, any fool can see his sort isn't fit to shine your boots!"

Touched by her loyalty, River twisted to face her, his smile warm and sympathetic. "I appreciate your desire to stick up for me, but when you consider what we're here for, how one old hatemonger treats me or what he thinks, really isn't very important, is it? Doesn't it make more sense to bite back your anger, pay him his price, and get on with what we came here to do?"

Aidan studied her hands which in her lap, then shrugged. "I guess you're right—this time. Still, I sure would have liked to tell him a thing or two."

River reached over and caught her chin, bringing her face around so she had to look at him. "Do me a favor, Little Fire. Don't waste your fire on things that don't matter in the long run. Save it for the important things. Like the story you're going to write exposing conditions on the reservations. I have a feeling we're going to need it more than ever before!"

Aidan grinned contritely. How could she stay mad when he looked at her like that? If his eyes just weren't so blue, and so old and tired, as if he didn't really believe what they were doing would actually make any difference . . . A wave of sadness washed over her. If it was the last thing she did, she was going to see River's eyes filled with hope again. "All right, I'll try," she said, leaning toward him to brush his mouth with a light kiss. "But let's go wire my folks and tell them where I am, and then get me out of this town fast, because this is one 'fancy hussy' who can't guarantee she won't set that simple-minded manure mucker's longjohns on fire if she sees him again!"

It was dusk when River drove the mules and buckboard over the Blue Creek bridge and neared the entrance to the Blue Creek Agency compound, five miles north of the Nebraska state line. He glanced cautiously at Aidan, wondering what she was thinking as her alert gaze took in the fortified wire fence that surrounded the agency.

Seeing her dismay, he knew a moment of shame. He deliberately hadn't told her about the guards at the agency gate or the fence that surrounded the reservation. In order for her to fully comprehend the plight of the once-free Indians now contained on the reservations, she had to experience it firsthand: the bigotry, the frustration, the hopelessness, and most of all, the feeling of being a prisoner in your own land.

"This reminds me of the warden's compound at the state prison I wanted to do a story on," she said with a slight shiver, though the evening was quite warm. "Of course, from what I heard about the way he and his guards treated the prisoners, he had more than sufficient reason to be afraid of them."

"Have you got a pass?" a blue-shirted member of the Indian police shouted from the other side of the gate. "No one comes through here after dark without a pass."

"Certainly, you're not suggesting we sit out here until daylight?" Aidan asked impatiently, leaning forward to peer past River at the guard.

The attitude of the uniformed Indian, probably still in his teens, immediately went from cocky to ingratiating. "You must be Miss Donovan," he said hurriedly fumbling with the lock on the gate. "I'm sorry. I didn't see you. When I saw this buckboard, I thought . . . I mean, we've been expecting *you*."

Aidan and River shot each other questioning glances. "Expecting me? I don't understand. How did you know—?"

"Welcome to Blue Creek Agency, Miss Donovan," a friendly male voice announced.

Looking up, Aidan spotted a smiling, middle-aged man striding toward the gate.

308

"Agent John Gimel," he announced cheerfully, nodding his head toward the gate in a gesture that told the young policeman to hurry. "Your publisher, Mr. Hearst, wired me that you were coming here to do a story for his paper on the great progress we've made in civilizing the Indians. I must say, I'm quite honored that you chose my agency as a model to write about."

"Mr. Hearst wired you? You must be mis—" The hard nudge in her ribs caught Aidan by surprise, and she closed her mouth, her gaze jumping from the agent to River, who gave her a barely discernible shake of his head.

Frowning, but knowing by the intense look in River's eyes that this was not the time to question his silent suggestion to change the subject, she turned back to the agent and smiled. "Please forgive my rudeness. It's just that it's been a very tiring trip, and your knowing my name before I've even been introduced is quite a surprise."

The young policeman swung the gate open and then stepped back to allow the buckboard to pass through. "Just drive it on over there," he ordered, pointing toward a small white house about a hundred yards away, across the large open area that was obviously the hub of the compound.

Without waiting for further instructions, River clicked his tongue and flicked the whip over the mules' backs. "Good girl," he said to Aidan out of the corner of his mouth as the wagon lurched forward.

"That makes me mad!" she fumed, her mind racing. "Why would Mr. Hearst tell Gimel I was coming? He knows my stories are successful because I don't let anyone know who I am. That way, I can see what's really going on. The minute people know a reporter is around, they're on their best behavior—and I have nothing to

309

write about."

"Obviously, that's Hearst's thinking too." River spit out in disgust. "He's put a kink in your plans—under the guise of helping you—and he won't have to print your story because you won't write it."

Snapping her head around, Aidan stared at him, aghast. "But why? He stands to gain as much from this as we do."

"You said yourself that he doesn't see it that way. He didn't want to print the reservation exposé in the first place. He only agreed to run it if you did the white-slave investigation in Chinatown. Now that he has the story he wanted, he's evidently having second thoughts about your reservation story."

"But he gave me his word," Aidan said, anger at her own gullibility causing a tightening in the pit of her stomach. "I can't believe he'd go back on it."

River laughed bitterly. "Welcome to the real world, Little Fire. You've just had your first lesson in understanding the white man's double standard when it comes to anything Indian. What are you going to do now, give up and go home or do you intend to stay?"

Aidan straightened resolutely and gave River a sly grin. "What do you think? Have you ever known me to let a change of plans stop me? I promised you this story, and I'm going to write it. *And* it's going to run on the front page of the New York *Journal* if I have to set the type myself! If it doesn't, Mr. Hearst will see himself exposed on the front pages of every other newspaper in the country as untrustworthy—along with the truth about these fenced-in *prairie prisons*. In fact, that will be a good title for my article: 'Prisons on the Prairies.' But whatever I call it, and no matter who doesn't want me to write it, I will do it—because it has to be written." Her expression soured. "You don't happen to have any ideas as to what

310

we're going to do now that I can't pose as a school-teacher, do you? Because I'm fresh out."

River raised his eyebrows in mock surprise. "I never knew you ran out of ideas!" He reached over and squeezed her hand encouragingly. "But between the two of us we ought to be able to come up with something," he added, pulling on the reins and bringing the mules to a halt in front of a freshly painted white house. Glancing over at her, he winked. "A smart lady told me not too long ago that there's nothing we can't do—together."

Confused by River's sudden change of attitude, Aidan smiled hesitantly. "Now who's being the optimist?" she asked with a grimace, indicating the approach of the Indian agent with a slight motion of her head and a roll of her eyes in his direction.

"I've had our guest cottage prepared for your use while you're here," Agent Gimel announced, drawing up to the buckboard on Aidan's side. "Of course, my cook will bring your meals." He extended a hand to help her down. "But your kitchen is fully stocked in case you'd prefer to cook your own. We just want you to be comfortable. If you need anything, all you have to do is ask."

Slicing an uneasy glance in River's direction, Aidan accepted the agent's assistance and climbed down. "I'm sure I will be quite comfortable, Mr. Gimel. It's lovely. But I hate to see you go to so much trouble on my account. I would have been more than happy to stay in the dormitory with the women who teach at the school."

"Nonsense, my dear," he said, tucking her hand securely in the bend of his elbow and starting up the steps to the porch of the little house. "I only wish we had known when you were arriving. I would have greeted you personally at the train and spared you the inconvenience of hiring a driver and riding in this Indian buckboard." He looked back over his shoulder at River and said,

311

"Just set Miss Donovan's luggage inside, driver. Then you can go. I'm sure you're anxious to get back to your village."

Astounded by Gimel's treatment of River, Aidan dropped her hold on the agent's arm. "This man isn't a hired driver. We met on the train, and when we discovered there wasn't another stagecoach today, he offered to bring me the rest of the way to the agency," she said, giving Gimel their prearranged story.

The agent patted her hand and gave her a patronizing smile. "There, there, my dear. Of course, you wouldn't have had any way of knowing who he was. It's amazing, when you get them cleaned up, put decent clothing on them, and give them a little education, some of them seem almost as white as you and me."

Anger flashing in her eyes, Aidan drew her diminutive body to its full height. "Some of *them?*"

"You still don't understand, do you, Miss Donovan?" the agent asked incredulously. "The man you rode here with—" He spoke in a whisper close to her ear and jabbed his thumb toward the wagon which River was already unloading. "—is a mixed blood." He gave her a mollifying smile. "Don't look so astonished, my dear. He's obviously tamed. But don't forget, no matter how they seem to have assimilated into the white culture, underneath they all have that same wild blood flowing in their veins. That's why—"

"Agent Gimel!" she interrupted her tone bristling with indignation. "You've got some—"

"If there won't be anything else, Miss Donovan," River blurted out pointedly, "I'll leave you now. I hope you enjoy your stay." He tipped his hat politely, then got back up on the buckboard.

Responding to his subtle reminder that this was not the best time to use her "fire," Aidan bit back the rest of her condemnation. Besides, at the moment she had a lot bigger problem than Gimel's biased thinking.

For some reason, River had decided to assume the role of the subservient Indian, and to leave before they had a chance to create an alternate plan; but she still had no idea of what she was going to do.

"Wait a minute!" she cried, running off the porch to the buckboard. "You can't leave!" she said, her face hardened into a threatening frown only River could see. "We haven't settled . . . I haven't *paid* you!"

"That's not necessary, ma'am. I was coming this way anyway." River lifted his hat an inch off his head again and raised the whip over the mules' rumps.

"No! You can't leave! You must be exhausted," Aidan insisted, refusing to let him get outside the compound before they had created a new plan of attack. "It will be better if you get a decent rest tonight. You can be on your way in the morning."

"I'll be fine, ma'am. But thanks anyway."

Her eyes blazed with a silent threat, though her voice hid her fury from the agent who stood behind her. "I won't hear of it," she declared, her dark eyes transmitting a warning. "You must stay. If not for yourself, then for your mules. They need to be fed and rested before you travel on."

Without giving River a chance to make another excuse, she flounced around to face the agent, who was obviously straining to disguise his irritation. "Please explain to him, Agent Gimel, that staying at the agency until the morning is the *sensible* thing to do," she pleaded, mustering a beguiling smile. "After he went out of his way to bring me safely here, I couldn't sleep knowing I repaid his kindness by turning him out."

A sick, conceding smile wormed its way across Gimel's round face. "Of course, we can quarter him with my

Indian police," he offered grudgingly. "But I'm sure he would prefer to get back to his own—"

"You're right," River said, a trace of amusement in his voice. "It will be better for the *mules* if I leave in the morning." He flicked his whip to start the mules forward. "I know the way to the stables."

Aidan stared after him in amazement. He could have at least given her a signal telling her when he'd be back and what he had in mind. Remembering where she was and who she was with, she faced Gimel again, forcing a smile. She would just have to improvise as best she could until she and River could talk again—but that had better be soon or their stories were going to clash.

"Now that I've done my good deed for the day, I think I'd like to get some rest myself," she declared, brushing past the agent and into the cottage, which she was surprised to see had electric lighting. "Oh, this is really quite nice," she exclaimed, glancing around the small parlor.

"We use this for visiting officials," Gimel said proudly, starting to follow her inside.

Pirouetting in the doorway, Aidan blocked it. "Thank you so much for your wonderful welcome, Mr. Gimel. I hope you won't think I'm being rude by not asking you in, but I'm really quite exhausted ... and a young woman traveling alone can't be too careful about her reputation, can she now?" She favored him with an enchanting smile. "Besides, I want to start touring your agency first thing in the morning. I've heard so many good things about the work you've done to civilize these poor Indians, I can't wait to see the results firsthand— and to write about them."

A flicker of discomfort flashed in Gimel's eyes, which he hastily covered with a friendly grin. "Of course, my dear. I, too, am anxious for you to see all of the advances that have been made since I became agent at Blue

Creek. In fact, I've crossed all appointments off my calendar for the next week so I'll be free to conduct your tour myself. If I do say so, I think you're going to be quite amazed at the accomplishments I've — *we've* — made in taming these savages."

Doing her best to disguise her growing dislike of the agent, Aidan gave him a half-smile. "I'm sure I will, as will thousands of *Journal* readers all over the country, Mr. Gimel! When I'm through, the entire nation will know your name and will be aware of what you and men like you are doing for these unfortunate souls."

Agent Gimel flushed with false modesty. "Of course, my own personal glory is not the important thing. Why, if you could have seen these savages when I came here, you wouldn't believe they are the same people." He snickered and shook his head. "Of course, they still have a long way to go before they're capable of taking care of themselves. They're like children. If you don't watch them every minute, they get into trouble. In fact, I see myself as a sort of parent to them, a parent who is here to guide and nurture them."

Aidan was sure she was going to be sick. Did he really expect her to believe this after the revealing way he had talked about her "driver"? She swallowed back a sarcastic retort and responded with a falseness equal to his. "Why that's beautiful," she gushed, even going so far as to wipe a nonexistent tear from her eye. "May I quote you?"

Gimel's chest swelled. "If you like."

"Oh, I would, Mr. Gimel. Now I really must get some rest. Thank you again for the delightfully surprising welcome, and for all your kindness. At what time shall I expect you in the morning? Bright and early, I hope! I don't want to miss a thing."

"Oh, you won't, Miss Donovan, I'll call for you at

315

seven-thirty. Will that be all right?"

"What took you so long?" Aidan hissed as River climbed through the back window of the darkened guest cottage. "I was about to come looking for you!"

"I had to wait until I was sure the way was clear. I was about to think your friend, Agent Gimel, was going to sit up reading all night long." His hands found her waist and drew her hips forward to meet his. "You weren't worried about me, were you?"

Catching the hint of playfulness in his voice, Aidan reared back and studied him. "What are you smiling about?" she asked suspiciously.

"I was just thinking about the sick look on Gimel's face when you cornered him into inviting me to stay the night."

"Well, you certainly weren't much help," she admonished him, fighting her own urge to grin. "You'd have just driven off and left me locked in this prison compound without a clue to what we were going to do."

River squeezed her and kissed her forehead. "I don't know what you were worried about. You didn't really think a little inconvenience like a fence could accomplish what a Cuban jungle, half a continent, and the San Francisco Bay couldn't, did you? Face it, Little Fire. You can't get rid of me."

Aidan eyed him suspiciously. "You're in an awfully good mood for a man who's just had all his plans go up in smoke. Do you know something I don't know? Or have you come up with an alternate plan?"

He gave her a secretive smile. She was right. He was in a good mood. In fact, he felt better than he had in years. All day, he'd watched Aidan, noting her reaction to the fenced-in reservation, the way she had fought to control her anger when Agent Gimel had made derogatory remarks about mixed bloods, and her contempt for the stableman in Chadron. And he had dared to hope that she was becoming as committed to his cause as he was.

Then, when she had vowed to do battle with Hearst if necessary, the most influential men in the country next to the President, River had known for sure, and that knowledge had changed his entire outlook.

In that moment when he'd truly known Aidan was on the reservation because she wanted to be, not because of the bargain between them, the great weight he had carried in his heart for almost eight years seemed suddenly lighter, even conquerable. Maybe it was just Aidan's everpresent optimism rubbing off on him at last; or maybe he had finally understood that in order to succeed he had to be willing to chance failing. But whatever it was, he liked the feeling, and he intended to hang on to it!

"Will you stop grinning like that? This is serious. We have to decide how I'm going to get out from under Agent Gimel's thumb to get the story I came for."

"You won't."

"What do you mean?" Aidan was growing more exasperated by the second. "How am I supposed to expose the corruption and deprivation here with Gimel watching me every minute of the day? You know I can't write the story that way. Everywhere he takes me will be all spruced up for my visit—just look at this house!" She waved her hand, indicating the nicely furnished room. "He probably expects me to believe the Indians live like this. And with him constantly at my side, no one will feel free to talk to me. Oh, he'll introduce me to people, but he'll have coached them to say what he wants me to hear. I simply can't get to the truth with him shadowing my every step."

317

"You're beginning to sound like me." River gave her a teasing peck on the nose. "I thought you didn't believe in 'can't.' "

Aidan gave him an exasperated glance. "I don't, but I do believe in avoiding head-on confrontations, unless there's no other way." Her eyes brightened. "I know! What about another agency? Aren't Pine Ridge and Rosebud near here? We could go to one of them."

River shook his head. "The agents on those reservations are more experienced than Gimel, which means they're probably better at covering up the truth. That's why I decided to bring you here."

He grinned mischievously and shrugged. "Besides, the minute the Rosebud or Pine Ridge agent spotted you with me, we'd be escorted off the reservation. Unfortunately, I'm known as a 'troublemaking mixed blood' over there. They can't force me to stay on a reservation because I'm not a full-blood, but they can control who comes onto a reservation. And believe me, they do, because they don't want to let a rabble-rouser like me rile up the 'well-behaved savages' on their reservations. They even discourage visiting between tribes for fear that someone will say something to set off the 'wild bloods.' "

Aidan's eyes widened. "They can't do that. This is the United States. Don't they realize the Bill of Rights guarantees citizens freedom of speech and the right to assemble?"

River couldn't hold back an amused chuckle. "In your world, maybe. But the United States doesn't consider Indians citizens, so they have no rights. Here, there is no freedom to speak out against injustice, and there's no right to assemble—without permission from the agent. On the reservations, the People aren't even allowed to gather to practice the old religions, for fear some old warrior who now has only his memories and his religion will incite the others to riot."

"But the law—"

"The agent is the law. He answers to no one except the President . . . who relies on the agent to tell him what is needed on the reservation."

River watched the fluid play of emotions on Aidan's face as disbelief swelled into outrage, then fleetingly dissolved into confusion and frustration, before hardening into resolution and conviction.

"Just tell me how you think we can get the proof we need, and I'll do it," she said firmly, her anger now harnessed by determination. "No one, including Agent Gimel, is going to stop us, and I'm not going to rest until we've exposed this terrible system."

"Because it will make you even more famous than you already are?" River suggested, his tone teasing. "Or because of our bargain?"

Realizing how selfish her original motives had been, Aidan grinned impishly and locked her arms around his middle. "Because it's the right thing to do—and because I wouldn't for the world pass up a chance to show you what a great team fire and earth make."

He nodded his head. "As long as earth doesn't smother the flames."

Shrugging, Aidan tightened her embrace and looked up into the blue eyes she had come to love nearly as much as River himself. "Even the brightest fire needs to be kept under control. Otherwise, it will burn down the very house it was meant to light."

Chapter Twenty-two

When Agent Gimel didn't arrive at the cottage at precisely seven-thirty the next morning as promised, Aidan grinned. The opportunity to look around Blue Creek Agency on her own might have come sooner than she and River had dared to hope. "After all, if he said he'd be here, he should be here," she told herself as she opened the door to the little house and peered outside.

Relieved to see no sign of the agent, she slipped out onto the porch, cautiously pulling the door closed behind her. Shading her eyes from the glaring morning sun, she hurried down the stairs and glanced over at the buildings surrounding the congested area at the center of the compound. She wanted to determine where the agent's office was, for she intended to begin her investigation by going in the opposite direction.

In the light of day, she saw that the compound resembled a town built around a square, and every one of the numerous buildings had recently been given a fresh coat of whitewash. "In the last few days, since you found out I was coming," she mused aloud. "I guess Mr. Gimel thinks if it looks good enough on the outside, I will assume everything's just as clean inside."

Across the way, she saw a building with about fifty blanket-wrapped Indians lined up along its front and side. Waiting for rations, she guessed. Certain it was the office, and the way she did not wish to go, she peered at the house to her right. Since it was by far the nicest building in view, she was sure it had to be Gimel's residence. Her choice of direction dictated by necessity, she pivoted to the left.

Beyond a row of small houses similar to the cottage she'd been assigned, she saw a cluster of large buildings and felt certain they must comprise the boarding school. Her heartbeat sped up at the thought of getting into the school and looking around without Gimel hovering over her. River was right, they might be able to use her exposure to their advantage after all.

Remembering the wonderful night she had spent with him, she smiled and glanced toward the building he had pointed out as the sleeping quarters of the Indian police. He had promised her he would be there or somewhere on the agency grounds. He planned to offer Gimel his services as an interpreter or a teacher. If that overture was refused, he had more than one friend at the agency who would help him find a way to stay — legally or illegally. But he had assured her he wouldn't leave the compound without her.

Satisfied that River was nearby, and that Gimel was nowhere in sight, she set off at a brisk walk toward the school building, determined to get inside before the agent showed up. Arriving at the front door only moments later, she took one last quick look around, drew a deep breath, adjusted the flat-brimmed little straw hat she wore, and then placed a gloved hand on the doorknob. Without further delay, she whisked open the door and stepped inside.

Temporarily blinded by the drastic contrast between

sunshine and the dark interior of the school, she paused to regain her sight. When her eyes had grown accustomed to the dim light, she found she was in a long, plank-floored hallway. The walls, like everything else she'd seen at the agency, had been freshly whitewashed, and at the far end of the hall were double doors with a sign above them indicating that they led to the stairs.

Becoming aware of a distant hum of voices reciting in unison, she started down the hallway, her mind cataloguing everything she saw. On both sides of her were doors, six in all, evidently leading to classrooms. She paused outside the first one and put her ear to it. Hearing nothing, she determined it was empty. Disappointed, though River had told her they'd arrived a week too early and the school was still closed for the summer, with the exception of a group of children who stayed here the year round, Aidan still wanted to see the room. Glancing up and down the hallway to be sure she wasn't observed, she opened the door and peeked into what, to her surprise, looked like a classroom in any public school—even nicer than some she'd seen. It, too, had been recently painted, but she knew there hadn't been enough time to secure desks and the other supplies before her arrival. They had to have been here all along, which caused her to wonder fleetingly whether River's estimation of the reservation school system might not be inaccurate. After all, all children went through periods when they hated school—any school. That didn't necessarily mean they were being mistreated.

"Begin again," a woman's impatient voice broke into the silence of the empty classroom, striking a discordant note in its peacefulness. Aidan turned back to the hallway.

" 'I pledge allegiance' — " The droning children's voices grew louder as Aidan neared the room from which they came. " — 'to the flag — ' "

As Aidan started to enter the room, the loud rapping of a ruler on a desk cut off the group recitation, and she stopped. "Eyes on the flag, Walter," the teacher's harsh voice ordered. "Now, begin again."

" 'I pledge allegiance to — ' "

Rap-rap-rap. "Walter, if you refuse to show proper respect for the flag of our glorious nation, perhaps you need a more tangible reminder to do so."

Aidan winced as she heard another tap tap tap of the ruler, because this time it sounded as if it were striking flesh. Certain that some unfortunate student was having his knuckles or palms hit, she held her breath as she waited for a child to cry. When no such response came, she frowned.

"Maybe an hour at the wall will teach you some respect, young man." The teacher's strident scolding came to Aidan over the shuffle of footsteps and the rustling of clothing. The errant student had evidently moved to the wall.

"Now, unless the rest of you want to join Walter," the teacher declared evenly, "I suggest we complete this practice without another interruption. The Superintendent and Mr. Gimel are coming to visit today, and they are bringing a very important guest. I expect your behavior to be exemplary. If anyone — I stress *anyone* — forgets his or her manners, then he or she will spend the next week in the basement, thinking about changing his or her ways. Is that clear? Now," she said," her tone artificially cheerful, "shall we begin again? 'I pledge allegiance . . .' Walter! Turn around! Or am I going to have to use the

323

strap?"

"He doesn't understand English, Miss Craddock," a young voice hesitantly explained. "This is his first time away from his family."

"Did I call on you, young lady? Perhaps you'd like to join—"

Aidan couldn't bear to listen to another word. "Good morning!" she sang out to the surprised students and their teacher, who all turned to face her as she burst into the classroom. "I'm Aidan Donovan of the New York *Journal,* and you must be Miss Craddock. Mr. Gimel said you were expecting me."

The flustered teacher glanced down at the lapel watch attached to her prim white blouse, then past Aidan to the open door. "Yes, but we were not expecting you until—"

Aidan rolled her eyes and feigned embarrassment. "I know. I'm early. It's a terrible fault of mine. I hope you'll forgive me, but when Mr. Gimel was delayed, I decided to come on ahead. I couldn't bear to waste a single minute when I could be absorbing the delightful ambiance of your school and all these beautiful children for my article." She stopped and glanced around her, seemingly unaware that she had interrupted the class at a very volatile moment. "It is all right, isn't it?" she asked, smiling sweetly at the teacher. "Mr. Gimel led me to believe . . ." Her expression changed from happy innocence to discomfort. "Of course, if you'd rather I leave . . ."

The teacher shot a nervous glance toward the door, then gave a Aidan a tight smile. "No, don't go. We would enjoy having you here. Can you say good morning to Miss Donovan, class?" she asked evenly.

324

"Good morning, Miss Donovan," the children chanted in expressionless voices. "Welcome to our school."

Clapping her hands together in pretended delight, Aidan returned their greeting. "Why, thank you, children. I'm very happy to be here," she gushed, hoping her tone of voice suited the part she had chosen to play for Miss Craddock's benefit. She pirouetted, obviously looking for something. "Perfect!" she exclaimed, spying an empty desk at the rear of the room. "Now, don't let me interrupt. I'll just sit back here and observe," she announced, hurriedly seating herself at the desk. "You won't even know I'm here."

Her bright smile remaining set, Aidan glanced from the obviously annoyed teacher to the dark-eyed, black-haired children who stared at her, wooden, manne-quinlike expressions on their faces.

They varied in age, some appearing to be as old as fourteen, while others could be no more than four or five. None of them wore any Indian jewelry or clothing, as if they had been *white*washed too. The boys looked like little men—white men—in stiff white collars that chafed their necks, and jackets that buttoned up the front to the collarbone. And, as if the stifling clothing wasn't enough to make them look uncomfortable, every boy had had his hair cut very short and combed into the current "civilized" style. The girls, too, displayed only the coloring of their Indian heritage. Otherwise, everything Indian had been erased from their lives. In fact, they all looked like replicas of Miss Craddock, with their hair parted in the middle and drawn back into knots at the napes of their necks, and their long-sleeved gray dresses.

"Please, go on with what you were doing. I believe

325

you were—" Aidan's voice broke as her eyes came to rest on a lone child who stood apart from the rest of the class, his face and frail body pressed to the wall from nose to knees. A hard knot formed in her chest, as she realized this must be Walter. Why, he was just a baby!

"What's this?" she asked in an artificially coaxing voice as she rushed to the little boy and knelt down beside him. "Hello, there. You don't really want to be over here all by yourself, do you?" She grasped the child's shoulders and gently turned him toward her, her heart breaking at the loneliness and confusion she saw on his innocent little-boy face. "My name is Aidan, and I don't want to stand by myself either. Why don't we stand together?"

"Miss Donovan," the teacher protested indignantly, "that boy is being punished for treasonous behavior, and I'll thank you not to interfere."

Walter's tear-filled black eyes gave Aidan a lost, pleading stare, and she ached to take his tiny body in her arms and run off with him—after she'd squashed Miss Craddock up against the wall and let her learn how it felt to be treated that way. But of course she couldn't. That wouldn't do Walter or anyone else any good.

Aidan smiled sweetly, swallowing back the rage building inside her. She'd been doing a lot of that the last twenty-four hours, and it was getting more difficult each time. "Oh, I'm sorry. I had no intention of interfering. I simply assumed he was over here all alone because he was unhappy and needed to hear a kind word." She stood up and looked directly into the schoolteacher's eyes, her cool smile never wavering. "However, as long as I have interfered, I simply must tell you that my curiosity is absolutely killing me. What in heaven's name could a child of this age possibly have done that is serious enough to be labeled 'treasonous behavior.' "

"For your information, Miss Donovan, Walter is four years old, certainly old enough to understand the importance of respect. And here at Blue Creek School, we do not take it lightly when a student, such as that boy, shows disrespect for the very things for which this country stands."

Aidan's eyes narrowed threateningly. "And what exactly are those things, Miss Craddock? Freedom and justice for all—except little Indian boys who've never been away from home before?" she asked sweetly.

Miss Craddock's eyes widened as she realized that Aidan had heard her chastise the child. "It's clear that you know nothing about these people," she wheezed haughtily, a tight forced smile narrowing her lips. "Minor displays of rebellious behavior, such as refusing to say the Pledge of Allegiance or to speak English, are just the beginning. They must be controlled with stern discipline from the very beginning, or they will only get worse."

"Is that why Walter was being punished? For not saying the Pledge of Allegiance?" Aidan smiled disbelievingly.

Miss Craddock glanced uncomfortably at the other students in the room. Their blank expressions indicated they were oblivious to the disagreement between the two women, but Aidan knew not one of them had missed a single word that had been exchanged. "That and his general demeanor," the teacher explained crisply. "He insists on using his Indian tongue, and refuses to speak English."

"Has it occurred to you that he only knows the one

language?" Aidan asked pointedly, the smile she gave the fuming Miss Craddock a cool one. Reaching for Walter, she drew him to her side, her expression daring the teacher to object. "That could be the reason he doesn't say the Pledge!" she declared happily, as if she had just made a discovery that would solve everyone's problems. "I have an idea! I'll help him! And it will make a wonderful human interest story. Why, I'll wager with a little help, Walter can be as respectful as the staunchest American—even as respectful as you are, Miss Craddock."

Bending down, Aidan took Walter's small brown hand in her own, doing her best not to flinch when she saw the red welts coloring his little fingers. *I'd love to take a ruler to her hands,* she thought vengefully, as she positioned Walter's hand over his heart and directed his face toward the flag. "We're ready any time you are," she said cheerfully, straightening and assuming the same stance as Walter, except that her left hand rested protectively on the boy's shoulder.

"Very well," Miss Craddock said tightly. She turned her thin, birdlike body toward the flag and placed her hand over her heart—an empty gesture as far as Aidan was concerned because it was quite obvious to her that Miss Craddock had no heart. " 'I pledge allegiance to the flag of the United . . .' "

With Miss Craddock's back to her, Aidan glanced down at Walter, who was staring up at her with adoring black eyes, and in that moment she knew why she had been brought to Blue Creek.

"We've got to think of a way to help him, River,"

Aidan declared that evening after she'd described what had happened that morning in the classroom—before Gimel had found her and whisked her off to see his office. "You should have seen Walter when I left him there. He looked so hurt and betrayed. I could tell he thought I'd come to save him from that witch of a teacher who rapped his knuckles with a ruler and made him stand against the wall. I can only imagine what other things she's done in the name of teaching children respect."

River stroked her bare shoulder as they lay together in her bed after making love. "He's just one of thousands of young children who are separated from their families every year and forced to go to boarding schools," he said pensively. "I know of a boy who was taken from his family when he was only six and didn't see them again until he was fourteen—and by then he hardly knew them."

"But why? Surely the government can see that an unhappy child isn't going to be a good student. Why can't they go to day schools like non-reservation children do?"

River shrugged. "Some do. The teachers are just as harsh and unyielding there, but at least those children can go home to their families at night. However, that doesn't serve the government's purpose—which is to eliminate the Indian way of life entirely. By taking the children from their own people at a young age, the authorities hope to drive everything Indian out of their minds and hearts: their language, their customs, their respect for their ancestors, their feelings about nature and the land, even their love of their parents. Then, after they remove the children from the influence of

329

their heritage and train them to think white, dress white, speak white, and act white, all they have to do is wait for the old ones who remember the old ways to die off; then the 'Indian problem' will be solved—because once the thing inside the Indian that makes him an Indian— his *nagi,* what the whites call his soul—has been killed, the Indian will be no more."

"Not if I have anything to say about it!" Aidan swore, tossing back the sheet and leaping out of bed. She snatched up her robe and put it on as she crossed the room. "And believe me, I have plenty to say! What's more, the whole country is going to hear it!"

"What are you going to do?" he asked, watching her through the open doorway as she turned on a light in the other room.

"I've decided not to write a story after all," she grunted, dragging her black typewriter case out from under the kitchen table. "It's going to be a series," she groaned as she hefted the heavy case onto the table, "and the sooner I write the first installment, the sooner the world is going to know what's going on here."

"But it's almost midnight. You've had a long day. Why don't you wait until tomorrow? Believe me, the story's not going anywhere."

"Hmm?" she mumbled, her attention already on the words she planned to put on the fresh piece of paper she was rolling into her newly purchased portable type-writer. "Oh! I'm sorry. What did you say?" She glanced back over her shoulder toward the bedroom.

River stood in the doorway, his fingers looped over the top edge of the doorframe, the admiring smile on his face indicating that he was completely oblivious to the fact that he wore only a breechcloth slung low on his lean hips. "I said, why don't you come back to bed?"

Aidan deliberately dragged her gaze up the long muscular length of him, then grinned. "No, you didn't. You said, 'Why don't you wait until tomorrow?' "

"Well?" he asked, sauntering over to where she sat facing the table. He bent over, lifted strands of red hair off her neck and kissed her behind the ear. "Why don't you? You know what you always tell me about all work and no play."

Giggling, Aidan swatted at her neck, then turned back to the typewriter. "Go 'way. We've already played. Now I need to work. I want to do this while the things you said and those I saw today are fresh in my mind."

He reached around from behind her and pulled her robe off her shoulders, his mouth continuing its assault on her back. "Mmm, I have something on my mind too, and it doesn't require a typewriter."

"River!" she admonished, leaning forward to escape his mouth. "Aren't you tired? Remember, you have to get up early tomorrow to start your new job as interpreter and allotment dispenser — or whatever it is."

"All the more reason for you to come back to bed. We both need to rest." He slid the robe down to the bend in her elbows and cupped her breasts from behind, whisking his thumbs over the nipples until they were hard and thrusting.

"Something tells me rest isn't what's on your mind," she murmured, leaning her head back and resting it against his middle.

"Something tells me you're right." He tipped her chair back on two legs and bent over her to cover her lips with his.

331

Unable to resist opening her mouth to savor the full wonder of his kiss, she raised her arms and wove her fingers into his thick hair.

Without warning, she heard the scrape of wood against wood, and in the same instant, she felt the chair legs slide out from under her. "No!" she screamed, unable to stop the instinctive squeal as she and the chair toppled over backward.

Shock, and her grip on his hair, passionate at one moment, frantic the next, joined forces and dragged River off balance. Fighting uselessly to regain his equilibrium, he staggered to his knees and fell forward.

Aidan struggled to work her way out from under his weight. "Get off me, you clumsy oaf!"

"Miss Donovan!" a man's voice shouted, as the sound of running footsteps pounded across the porch. "I heard a scream! Quick, break down the door!"

Aidan's and River's heads snapped toward the door in time to see it come crashing into the room.

"What is it?" Gimel roared, brushing past the two Indian policemen who stood paralyzed in the doorway, gaping at the couple on the floor. "Oh, my god!" the agent gasped, as he saw what his men were staring at. "Don't just stand there! Get that filthy savage off her!" he bellowed.

The policemen lunged at River with wooden clubs, hitting him on the side of the head and in the kidney area of the back before he could get into position to defend himself.

"Stop!" Aidan shrieked hysterically, as River collapsed, unconscious, and rolled off her. "You're going to kill him!" Instinctively, she threw her half-clothed body over his head and shoulders as an Indian club came down toward his rib cage.

She held up her arms to block the blow, and pain exploded in them, sending a wave of nausea through her. "Stop," she pleaded, driven by fear and agony.

"Kill him, not her!" Gimel dropped to the floor beside Aidan and pulled her off River. "There now," he soothed, gathering her into his embrace. "It's all right. That animal won't hurt you again. I'm going to see that he never hurts anyone again! Get him out of here!" he said to his men. "I want him in chains. Everyone on this post is going to see what happens to rapists!"

"No!" Aidan protested. She freed herself from Gimel's grasp and reached for River. "You can't take him. He's wounded. You have to get him a doctor!"

Stunned, the agent sat back on his heels. "My god, woman! Do you hear what you're saying? This animal was on the verge of raping you, and you want to get him a doctor? I realize your innocence gives you an unnatural sympathy for the Indians, but protecting the man who would have abused you is carrying Christian charity to the extreme—even for a woman of your uninformed and liberal leanings. I will not allow it."

Wrapping an arm around Aidan's shoulders, he drew her away from River, then nodded at the policemen who had frozen in place when Aidan had ordered them to stop. "Take him. I'll be along as soon as I get this poor hysterical girl calmed down. And send Dr. Quaid over. She probably needs a sedative."

"No!" Aidan fought the agent's hold on her. "You don't understand!"

"I do understand, my dear. You've had a shocking experience. But it's over now. Just try to relax until the doctor comes!"

333

"Will you listen to me? He wasn't raping me! He—"

"That's good. We'll just forget it ever happened. That's the best thing to do."

"Why can't you understand? He wasn't forcing himself on me. He was—" Aidan stopped in midsentence. She couldn't very well tell Gimel what had really happened. He would run them both off the reservation—River for being a half-breed with the audacity to touch a white woman, her for sharing her favors with him. Unless . . .

"He was here because I asked him to come," she blurted out. "He's my husband!"

"Husband!" Gimel dropped his hold on her as if he'd just realized he was holding an armload of filth of the lowest order. "You don't mean that. You're delirious."

"I'm not delirious or hysterical or anything else. He's my husband!"

Gimel studied her for a long time, as if weighing the consequences of believing her or not believing her. He finally asked, "Why, if he is your husband, didn't you tell me this when you first arrived?"

Aidan stared dumbfounded at the agent. *Think fast. River's life depends on it, because if Gimel doesn't believe you, he'll see that River's hung before morning—or worse.*

"Because, uh—" Noticing Gimel's lust-filled gaze lower to where her robe gapped, she stopped speaking and clutched the front closed as she scrambled out of the agent's reach. "—because when we arrived the things you said gave me the distinct impression that it would be close to impossible for us to work together if you knew the truth. Of course, now, after getting to know you a little better, I realize you were only concerned about my safety when you assumed my husband was a

334

stranger, and that you didn't mean to be cruel. Since you know the real situation, if you don't want me to do a story on you and this reservation, I'm sure Mr. Hearst will understand. But your decision regarding that won't change the fact that I am married and that my husband was *not* forcing himself on me."

"If you are indeed married to this . . . man—" Gimel's lip curled as he glanced down at River, who moaned weakly. "—why aren't you wearing a wedding ring?"

"My wedding ring?" Aidan repeated in a frantic play for time. "I took it off on the train to wash my hands. The coach lurched suddenly and my ring slipped into the sink and went down the drain before I could prevent it. I'm afraid my gold band is now lying in a bed of cinders on the tracks somewhere in Wyoming."

The agent's mouth stretched into a grim, knowing line, but Aidan was reasonably sure he wouldn't accuse her of lying outright . . . not if he still hoped to get the national recognition her article promised to attain for him and his agency. And not if he didn't want her to expose him as a bigot who hated the very people he was supposedly protecting. He certainly couldn't risk that getting out if he had any political aspirations.

"Perhaps the entire incident is best forgotten," Gimel said with an insincere smile. With an annoyed motion of his head, he signaled his men to leave. "*Neither* of us would want any *false* impressions of ourselves to be circulating, would we?"

"No. I don't think that would be advantageous to either of us," Aidan replied coolly.

"Ohhh . . ." River stirred where he lay on the floor. "Aidan?"

She crawled over to him and lifted his head onto her lap. "I'm here. Just lie still. Everything is going to be all right." She directed a purposeful glance up at the agent. "Mr. Gimel is going to send for the doctor!"

The agent studied her, his mouth twisted by indecision, as if he might yet change his mind about how to deal with the situation.

Aidan waited breathlessly as his prejudice warred with greed and a desire for personal glory.

He headed for the door. "Yes, of course. I'll get him right away. I'll also send someone to repair the door."

Chapter Twenty-three

The next morning, Aidan rolled over in bed and reached out to reassure herself that River was truly safe. In her dreams, she had relived the horrors of the night before, but in them, she hadn't been able to stop Gimel and his policemen from hurting River even more.

When her hand found only a pillow where River's head should have been, a cold wave of fear washed over her. She sprang upright in the bed, her eyes wild with panic. "River!" she called, her heart pounding with dread. What if she had only dreamed she'd convinced the agent River wasn't raping her? What if they'd given her a sedative after the club struck her arm and she hadn't saved him at all? What if they'd taken River away and . . . ? She cannoned out of bed and raced across the floor toward the front of the cottage. "River!"

"Little Fire! What's wrong?" His voice was breathless with alarm as he rounded the corner and collided with her.

Aidan stopped and stared up into his bruised and worried face. "You're here!" she told him, wrapping her arms around his neck and covering his naked chest with grateful, teary kisses. "Don't ever do that to me again."

"Do what?" He tightened his embrace on her shuddering frame.

"Leave without telling me where you're going," she said

shakily.

"I was just in the bathroom shaving," he told her, meanwhile caressing her and rocking her the way one would a frightened child. "That's hardly leaving, is it?"

Embarrassed, Aidan shook her head. Then the fact that River was partially dressed dawned on her. She pushed back from his embrace to confirm that he was wearing trousers and boots. Only his shirt, coat, and tie were missing. "What are you doing?"

"I'm getting dressed to go thank Gimel for his understanding, and to convince him I still want to work for him."

"Thank him?" Aidan gasped, her eyes round with anger. "How can you even think about doing such a thing after what he did to you? To us?" She gently placed the palm of her hand on the nasty bruise on the side of his face. "When I think about what he was going to do to you, I want to pulverize him."

River kissed her forehead. "And you will, with your typewriter and paper. But, my little 'wife,' not until we have proof that reservation funds and allotments are being misdirected and used to benefit others while the Indians are being cheated. That is why I want to keep on working for Gimel."

Still afraid to have River anywhere near the agent, Aidan shook her head. "I don't want you to go. You didn't see the look on Gimel's face last night. He wanted to kill you. He backed off when I told him we were married, but it was clear that his feelings hadn't changed. If anything, his hatred is stronger."

"All the more reason for me to go. I want to get this done and see you safely out of here—as soon as possible."

Seeing that he was determined, Aidan tried another

338

tack. "At least wait one more day. The doctor told you to rest. You might complicate your injuries by getting out of bed so soon."

River smiled sympathetically at seeing her worried look. "He also told me that nothing was broken, and that other than some bruises I'd be good as new this morning. Tell you what. Why don't you spend today writing . . . since your work was interrupted last night? I'll check in on you at lunch time if I can."

Knowing he was right, Aidan nodded her head and turned back toward the bedroom. They had come here to do something important, and they couldn't let a minute go to waste, or allow anything to stand in their way. Still, she couldn't bear . . .

"River!" she pleaded, spinning around and running back into his arms. "Be careful. I don't know what I would do if you didn't come back."

He hugged her tightly. "Don't you worry about me, Little Fire. As long as I know you're waiting for me, I'll always be back. After all, now that you've compromised your reputation to save my neck, the least I can do is come back and make an 'honest woman' out of you."

It took a moment for Aidan to absorb the meaning of what he had said. "You mean you want to . . . "

He raised his eyebrows expectantly and smiled. "Marry you."

"To protect my reputation?" she asked, fighting the joy that surged through her, urging her not to question his motives but to just say yes.

"Can you think of a better reason?" he asked innocently. "It's really the only sensible thing to do, since neither one of us has much luck at staying out of trouble and we take turns bailing each other out of it."

" 'The sensible thing to do'?" she repeated softly, his words ramming hurtfully into her. "The *sensible* thing to do!?" she said again, her voice rising as indignation overcame her hurt. "You want to marry me because it's the *sensible thing to do?!*" Her umbrage blossomed into full-blown anger. "You conceited, obtuse dolt! I don't need you or any other man to make an honest woman of me! Why, I wouldn't marry you if you were the only man on earth — because it was the 'sensible thing to do'!"

She spun out of his arms and stomped toward the bedroom. "I should have let Gimel's men grind you to a pulp. Maybe they would have beaten some sense into that *sensible* head of yours. Lord knows I haven't been able to, not if you think the threat of a tarnished reputation would be enough to make me marry a man who didn't lo —" She plucked the sheet up from the foot of the bed, then picked up a pillow. "Sensible, indeed," she muttered, pounding the pillow vengefully, then slamming it into place before tramping angrily around the bed to straighten the sheet on the other side.

"Would you marry me if I said —"

Snatching up the second pillow, Aidan glared at him. "I wouldn't marry you if —"

"— I love you and if —"

Aidan's mouth dropped open. "What did you say?" she asked, her fingers tightly gripping the pillow.

"— I said I can't live without you."

"You didn't!" she exclaimed, her mouth splitting into a wide grin. "You asked if I'd marry you if you said you loved me."

"Well, would you?"

Aidan shrugged her shoulders and placed the pillow on the bed. She continued to tuck in the sheets. "I might

340

consider it . . . if you could convince me you weren't telling me you love me just because it's the 'sensible' thing to say."

"What if I told you that loving you is the most irrational, unreasonable, unsensible thing I've done in my orderly, serious life, and that thinking of a future with you as my wife threatens every practical instinct I possess, but I don't care about practical or logical or sensible. I just care about having you for my wife and by my side for the rest of my life. What would you say then?"

She grinned saucily. "In that case, Mr. Blue Eagle, I would have to agree with you. Marrying me is definitely the only 'sensible thing' you can do, if you are to have any chance at all of being rescued from the hopelessly dull existence that awaits you without me in it!"

"Is that a yes?"

Aidan climbed onto the freshly made bed and crawled across to him, her smile challenging. "What do you think?"

Blue Creek Indian Reservation, South Dakota—August 1898. Lurking behind the misleading façade of freshly painted buildings, kind smiles, and well-equipped schoolrooms, is a cruel and invisible evil. . . .

Aidan paused as she read over the article she had composed that morning after River had left. "Evil's too obvious," she muttered, picking up her eraser and deleting the word from the line of typed letters. She thought for a minute, then rolled the typewriter carriage back to the newly blank space on the page and inserted the word "force." "Yes, that's better," she declared with a satisfied smile as she resumed her editing.

341

. . . a cruel and invisible force at work on the Indian reservations of America. Like the vampires of folklore, this force is slowly, quietly draining the life from an entire . . .

A sound from the bedroom interrupted her concentration, and she glanced up from her work. There it was again. A light tapping. Curious, she pushed back her chair and went to the bedroom door. The sound came again. Her gaze shifted to the glass window, partially raised below the half-drawn shade. Nothing unusual there. Just the shrub someone had planted to give the bedroom's occupants additional privacy when the shade was up.

"You're getting awfully jumpy," she said to herself with a laugh. She started to go back to the typewriter, but something made her cross to the window instead. It was probably just a branch hitting the outside wall, but she knew she wouldn't be able to relax until she knew for certain.

As she neared the window, a small brown fist jabbed into view, rapped quickly on the glass, then disappeared.

"What in heaven's . . .?" Racing to the window, raised it all the way and peered out. There, crouched in the shrubbery, was a young Indian girl—a student from the school, judging by the way she was dressed. "Well, hello! Who are you?"

The girl's black eyes shifted furtively from left to right, then she slowly stood up, taking care to stay hidden in the greenery. Though she was small framed, it was evident that she was in her teens. "I am Patricia Kind Heart," she said. "Walks Proud needs you."

"Walks Proud?" Aidan asked, motioning for the girl to come into the cottage through the window.

Patricia shook her head. "I must go back before I am missed," she whispered. "Miss Craddock calls him Walter."

Fear squeezed painfully in Aidan's chest. "Walter needs help?" she choked out. Without hesitation, she hiked up her skirt and swung a leg over the sill to climb outside. "What is it?"

Patricia shrugged her shoulders, her large eyes filled with tears. "He would not stop crying after you left yesterday, so Miss Craddock strapped his back and put him in the school basement until he 'learns to respect authority.' " Her eyes, almost on the same level with Aidan's, projected a plea for help. "How can he learn anything but hatred when he does not understand what has happened to him, Miss Donovan? He only knows that he was taken from a home where he was loved and protected, and put in a place where the white teacher barks orders at him in a strange tongue and then hits him for not understanding. I do not know what to do. If he stays at the school, I do not believe he will survive. Will you help him, Miss Donovan?"

"Of course, I'll help him. Let's go." She took the girl's elbow and turned her toward the school. "Take me to him."

"If we stay behind the buildings and off the main square, no one will see us," Patricia whispered, leading the way out of the shrubbery, crouched and running.

Glancing over her shoulder for one last time to be sure it was safe, Aidan made a furtive dash for the rear of the next cottage, where Patricia waited for her.

Giving each other uneasy grins that said, So far, so good, they took off at a fast clip, skirting the back yards of the nearby houses, which Aidan had decided were the living quarters of the teachers and school staff still on summer vacation, since most of the dwellings seemed to be empty.

As they passed the last cottage, Patricia stopped. "That's the laundry," she explained, pointing past the rows of clotheslines to the building behind the school. "Next to that is the kitchen and dining hall. Everyone will be in there now, so the way into the school should be clear."

Patricia started for the back door of the school, but Aidan stopped her by tugging on her sleeve. "Wait a minute," she said.

"We must hurry. There's no time to lose. I told Miss Craddock I was sick and was going to the outhouse, but she will come looking for me if I do not return soon."

"Then you go on. There's no need for you to get caught. I can go the rest of the way by myself. Are the basement stairs just inside the back door?" Aidan asked, a plan beginning to form in her head.

The girl glanced nervously at the school, then back to Aidan and nodded. "On the right. He is in the third storeroom from the stairs."

"You go on to lunch. I can find Walter—I mean Walks Proud—myself. But I'll wait until I'm sure you've had time to get safely into the dining room. By the way, Patricia, what will Miss Craddock think if Walter just disappears from the school?"

The Indian girl hesitated, then smiled. "She'll think he ran away, like many do every year, especially when school first starts. After she files a report on him, she will let the Indian police worry about him."

"What about you, Patricia? Do you want to leave here?"

The girl nodded her head. "Oh, yes, I long for the day. But I will graduate the end of this next school year, and at that time, I will be able to apply for a teaching post in one of the reservation schools. I want to teach little children like Walks Proud to live in the white man's world, while keeping their dignity and their Indian traditions."

Aidan smiled, though tears came to her eyes. "You are well named, Patricia Kind Heart, and I know you will be a wonderful teacher. I wish you well."

"Thank you, Miss Donovan."

"Thank *you,* Patricia. Now go on back before that old prune of a teacher comes out here and takes a strap to the two of us!"

Aidan stayed hidden until she heard a screen door slam in the area of the dining hall. Then she made a quick dash for the clotheslines that ran along the short side of the laundry building. Weaving her way between wet bedsheets, she worked her way to the end of the clothesline nearest the school.

Peeking out from behind the wash, she saw that the way was clear, then made a run for the porch steps. She opened the screen door, and slipped inside. Catching the door before it could slam, she eased it shut, and was relieved that no one was in sight. Being seen by even one person would ruin everything.

Spying the basement stairs, she hurried down them, pausing only a moment at the bottom to again check to be sure she was alone. Safe so far, she ran to the third door and gingerly slid the bolt out of its housing. Holding her breath, she eased the door open.

Inside the dim room, huddled on a cot in a corner, she saw the boy she'd come to get, and for a moment she couldn't move. He looked so tiny and helpless. How could anyone use a strap on his little back . . . or leave him in this damp basement? No wonder tuberculosis caused the deaths of so many children on reservations. "Walks Proud," she whispered, hurrying to the desolate little figure on the cot. "I've come to take you away from here."

The boy lifted his head, his expression as wooden as those of the children in the classroom. But when he recognized Aidan, his dark eyes filled with tears and his bottom lip began to tremble. "*Ina,*" he said and sniffled.

Gathering Walks Proud into her embrace, Aidan rocked him. "Yes, yes, little one. I will take you to your *ina,*" she replied, recognizing the Lakota word for mother, from her own mother's teachings.

Burying his dark head against her breast, Walks Proud cried silently, his skinny arms clinging desperately to her neck. "Go on and cry, my *cikala ohitika,*" Aidan said, reasonably certain she remembered the Lakota words for little brave. "I won't let them hurt you again."

Wishing she could wait until Walks Proud stopped crying, but knowing they must get away, she secured her hold on his body and caught him behind the knees. Lifting his light weight, with the assistance of his death grip on her neck, was easily accomplished, and she ran back to the door.

After making certain the way was clear, she shifted the boy's weight to her hip to free a hand, then slipped back in to the main basement and ran for the stairs. She paused at the head of them to listen before stepping out into the open. Luck was still with her; the building had a hollow emptiness to it. Tightening her hold on the tiny body in her arms, she peeked out the back door, then made a frantic rush for freedom.

Once outside and safely surrounded by flapping wash, she paused to catch her breath. It was then she heard the muffled sounds of men's voices in deep conversation coming from behind the laundry.

Cocking her head to the side and listening, she looked back toward the school to see if there wasn't another way to get out of the school yard without going past the men. Unfortunately, passing them was the only way to get back to her cottage without walking part of the way in the open. She listened intently. Maybe they weren't as close as she had thought. After all, their words were not distinguishable. She couldn't even tell what language they were speaking. All that came to her was the deep hum of conservation.

Deciding she had no choice but to chance slipping unnoticed past the men, Aidan placed her forefinger to her lips, warning Walks Proud to be very quiet. Then she started toward the back of the laundry building. Telling herself that if the men saw her feet, they would assume she was a washing woman checking the laundry, she cautiously worked her way down the line of wash.

But despite her attempts to remain calm, she knew that with every step she took, the danger increased. She felt as though the next time she put her foot down a loud alarm would sound, announcing her presence.

Her every nerve stretched to the limit as she waited to hear that she'd been discovered, Aidan reached a point even with the back wall of the next cottage. She allowed herself a sigh of relief and gave Walks Proud a reassuring squeeze. All she had to do now was run back to her own cottage, and she and Walks Proud would be safe.

Call it a natural nose for news as her father had, or woman's intuition, as her mother had, or even a sixth sense, as her grandmother had, but just as she started to make that final dash to safety, something told her she couldn't leave yet — not until she'd determined who the men behind the laundry building were.

Appalled at herself for even considering taking such a risk, she started to ignore the hunch. After all, her hunches were wrong just as often as they were right. *But what about the times they were right?* a little voice inside her asked. *What if this is one of those times?*

Begrudgingly giving in to her instinct, Aidan turned back toward the laundry-building side of the wash. Cautiously, she peeked through a gap between two sheets on the clothesline.

Immediately, she spotted the two men she'd heard talking, and her breath caught in her chest. Gimel! Gimel and a man she recognized as the manager of the agency's general store, where Indians could buy things not given to them in allotments.

Though they had their backs to her and kept their voices low, the men were much closer than she had expected, and she could make out almost everything they were saying, if she listened very carefully.

Walks Proud squirmed slightly in her arms, and she held her finger up to her lips again and shook her head.

"I don't care what you do with it, Jackson," the agent was saying. "Just get this stuff out of sight until I can get rid of that newspaper bitch and the breed she *says* is her husband."

"All right," Jackson grumbled. "But I don't like havin' her snoopin' around out here. What if she sees somethin' she ain't supposed to see? And I still got the feelin' I seen that breed before. What'd you say his name was?"

"Stop worrying," Gimel chided him. "I plan to keep them both where I can watch every move they make. If either one of them does anything that indicates they're not here for the reasons they claim, I'll know it. In the meantime, you just get those allotments hidden until I give you the word it's okay to move them into the store and sell them. I don't want that breed to recognize any merchandise for sale in your store as something he might've seen when the supplies were unloaded from the government wagons yesterday. I paid a fat politician too much for this appointment to let a liberal, Eastern newspaper whore or her rutting breed of a husband ruin it for me. I'll see them both dead first."

Shock and terror united to set Aidan's feet into motion. Clutching the boy to her, she spun around and burst out of the billowy shelter of the sheets to race wildly for the safety of the cottage. She knew only that she had to get to River. He would know what to do. He would think of a way to get them away from here.

By the time she was safely hidden behind the shrub outside her open bedroom window, her chest was rising and falling laboriously, her side was cramping, and her arms quivered from the strain of running with the extra burden of Walks Proud. She was afraid she didn't even have enough strength left to lift the child's light body through the window, much less climb in herself.

Sucking large gulps of air into her deprived lungs, she sagged against the back wall of the house and slid down to the ground. She would just have to rest a minute to regain her breath before she went inside.

As she looked down at the boy in her arms, he stared at her with large wondering eyes. She tried to smile, but could only nod her head as she continued to gasp for air. "Good boy," she panted, rolling her head back against the painted boards of the cottage and closing her eyes. What were they going to do now? She and River were already in danger, and she had just added kidnapping to Gimel's growing list of reasons to distrust her.

She laughed softly. "My father used to tell me, I could be buried up to my eyebrows in horse ma—" She caught her-

349

self, remembering Walks Proud, though she knew he didn't understand a word she was saying. "Trouble," she amended with an apologetic grin. "I could be up to my eyebrows in *trouble* and still talk my way out of it so I'd wind up 'smelling like a rose.' But I've got news for dear old Dad, *cikala ohitika,* if Gimel finds out I've got you, my smelling-like-a-rose days are numbered, because this is one thing I don't see how I'm going to talk my way out of."

"What the hell are you doing?" an angry male voice hissed from above her.

Aidan's head bumped back against the wall as her frightened glance flew upward. Recognition and relief coursed through her. "River!" she yelped struggling to stand up. "Thank God. I thought it was . . ."

"What're you doing with that kid?" he asked, leaning out the window to help her.

"Please don't be mad at me," Aidan pleaded, her brown eyes wide, her bravery suddenly deserting her. "I couldn't leave him there. I didn't know what else to do."

Taking in Aidan's disheveled state and the cringing Indian boy clinging to her, his anger dissipated into serious concern. "Here, give him to me." He reached for Walks Proud. "Does anyone know he's here?"

As River's hands neared him, Walks Proud's black eyes widened in terror. *"Ina!"* he quailed, shrinking back from River's touch. His grip on Aidan's neck became a stranglehold and he pressed his face against her sweat- and tear-soaked bodice. *"Ina,"* he pleaded, his voice muffled.

"Shh, shh, *cikala ohitika,* it's all right," she soothed, patting his tense little body as she raised her eyes to River in a plea for understanding. "We'll find your mama."

"It looks to me like he thinks he already has," River mumbled. A worried frown on his face, he threw a long leg

350

over the sill and climbed out the window. "Maybe if I'm out here, he'll let *you* put him inside. But for God's sake, keep him quiet!"

Aidan nodded. "Shh, shh, sweetheart. No one is going to hurt you," she murmured against the boy's ear. "What's the Lakota word for safe?" she asked River out of the corner of her mouth.

"Tan-yan, he whispered, enunciating each syllable.

"Tanyan," Aidan repeated to Walks Proud. "You are *tanyan.* Safe! But you must be very quiet," she cautioned, holding a finger to her lips and saying, "Shh. Very very quiet."

"E-ni-la," River said next to her ear.

Giving him a grateful glance, Aidan said, *"Enila,"* praying her uneducated tongue wasn't butchering the language so badly that Walks Proud didn't understand her Lakota any better than her English.

Chanting the words for safe and quiet over and over, Aidan peeled Walks Proud's thin legs from around her waist one by one. Then, before he could get his spindly little limbs around her again, she heaved the lower half of his tiny body through the window, groaning as she did so. But when she tried to get him to release her neck, he balked, and struggled to climb back outside. *"Ina!"*

"No, no, little brave—*Hiya, hiya, cikala ohitika"* she crooned, casting a desperate glance in River's direction. "Help me."

Shaking his head hopelessly, he scooped her legs and bottom up in his arms and shoved her through the window, unintentionally catapulting Aidan and Walks Proud into the cottage in a tangle of arms, legs, full skirt, and petticoats.

River then climbed through the window, slamming it

351

shut behind him and pulling down the shade with an angry tug.

Slowly, so he might gather his thoughts, he turned to face her, a dark scowl on his face. "Now!" he said, whisking her and Walks Proud up in his arms and plopping them onto the bed, "will you please tell me what this is all about? Because if it's half as bad as it looks, Aidan, we're in deep trouble." He threw a hesitant glance at the little boy Aidan clutched protectively, then shook his head. "Deep trouble!"

Chapter Twenty-four

Aidan stiffened indignantly. "Don't you think I know I've made things worse?" She gently removed Walks Proud's arms from around her neck and smiled reassuringly at the boy, keeping her tone cheerful for his benefit despite her annoyance. "But I didn't have a choice! I had to take him!" she said through her teeth-grinding grin. Turning the boy around on her lap so his back was to her, she added sarcastically, "Given your great wisdom, tell me what you would have done differently if . . ."

She lifted the youngster's shirt so she could check his back for marks left by the strap Patricia Kind Heart had said Miss Craddock had used. Her eyes narrowed at what she saw, and she swallowed loudly, then looked up at River, her eyes filled with pain. The corners of her mouth turned down in an effort not to cry, her bottom lip quivering. ". . . if you'd known about this?" she said harshly, angling Walks Proud so River could see his back. "Would you have been able to leave him there?"

Outrage forming in his blue eyes, River stared at the three bright red welts that streaked across the thin, brown back from bony shoulder to waist. He shook his head and sat on the bed beside Aidan. "No, you couldn't leave him there," he admitted, reaching out and stroking the boy's freshly cut black hair.

Walks Proud didn't move. He just rested his head against Aidan's chest and watched the strange man who looked like one of the People but had the light eyes of the *wasicun*.

"Poor, brave little man," River said in Lakota, his memories of the half-frozen children who had miraculously survived Wounded Knee suddenly as vivid as they had been a week after the massacre. They, too, had been betrayed by the people sent to help them, and they'd had that same lost look in their eyes. "You don't need to be afraid anymore. No one will hurt you again. We'll take you to your mother and father."

Walks Proud sat up straight and looked at Aidan, showing more life than she'd ever seen him display. *"Ate?"* he asked, glancing shyly at River out of the corner of his eye.

She smiled and raised her eyebrows at River. *"Ate?"* she repeated. "You didn't just tell him you were his father, did you?"

Rattled, River shook his head and waved a hand in denial. "No, no, no. I didn't say *I* was his father. I told him we'd *find* his father."

Before he could gather his wits enough to explain in words the little boy could understand, Walks Proud strained away from Aidan and leaned toward River. *"Ate."*

"Maybe I'm not the only one who needs to brush up on my Lakota, *Ate,* because I don't think you said what you thought you were saying," she laughed, handing Walks Proud over to River. "It looks like we're suddenly a family, doesn't it? We've got an *ate,* an *ina,* and a *cikala ḣoksila.* A mama, a daddy, and a little boy. What

354

more could we ask for?"

Taking care not to touch the welts on Walks Proud's back, River held the boy close and shot Aidan a sick, forlorn grin. "Nothing, except maybe wings to fly us out of here. You don't happen to have any in your suitcase, do you? Because if you do, now is definitely the time to get them out."

Enfolding River and Walks Proud in her embrace, Aidan nuzzled River's neck. "Just the ones loving you put in my heart."

His thoughts a jumble of apprehension and love, River caught her chin and lifted her face so he could look into her eyes. "With those and the ones you put in my heart, we'll find a way. I give you my word, *Cikala Peta*—Little Fire. I'm going to keep you both safe."

His lips covered hers to seal the vow.

Just then, heavy boots clomped onto the porch of the cottage, and the heads of the three on the bed twisted toward the front room, their expressions disturbed.

The urgent hammering of a fist rattled the door, and panic struck River and Aidan. Their eyes silently questioning, they looked at each other, then down at Walks Proud, who was already trembling and hiding his face in River's shirtfront. "Shh . . . *enila,*" they said to the child at the same time.

Handing Walks Proud to Aidan, River tiptoed into the other room. Again, the door shook under the impact of the unknown visitor's fist. Carefully easing the edge of the living-room shade aside, River peeked out. Then he quietly hurried back to Aidan. "It's Gimel. And he's got a woman with him." He took Walks Proud from her and prodded her toward the other room.

"Oh, River, what are we going to do?" she moaned,

allowing herself to be guided to the kitchen table where her typewriter was.

"Sit down," he ordered in a rough whisper, pushing her into the chair. "Just look like you've been there all morning."

Another series of knocks shook the door. "Miss Donovan. Open this door."

"Ask who it is?" River hissed, dropping to the floor and lifting her skirt.

"What are you doing?" she whispered.

"Dammit, Aidan, just ask who it is?"

"Who is it?" she called, her quavering voice high and unnatural.

"Good girl," he murmured. Positioning Walks Proud in the space between the backs of her knees and the legs of the chair, he instructed him in Lakota to be very quiet and not to move.

"Agent John Gimel. I must talk to you immediately. Please open the door."

"Tell him just a minute," River ordered, arranging her skirt and petticoats to conceal the small boy hovering against the backs of her calves.

"Just a minute!" Aidan called out, her voice having regained a degree of normalcy at the knowledge that Walks Proud was out of sight.

River stood back and walked around her, checking her skirt from every angle. Stopping, he lifted her hands and placed them on the typewriter keys. Satisfied, he quickly glanced into the bedroom to be sure they hadn't forgotten anything, then hurried to the door. One hand on the knob, he turned back to Aidan, drew a smile on his own face with a forefinger, then swung open the door.

"Agent Gimel," he said humbly. "We didn't expect

you. Is there something wrong with the work I did this morning? If there is, I hope you'll give me a chance to correct it."

"Relax, Edwards," Gimel snarled, giving River an off-hand glance as he brushed past him into the room. "It's your 'wife' I'm here to talk to, not you."

"Of course." River stepped aside and winked encouragingly at Aidan.

"Miss Donovan—" Gimel glanced over his shoulder at River. "—or should I call you Mrs. Edwards?" His revulsion at the idea was undisguised.

"Either one will do," Aidan said generously. "I write under the name of Donovan, but I'm Mrs. Edwards in all my other dealings. What can I do for you? After last night, I—"

"Miss Donovan," Gimel broke in, "I'm not here to discuss last night. As far as I'm concerned the entire matter is forgotten. I've come for quite another purpose." He turned to the door. "Miss Craddock," he called. "Will you come in now?"

"Why, Miss Craddock," Aidan exclaimed as the schoolteacher swept haughtily into the room, her small eyes taking in everything. "What a pleasure to see you again. Won't you sit down?"

"This is not a social call, Miss Donovan."

Aidan could feel Walks Proud start to shake at the sound of the teacher's voice. Swallowing the lump of fear in her own throat, she brought her calves back to touch him reassuringly. "It's not?" she asked. "Then why are you—"

"We've come to discuss an important matter," Gimel interrupted. "Miss Craddock has made some very serious allegations against you, and it is most urgent that we

357

clear them up as soon as possible."

Aidan stiffened. She licked her lips and glanced uneasily at River, who stood poised to step in should she need him. Drawing strength from the love she saw in his eyes and the encouraging grin he sent her, she managed to speak. "Allegations? I don't understand." Her eyes widened with sudden recall. "Surely, you don't mean that little disagreement we had yesterday, Miss Craddock? If that's the case, I apologize. I realize now that I overstepped my bounds as a guest in your classroom."

Her lips compressed in a tight, angry line, Miss Craddock drew an offended breath through flared nostrils. "I hardly consider your rude intrusion a 'little disagreement,' Miss Donovan. However, we've come about a matter of far greater importance. I have reason to believe you abducted a student from the school this morning, and we have come to demand his immediate return."

"Mr. Gimel," Aidan huffed, leveling an accusing stare at the agent, "am I expected to sit here and submit to this vindictive woman's libelous accusations? Do I strike you as the kind of woman who would resort to kidnapping an innocent child simply because I disagree with a teacher's methods of instruction, no matter how harsh or barbaric I find those methods to be? Besides, why would I resort to breaking the law to create problems for someone I disagree with, when the United States Constitution guarantees my right to do it legally through the press?" She paused and smiled tauntingly. "That is, if I were the sort of unforgiving person who would take advantage of her position with Mr. Hearst, and the protection of our hallowed Bill of Rights, to do something like that — which, of course, I'm not."

358

"Now, now, Miss Donovan," Gimel said, his ingratiating tone telling her that he hadn't given up on the idea that if he stayed in her good graces, he could gain something from being featured in a story run in Hearst's papers. "You must forgive Miss Craddock's choice of words. No one is making an accusation. She is simply distraught over the fact that one of the students placed in her care has disappeared this morning. We only hoped you might know something that would help us to locate the boy."

"Me? Why would I know where he is? I've been here, working at my typewriter all morning."

"Because the boy who is missing is Walter Proud, the student with whom you undermined my discipline yesterday morning," the teacher announced.

"A coincidence, Miss Craddock, nothing else; but it's hardly a reason to blame *me* for *your* failure to provide proper supervision for your charges. Has it ever occurred to you that the child simply ran away? I understand that's a constant problem in all reservation schools—which, now that I think of it, wouldn't look too good on the report the superintendent files with the Bureau of Indian Affairs." Aidan's eyes lit with sudden knowledge. "Now I see why you're trying to place the responsibility for the boy's disappearance on me. You don't want another runaway child on *your* record! That's it, isn't it? You thought you'd protect yourself at my expense. But, unfortunately, Miss Craddock, I'm not a helpless little Indian student who can be accused and judged and punished without having any defense—except to run away."

"He didn't run away, and you know it." Miss Craddock seethed. "I insist you turn that boy over to me this

359

instant, or I'll—"

"Mr. Gimel," Aidan said, turning to the agent, "at first, I found this slightly amusing, but I'm beginning to become quite bored with the entire matter. I've told both you and Miss Craddock that I know nothing about her missing student. However, to put your mind at rest and to show that this irrational woman's ridiculous accusation is based on a desire to protect herself and to injure me because of some imagined insult, I insist you search the house. But forgive me if I don't accompany you. I have work to do." She turned back to her typewriter and with a flourish, snatched her article out of the machine. Inserting a clean sheet of paper, she glanced back at Miss Craddock. "Well, go on." She started typing.

"Very well," Miss Craddock said, moving toward the bedroom. "Are you coming, Mr. Gimel."

Torn by indecision, Gimel glanced from the teacher to the reporter.

Aidan looked up. "Mr. Gimel, do you suppose you and I could set aside a time when I can come to your office to discuss your personal background and beliefs. I've decided to do a series, with one article about the agency itself, one about the people who depend on it for their survival, and one about the man who runs it so effectively."

His greed for personal glory obviously more important to him than Miss Craddock's missing student, Gimel smiled. "As a matter of fact," he said, "I believe I have some free time this afternoon, if you'd like to come then . . . say about three."

"That will be fine. I'll see you at three. But do go on and help Miss Craddock with her search. I didn't mean to interrupt."

"I don't really think this is necessary, Miss Craddock," Gimel declared. "It's obvious, Miss Donovan knows nothing about the boy. We should leave her to her work. Sorry to have disturbed you," he said to Aidan as he grasped the flabbergasted teacher's arm and propelled her toward the door.

"But I tell you, she knows where he is!" Miss Craddock protested, her angry gaze boring into Aidan.

"That's quite enough," Gimel snapped. He gave River a begrudging nod. "I assume you'll be back on the job shortly, Edwards."

"Yes, sir, Mr. Gimel. I'll be right there," River said, opening the door so their "guests" might exit. He watched the pair until they stepped into the street, then shut the door and sagged back against it. A smile on his face, he mouthed the words, "good girl."

Aidan started to lift her skirt, but River held up a hand to stop her and went to the window. "Let's just be sure," he whispered. Lifting the blind, he peeked out, then hurried to the table. "It's okay. They're across the street, and she's still lambasting him," he announced, dropping to the floor beside her chair.

Aidan, her heart still pounding, flipped her skirts up into her lap to expose the little figure huddled there. *"Washtay hoksila—*good boy," she giggled as River drew Walks Proud out of his hiding place. Sliding from her chair to the floor, she hugged Walks Proud and kissed his face, saying *"Washtay cikala ohitika—*good little brave!"

"You were both great," River said, drawing them into his embrace. "I almost felt sorry for Miss Craddock. She didn't stand a chance when you went after her, Little Fire."

Aidan shook her head. "I couldn't have done it without the two of you. Walks Proud was so quiet, I almost forgot he was there. Except for his trembling, he didn't move a muscle the whole time. *Washtay cikala ohitika*— good little brave," she repeated, her smile glowing as she gave Walks Proud another kiss. "And as far as '*Ate*' is concerned," she said, gazing lovingly into River's blue eyes, "without you there giving me your strength, I would have fallen apart in the first two minutes after Gimel came through the door."

At the mention of the agent, they both grew serious, and River shook his head. "All we did was buy ourselves a little time to find an answer to our problems. You do realize that nothing's changed, don't you, Little Fire?"

"Yes, my serious Lakota brave, I know," she said sadly, cupping his tanned cheek in her palm. "And there's still something I haven't told you. Coming back from the school, I overheard Gimel talking to the trading store operator. Did you know that man takes the supplies the government sends to the Indians and *sells* them in the store?"

River nodded. "Yes, but without tangible evidence, we can't do anything. I was hoping to get some while I was working for him."

Aidan winced, feeling guilty that she had caused his plan to go awry, and now she had even worse news for him. "That's not all I heard him say, River."

As he sensed her apprehension, a chill of foreboding shuddered through River. "Go on."

"Gimel told the trader, Jackson, that if either of us does anything that indicates we plan to expose what he's doing here, he intends to have us killed."

"That does it!" River exclaimed, bolting up from the

362

floor. "Get our things packed. I'm taking you out of here today." He crossed to the door.

Whisking Walks Proud up into her arms, Aidan ran after him. "What are you going to do?" she asked, catching his arm. "You don't intend to confront him, do you? You know what he's capable of!"

River's expression gentled as he looked into her frightened face. "Don't worry, *Peta,* jumping into the *fire* is more your style than mine. Besides, now that I've suddenly got a family to think about, I can't very well get myself killed, can I?"

Aidan threw her free arm around River's neck and buried her face against his shoulder, almost crushing Walks Proud between them. "Oh, River, I love you so much. Can you ever forgive me for turning your life into such an ungodly mess?"

He kissed her tearful face, then ruffled Walks Proud's hair. "I wouldn't have missed it, Little Fire. You've brought more *life* into my life than I ever thought possible." He gave her another kiss. "I've got to go. You just get packed and be ready to leave when I get back. I'll try to be here about five or six." He opened the door a crack and looked out, making sure Aidan and Walks Proud weren't exposed. Finding the way clear, he turned back to her and grinned. "By the way, Little Fire, I don't want you to step out of this cottage for one minute until I get back. Is that understood?"

"What about my appointment with Gimel? He'll know something's wrong if I don't go."

River shook his head. "I mean it, Aidan. Not a single step! Don't worry about Gimel. I'll explain to him that you weren't feeling well—after your unsettling encounter with Miss Craddock—and that you would consider it a great favor if your meeting could be postponed until some time tomorrow. I mean it, Fire! Don't go out for any reason!"

"I won't," she answered with a salute, not even resenting his order. Right then, she just liked being taken care of. "I promise."

"You take care of her, Walks Proud," he said to the child, who yawned sleepily and rested his head on Aidan's shoulder. Laughing, River gave the boy an extra hug and a kiss on the cheek. "We men have to keep our women out of trouble, don't we?"

An hour later, as River stood on the long loading dock of the agency allotment depot, checking permits and marking off names on a list of those eligible to receive supplies at the Blue Creek Agency, John Gimel watched him from his office across the alley. "Are you certain?" he asked the man beside him. "You could be mistaken."

"Believe me, Gimel, I'm not making a mistake. I don't care what he told you, that half-breed you hired has a degree in law from Harvard. He was Theodore Roosevelt's personal aide in Cuba, and his name is River *Blue Eagle!*"

"The son of Daniel Blue Eagle, the red bastard who spends all his time preaching Indian Rights and campaigning for the Indians to be allowed to run their own reservations?"

A triumphant smile lit Scott Percy's face, and he sat back in his chair. "The one and only," he said, removing a silver case from his breast pocket and taking out a cigarette. "Face it, Gimel, that breed and his girl friend

364

aren't here to write any glowing reports about you and the way you run Blue Creek Reservation." He inserted the cigarette between his lips and lit it. "Quite frankly, old man . . ." He threw back his head and blew out a puff of smoke. ". . . they're here to crucify you—and every other white man who has devoted his life to taking care of these mangy, ungrateful redskins. To put it bluntly, my friend, they intend to nail your ass to the wall, and I can guarantee you that they won't stop until they've succeeded. Unless you do something about it."

Gimel's eyes narrowed angrily as he watched River move easily down the line of raggedly dressed squaws, stopping to talk and listen to each one. "We'll just see who gets whose ass," he vowed, dropping his hand away from the shade and turning back to his visitor. "And what about you, Mr. Percy? What do you expect to get out of this? Money?"

Scott tilted his head to the side and lifted his eyebrows, giving Gimel a cocky, you-caught-me grin. "But not yours, Gimel. I'm after a much bigger fish."

"And you expect me to help you catch that fish?"

"It's only fair. I save your hide, you help me catch the fish I want."

"Which one? Blue Eagle or that Donovan slut?"

"Both of them. Their disappearance is going to be my ticket to the biggest fish of all—William Randolph Hearst—at the same time it saves this nice little setup you've got here."

Gimel eyed the writer suspiciously, still not certain he was ready to incriminate himself by acting too interested. "What exactly do you mean by disappearance? It's not as if they're two drifters who can just drop off the face of the earth without anyone noticing."

365

"That's the beauty of my plan. With your help, I'm going to see that the entire nation 'notices' every sordid detail of their love affair—and the tragedy that ends it—through my article in the New York *Journal*—the same article that will portray you as a modern-day saint and hero."

"Go on." Gimel wasn't yet ready to trust Scott Percy, but if the man could show him a way to get rid of Blue Eagle and Aidan Donovan without implicating himself, he was certainly going to listen. He studied Percy thoughtfully, his fingers forming a steeple and tapping at his lower lip. "I must admit, you have aroused my curiosity. Exactly how would this, uh, tragedy come about?"

Scott took a final drag on his cigarette, then ground it out and leaned forward. "First of all, I think it would be very good for your 'saintly image' if you sent your Lakota-speaking rations clerk out with a wagonload of supplies to be distributed to poor families in an outlying village on the reservation, families who you've just learned have no way to come to the agency to collect them.

"And, as long as Blue Eagle's going anyway, why not let Miss Donovan go with him? That will be a big help to you since you don't really have time to take her on a tour of the reservation, because of your busy schedule here at the agency. 'Kill two birds with one stone'—in more ways than one."

Beginning to understand the direction in which Percy was heading, Gimel nodded his head. "Are you suggesting the two lovebirds have an unfortunate accident while they are gone?"

"Except that we're going to take one step further.

366

Think how much better the story will read if a band of renegade Indians descends on our hapless lovers, steals the supply wagon the 'kind' agent sent out—killing the lovers in the process—and then disappears into the Badlands, from whence they came."

"Go on," Gimel said, his eyes dilating with excitement.

Percy smiled, knowing his instinct about Gimel had been right. "Upon hearing of their unfortunate deaths, a newspaper reporter—yours truly—who has been a friend of the dear departed since he met them in Cuba, comes to Blue Creek to write the story of their tragic end. While here, *I* find Aidan Donovan's 'notes'. . ." He raised an eyebrow suggestively. ". . . describing the wonderful things being done for the Indians on this reservation, all because of one great man, Agent John Gimel." He paused to shrug helplessly and throw out his hands. "What can I do, but write the story she would have written . . . if she hadn't been cut off in her prime?" He leaned back in his chair and waited for Gimel's reaction.

His upper body rocking slightly, the agent watched Percy without speaking for several seconds. Finally he spoke. "I'm not suggesting I'm interested in going along with your plan, Mr. Percy, but just for the sake of curiosity, if I were, what guarantee do I have that you wouldn't betray me?"

Percy laughed. "The same guarantee I have that you won't call in your Indian police and have me thrown in jail for even suggesting it. None. But face it, Gimel old man, we need each other, and if one of us lets the other one down, we both lose."

"Still, and again for the sake of curiosity, what would I be expected to do . . . besides sending the clerk and the woman out onto the reservation?"

367

"All you need to do is find me a half-dozen men who feel the same way you and I do about keeping the Indians in their place — and control of the reservations in the right hands. Then send the breed and his bitch on their way, and you can sit back and relax. I'll take care of the rest."

"I must admit you've thought of everything, Percy. I'm very impressed by your thoroughness. I have just one more question."

"Feel free to ask it."

"What's your real motive? Mine, as you so astutely realized, is survival, but I can't quite figure yours out."

A pleased smile snaked across Scott Percy's face. "Let's just say Aidan Donovan has been a thorn in my side for some time now, and the only way to rid myself of that thorn is to *cut* it out!" He held out his right hand. "Do we have an agreement?"

Gimel glanced from Percy's extended hand to his smug face; then he took the reporter's hand. "We have an agreement."

Chapter Twenty-five

Aidan stared down at the boy sleeping in her bed, her heart filled with tenderness she'd never imagined existed. It was similar to the way she felt when she thought about River and how much she loved him. But not quite.

This was a feeling so unique and sweet that she, who made her living with words, was at a loss to describe it. Yet she knew it filled her with a warm, sweet glow, and she would give her life before she would ever again allow anyone to hurt this beautiful child.

Turning back to her packing, she rearranged her trunk so her typewriter would fit inside, then covered the case with articles of clothing, things she thought they needed most—jeans, shirts, sturdy shoes, stockings, a sun hat, gloves. The frivolous dresses and hats she had worn in San Francisco lay discarded at the end of the bed. River hadn't told her what to bring, but she was sure, since they were to leave without being noticed, he would probably want her to pack lightly.

Glancing at Walks Proud, she paused and smiled. "Poor little baby. You were exhausted, weren't you?" she said, remembering that he'd hardly been able to stay awake to eat the lunch she had fixed or while she had rubbed ointment on the welts on his back. She brushed a lock of coal black hair off his forehead. "This is probably the first time you've felt safe since you came here."

A pang of guilt stabbed her. What if she had only made things worse by bringing him here? If anyone found out she and River had Walks Proud, he would be taken from them and would again know the agony of being confused and alone—and feeling betrayed. Being wrenched away from them and put back in the Blue Creek Agency school would be devastating to such a tiny fellow who had already gone through so much. He might never trust anyone again. She's even heard reports that students as young as six years old had committed suicide because they could not bear being cut off from their families. "That won't happen to you, little brave. River and I won't let it."

The thought that she had let River down brought a twinge of regret. If they just could have gotten some proof that Gimel and Jackson were selling government supplies to the Indians instead of dispensing them free of charge, as the government intended . . . Of course, she had overheard Gimel and Jackson, but it would be their word against hers. No, they needed something else, something indisputable. Something like . . . Aidan's gaze flew to the dresser.

"A photograph!" she exclaimed, grabbing up the Kodak box camera she had used to take pictures of Walks Proud, front and back after she had bathed him, so she would have a record of the welts on his body even after they had disappeared. Of course, there was a good chance the photographs wouldn't turn out because she had dared to open the blind only for a couple of minutes and the light might not have been bright enough. But pictures of the trading store would come out because she could photograph the merchandise displayed on the front porch—outside and in full sunlight. Surely a number of the items for sale would be recognizable as having been issued by the government, and then she would have something to substantiate what she had seen and heard.

Suddenly, a memory broke through Aidan's excitement and brought her back to reality. She had promised River she wouldn't leave the cottage until he got back, and, more importantly, she couldn't leave Walks Proud alone. If he woke up and she wasn't nearby, he would be terrified.

Her shoulders slumped, not because she now had a responsibility and couldn't go running off whenever the mood struck her, but because after all River had done for her, all he continued to do for her, she couldn't give him the one thing he needed, proof that John Gimel was stealing from the Lakotas on the Blue Creek Reservation.

Dejected, she went into the well-stocked kitchen and began to gather up canned goods, dropping them into the pillow case she had taken off the bed. She didn't know what River's intentions were, but she was resolved to be ready for anything.

As if her thoughts of River made him materialize, suddenly he was there, standing inside the door, his gaze raking over her as though he were taking inventory to be sure she was still safe. "Hi," she greeted him in a low, husky whisper.

"Hi," she said with a tired smile, the worried expression on his face relaxing only slightly as he set down a bundle. "Did you miss me?"

Grinning impishly, she shrugged. "Oh? Have you been gone?"

His smile widened, but his eyes didn't lose their worried look. "Get over here, woman," he ordered, holding out his arms to her. "You need to learn the proper way for a 'wife' to greet her 'husband' after he's been slaving all day at the salt mines."

Laughing, she ran into his embrace. "Is this any better?" she asked, covering his neck with eager kisses.

"Much." He pulled her hard against him and kissed her. Ending the kiss slowly, he leaned his forehead against hers and laced his fingers together at the small of her back. "How's the boy?"

"He's fine. He's been sleeping most of the time since you left. Poor little thing. I wouldn't be surprised if this isn't the first time he's felt secure enough to sleep soundly since he's been here."

"I just hope we can keep him secure." He removed her hands from around his neck and led her over to the sofa. "We need to talk."

"What's wrong? Aren't we leaving?"

"Gimel wants me to take a load of rations to an outlying village east of here, to some families who can't come in for them. And to make it even better, he suggested I take you with me so that you can see some more of the reservation."

Aidan looked at him, confused by his odd mood. "Isn't that good? Doesn't it mean he's decided to trust us?"

River shook his head. "I wish I could believe that. But I'm afraid it's just the opposite. Gimel's attitude toward me changed a bit too suddenly for me not to suspect he's up to something. He was actually friendly. He even called me 'my boy.' Mark my words, Fire, something happened this afternoon to convince Agent Gimel that he needs to be rid of us—permanently."

"You mean he . . ."

". . . doesn't plan for us to return safely from this little excursion he's sending us on."

Understanding dawned in Aidan's eyes. "And if something should happen to us miles from the agency while he's here, in plain sight and with plenty of witnesses, no one would be able to connect it to him. Right?"

"Right."

"Does he know you suspect he's up to something?"

River shook his head and blew out a disgusted chuckle. "He's convinced I don't have any idea that he suspects the real reason we're here."

"What did you tell him?"

"I told him I was honored that he trusted me to do the job, and promised him I wouldn't let him down."

"But we're not going to go, are we?"

"We're going, but not when he expects us to."

"What does that mean?"

"It means we're going tonight after he's in bed, instead of tomorrow morning at eight as he planned. Then, once I get you and Walks Proud off the reservation, I'm coming back for the proof I need to confront that bastard face-to-face and put him in prison."

"There you go again, making plans without taking what I think into consideration. I thought we were in this together—partners. That means we share the good and the bad, River. Besides, what makes you think I'm willing to sit safely in a hotel room in Nebraska, waiting to receive word that you've been killed on the Blue Creek reservation?"

"Aidan," he said, standing up, "it's been a long, trying day, and it's going to be an even longer night. Quite frankly, I'm just not up to arguing with you right now. I'm going to take a bath, and then I'm going to sleep.

373

Be packed and ready to leave around midnight."

Aidan stared after him as he disappeared into the bathroom and slammed the door behind him. "Damn you, River," she muttered. *I'm going to show you once and for all that I can carry my weight in this partnership. You want proof that Gimel is a crook, and I'm going to get it for you.*

With a smug smile, Aidan snatched her hat off the coat rack and plopped it on her head. Grabbing up her purse and a carryall, she went into the bedroom, quietly put her box camera into its case, then draped the strap across her shoulder.

When I get the roll of film developed, I'm going to have more proof than you can imagine. She patted her camera case affectionately, more grateful than ever before that the lightweight Kodak came with enough film to take one hundred pictures before she had them developed. It was so easy to operate, and when she had used all the exposures, all she had to do was mail the camera, the exposed film still in it, back to Eastman Kodak Company in Rochester, New York, where her pictures would be quickly developed and returned to her, along with her camera, reloaded with a new roll of film.

Of course, it wouldn't be so convenient if she owned only one camera and needed to take pictures of something important while it was in Rochester. But she didn't have to worry about that. She had three of the handy little contraptions.

Aidan tapped lightly on the bathroom door. "River?"

"What?" he asked wearily.

"Listen for Walks Proud, will you? I'm going to run over to the trading store and get something we need."

Without waiting for an answer, because she knew what it would be, she made a dash for the front door.

374

"Aidan!" She heard the sloshing of water as he evidently sprang upright in the tub. "Don't you—"

"I'll be right back!" she called, whipping through the door as if she hadn't heard his protest. "After I get what I need from the store," she added with a satisfied grin as she hurried off the porch and into the street.

Jackson's Trading Store was a white clapboard structure with a flat roof and a boardwalk that stretched across its front and around one side. Scattered along the walk and on the ground were Indian men and women, some congregated in small groups, others considering the various items displayed for sale. In the street around the store were several dilapidated buckboard wagons, a few empty, others already loaded, but none of them looked as if they could make it very far without falling apart.

Glancing over her shoulder to check the sun's location, Aidan unsnapped her camera case and took it out. "Perfect," she said, looking into the viewfinder to determine whether she should move closer or step back to get the whole building into the photograph.

Having settled on the proper distance, she took several exposures of the entire store from different angles then moved in closer, intending to take photographs of specific merchandise while Indians were buying it. Just then she saw a white-shirted, short-haired Indian man holding a sack of flour on his shoulder, his hand held out to an Indian woman who had three small children clinging to her skirt. "Don't move," she muttered, framing the scene in her camera. As the woman put something in the Indian store clerk's hand, Aidan pressed on the button that opened the shutter of her camera. Hurriedly rolling the film forward, she took another picture of the clerk shifting the flour sack to the shoulder of a teenage boy

375

who was obviously with the woman.

Click. Wind. Move to a new location. Click. Wind. Move. Over and over, she took pictures of transactions, certain some of these must be illegal sales, moving nearer to the store with every picture. Wanting to get even tighter shots, Aidan approached a young woman who carried a baby on her back and looked wistfully at the display of canned milk for sale.

"Excuse me?" she said to the woman. "Do you speak English? I'd like to take a picture of you and your *hoksi cala*. You and your baby." She used her free hand to illustrate her words.

The Indian mother directed a sad-eyed stare at Aidan, giving no indication that she understood but remaining still while Aidan got set and took the picture.

"Washtay," Aidan said with a smile. She dug in her purse, pulled out a fifty-cent piece, and handed it to the woman. "Thank you — *ha ye.*"

During the next few minutes, Aidan handed out all the money she had in her purse as Lakota men, women, and children eagerly posed for her — and for her coin — each time in front of a different item for sale. On film, she captured a boy peeking curiously into the oven of an iron stove, a girl looking longingly at a jar of licorice, men studying harnesses and plows and farming equipment, and women buying various foods they had only looked at until she had paid them to pose for her. Her camera also caught some of these same women gazing at large cooking pots or holding yard goods up to their children. One of them, a pretty young woman, had even been photographed trying on a large flowered hat.

Just as Aidan was about to finish up, everyone on the boardwalk suddenly became quiet. She looked up to see the Indian clerk pointing her out to a man she recognized as Jackson.

"Hey, lady!" Jackson shouted as he bounded off the porch and came toward her. "What do you think you're doing?"

"Why, I'm just taking pictures of people for my newspaper," she explained, dropping her camera into the case and snapping it shut. "Is there a problem?"

"Yeah. I don't like no one takin' pictures o' my store without my permission. Gimme that camera." He made a grab for the case.

"I will not!" Aidan exclaimed, snatching up the camera and holding it against her bosom with both arms. "This store and this street do not belong to you. The government owns them, and I'll take pictures anywhere, and of anyone I please."

"We'll jest see 'bout that, little lady." Jackson stepped closer and reached for the camera. Grasping the strap on her shoulder, he gave it a jerk, pulling her forward as he took the camera from her and turned to walk away.

"Give me my camera!" Aidan shrieked, running after him.

"Give the lady her camera, Jackson," a deep, familiar voice ordered.

Jackson immediately stopped and looked around. "But—"

"Didn't I tell you Miss Donovan was here as my guest and that she was to be shown every courtesy? Now give her the camera."

Jackson begrudgingly pitched the camera at Aidan, but she reacted faster than he had expected and managed to catch it. Giving Jackson a triumphant grin, she turned away from him. "Thank you, Mr. Gimel. I can't imagine why this man is acting like this. I only wanted pictures of the Indians shopping, just like civilized

377

people, to show how they've changed since the old days when they were raiding homesteads and stealing what they needed from innocent whites."

"Yes, well, I'm sure Mr. Jackson didn't understand. I hope you will accept my apology for his ungentlemanly and inappropriate reaction to your picture-taking," Gimel said smoothly.

An involuntary shiver tripped up Aidan's spine, as she was hit by the realization that this was indeed a very dangerous man and that she and River must escape from his influence at all costs. She hazarded a glance at the scowling Jackson, then nodded her head. "Of course, I accept your apology" she said placatingly, wanting to get as far away as she could from these two men as quickly as she could. Then an idea struck her, and she knew she couldn't leave just yet.

"I've just had the most wonderful thought! I was going to take your picture when I interviewed you, but would you be willing to pose for me now? Maybe talking to Mr. Jackson or one of the Indians?"

Jackson glowered at her and shook his head. "You ain't takin' my picture!"

"Come on, Jackson." Gimel clapped the disgruntled storekeeper on the back. "What harm will a photograph or two do . . . unless you're afraid your face will break Miss Donovan's camera? Where would you like us to stand?"

Aidan glanced at the afternoon sun descending in the western sky. "I think I will have the best light over there." She pointed directly at the front corner of the store, where she would have a full view of both the front and side porches. "The light is perfect there."

Before she was through, Aidan had taken several pictures of the two men standing in front of the store, and

378

she'd even gotten one of Gimel handing a harness to an Indian man.

"I really must be going now," she finally declared, putting her camera away. "My husband will be wondering where I've disappeared to. But thank you for helping me — once more. You have been wonderful to me since I've been here; and believe me, I won't forget all you've done to make my article successful — like arranging the trip to the Indian village tomorrow. I'm really looking forward to that!"

"No thanks are necessary, Miss Donovan. I've been glad to help. I would offer to escort you back to your cottage, but Mr. Jackson and I have some business to discuss. So I bid you good day, but I will look forward to seeing you in the morning, before you and Edwards leave."

"And I will look forward to seeing you." Fighting the desire to break into a run, she started back to the cottage.

A few minutes later, her heart still beating a rapid tattoo against her ribs, Aidan ran up onto the front porch. As she wrapped her fingers around the doorknob, it was wrenched from her grasp.

"Where the hell have you been?"

Stung by his anger, Aidan lifted her chin and brushed past River. "I told you I was going to the trading store."

"And I told you not to go anywhere," he growled, kicking the door shut and wheeling around to face her. "And you agreed you wouldn't."

"I assumed you meant while you were gone," she said, ripping her hat from her head and tossing it onto the table. You certainly didn't think I had agreed never to go anywhere without you ever again, did you? Besides, I don't know what you're so upset about. I'm back now, and none the worse for wear."

"Have you completely forgotten what I told you earlier?" He grasped her upper arms and brought his face down to hers. "Gimel wants us dead!"

"I haven't forgotten. But if you're right ¡about Gimel wanting it done miles from the agency so he won't be implicated, I couldn't have been safer."

River dropped his hands in resignation and strode away from her. "I don't know why your queer sense of logic never fails to amaze me. But fool that I am, I keep being caught off guard by it."

Aidan balled her fists on her hips and assumed a belligerent feet-apart stance. "So I have a 'queer sense of logic,' do I? Next, I suppose you're going to tell me that it's perfectly sound logic to leave here without having gotten the proof we need against Gimel, so that you have to come back alone and risk your life . . . when I was able to get it with no risk whatsoever!"

River stopped midway in his retreat to the bedroom. "What did you say?" he ground out, turning to face her again. "What are you talking about?"

Aidan grinned tauntingly and waved her hand back and forth. "Uh-uh." She sauntered past him toward the bedroom, shooting a mischievous look over her shoulder. "You think my logic is queer, remember?"

"Dammit Aidan!" He wrapped steely fingers around her arm and brought her progress to an abrupt halt. "What did you find?"

Her smile secretive, she shrugged her shoulders and twisted her arm free. "Probably nothing that would interest someone who thinks my logic is 'queer.' " She dangled her camera case out to her side, goading him. "But I have no doubt Mr. Hearst will be fascinated."

"You got pictures? Of what?" In his voice was a mixure of excitement and worry.

Aidan whipped the camera out of his reach and headed into the bedroom, removing the camera from its case as she did so. "Not until you apologize for saying my sense of logic is queer!" She dug a second camera out of the trunk she'd packed earlier, then put the camera with the exposed film in it in the trunk, cushioning it with protective layers of clothing.

"All right! I apologize for saying you have queer logic. Now tell me, what did you take pictures of?"

Tired of teasing him, she dropped the second camera into the case and snapped it shut. "What would you say if I told you I got pictures of Indians *buying* various items at the trading store that they probably should be getting for nothing?"

Before he spoke, River stared at her for a moment as he absorbed what she had said. "You really took pictures?"

She nodded. "With my trusty little Kodak. I even got Gimel and Jackson to pose in front of the store for me. Jackson is not only the storekeeper, but he's the man I saw talking to Gimel this morning. Now what do you think of my logic?"

Torn between concern over what might have happened to Aidan and excitement because the photographs would probably provide the proof they needed to take Gimel to court, River shook his head. "I don't know whether to hug you or throttle you! You took a big risk."

She nodded toward the head of the bed and grinned. "I think you'd better hug me, because our little brave may not like to see his *ate* throttle his *ina*." She went to the side of the bed closest to the window. "Good 'morning,' *cikala ohitika*. Did our silly arguing wake you up?" he asked, lying down and drawing the still-drowsy boy

381

into her embrace. "Anyway, hugging's a lot more fun, isn't it, my little brave?" She tweaked his nose and kissed his forehead, then smiled lovingly up at River and gave the mattress on the other side of Walks Proud a pat. "Come on, my grown-up brave, lie down with us. Didn't you say earlier that you might take a nap?"

Laughing, River lowered his large frame onto the bed and slipped an arm around Walks Proud and Aidan. "I guess I'm going to have to get used to living with a woman who has a mind of her own."

"Because you're finally willing to admit I might not be scatterbrained after all?" she asked, lifting her hand to brush back a lock of obsidian hair from River's forehead.

"Because you're my heart and I can't live without you."

Touched deeply by his confession, Aidan blinked back tears. "And you, dear River, are my soul—my *nagi*."

Chapter Twenty-six

Aidan opened the bedroom window at the back of the cottage and peered out into the ebony darkness of the moonless night. For a moment she listened for any unusual sound, then she lowered a cloth bag filled with things she absolutely had to take: a spare blanket, bread, a canteen of water, some oranges for Walks Proud, a few first-aid supplies, the article she had written at the Blue Creek Agency, and two of her cameras.

Everything else had to be left behind, which for the most part didn't bother her. As long as she had the film she'd exposed and some yet unexposed in one of the cameras she was taking, she didn't mind leaving the third camera behind. And as far as her clothes were concerned, she didn't deem them an important loss. Right now, she only needed garments that would keep her modesty intact. However, while she could be perfectly happy with a minimum of clothing, leaving her typewriter behind was a different matter. She had sworn in Cuba, she'd never be without one again, and a new one would definitely be her first purchase when they reached Rushville, Nebraska, in the morning.

Satisfied that it was safe to proceed, she followed the bag out the window. Quickly checking the area again, she turned back to lift Walks Proud out and set him on the ground. She held a finger to her lips to remind him to be quiet, then hefted the supply bag. Draping it strap diagonally across her chest, she positioned it weight on one hip before wrapping a blanket over he head and around her shoulders. Holding back the edge of the blanket with her arms, she picked up Walk Proud, enfolding his undersized little body in the blan ket.

"*Washtay*—good," she said softly as Walks Prou wound his arms and legs around her neck and waist She tucked his head under her chin and drew the blan ket together over him, smiling reasurringly, though h couldn't see her face. "All right, little brave, this is it We're going to leave this bad place." Taking a deep fortifying breath, she scurried from behind the shru and into the open.

Her eyes and ears alert to every sight and sound, sh made her way past the back of Gimel's big white hous and several other buildings before she came to the alle where River had told her to wait for him to drive past i the wagon.

"So far, so good," she mumbled, sagging back agains the wall at the corner nearest the main street of th compound. She gave the little leg wound around he waist an affectionate pat. "*Washtay*," she whispered Though the added weight of the bag and the little bo couldn't have amounted to as much as she'd carried i Cuba, Aidan's arms and shoulders ached, and her lung expanded and deflated as though she had run up a hi carrying a much heavier load.

Catching her breath a bit, though her heart had yet t stop thrumming painfully in her chest, she peeked ou from her hiding place—and saw what she was lookin for: the loaded agency wagon being pulled by a team o horses driven by a lone man, a hat pulled low on his head.

"Hipi—he is here," she whispered, giving Walks Proud a bolstering squeeze. She waited in the shadows behind the rain barrel until the jangle of harness and the clatter of wagon wheels told her the horses would appear at the alley exit in the next instant. Holding her breath, she checked her instinct to run out of her hiding place and wait in the street.

Then came the sound she had been waiting for, the creaking of the wagon as it rolled into view and stopped, blocking the alleyway. Still she didn't move, though every nerve in her body screamed for release, like a rubber band stretched to the limit.

Go on, she silently urged the driver who sat erect in his seat, his head slowly turning in every direction except up the alley. *Give the signal, dammit.*

Finally he took off his hat, smoothed back his hair, and put his hat back on his head.

Aidan bounded out of the shadows and made a dash for the waiting wagon. "It's about time," she hissed, heaving Walks Proud onto the box, then following behind him.

"Have you been here long?" River asked, his lips not moving as he continued to glance up and down the street.

"It probably seemed a lot longer than it was," she admitted, settling herself and Walks Proud into the narrow space at River's feet and covering them both with the blanket. They had decided that explaining why he was leaving the agency at this time of night would be easier if the guard at the gate thought he was alone, and they had already told Walks Proud that he must be quiet and do whatever they told him without questioning it.

"Everybody comfortable?" Without waiting for an answer, River clicked his tongue at the horses and guided them across the square, deciding it was best to take the extra time and follow a roundabout route to the agency gate, instead of going past Gimel's house and the police headquarters.

"Other than feeling like I'm in a sweat lodge built for the wee folk, I am." She laughed, her breathing and heart rate already resuming a more normal rate. Even though they still had to get past the guard, she realized she felt safe for the first time since River had left them to hitch up the horses to the wagon over an hour before. Just knowing he was there gave her an invincible feeling that she'd not known since she'd taken Walks Proud out of the school basement. "How about you? Are you all right?"

"Me?" River asked with forced casualness. "Never better. But then, I'm not the one in the 'sweat lodge.' "

Suddenly, an uncomfortable sense of foreboding washed over Aidan, "River?"

"Little Fire," he answered.

"I just want to tell you that no matter what happens, the months we've been together have been the best part of my life, and I'll never regret one moment we shared."

"You sound like you don't think we're going to get out of this," he said teasingly, though his tone published his own worries.

"That's not true. Remember me? I'm the one who said we can do anything as long as we're together. I just wanted you to know how I felt . . . in case."

"Well, I'm going to do my damnedest to make sure there's no 'in case.' " Though she couldn't see his face, she could hear the smile in his voice.

"I have no doubt you'll do it. You've never let me

down yet. Look at all we've been through, and we've always come out of it 'smellin' like a rose', as my Da always says. We'll get out of—"

"Shh." His terse hiss cut her off in midsentence. "The gate's just ahead."

"Halt!" the Indian policeman on duty called out. "Where do you think you're going?"

"To *Sapa Mato's* camp, east of here, to deliver these rations," River answered in Lakota. Even though he knew the policeman had taken an oath to protect the agent, above all others, and that he would not hesitate to kill anyone who threatened Gimel, even his own kinsmen, River hoped the fact that they spoke the same language would make the guard less suspicious.

"I do not believe you," the guard answered, his tone making it obvious that he took his authority seriously, and wouldn't be fooled by any friendly overtures River made, no matter what language they were in. "The agent says everyone who receives rations must come to the agency to get them. Unless I have other orders from him, there are no exceptions, not for Black Bear and his band or any others."

River shrugged. "It's your funeral. Not mine." He acted as if he were about to turn the wagon around, then hesitated. He nodded toward the little guard shack. "Do you have a telephone to the agent's house in there?"

"Yes."

River secured the reins and stepped down from the wagon. "Tell you what. I'd hate to see you lose this good job and regular pay just because of a misunderstanding. Why don't you call him and verify my orders."

Indecision crossed the policeman's young face. "He is sleeping. He will be very angry if I wake him."

"Not as angry as he's going to be if I don't take these

387

rations out to Black Bear's camp and get back here right away. But, as I said, it's your funeral." He started to turn back toward the wagon.

"Wait. I will call." The guard stepped into the guardhouse. Picking up the cone-shaped earpiece of the telephone with one hand, he grabbed the crank handle with the other.

That was all the opportunity River needed. Without hesitation, he brought the butt of his revolver crashing down on the guard's head. Not waiting for the man to fall all the way to the floor, River ripped the telephone wire from the box and began to bind his hands and feet.

Grabbing the gate keys, he ran to unlock it, then leaped back into the wagon. Yelling at the horses, he cracked the whip over their heads. "So much for making a subtle getaway," he grumbled. "You might as well come out now. It's just a matter of time until that guard sounds the alarm."

Aidan didn't wait for him to say it again. She threw the blanket off herself and Walks Proud, and scrambled up to the seat beside River. "What happened?" she gasped, drawing the little boy onto her lap, despite the bouncing, of the speeding wagon. "I thought I'd go crazy not knowing what was going on. If you hadn't come back when you did, I don't think I'd have been able to stand it another second."

"I had to hit the guard and tie him up. Our only chance now is to get to those buttes over there—" He pointed to the west. "—before his relief comes or he gets loose on his own. One way or another, we're not going to have time to make it to the state line before Gimel knows we're gone and comes after us."

His ominous tone sent tentacles of dread skittering through Aidan, and a violent shudder shook her. She

388

ghtened her hold on Walks Proud and squinted into
ne distance, trying to spot the jagged line of flat-topped
ocks rising from the floor of the plains and easily seen
rom the agency during the day. "How far is it?"

"Maybe a little less than an hour, if the horses don't
ive out or the wagon doesn't break down."

"And if we make it to the buttes? What then? Will
ney be able to find us?"

"If we can get in there and off the road, we might
:and a chance of losing them," he explained doubtfully.
I spent a lot of time there with my grandfather when I
·as a boy, so I know several good places to hide."

"I just thought of something!" Aidan announced glee-
.lly. "Won't Gimel expect us to take the road south
nce that's the fastest way off the reservation?"

River nodded. "That's what I'm hoping for. By the
me he realizes he should have overtaken us, he'll have
) backtrack to pick up our trail. Hopefully, it will give
s time to lose them. The only thing we have to worry
bout is that he'll send his Indian police after us and
ur trail won't be easy to hide from them."

Aidan grinned and squeezed his arm. "I'm not wor-
ed. I know we're going to be all right."

Whimpering softly, Walks Proud squirmed in her
rms. She shifted him around so he could straddle her
ip and use her bosom as a pillow for his head. "Poor
ttle boy," she cooed, rubbing his back. "That's the first
)und he's made. Are all Indian children so well be-
aved?"

"They're trained from infancy not to cry or make
oise when there's danger."

"But he doesn't understand us. How does he know?"

"He senses it from your voice; and because he trusts
)u to take care of him, he won't make a sound if you

tell him not to. I told you, he thinks you're his *ina*."

"River, what will happen to him if we don't find hi
parents? I was thinking . . . maybe he was at the board
ing school because he has no parents."

River glanced over at Aidan, his love for her a physi
cal ache in his chest. How could he ever have though
she was a selfish, spoiled little white girl who cared onl
about having fun and getting what she wanted?

He shook his head. He was the one who had bee
selfish. And because of that selfishness, he had force
her to take up his fight without giving a thought to he
needs, or to the danger she would be in—or the good h
would be stealing from the world if anything happene
to her while she was fighting his battle.

Studying her sweet face, he hurt anew. Even if the
escaped being killed by Gimel, he didn't see how h
could protect her optimistic faith in herself and in him
There was just too much ugliness for her to see, and sh
was going to become more disillusioned each day sh
stayed on the reservation. No matter how much h
wanted her with him, he had to get her away.

"River? Are you in there?" Aidan asked, waving he
hand in front of his eyes. "I asked you what will happe
if we don't find his parents."

He nodded and gave a sad chuckle. Sooner or later h
would have to tell her the truth: Walks Proud probabl
had no parents or relatives to claim him, and India
children this young had a very high death rate—espe
cially puny ones like Walks Proud. The odds wer
stacked against him. It didn't matter what took Walk
Proud, the chances were that something would: measle
tuberculosis, malnutrition, or just losing the will to liv
because his spirit had been broken by a hard life.

But right now, he couldn't bring himself to destro

\idan's vision of a happy ending, one she thought she \ould bring about by sheer will and determination.

He reached over and ruffled Walks Proud's dark hair \nd grinned at him. "If we can't find them, I'm sure \nere are lots of kind Lakota families who'd love to \dopt such a *washtay, ohitika cikala wicasa.*

"Good, brave little man," Aidan translated, kissing the \op of Walks Proud's head, then moving her lips to \:iver's hand. "And good, brave *grown-up* man. Have I \old you, I love you?"

"Yes," he said with a sad smile, feeling another surge \f guilt for putting her in danger. "But right now, I \an't think of anything I'd rather hear."

She caught his chin and turned his face to hers. \River Blue Eagle, I love you with my *cante,* my *nagi* \nd my *woniya*—my heart, my soul, and my life. And \' I should die this very minute, I would die happy, \ecause I'm with you and you love me."

Agent John Gimel grunted and rolled over onto his \ack. He patted the empty space beside him in the bed. \Winter?" he called out. "Aren't you going to do some-\ning about that infernal pounding?"

As if in answer to his question, the knocking stopped. \That's better," he mumbled drowsily. "Now, come back \o bed."

When his live-in housekeeper and mistress, a gift from \ chief wanting extra favors, didn't return immediately, \Gimel roused slightly. Now that he was awake, he could \ear a deep agitated voice coming from the entry hall, \nd he knew immediately it meant trouble.

Tossing the sheet off his portly frame, he sat up and \wung his feet onto the floor. Leaning forward, he raked

391

his fingers through his hair. "This had better be important for someone to ruin the first decent night's sleep I've had since that Donovan bitch got here." A ripple of smug satisfaction charged through him at the thought of being rid of her and her half-breed lover once and for all. "Thanks to Scott Percy's little plan," he said, shrugging into his dressing gown. *Shame he won't be around long enough to enjoy the fruits of his cleverness.*

"Agent Gimel," Winter whispered, cracking the bedroom door to peek in.

"It's all right, Winter, I'm up. What is it? It better be something more important than backed-up plumbing in the dormitory."

"It is the police chief, Red Arrow, to see you," she said, continuing to speak in hushed tones. "He says there has been some trouble at the gate and he must speak to you immediately."

"Trouble at the gate?" Gimel slid his feet into his slippers. "What kind of trouble?"

The pretty Indian girl shook her head. "I do not know, Agent Gimel, sir."

He smiled and cupped her chin in his hand, lifting her face upward. "How many times must I tell you it's all right to call me John when we're alone?"

"I forget . . . John," Winter explained shyly. "I will do better."

Gimel kissed her pouting lips and chuckled. "Go on back to bed. I'll take care of this matter and join you shortly."

He hurriedly left the room and started down the stairs to the entry hall. "All right, Red Arrow, what's the meaning of this?" he asked midway down as he saw his chief of police waiting below. "Whose band is acting up tonight? If it's Crooked Leg again, he's going to—"

392

"It is not Crooked Leg, Agent Gimel. It is that mixed blood who brought the white woman to the agency two days ago, the one you hired as rations overseer."

As if he'd been wired with electricity and the policeman had hit a switch, alarm crackled through every nerve in Gimel's body. "What about him?"

"He's gone."

"Gone? What are you talking about?" the agent growled, a sudden vicious pounding in his right temple reverberating through his brain.

"He was driving a supply wagon full of rations that he said you ordered him to take to Black Bear's camp east of here; but when the guard on duty tried to call for confirmation, Blue Eagle knocked him out and tied him up."

"Damn!" Gimel glanced at the tall grandfather clock that stood in the hallway. "What time did this happen?"

"The guard guessed it to be about midnight. He was on duty from eleven to three, and he thinks about an hour had passed when Blue Eagle came through. But since he can't tell time by a clock, and there was no moon, he is not sure."

The pain in Gimel's head pulsed and throbbed, as if it were a live, tangible presence straining against the confines of his skull. Rubbing his fingers into his eyes, he massaged his temples with his thumbs. "I assume the woman was with him."

"No sir. The guard said he was alone."

Not trusting the frisson of relief that ran through him, Gimel shook his head. "He must have hidden her." He started back up the stairs. "While I dress, go get that newspaper fellow, the one who arrived today, and have him meet me where the woman was staying — immediately."

393

"Yes, Agent Gimel." The police chief saluted smartly, then turned and bolted out the door.

Minutes later, Red Arrow was back with a bleary-eyed, hurriedly dressed Scott Percy. "What's going on?" Percy asked as he approached Gimel, who was pacing back and forth in front of Aidan's cottage.

"Blue Eagle's gone, and you can bet he took that bitch and her damaging story and pictures with him!"

"Gone? Are you sure?"

"Do you think I'd be standing out here in the middle of the night if I weren't?" Gimel hissed. He stomped onto the porch of Aidan's cottage.

Percy ran after him. "He must have realized you were on to them."

Gimel paused at the door and slid an incredulous glance down his nose at the reporter. "Of course, he did, you fool! Thanks to your clever plan, they not only got out of here with information that could cost me everything, but even with pictures I let her take because I was sure the film would be destroyed! And who knows what other pictures she took when she was snooping around the agency!"

His sleepy mind finally beginning to rouse, Percy shook his head. "Maybe it's better this way."

"I knew it! I gambled my future on the scheme of a crazy man." Gimel kicked the latch, sending the door flying in.

"Wait a minute!" Percy insisted, following the agent into the dark cottage. "Hear me out."

Gimel flicked on the light switch and looked around, immediately spotting the pillowcase filled with canned goods on the kitchen table. "Looks like they weren't planning on a long trip, doesn't it?" He glowered at Percy. "But that's no surprise, is it? Since it's less than

394

six hours to the nearest town—and telegraph office—in Nebraska." He stormed across to the bedroom and flipped on a second light.

"She left her clothes and trunk!" Scott said, his new plan becoming more appealing every instant. "Obviously, they were in a real hurry—which means they took the road south since that would be the fastest way to get to the state line."

"Of course, it does." Gimel's gaze fastened on a box-like object on the bureau and his mouth split into a grin. "Son-of-a-bitch! She didn't take the camera!" He made a dash for the incriminating evidence.

Percy followed close behind the agent. "Let me see that," he said, making a grab for the camera. Gaining possession first, he examined it, then shook his head. "That's what I thought."

"Give me that!" Gimel snarled, snatching the camera out of Percy's hold. "I'm going to get rid of it right this minute." He held it over his head as if to throw it.

"I hate to tell you, Gimel, old friend, but you'll be ruining a perfectly good camera and a roll of unexposed film. The camera you want is evidently on its way to Nebraska—along with Aidan Donovan and the end of your career as an agent if we don't stop them."

The muscles in Gimel's face sagged as he brought the camera down to examine it. "That can't be. I know it's the same camera I saw her use."

"Sorry," Percy said, his voice artificially sympathetic. "Any reporter with an ounce of sense carries a spare camera. And Aidan Donovan has more than an ounce of sense. She might leave her clothes and food behind, but she'd never leave evidence supporting her story." He waited a moment for Gimel to absorb the truth, then went on. "Now, are you interested in how I think we can

395

still save your skin and my story — and get rid of Aidan Donovan and River Blue Eagle?"

"Go on."

"If he left the agency with a load of rations without your permission, that's stealing government property, isn't it?"

"Yes, but . . . "

"And if someone steals from the agency, what would you do?"

"Send my Indian police after them, but they've already got at least an hour's head start."

"On the other hand, a loaded wagon travels about half as fast as men on horseback — especially Indians on horseback."

"Indians who will get a generous reward if they catch the culprits before they get off the reservation," Gimel added, hope growing in him as the mechanics of Percy's new scheme began to take shape in his mind.

"If Blue Eagle resists arrest, which I have no doubt he will, the police might be forced to kill him . . . and if the woman happens to get caught in the crossfire, it certainly would be an understandable accident."

"Red Arrow!" Gimel shouted as he crossed to the door of the cottage.

"Yes, Agent Gimel, sir," the Indian immediately replied, bounding into the room as though he'd been just outside the door waiting.

"I want you to lead a patrol after the man who stole our supplies. I have reason to believe he took the road south and has the woman with him. If he resists arrest, kill him, but don't let him get off the reservation. There will be a reward — gold pieces and extra rations — for you and your men when you bring him in or bring me proof he's dead."

396

"Yes, sir!" Red Arrow spun around to leave.

"One more thing, Red Arrow," Percy called out. "I'd like to ride with you. If Agent Gimel approves, of course." He glanced questioningly at Gimel, then purposefully directed his gaze to the camera in the agent's hands.

"Yes," Gimel said. "That might be a good idea . . . so you can write about my fine police force in action."

"I'll go get ready to ride," Percy announced, hurrying past the Indian police chief and into the night. "I'll be at the stables in five minutes. Have someone saddle a mount for me."

Chapter Twenty-seven

"Why are we stopping?" Aidan asked River as he reined in the horses.

He pointed toward a coulee between two buttes. "A hundred yards back, on the left, there's a large jagged boulder about nine feet tall. Behind it, there's a narrow fissure in the butte that you can follow to a group of caves on the other side. I want you to take the boy and wait for me there."

"Where will you be?" Her voice quivered slightly.

"I'll be back after I get rid of the wagon. Now, go on. We don't want them to realize we stopped here."

"Then let us go with you."

"Fire, we don't have time to argue." He gave her a little prod.

Knowing by the set of his mouth that arguing with him wouldn't do any good, she climbed down and held up her arms so he could hand Walks Proud down to her. "I still think we would be—"

He interrupted her. "Do you remember when we were kids and we played tracking games?"

"Yes, but—"

"I want you to get rid of any indication that the horses stopped here, and then be sure to cover your trail when you leave. Can you do it or have you forgotten how?" he asked, glancing apprehensively over his shoulder to see if anyone was following them yet.

"Of course I haven't forgotten," she answered indignantly, "but I think we should stay together. What if we get lost and you can't find us?"

"You keep telling me you can do anything, so here's your chance to prove it." Giving her no more time to argue, he flipped the whip over the horses' rumps and set the wagon into motion. "I'll be back in about an hour," he hollered as he headed the team north. "And don't forget to do something about the horse droppings!"

Aidan's gaze immediately fell to the fresh evidence one horse had left behind. Aware that even the most novice tracker would know piled manure meant a horse had been standing still when it was dropped, she realized she had no choice but to do as River told her. "Thanks a lot," she grumbled. Setting Walks Proud down on a boulder, she glanced around for something to use as an improvised shovel and rake.

When she had finished the unpleasant task, she pointed to the coulee and told Walks Proud to go on ahead of her, using her hands to make him understand what she wanted him to do. Then, with Walks Proud leading the way into the split between the buttes, she walked backward, brushing away any traces of their footsteps with the branches of a dead sapling.

By the time she found the jagged rock she'd been looking for, her back was aching from stooping over to sweep the trail. She shooed Walks Proud into the narrow opening, then gave the path an extra pass with her "broom." Satisfied she'd done the best she could, she backed into the fissure, dragging the dead tree top into

399

the opening and wedging it there.

"This is just wonderful," she complained. "How are we supposed to find his caves, if I can't see my hand when it's in front of my eyes?" She rummaged blindly in her bag of emergency supplies, looking for the candle and the tin of matches she was certain she had packed. "Aha!" she exclaimed when the candle was lit. "That's a little better."

Looking ahead into the dark crack in the mountain, a wave of uncertainty washed over her. *This doesn't look wide enough for anyone to pass through. Maybe it's the wrong fissure.* She glanced back, thinking that maybe she should go back out to the coulee and see if she could find another jagged rock nine feet tall. But since this was the only one she'd seen she decided to follow it and see where it led. If it fizzled out, she could turn around and look for another one.

She took a deep breath, adjusted the supply bag on her hip and its strap on her shoulder, then grasped Walks Proud's small hand and guided him behind her. "Just hold onto my skirt," she told him, indicating what she was saying by wrapping his fingers around a clump of the material. *"Washtay,"* she whispered when she felt him grab a second section of her skirt with his other hand. "Good, smart boy."

Shuffling first on one foot, then the other, from side to side over the rocky floor of the crack in the butte to test the ground, she held the candle with its bandana holder, out in front of her as she started forward, using her free hand to feel her way along the bumpy wall. "Something tells me if this is the right place, River's forgotten how small it really is. In fact, I don't see how he plans to fit through here."

"Ina," Walks Proud whimpered, his tone pitiful.

*"Ohan, ohan, cikala ohitika—*yes, yes, little brave. *Hipi—*I'm here," she soothed, her own voice shaking with uncertainty. It didn't even cross her mind to remind him she wasn't his mother.

"Ate?"

Nor to deny that River was his father. *"Ate* will be back soon. Don't worry, he'll be here." *I hope,* she said to herself as she inched her way deeper into the dark bowels of the butte. "It won't be long now." *And if he's not here by morning, we'll go back to the coulee and look for him.* She pictured herself waiting interminably with Walks Proud deep in the mountain, and River not being able to get to them because of his size.

Twice her candle flickered out, and they had to stop while she relit it with trembling hands before they could move on. But the fault in the rocky butte continued, remaining just wide enough and high enough to accommodate her small size.

Aidan was slow to realize the the floor of the narrow path she was following into the mountain was gradually taking them uphill. Finally, after what she guessed to be at least a half-hour inside the butte, the walls on both sides of the trail suddenly angled away from the path, leaving them standing in what looked like a large round room.

"Well, I'll be." She raised the candle higher so she could better view her discovery. "I feel as though we've stepped back through time," she mused aloud, awestruck. Her eyes darted over the chamber walls, taking in the crude painting and carvings decorating them. "Or been hurled into a Jules Verne adventure story. It's as if nothing has been disturbed for hundreds of—"

401

"Ina, Ina!" Walks Proud tugged excitedly on her skirt.

"Walks Proud!" she chuckled, turning to kneel and hug him. "I'm sorry. I almost forgot you. It's just that this is the most amazing place I've ever se—"

"Mahpiya, Ina!" he announced, pointing upward.

"Sky?" she repeated in English, tipping her head back so she could see in the direction he was indicating. "You're right!" she squealed as she spotted the softly glowing opening high above their heads. "It is the *mahpiya!*"

Together they stared in awe as the curtain of low-hanging clouds that had dulled the sky all night parted to expose a brilliant quarter moon and one bright star.

She blew out the candle, not wanting anything to spoil the beauty of the sight. "It's as if God has sent an omen, Walks Proud." As she spoke, she realized she now believed that River would find them. "You can almost hear God telling us not to be afraid because He's watching over us."

Frowning because he didn't understand what she'd said, Walks Proud clasped her cheeks between his palms and turned her face to his.

"I keep forgetting you can't understand anything I say," she said apologetically, sitting down and drawing him onto her lap. "Let me see if I can remember enough Lakota words to make it clear."

Using a combination of hand signals she remembered from summers spent in the village of the people who'd adopted her mother, and English and Lakota words, Aidan tried to translate what she had said. *"Wakan Tanka* gives—*otuhan*—to *Ina* and *Manni Yuskanyan*—Walks Proud—his good luck sign—*wotawe*—to tell us—*hipi*—he is here and will keep us safe—*tanyan."*

She knew that the literal translation of the Lakota words wasn't quite what she'd meant, but evidently it had satisfied Walks Proud because he looked back up at the sky and sighed. *Tanyan,*" he said softly.

The faraway crack of thunder broke into their magical moment, and Walks Proud flung himself around in her arms, tumbling her over onto her back. "*Hiya, hiya*—no, no," she giggled as she struggled to disentangle herself and sit up. "The *wakinyan* won't hurt us. They will keep us *tanyan* if they bring rain and that is *washtay.* It will stop the bad men."

She struggled to her feet and pulled Walks Proud to his. "But if it's going to rain, we'd better find somewhere else to sit because, in case you didn't notice, we've got a giant hole in our roof!"

She lit the candle again and held it close to her so she could check the time on her lapel watch. A twinge of apprehension seeped into her mind when she realized over an hour had passed since River had left them. But she shook her head, refusing to let worry overcome her for even a minute. She would put her faith in her good luck sign until River came.

"*Ate* said there were caves, so if we're in the right place, there must be at least one more— Aha! There it is!"

She led Walks Proud across the chamber to the narrow archway she had spotted. Holding the candle ahead of her, she surveyed a smaller version of the large main cave—minus the "skylight." "Our bedroom, your majesty," she announced, bowing and extending her arm in a wide arc of welcome.

Within minutes, they had found two more small rooms behind the "bedroom." The chamber farthest back in the cluster of caves even had a trickle of fresh water coming down one wall to pool in a natural rock basin before it spilled over the edge and disappeared into the floor. "All the comforts of home," she said admiringly.

By the time, they had bathed and eaten and taken care of their personal needs, Aidan was more than ready to lie down beside Walks Proud on the pallet she had made in the first room off the main chamber. She fully intended to wait up for River, however if Walks Proud beat her to sleep, it was only by seconds.

Aidan came awake with a start, her eyes round with fear as they focused on the flickering, diffused light coming from the doorway to the next room. *It has to be River,* she assured herself, gently easing out from under the blanket, and placing it back over Walks Proud.

On her toes, she crept along the wall toward the entry to the third cave. Not only did she want to keep from waking Walks Proud, she had to be sure it truly was River and not someone else who used this hideout. Perhaps there was an entrance on this side of the butte, and she hadn't noticed it.

Slowly, quietly, she approached the doorway, then cautiously peeked into the second small room. Finding it empty, she tiptoed across it to peer into the fully lighted rear cavern.

There, a man dressed only in a breechcloth was bending over and washing himself at the stone basin, his back to her. "You sure took long enough," he said in a low whisper, peering back at her from under an arm, mischievous smile on his face.

404

"River!" She ran into the room and pounded her fists
his back. "You scared me. I thought you might be a
ar."

He cocked an eyebrow. "With a kerosene lamp?"

"Well, maybe not a bear, but you could have been one
Gimel's men. You're just lucky I didn't have a gun,
you'd be dead right now."

She stopped and glanced around, noticing several bun-
:s stacked on the floor. They hadn't been there earlier.
/hat's all that?"

"Just a few items I thought we might need." He
ned his attention back to his bath.

"How did you bring it in here without my hearing
u? And for that matter, how did you fit through that
ncil-thin crack you sent us up. It was a close enough
ueeze for me."

"I came in the back entrance," he explained, indica-
g a ledge a few feet above their heads. "There's a
indow' up there that looks straight down the south-
st side of the butte to another coulee."

Remembering the gradual incline she and Walks Proud
d ascended earlier, she asked, "Exactly how far down
that?"

"Maybe forty feet, give or take a few."

"Forty feet? How'd you get up here? Is there another
der fissure?"

He shook his head. "Just a rope vine and a few hid-
n handholds an ancient tribesman must have carved
t generations ago."

"You carried all those packs forty feet up the side of
e butte with only a vine to hang on to?"

"Not all at the same time. It took me a couple of
ps," he said with a cocky grin, then returned to his

405

bath.

"But why?"

"You said it yourself," he laughed, cupping water [in] his hands and splashing it on his face, neck, and ches[t.] "I wasn't able to fit through the narrow crack you an[d] Walks Proud followed." He groped blindly for the tow[el] he'd evidently taken from one of the supply packs.

"You know that's not what I meant. Here," she sai[d,] handing the towel to him. "Why did you bring all the[se] supplies up here? What do we need them for if we'[re] going to leave tomorrow night? We are still going [to] Nebraska after we get some rest and it turns dark aga[in,] aren't we?"

"That's my plan, but when I got ready to dispatch th[e] wagon, I decided it might not be such a bad idea [to] hang onto a few things — just in case." He stretched th[e] towel between his hands and looped it around her wais[t,] hauling her toward him. "Come here and warm me u[p,] Fire. That water is cold."

"Not so fast, River Blue Eagle," she scolded stern[ly,] flattening her palms against his smooth chest in pr[e-] tended protest, though she had great difficulty thwartin[g] the grin that wanted to curl her lips. "What do y[ou] mean by, 'just in case'?"

He shrugged and slid the towel lower on her body [to] pull her hips forward. "Just in case we get hungry f[or] something other than bread and oranges before we lea[ve] . . ." He bent his head so his tongue could trail alo[ng] the outside rim of her ear. "And . . ."

"And?" she prompted, unable to stop herself fro[m] tilting her head to the side to give his mouth bett[er] access.

"In case it rains and we need to stay here an extra d[ay]

two," he murmured against her neck. "And . . ."

"Go on," she encouraged, fanning her hands over his
est.

"If Gimel's government police don't fall for the false
ail I left and they figure out we're somewhere in these
ttes—" He dropped the towel and brought his hands
ound to the front of her dress intent on unfastening
e buttons at the top of her bodice. "—we'll be able to
ld out until they give up, and it's safe to leave."

"What if one of them knows about this place and
mes here?" Aidan's eyes drifted shut. She found it
ore and more difficult to concentrate on the serious
estions she wanted answered.

"From the looks of the cave, no one's been here since
y brother and I last visited. But unless they've got
me very small men with them, they'll have to come in
e way I did, and I've left a trap or two along the way
." Freeing her arms from the sleeves of her gown, he
dicated a bell hanging from the ledge above their
ads. "Including that cow bell. It'll ring if anyone de-
des to climb the vine."

She twined her arms around his shoulders and tangled
r fingers in his wet hair. "Sounds like you've thought
everything." Her tongue tickled a bulging pectoral
uscle. "Except one."

"What's that?" He tugged her camisole downward,
eeing her breasts.

"If there's a hole up there, won't someone see the
ht?"

"Uh-uh. It's recessed, and there's a ledge that obscures
e window from the ground. Besides, I covered it with
blanket." He hunched down and opened his lips to her
raining nipple. He drew it hungrily into his mouth,

twirling his tongue around the erect crest.

Sparks of fire raged through Aidan.

"Maybe we should turn it out anyway," she sighed, her reserve of rationality nearly depleted. "Just in case . . . mmm . . . I mean . . . yes . . . we wouldn't want . . . ohhh . . ."

Releasing her breast, he reached out for the lamp and doused the light with a flick of his wrist, cocooning them in total darkness. "Is that better?"

Aware of his hands at the ties and waistbands of her skirt and drawers and petticoat, she smiled. *"Washtay,"* she whispered, as he whisked her clothes down her slim body. "It's as if we're the only two people on earth."

She heard the rustle of clothing as he removed his breechcloth. Then his mouth was back at her breast, his hands massaging her buttocks with hard, kneading squeezes.

His tongue and hot breath trailed down the center of her body, touching, licking, teasing until she felt the heat on the curls of her womanhood. "Ah," she moaned as his tongue, scorching and bold, probed the folds of her passion.

Her body rocked gently into the intimate caress of his mouth, her fingers digging urgently into the corded muscles of his shoulders. Then it was happening, the swelling, stretching, coiling at the very center of her. Every thought, every nerve, pinpointed on that glorious core of elemental need. "Oh, God," she hissed, throwing her head back and panting raggedly. Instinct thrust her hips forward in an ardent plea. "I can't bear it . . . can't. . . . Oh, please . . . ohhhhh!" She sagged helplessly, but his strong grip kept her standing.

Kissing his way up the lightly perspiring center of her

408

body, he stood up and leaned back against the edge of the water basin. His legs stretched out in front of him, he lifted her so she straddled them, bringing her pulsing, wet heat down onto his strength with one mighty thrust.

"Ahh," he moaned as the sheath of her sex closed around him.

"Oh, River, I love you so much," she rasped, locking her ankles beneath him and winding her arms around his neck as she opened her mouth to his.

Their tongues mating erotically, he curved his fingers into her waist and lifted her upward, raising her almost the entire length of his manhood, until only the throbbing tip remained inside the boiling heat of her body. Then, his tongue mimicking the motions of his hips, he speared high into her, to again fill her to exquisite capacity.

Desperate for air, Aidan arched her neck back, gasping, as over and over she was lifted off him, then forcefully brought back down onto his demanding strength.

She was on fire, burning hotter and hotter with each relentless thrust into her. Her words were incoherent whimperings of his name, her love, and her need.

Suddenly, the accommodating, yielding clay of her body wrenched in a violent contraction. Beyond sanity now, she rode him from the darkness of the cave into a shower of brilliant light.

Too weak to keep her arms around his neck, she let them fall at her sides, her legs hanging limply over his lap.

His hips still rocking beneath her, he lay her back on his extended legs and touched her where their bodies were still joined, his still hard and erect.

"Nooo," she gasped, reaching to stop him, her flesh

flaming anew. "Please. I can't bear . . ."

Pushing her hands out of the way, he relentlessly stroked and caressed despite her protests. Then it was happening, that explosive journey from darkness into light as the fire she was certain had burned itself to extinction, reignited yet again, to burn mercilessly through her veins.

No longer able to withstand the torture of waiting, River gripped her thighs and buried himself deep in the raging core of her. There was no restraint on his part. Harder and harder he thrust.

Then, with one final surge, he spilled his love deep inside her, to mingle and become one with the fluids of her body as she again achieved the ultimate glory.

Her energy spent, Aidan stayed as she was until he leaned forward and brought her up to lay her head against his chest. The only sounds she heard were labored breathing and the pounding of their racing hearts.

River slid down to the floor of the cave, carrying her with him. "Did I ever tell you that when we were kids, I daydreamed of bringing you here and being with you like this?"

"When we were kids? I didn't know 'kids' even knew about things like this."

"Maybe not girls, but boys do—especially a thirteen-year-old boy who's spent the summer chasing and wrestling and playing with a twelve-year-old girl with long red braids, and touching her every chance he got. I don't think I slept through a single night that summer without having at least one *very* realistic dream about you being here—naked and at my mercy!"

"I had no idea. You always treated me just like one of the boys. In fact, more than a few nights, just before I

410

went to sleep, I imagined you catching me in the woods to declare your undying love and steal long, passionate kisses from me." She chuckled and kissed his chest. "Nothing quite so grownup as what you had in mind, of course—but then you were a whole year older than I was. And you'd been off to school in the East. Not only were you the handsomest boy I'd ever seen, you were a real man of the world in my eyes!"

"And you were the prettiest, liveliest bundle of energy and intelligence and fun I'd ever known—you still are."

She rose up and kissed his face. "River?"

"Mmm?"

"When we met again, why did you act to unhappy to see me? It was as if you were angry with me."

"It wasn't you, Little Fire. It was what you and your family stood for. From the moment I saw what happened to our people at Wounded Knee, saw those frozen bodies stripped and thrown into that common grave, I didn't allow a day of my life to pass without reminding myself how much I hated whites for what they had done to my people. I even hated the part of myself that was white. It was as though I had to stay on guard every minute, or it would seep into my very soul and destroy the part of me that is pure Lakota, the way the whites have oozed over the continent, like a deadly cancer, devouring and destroying the Indian way of life, and the very essence of the Indian—his spirit."

She felt him shrug, and she could hear the pain his words were costing him, so she said nothing.

"So I built a wall of hatred around myself to protect the only part of me that I believed was good, and I vowed to never rest until I had found a way to keep all my people safe from the whites and to make their spirits

411

whole again, in the way I had protected my own Indian heart."

He hugged her and released a chuckle. "But then you exploded back into my life—wearing a mustache no less!—and without a moment's hesitation or any consideration for the years I'd spent creating my nice solid wall, you bulldozed right through it as if it had never been there."

"Are you sorry?"

River shook his head and kissed her forehead. "What do you think? If you hadn't broken through that wall, I might never have realized that by walling out the rest of the world I had walled myself into a narrow and unyielding prison so small and confining that I couldn't go anywhere but in circles. You set me free to move forward, and I'll be forever grateful to you."

"I remember a few times when you weren't all that appreciative of my tactics."

He patted her bottom and snorted with laughter. "It's not that easy for a man to learn the foundation he's built his life on is burying him alive."

"Or for a woman," she admitted. "When I think how indignant I was when you called me a spoiled little white girl who didn't care about anything but myself, I still cringe with shame."

"Don't be too hard on yourself. I was wrong."

"No, you weren't. I'd convinced myself what I wanted was right, maybe even noble, but it was still a case of going after what *I* wanted. You've taught me—" Her voice cracked with emotion. "—that I've been given a precious gift, and that I have to use it to help people who can't always help themselves, people who are suffering, or I will never be happy."

412

"Speaking of suffering," River said with a soft groan. "This gravel floor is getting sharper and more vicious by the second. In fact, my butt feels like it's been peppered by a shotgun. Do you suppose we could continue this conversation later?"

"Oh, you poor thing," Aidan soothed, rolling off him and helping him up from the ground. "I guess confession isn't quite as good for the bottom as it is for the soul, is it?"

Groping for her in the darkness, he caressed the roundness of her buttocks and pulled her against him. "It hasn't done yours any harm. In fact . . ." His mouth closed over hers in a kiss that erased the last traces of pain from his soul and his body.

Chapter Twenty-eight

"*Ina! Ate!*" Walks Proud cried when he awoke in the morning, his high voice sounding terrified. "*Ciciye!*"

Aidan rolled over and drew Walks Proud onto the blanket she and River had placed beside his when they had finally been ready to sleep. "Shh, shh, *Hiya ciciye!*—there's no boogeyman. *Manni Yuskanyan tanyan!* Walks Proud is safe."

"*Ate?*" Walks Proud whimpered, burying his teary face against her neck as he nestled closer in her arms.

"*Hipi*. He is here."

"Who's making all that noise in my cave?" River roared in a deep Papa-Bear voice. He flopped over onto his back and reached out to pat the little boy's head.

"*Ate!*" Walks Proud squealed, scrambling across Aidan and finding River in the dark, the way a newborn puppy finds its mother without the advantage of sight. He threw his arms around River's neck and squeezed tightly.

"*Hihani washtay, Cikala Mato* . . . good morning, Little Bear." River yawned, adjusting Walks Proud over his chest and returning his hug. "Were you a good boy while I was gone?" he asked in Lakota, reaching out to squeeze Aidan's hand. "*Hihani washtay, Ina Mato.*"

Sitting up and straddling River's chest, Walks Proud

414

started jabbering excitedly—so fast that Aidan couldn't even identify familiar words.

"Ohan, oha ohan, hipi—yes, yes, I'm here," River laughed, patting the exuberant Walks Proud on the back.

"That's the most I've ever heard him say," Aidan chuckled. "What's he telling you?"

"He says you told him I would come, and that he wasn't afraid because *Wakan Tanka* sent you a sign from the sky in the form of the moon and a star to tell you he would watch over you until I came back. The Baby Bear wants Papa Bear to know that he was very brave and helped *Wakan Tanka* keep Mama Bear safe."

"Oh, he does, does he? Why, that little devil." Aidan paddled Walks Proud's bottom affectionately. "He tricked me. All this time, I thought I was taking care of him."

"Speaking of taking care of things, I notice you haven't made him understand that we're not his parents," he said out of the corner of his mouth, continuing to massage the thin little back that could be spanned by one of his own large hands.

Aidan snuggled into the curve of River's arm and rested her head on his shoulder. "I just haven't had the heart to do it. He was so scared, and it seems to make him feel safer if he thinks we're a family, so I thought it would be better to wait until we're in a more settled situation."

"The longer you put it off, the more difficult it's going to be on him."

"I know. It's just that I . . ." She stopped, unable to admit how hard giving up Walks Proud was going to be. She knew she had no right to think about adopting him,

415

but she couldn't help secretly wishing they wouldn't locate his parents. Of course, she realized it was a ridiculous idea. People didn't just find lost children and take them home to raise like stray puppies. Somewhere, Walks Proud's real parents were looking for him. Still, she couldn't help feeling that he already belonged to her, was hers as truly as if she'd borne him.

"Just that you what?"

"Just that I think you should do it. You can speak his language fluently, while I just remember a few specific words, and I'm not even certain I'm using them correctly. Everything I say to him comes out in a mishmash of English and hand signals and Lakota words that may, or may not, mean what I think they mean."

"Well, however you're communicating with him, it must be right, because this happy little cub is certainly not the frightened boy he was yester—"

River's grip on her tightened, and the muscles in his arm and shoulder tensed beneath her cheek. "What is it?" she asked.

"Shh!" he hissed harshly, shoving Walks Proud at her and cannonading up from their blanket in one fluid motion. "Someone's out there."

Aidan put a finger to Walks Proud's lips, then sat up. *"Enila*—quiet," she whispered against his ear.

"Just stay there," River ordered in a rough murmur. "I'll be back."

Aidan nodded her head, though she knew he couldn't see her in the dark. She was tempted to light the lamp, but thought better of it. She was thankful that River had removed the covering from the last cave's window before they'd gone to sleep, since the opening let just the tiniest thread of light seep into the cave where she sat rocking Walks Proud.

After silently watching the archway leading to the rear caves for what she was sure must have been a full ten minutes, Aidan realized her legs and feet had gone to sleep. *"Enila,"* she reminded Walks Proud, setting him aside and standing up to stamp the circulation back into her limbs. Then, picking the boy up, she moved quietly to the archway to see if she could determine what was taking River so long.

The middle chamber of the three caves received more light than the one they had slept in, and Aidan could actually make out shadows and outlines—enough to see that River wasn't in there.

Giving Walks Proud a kiss on the nose and placing a reminding finger to his lips, she crept across the second cave to peek into the very back room.

Her heart leaped violently in her chest and she swallowed back the panic that rose in her throat. River wasn't in this cave either.

"River?" she whispered, unable to keep her silence. "Are you here?"

In response to her question, she received an angry, "I thought I told you to stay put," from above her head.

She looked up at the window ledge just as River's head and bare shoulders popped into view, his expression dark and scowling.

"You've been gone so long. I had to know what's happening!" she insisted, running to stand below him.

Realizing he had to tell her sooner or later, River gripped the ledge and somersaulted down to the floor, landing on bare feet with the silent grace of a cat. "Gimel's Indian police are down there looking for us." He snatched up his trousers and climbed into them. "It

417

didn't take them as long as I'd hoped it would to figure out we came into these buttes." He reached for his boots and socks.

"What are you going to do?"

"I'm going to wait until it's clear, and then I'm going to go down and lead them off on another trail."

Her heart pounding with fear, Aidon caught his arm. "You can't do that. They'll shoot you. Let's just wait until they give up and leave—like you planned. Obviously, they don't know about the cave or they'd be up here already."

"They're too good at tracking. It's just a matter of time until they figure it out," he said, firmly removing her hand from his arm so he could finish dressing. "I'm sorry, *Peta*. There's no other way." He strapped a gun belt on his hips and checked the revolver's load.

"Then let us come with you."

He shook his head. "You know I can't. I can move faster if I'm alone. Anyway, I don't want to chance you getting caught. I'm depending on you to get your story and those pictures to the newspapers. Or everything we've done will have been in vain. Our only chance is to separate so I can act as a decoy and lead them north. I want you and Walks Proud to head south into Nebraska as soon as it's dark."

"But what if they catch you?"

Ignoring her question, he curved his fingers around the back of her head and pulled her to him, covering her mouth with a hard probing kiss. "I love you, Little Fire . . . *Cikala Peta*. You've made me whole. You gave me back my heart, my life, and my soul, when thought they were lost forever."

His words sounded so final, as if he didn't think he

would see her again, and desperation such as she'd never known filled her. "Please don't go!" she pleaded. "We'll think of another way. I need you with me. I can't get there without you."

"There is no other way. How many times have you told me how strong you are, that there's nothing you can't do?"

"I'm only strong when I'm with you! I beg you, River. Don't go out there! I don't want to go on alone."

"You have to, *Peta*. Besides, I have it on good authority that you won't be alone." River kissed Walks Proud on the forehead and told him in his own language, "Take care of *Ina,* son. The Lakota people and I are placing our futures in your hands."

"*Ate!*" Walks Proud reached out to cling to River's neck as though he sensed there was a possibility of not seeing him again.

Vowing not to let River see her fear, Aidan pried the little boy from his neck. "*Ate* must go, little brave. But we will have him in our hearts," she whispered tearfully, her eyes on River though she spoke to Walks Proud. "I love you, River Blue Eagle. And I'm warning you, if anything happens and you don't come back, I'm going to track you down and make you pay. Do you hear me?"

"I hear you, Little Fire," he said with a grin. "And I promise you I'm going to do everything in my power to make sure that doesn't happen." He kissed her again, then reached up to the ledge and pulled himself onto it. He turned back to look down at her, doing his best to keep up a façade for her benefit. "Cut the vine once I'm down. Then go out the way you came in. Just be careful and don't worry. I'll see you in Rushville in a couple of days."

Throughout the day, Aidan did her best to stay busy.
But besides eating, napping, and changing into the clean
clothing River had brought them in the packs of supplies, there hadn't been anything to do except pace and
worry — and pray.

She brushed Walks Proud's dark hair back off his
forehead and kissed him after she finished buttoning his
plaid cotton shirt. "There! That's much better than that
awful stiff collar they made you wear at the agency, isn't
it?"

"Washtay," he said, running his hand over the soft
material, almost as if he had understood her.

"Yes, good," she agreed with a sad smile, caressing his
smooth cheek. "And you're good. A good brave little
man. *Washtay ohitika cikala wicasa.* If you hadn't been
here today, I would have gone crazy for certain." She
sighed and drew him into her arms. "Oh, Walks Proud,
I'm so afraid. I love him so much."

Walks Proud reared back and sandwiched her face
between his small palms. *"Ate, hipi."* He put one hand
on her chest and the other over his own. *"Cante."*

"Father, he is here. In our hearts," Aidan translated
through a trembling smile, tears rolling down her
cheeks. *"Ohan.* He will always be in our hearts, and no
one can take that from us, can they?"

Wiping at her tears with the backs of her wrists, she
sniffed and stood up. *"Hiyupo* . . . let's go. *Ate* is depending on us."

She took a last look around the large cavern to be
sure she hadn't forgotten anything, then glanced up at

420

he star-studded piece of sky above their heads. "Please, dear Lord, watch over us all tonight, and keep us safe. We place our lives in Your hands."

Picking up the supply bag and adjusting the strap diagonally across her chest, she patted her pocket to be certain the matches and spare candles were still in it. Then she picked up the lantern and, with her free hand, wrapped Walks Proud's stubby fingers around the folds at the back of her skirt. *"Hiyupo!"*

Nearing the turn she gauged to be only a few feet before the exit from the narrow passageway, Aidan paused and squatted down beside Walks Proud. She held his face near hers. "You must wait here while I check to make sure it's *tanyan*." Giving him a quick hug and a kiss, she stood up and started away from him. "I'll be right back."

Walks Proud started to grab her skirt and follow.

"Hiya No! *"Enaynka.* Stay here," she repeated, pulling her skirt free of his grip and placing her open hand to his chest, stopping him. *"Enaynka.* I will return."

She sensed that Walks Proud understood he wasn't to come with her by the way the forward push of his little body eased against her hand. But she was just as certain that he thought she wouldn't be back, and the hurt he was feeling tore at her heart, though she knew it would only have to last a minute. She considered taking him with her just to save him from experiencing even that one minute of fear. But something warned her not to do it, no matter how tempted she was. She would just have to hurry to make his moments alone as short as possible. She turned out the lantern and said, "Brave boy," in

421

Lakota, then hurried forward.

Shuffling through the remaining dark feet of tunnel as quickly as she could, Aidan used her hands to "see" her way out. She slowed her steps at the entrance to the butte and listened intently. When she heard nothing out of the ordinary, she crept closer and peered out into the coulee. Bathed in starlight, it seemed almost bright compared to the dark mountain crack she was in. Seeing no danger, she took another step forward and poked her head and shoulders out into the open, glancing cautiously from left to right. Everything was clear, but she couldn't get rid of the feeling that all was not as it seemed. She took a step out into the trail, then a second one.

Suddenly, she realized what was wrong. Someone had removed the dead sapling she had wedged in the entrance to the crevice.

"Miss Donovan, I presume," an oily voice said, to the accompaniment of a click that sounded like a revolver being cocked. "We've been expecting you, but we knew if we were patient you'd get tired of your cramped quarters and come out."

Aidan's head bobbed up, her eyes focusing on the spot from which the voice had originated, as the silhouette of a man's head and shoulders materialized above a boulder on the opposite side of the trail and to her right.

Instinctively, she started to fall back into the cleft in the butte.

The sound of a second revolver being readied for the kill cracked through the air from her left. "I wouldn't do that if I were you," a voice she recognized as Gimel's ordered.

422

Aidan froze, her frightened gaze zigzagging from man to man as she frantically tried to decide what was best. She could turn and dive back into the tunnel, but what about Walks Proud? If they fired into the butte, the bullets could ricochet off the solid walls and hit him. Or if they downed her, what would it do to the little boy to see her killed before his eyes? She simply couldn't chance it!

"*Hiya tanya, Manni Yuskanyan!*" she screamed warning, Not safe, Walks Proud. "*Enila, cikala ohitika!*" Quiet, little brave. *Enila! Hiya tanyan. Ciciye, hipi!*" The boogeyman, he is here. "*Enila!*"

"What's she saying?" The man on the other side of the divide stepped out from behind the boulder and started toward her.

"How the hell should I know," Gimel snarled. "I don't understand that Indian crap."

"*Enila! Hiya tanyan! Enila, cikala ohitika! Hiya tanyan!*" Aidan chanted loudly, praying Walks Proud could hear her and would do as she instructed. Quiet, little brave. Not safe. The boogeyman is here.

"Shut up, bitch!" Gimel ordered, slapping her across the face with a mind-reeling blow made with the back of his hand, as he stepped in front of her and jabbed his gun at her stomach.

The second man drew near. "Besides, if you're trying to call that Indian buck of yours to come help you, you're wasting your time. You're too late. He can't hear you."

Groggily, Aidan raised her head and looked at the man she hadn't been able to place. Her expression filled with recognition. "I know you!" she slurred, studying him through cloudy vision. "You're that reporter from the Tampa docks. You tried to discredit my Cuba story, then helped Chu abduct me. What do you mean, I'm too late?"

Scott Percy shook his head in mock regret. "It seems that poor half-breed bastard simply went crazy. Not only did he kidnap and rape William Randolph Hearst's star reporter, but he murdered her and left her body on the plains to be devoured by wild animals. Fortunately for decent people everywhere, that savage maniac has been caught and will be tried and hung before the night out."

Agony and fear for River squeezed at Aidan's gut. "You're the one who's crazy. River hasn't been arrested."

"Oh, I'm crazy, am I?" He held up a shirt identical to the one River had been wearing when he'd left them. "Recognize this?"

Knowledge knifed through her like an electrical shock. Scott Percy wasn't lying. He had River, and he was going to kill him.

Think, Aidan. You've got to do something! she told herself, clenching her fists so tightly that her fingernails cut into her palms. *Think.* "Why are you doing this to me, Mr. Percy?" she asked, resorting to a delaying tactic. "I understand why Mr. Gimel doesn't want me to leave the reservation alive, but why you? And why have you followed me across the country and back again, doing everything in your power to destroy me?"

Percy threw back his head and laughed. "Because you owe me, bitch." He clutched at her arm and started to drag her farther out into the open.

But Aidan dug in her heels. "What are you talking about? How could I owe you anything? Except from distance, I've never even seen you before tonight?"

He shoved his face up close to hers, his mouth curling into an ugly sneer. "Well, take a good look, sweetheart, because this is the face of the man who's going to write your obituary. It's the face of the writer whose name is going to be on the front page of the New York *Journal* where it belongs—in the space you stole from me."

Aidan glanced nervously at the entrance to the butte to be sure Walks Proud was still out of sight, then directed her attention back to Percy. She might have to dive back inside and take her chances with ricocheting bullets, after all, because if she stayed here, her risks looked even worse.

"Mr. Percy, I had no intention of stealing your position with Mr. Hearst," she said, "but if you'll let me go, I give you my word I'll recommend that Mr. Hearst hire you to write for the *Journal* in my place. I'll even give you the story I'm doing now, and it's bigger than anything I've done yet. When the country finds out what's been going on here—"

"Shut up. Let's get this done before the others get back from retrieving the supply wagon," Gimel ordered, reaching for Aidan's bag. "Those dumb-ass Indians of mine won't be too willing to hang that breed if we don't find her body' and show it to them. Where's that camera, girl? In here?"

"You want my camera?" With a speed and strength she didn't know she possessed, Aidan lifted the strap over her head and shoved the bag at Gimel's chest. "Here!"

Taken off guard by the force of her blow, Gimel stumbled back and bumped against Percy's arm.

Aidan heard the revolver fire, but she didn't wait to see if it had hit anyone. She dove back into the fissure

425

in the butte, scrambling on all fours toward the turn where she had left Walks Proud. Above the roar of her own pulse, she could hear Percy yelling at her. "Run back into your dark hole, bitch. I'm glad you like it so much, because you've just chosen your own tomb!"

She heard the ranting man yelling after her, but she didn't try to understand what he was saying. She was too intent on getting to the other side of the butte before they could go around it.

Relieved to find Walks Proud where she had left him, she grabbed him and the lantern in one synchronized movement as she bored deeper into the tunnel. *"Washta hoksila!"* she panted, slowing her retreat to a rapid walk now that she had gotten out of a direct line of fire from the entrance. "Good boy!"

Deeming it safe, she paused to light the lantern, then hurried toward what she prayed was safety. Her progress through the fracture in the butte was much quicker than it had been the night before, and she arrived at the large cavern within a matter of minutes.

As they crossed the roomy cave, Walks Proud raised his head from her shoulder and sniffed the air. *"Ina Peta!"*

"Yes, Fire," she agreed absently, thinking only a four-year-old would choose this particular moment to remind her of the name River sometimes called her.

"Peta! Peta!" Walks Proud repeated, pointing back at the tunnel they had exited.

Just then, the smell of smoke assaulted Aidan's nostrils, and she pivoted around in time to see a cloud of gray roll into the large cave from the mountain fault. Panic overrode her for an instant, and then she relaxed, a bitter smile on her face.

426

"Don't worry, little brave, *Wakan Tanka* is still watching over us. *Hipi*." She patted his shoulder and indicated he should look up to the skylight, through which smoke was already spiraling out of the butte. "They think they've gotten rid of me for good by trapping me in the tunnel. But we've fooled them, haven't we? They don't know about our 'back door.'"

She ran through the two smaller rooms to the rear chamber. Standing Walks Proud on his feet, she quickly set down a blanket and hung it over the entrance so that any smoke that found its way back this far wouldn't go out through the window and give away its existence. Retrieving a rope from the supplies River had brought, she tossed it up onto the window ledge. Next, she lifted Walks Proud up to the ledge. Then, stacking the supply bags and climbing up on them, she dragged herself onto the ledge.

"I sure do wish I hadn't cut that vine," she complained as she peeked down toward the ground.

Saying a silent thank you to her father's friend, a tired sailor, who'd taught her how to make several kinds of knots, she began tying nonslip bowline knots every two feet or so along the rope. When she was through, she secured one end of the rope around the base of a large boulder and turned back to Walks Proud. "I wish I could tell you I've climbed down ropes all my life and this is going to be easy. Unfortunately . . ." She looked out the window again and threw the knotted rope down to the ground.

"Okay, little fellow. This is it." She lifted him onto her back, helping him to wrap his arms and legs around her. "We're going to go for a piggyback ride."

Again reassuring herself that no one was waiting be-

427

low, she took a deep breath, gave the rope a testing pull and lowered her legs out the window, Groping for the first loop with her foot, she found it and hurriedly stepped into the makeshift stirrup, shifting all her weight to that foot. Hand over hand, she slid down the rope until her other foot located the second loop and got firmly set in it. Then she freed her foot from the first ring and sought the third loop.

Her hands burned from the coarse rope, and she was nearly blinded by the salty sweat that poured from her brow, causing her to make the descent strictly by feel. Every cautious inch she moved down the makeshift ladder, the weight on her back seemed to double, but she didn't stop.

Having lost count of how many steps she'd taken, an afraid to look down, Aidan searched for the next loop with her foot. This time she found no dangling stirrup Instead, her boot toe touched the ground.

Afraid to trust her feelings, she snapped her eyes open and ventured a look down.

"We did it, Walks Proud!" she exclaimed, forgetting the importance of being quiet as she jumped the rest of the way down. "Oops!" She slapped her rope-burned fingers to her mouth and giggled nervously, the tension she'd experienced while climbing down the rope finding some release. "I mean, we did it!" she whispered, disentangling the clenched arms and legs from around her neck and waist and lowering Walks Proud to the ground.

"Now, all we have to do is find out where they're keeping River and get him back," she said, her light tone belying the desperation that threatened to overwhelm her.

She took Walks Proud's hand in hers and walked a ew steps in one direction, then turned around and went n another. The futility of her situation hit her all at nce. She had no idea which way to go to find River. rustrated, she looked up at the sky, as if she would ind an answer in the stars. "Help me," she begged. What should I do?"

And the answer came to her as if one of the stars had one off in her head. Gimel had said that when his ndians came back with the wagon they'd want to see er body before they would hang River. If that were the ase, they would be able to lead her to River.

Squaring her shoulders, she and Walks Proud started round the butte toward the coulee where she had left imel and Percy. "Aren't they going to be surprised hen I show up at my own funeral?"

She managed an ironic chuckle. *"Hiyupo, Cikala Mato. Let's go get our Ate. There are some wasicuns on e other side who need to learn that if they play with is Fire, they're the ones who are going to be burned!"*

Chapter Twenty-nine

River watched in horror from the government suppl
wagon as two Indian policemen dragged John Gimel'
body from the entrance to the secret caves, where it ha
been wedged. With the unplugging of the narrow open
ing, a giant cloud of gray smoke billowed out into th
coulee, obscuring the men, the ground, the sky, and th
steep rock sides to the gorge.

"Nooo!" River bawled, hit full force by what smoke i
the passage meant. Straining against the ropes tha
bound his wrists behind his back, he bolted to a stand
ing position. "Little Fire!" he wailed, his eyes stingin
with tears as smoke continued to pour out of the butte
"Little Brave!"

River felt a gentle tug on his hands, and at the sam
time he heard a small voice speak to him from behind
"Ate, hipi."

"Cikala ohitika?" River twisted his head to the sid
amazed to find the tiny black-haired boy standing in th
wagon bed behind the bench and smiling up at him
"You're alive!" he rasped hoarsely in Lakota, afraid t
believe the boy wasn't an illusion.

430

"*Ohan!*" Walks Proud said, struggling with clumsy little-boy fingers to untie the ropes on the man's wrists.

Relief washed over River at the sight of the boy. If Walks Proud was safe, Aidan was, too, because she would never let him be separated from her. Unless . . . "*Ina!* What about *Ina!* Why aren't you together?"

"*Ina* is safe. We come to make *Ate* safe," the boy answered in his own language.

As the fear in his taut nerves subsided, River felt the bindings on his wrists loosen slightly, and he sagged down onto the bench, not only to make it easier for Walks Proud to work, but because the moments of agonizing fear had taken a toll on his strength. "Good boy," he said, his chest still heaving as if he'd been running hard. He twisted his hands against the loosening ropes. "That's almost got it. Just a little bit more. Are you sure *Ina's* safe? How did you get past the fire?"

"We go out back like *Ate.*"

"How? The vine was cut."

"*Ina* make new vine with rope and 'piggyback-ride'—" He said piggyback-ride in English. "—Little Brave down rope—like *Unktomi,* the tricky spider-man," the child explained proudly as he worked a loop of rope over River's thumb.

The rope slid off River's hand, and he quickly worked the other one free. "Good boy." He leaped down from the wagon and held his arms up to Walks Proud. "Quick! Take me to *Ina.*"

An eerie hush suddenly fell over the smoky coulee, and River instinctively looked up to see what had caused it.

Gimel's men, who had been running in frantic circles since they'd made their bizarre discovery of the agent's

431

body, shouting orders and arguing about what to do stopped everything to gawk in awed silence at the entrance to the divide.

"*Ina*," Walks Proud announced gleefully, pointing his finger to the east.

River's mouth dropped open as he at last witnessed what held the policemen entranced. "Oh, God, Little Fire, what are you up to now?"

"*Wanagi!*" Walks Proud giggled, his dark eyes dancing with delight as he and River watched the white-clad form of a woman glide through the clearing smoke toward the enthralled gathering, her arms held out from her sides as if inviting them all into her embrace.

River shook his head in wry disbelief at the perversity of Aidan's latest stunt. Who but Aidan Donovan could have conceived such a grimly humorous plan? For that matter, who but Aidan would have the blind audacity to pretend to be her own ghost and walk unarmed into a coulee full of potential killers? And who else would ever believe this crazy scheme might actually work?

"Only a man who's crazier than she is!" River complained in an amazed mumble.

Aidan bestowed what she hoped was an ethereal smile on the awestruck Indians before her. "Do not be afraid," she called to them in her most haunting voice, using a mishmash of Lakota, English, and sign language. "I have not come to harm you. I am Little Fire, the woman of River Blue Eagle, and the daughter of Gentle Fawn. I am of the Lakota People, and I have come to tell you the truth about the *shica wasicun*—the bad white man—you call by the name John Gimel."

The Indians glanced uneasily at each other, then back to Aidan, but none of them made a move to back away or to advance on her. Emboldened by their reaction, she went on.

"The *shica wasicun* John Gimel, has tricked you. He has been stealing from the Lakota people—your rations, your freedom, your cattle, your money, your land, and your dignity. That is why River Blue Eagle and I have come here, to help you reclaim what is yours. When Agent Gimel learned we were here to see that he was punished for what he was doing, he made plans with another evil white man to kill me and to blame River Blue Eagle for my murder so that you would be tricked into hurting the very man who came here to help you."

There was a slow buzz of conversation among the policemen as those who spoke English translated for those who did not understand, and Aidan waited a moment for it to die down. Then she went on.

"River Blue Eagle did not kill me as John Gimel wanted you to believe. Now another injustice is about to occur, and only you can stop it. It is even more terrible than one innocent Lakota being punished for a murder. Right now, the other evil white man is riding for Nebraska to claim that all of you turned on Agent Gimel and killed him, and that you must hang for the murder *he* himself committed."

A roar of indignation rose from the men as one by one they understood the truth of her words. One of them stepped forward to protest. "And even though we are many while he is one, the government will believe the *wasicun* over us. She is right. We will be hung. We must leave here."

Aidan held up her hands to hush their worried shouts.

433

"Enila . . . quiet. I told you I have come to help you. You must not run and hide. Instead, you must go after the *shica wasicun* and bring him back to the agency to be punished by the white man's law."

"But no one will believe us! They will say we are lying to protect ourselves. We will be hung."

"Hiya! No! There are two among us the *wasicuns* trust and will believe over the evil white man who killed the agent and left you to die for his crime. If these trusted two speak to the authorities on your behalf, you will be believed. You will not hang. Instead, you will receive a reward. But if you run away, there will be nothing that can stop the *wasicuns* from hunting you down, and you will not be the only ones who suffer. Indian people all over the land will pay for this crime that they, like you, did not commit. The *wasicuns* will say another uprising is coming, and will send the soldiers again. We can only fight them the way I have told you—with the truth and by using their own laws to see that justice is done."

Shouts of, "Who are these two the whites will believe?" and "Tell us who they are?" echoed off the canyon walls.

Aidan extended a hand toward the supply wagon that had gone unnoticed throughout her performance. "River Blue Eagle, the son of Daniel Blue Eagle and the grandson of Man of the People, is the man who will speak for you. Already, he is known and believed by important white men as far away as Washington, where the White Father lives. He is educated in the white man's laws and they will listen to him. And I, *Cikala Peta,* the *winyan* of *Mni Tanka Tru Wanblee* . . . the woman of River Blue Eagle . . . will write words for the *wasicun* newspa-

434

pers that will tell the world the truth about what happened here. And whatever I write will be believed because I am known throughout the white world to be honest and truthful."

"You? But you are not real. You are a *wanagi!*" one man protested. "And you are white."

"A ghost?" Aidan repeated. *"Hiya . . . I am hiya wanagi.* I told you, I am the woman of River Blue Eagle, and I am only flesh and bone—like all of you." She took a step forward, her hands reaching out to them. "And though my skin may be white, in the part of me where it is important—in my *cante* and in my *nagi*—my heart and soul, I am Lakota."

"Is what she says true?" a man asked, turning to River for confirmation. "You will speak for us in the *wasicun's* court and see that the *shica wasicun* hangs for his crime?"

His face solemn, River nodded. "The words of *Cikala Peta* are true. We will speak for each of you, for the Lakotas as a nation, and for all the People all over this land. I swear to you on the grave of our *wakicagapis*—dead relatives—who died at Wounded Knee, that we will not stop speaking and fighting for the right of the *ikce wicasa* . . . the Indian . . . to be free."

A cheer rose from the men, and they started running for their horses. *"Hiyupo!* Let's go," they shouted over and over.

In the midst of the scurrying to mount up, Red Arrow, the police chief, guided his pony to where River stood, Walks Proud still in his arms, "We will trust you and your woman, River Blue Eagle. And we will bring back this evil white man to the agency to be punished by the *wasicun's* law."

435

Wheeling his horse away from River, he raised a hand and signaled his men to ride. Though they all knew they were about to enter into a kind of war the People had never fought before, and that the battle would be long—a bloodless battle in the white man's courts—the police chief gave the ancient battle cry of the Lakotas as he rode south after Scott Percy. *"Hoka hey!"* he shouted. "It is a good day to die."

In a swirl of dust and lingering smoke, the riders cleared the coulee, leaving River and Aidan and Walks Proud alone with the supply wagon.

Aidan looked at River and grinned, though she made no move to go to him. "Go on," she challenged. "Yell at me. Tell me what a stupid stunt that was and that I took a terrible chance and . . ."

River stood Walks Proud in the supply wagon and told him to stay there; then he strode toward her, his expression impossible for her to read.

"Well? Aren't you going say anything?"

He nodded, continuing his purposeful stroll toward her, the gleam in his eyes hard and threatening, but still he didn't speak.

She took an instinctive step backward. "I'm warning you, River. There's nothing you can say to make me sorry I did it. No matter what you think about my tactics, you can't argue the fact that they worked!"

"Do you really want to know what I think?" he ground out through clenched teeth, the muscle in his lower jaw bunching and relaxing as he clasped her upper arms and hauled her hard against him.

"Uh-huh." Her expression was not quite so defiant and daring now.

"I think you are the most audacious, rash, foolhardy,

436

stubborn woman I've ever known." He paused, unable to disguise his happiness any longer. "And I don't know whether *Wakan Tanka* gave you to me as a punishment for some sin I committed or as a reward for a good deed, but I will spend the rest of my life being grateful that you are mine. I love you, *Cikala Peta,* my *ohitika Lakota winyan.*"

"Then why don't you kiss me and show me how much?" she teased, winding her arms around his neck. "Because I'm one *winyan* who can be told and told, but until I'm shown, I'm never completely convinced."

A sly grin curved his lips, and he started to comply with her request, then hesitated. "Just one more thing, Little Fire."

Her eyes already closed in anticipation, she opened them lazily. "What's that?"

"The next time you decide to play the part of a ghost, wear a sheet. Because if you *ever* again walk into a group of men wearing nothing but your underclothes, I intend to *show* you how I feel until you can't sit down. Do I make myself clear, Mrs. Blue Eagle?"

"Perfectly clear, Mr. Blue Eagle. The next time I'm called on to save your neck, I'll just tell whomever it is that's going to hang you I can't attend unless they give me proper notice—so that I can have the correct costume on hand for the event and don't have to improvise. Does that meet with your approval?"

He threw back his head and laughed, loud and hard. "Little Fire, Little Fire, Little Fire. I doubt very seriously that your approach to getting things done is ever going to quite meet with my approval. But I intend to spend the next fifty or sixty years finding out. Because no matter how *witko*—crazy—you are, I love you and

437

hope you never change!"

"Ate, Ina!" a little voice interrupted.

In answer to the urgent tugging on their clothing, Aidan and River looked down at the smiling face raised to theirs. Together they knelt and took the child in their arms, each of them kissing one of his cheeks.

"I guess this kind of interruption is something we're going to have to get used to," River said, grinning at the two of them.

Aidan frowned, her disappointment obvious. "Oh, no! How did you find out? I was planning it for a surprise!"

"You know about Walks Proud's family?"

"Walks Proud? What are you talking about?"

"What are *you* talking about?"

"You go first. What about Walks Proud's family?" She possessively hugged Walks Proud, her heart already twisting with regret at the thought of giving up the little boy she'd come to love so much.

"He doesn't have anybody. The man who drove the wagon back here, told me his father was hung in Indian Territory for stealing horses—before Walks Proud was even born. And his mother died giving birth to him. Since then, he's been raised by his only relative, a grandmother. She brought him to the agency when she came to pick up rations last week. But evidently, the long trip in the heat, and the even longer wait on the rations line, was too much for her, because she just collapsed and died. That's how he ended up in the school. I guess no one knew what else to do with him."

Aidan's expression revealed her anguish at hearing all the tragedies in Walks Proud's short life. "Well, no more!" she said, pulling the little boy closer into her protective embrace. "You never have to be alone or

438

afraid again, Little Brave. From now on, you have an *ina* and an *ate* to love and care for you. We're never going to let anything hurt you again."

"Not so fast, Fire, the tribe might not want us to adopt him. You're white, and I'm only one-quarter Lakota."

She tilted her head to the side and directed her most beguiling look up at him. "But you'll be able to make them understand that we belong together, won't you? I know you won't let anyone take him away from us."

River smiled sheepishly at her expression of blind faith in him. "I give you my word, if I have to take our adoption petition all the way to Washington, I'll fight anyone who tries to separate us from him. We're a family, and we'll stay together."

Unable to contain his happiness, River patted his bare chest and said in a falsely deep voice, "*Ate Mato* . . . Papa Bear." He kissed Aidan's lips and, in a higher voice said, "*Ina Mato* . . . Mama Bear." He ruffled Walks Proud's hair and finished in a normal voice, "And *Cikala Mato* . . . Little Bear."

Aidan giggled, then patted her tummy and said in a tiny little voice, "And *Hoksi Cala Mato* . . . Baby Bear."

Speechless, River stared at her.

"Well, aren't you going to say anything?"

"A baby?" he asked, his expression reverent as he reached out to cup her face in his hand. "Our baby? Are you sure? Why didn't you tell me?"

"I wasn't certain until recently, and the time never seemed right."

Hugging her and Walks Proud, River announced. "We're going to have a baby, Walks Proud!"

Suddenly his expression sobered. He leaped up from

439

the ground and bent to gently help Aidan rise, as though she were very fragile. "Now that you're going to be a mother, I hope you realize you must start behaving with a little caution."

"I thought you just told me you hoped I'd never change," she taunted, allowing him to hover protectively over her.

He cleared his throat. "I was speaking figuratively. For instance, what's this Walks Proud told me about your climbing down a rope with him on your back? I want your word, right now, that you won't pull any more daredevil stunts like that."

She smiled and leaned into the curve of his arm, letting him lead her toward the wagon. "Yes, dear," she said sweetly, grinning up at him, her dark eyes wide with sincerity. "I give you my word that as long as I'm expecting, I won't climb down any more ropes or buttes with a four-year-old on my back."

He studied her warily, recognizing that guileless look of hers . . . and knowing exactly how far he could trust it. "And no other crazy stunts either."

She drew an *X* over her heart with her forefinger. "Cross my heart and hope to die. I swear, no more rope climbing and no other crazy stunts, unless . . ."

"Aidan, get that look out of your eyes. I'm serious about this. I don't want you taking any more chances."

"I give you my word, I'll never take another chance as long as I live—" She grinned and gave Walks Proud a mischievous wink. "—unless it's *absolutely* necessary."

River rolled his eyes heavenward. "I can see we're going to have to keep a very close eye on *Ina,* Walks Proud."

And I can see the first thing I'm going to have to

440

teach Walks Proud is that we don't have to tell Ate every little thing that happens. Not when he'd just worry needlessly.

HEKETCHETU . . . IT IS FINISHED

Epilogue

**BLUE CREEK RESERVATION,
SOUTH DAKOTA — *Spring, 1904***

Wiping ink-stained hands on her apron, Aidan Blue Eagle stepped out of the *Lakota Centurion* office. "Walks Proud, run over to the school and tell Patricia Kind Heart that she and her students need to start putting their luggage into the wagons. We don't want to miss our train." She wiped a curly wisp of red hair out of her eyes with the back of a wrist and turned to go back inside.

Walks Proud leaped up from the porch, his five-year-old twin brothers in tow. *"Ina!* The wagons are all loaded," he replied, with as much patience as any ten-year-old could muster when, on the verge of embarking on the adventure of a lifetime, he was being held up by a parent's timetable. "Everyone's ready but you — and you're not even dressed yet," he scolded.

"Hiyupo! Let's go," the twins shouted in unison, running to their mother and tugging on her skirt. "The others are waiting!"

Properly chagrined by her children's reminder that she was always the one who was late, Aidan smiled apologetically at her three boys. Handsome in new broadcloth suits

442

designed to display pride in their Indian heritage while still conforming to the fashions of the day, they brought a lump to her throat. How could one woman be so lucky—or so happy?

She caressed the two black-haired heads on either side of her, and told Walks Proud, "Just let me tell David Spotted Back a couple more things, and then I'll go change."

"Peta," River said as he approached the little group on the porch, a tolerant grin on his face, "David has worked here since the day you started the paper four years ago. He knows as much as you do about it. Now, come on, your fourth *hoksi cala* is in perfectly capable hands."

Aidan made a face at her husband of six years. "You certainly know how to make a *winyan* feel essential, Agent Blue Eagle! How would you feel if I told you someone else could run this agency as well as you?"

"I'd say you're probably right—at least for the two weeks we're going to be gone! But if you're really worried about how essential you are, just look over at that crowd of expectant faces in front of the school, not to mention these three wild Indians. They all know if you hadn't found financial backers for this special trip, the graduation class wouldn't be going to the World's Fair in St. Louis. And believe me, by the tone of excitement I detected when I passed the wagons, if you weren't essential, they would have left without you an hour ago. Now, go get ready, or I'm going to revert to the ways of my ancestors, throw you over my shoulder, and take you as you are—ink-blacked face and hands, work dress, unbrushed hair, and all."

Grinning, Aidan removed the apron and tossed it over the porch rail. "You wouldn't dare."

A mischievous twinkle lit River's blue eyes. "Oh, wouldn't I?" He took a menacing step toward her. "Don't forget what John Gimel told you. No matter how civilized we may seem, underneath our tamed exterior, we've still got that 'wild Indian blood' flowing in our veins."

"Ohan! Ohan!" the three little boys cheered. "Do it, *Ate!*" they squealed. "Go on! Put *Ina* over your shoulder!"

River dropped his glance to his giggling sons and chuckled. "Maybe we ought to give her one more chance to redeem herself and go on her own. What do you think?"

"Aw," the three groaned in disgust.

"Aw," Aidan mimicked, turning the children around and prodding them off the porch. "Go over to the school and tell them your *ina* will be there in fifteen minutes, ink smudged or not — and walking on her own two feet."

"Promise?" Walks Proud asked warily, for experience told him Aidan's fifteen minutes wasn't always in line with everyone else's.

Aidan crossed her heart with an inky forefinger. "I promise."

River wrapped a proprietary arm around his wife's shoulders. "And I'll see that she keeps her promise!" he declared.

"Yea!" the twins shouted, skipping off the porch.

"Hiyupo" Walks Proud yelled, breaking into a run for the school building, his little brothers close on his heels.

"Ohan, hiyupo, Mrs. Blue Eagle. We've got a train to catch and a World's Fair to see!"

"And this, my handsome Lakota husband, is only the beginning!"

SPECIAL THANKS

I wish to thank Ted Hamilton at Oglala Lakota College in Kyle, South Dakota; Irving Tail and Cornelius Kills Small at the Oglala Lakota Tribal Office on the Pine Ridge Reservation, South Dakota; Brother Simon at the Red Cloud School in Pine Ridge; Chuck Hill at the Sinte Gleska College on the Rosebud Reservation, South Dakota; and Lois Latimer at the Tampa Historical Society in Tampa, Florida.

Over and over, they have gone out of their way to get me the exact information I needed; and no matter how crazy or inconsequential my questions may have seemed to them, not one of these kind people ever lost his or her patience — or sense of humor. Thanks to you all.

AUTHOR'S NOTE

When writing historical fiction, I make every effort to keep my details as factual as I can, however, there are times when I find "bending" the facts is necessary for the good of my story. For instance, I took liberties with the officers' sleeping arrangements on the train to Florida. Though it is true the train had one Pullman car for their comfort, my research led me to believe that instead of individual compartments with private bathrooms, that car contained pull-down sleeping berths above seats that also converted into beds, both of which were equipped with curtains for privacy.

By the same token, Blue Creek Indian Reservation is fictional and was created strictly for this story because I wanted to represent the conditions that existed on reservations throughout the system, rather than concentrate on one actual location, in which they might have been better or worse than on my imaginary reservation.

LAKOTA DICTIONARY

AJUSTAN: Leave it alone

ATE: Father

CANTE (Chante): Heart

CICIYE: Boogeyman

CIKALA: Little

ENAYNKA: Stay

ENILA: Quiet

HANHEPI: Night

HANHEPI WI: Moon (night sun)

HA YE: Thank you

HEKETCHETU: It is finished

HIPI: I am or he/she/it is here

HIYUPO: Let's go

HIYA: No

HOKSI (hokshi): Child

HOKSI (hokshi) CALA: Baby

HOKSILA (hokshila): Boy

IKCE WICASA (Wichasha): The Indians, The People

INA: Mother

KOLA: Friend

LAKOTA: Sioux

MAHPIYA: Sky, heaven, clouds

MANNI: Walk

MATO: Bear

MNI (Mini) TANKA: River

NAGI: Soul, spirit, essence

OHAN: Yes

OHITIKA: Brave

OTUHAN: Giveaway

PETA: Fire

SAPA: Black

SHICA: Bad

SKA: White

TANYAN: Safe

TRU: Blue

WAKAN TANKA: Great Spirit
WAKICAGAPI: Dead Relative
WAKINYAN: Thunderbirds
WANA: It is beginning
WANAGI: Ghost
WANBLEE: Eagle
WASHTAY: Good
WASHTAY HIHANI: Good morning
WASICUN: White man
WICASA (Wichasha): Man, mankind
WICINCA (wichincha): Girl
WINYAN: Woman
WITKO: Crazy
WI: Sun
WONIYA: Life, Breath
WOTAWE: Good luck charm
YUSKANYAN: Proud